Remember Me

Karen Vickers

Remember Me
© Karen Vickers 2025

ISBN: 978-1-923512-02-3 (Paperback)

A catalogue record for this book is available from the National Library of Australia

Dedication

To Kris,
who planted the seed, lit the spark and
believed I could be a writer.
Thank you.

Chapter 1

Friday, September 8th

The scorching sun warmed the car as I drove towards the picturesque seaside town of Cape Gorge. In a few months, it would be summer, and the calming blue ocean felt like the perfect place to start my new life. I'd spent the past five days on the road, driving almost non-stop, desperate to reach my destination without a single glance back.

In two days, I'll be on the beach, watching the sunset, with a delicious cocktail in my hand. I thought, as I cruised along the weathered black bitumen.

With images of the ocean flashing through my mind, I shifted impatiently in my seat as my excitement increased, and with a huge grin on my face, I turned up the radio and sang along to the upbeat song.

Navigating my way through a small town, still singing loudly, I approached a quiet intersection. As the traffic light was green, I kept my foot on the accelerator, not seeing a reason to slow down.

Suddenly, out of the corner of my eye on my right, I spotted a large black car hurtling towards me, running the red light.

Before I had the chance to hit the brakes or swerve, the car slammed into mine with a terrifying crunch.

The force of the collision crumpled the hood, cracked the windscreen, and rammed the engine block towards me. A burst of pain shot through my right shin as the brake pedal launched forward and broke my bone, I screamed in agony.

The momentum of the impact flung me against the seatbelt and as it locked, the belt dug sharply into my chest, forcing the breath out my lungs with an abrupt whoosh, silencing my howl.

Although the seatbelt stopped me from flying out the windscreen, my head snapped forward, slamming heavily into the steering wheel. Pain erupted through my forehead, blinding my vision.

The momentum of the other car, still ploughing into me, sent my car spinning violently across the asphalt—the wheels squealing loudly in protest.

Seconds later, my car bounced over the curb, on the opposite side of the intersection, and crashed into a traffic pole. Pain, nausea, and adrenaline ravaged my entire body, but before I had time to fully comprehend what happened, I blacked out.

Chapter 2

Sunday, September 10th

Drifting towards consciousness, in a half awake half dreaming state, I automatically swallowed but to my shock, felt an obstruction in my throat. Fear kicked in as my eyes flew open and instinctively gagged. Overwhelming panic surged through me as I reached to my mouth, trying to grasp whatever was lodged in my throat, threatening to choke me.

"Easy does it, easy!" A female's voice called out. Through the terror, I felt strong, yet gentle hands grip mine and pull them away from my face. "You're okay. You're okay. I've got it."

Turning my head, my blurred eyes focused on the face of a young girl and not recognising her, I frowned in confusion.

"Who...?" I tried to say, but the obstruction in my throat muffled my voice.

"It's okay," she repeated. "I'm a nurse here at Parker Hospital. You're in the Intensive Care Unit and you're safe." She paused and smiled at me again. "You have a breathing tube down your throat. We had to intubate while you were unconscious in theatre–that's what you can feel. Try to relax, so I can pull it out."

"She's awake?" I heard another voice say as a second female came into view behind the girl next to me.

"Yes, can you call Doctor Wright, please?" asked the young nurse. The second lady disappeared as quickly as she had arrived, leaving me feeling more confused.

"I'm going to remove the tape on your cheeks and then I'll pull the tube out, okay?" The nurse moved quickly, pulling the tape free. "Alright. On three, I want you to cough."

I looked at her with wide eyes, feeling my breathing increase. As though seeing my panic, the nurse held my gaze, nodding slowly.

"Ready? One, two, three, cough."

I braced myself and forced out a cough as the nurse pulled the tube out in one swift motion. Unfortunately for me, not only did my gag reflex kicked in as the tube scraped along the back of my throat, but it triggered sharp pains shooting through my chest. I squeezed my eyes shut breathing through the pain, fighting back the urge to vomit and not pass out at the same time.

After a few seconds, my stomach unclenched, my throat relaxed and the urge to throw up eased.

"Don't talk just yet. Your throat will feel dry and tender," the nurse said, smiling warmly.

Although the breathing tube was gone, I could still feel something in my throat each time I swallowed. To add to the chaos, my nose itched terribly and when I lifted my hand to scratch it, my fingertips felt a small tube protruding from my nostril.

Once again, the nurse eased my hand away from my face again. "Leave that there. It's a feeding tube," she said patiently, though there was a subtle warning in her tone.

I was only vaguely aware of her words, as aching pains, I was not feeling before throughout my body intensified, bringing with it a sudden and acute alertness. A dull throb pulsated through my head with every breath and, trying to adjust my uncomfortable position, I realised I couldn't move my right leg. Gasping, I winced as another sharp pain emanated from within my chest.

"Try to keep still," the nurse said politely, laying her hand gently on my shoulder. "I know you're very confused right now."

I blinked a few times, trying to focus on my surroundings, but my eyes felt so heavy. Through the groggy veil, the room seemed large from where I lay, and the off-white walls were far too bright under the ceiling lights.

Slowly turning my head left and right, I noticed I was not alone. There were other beds in the room, each one occupied with a person, surrounded by tubes and machines emitting constant beeps and noises. The sight brought me no relief, in fact, it only heightened my confusion.

"What happened?" I whispered hoarsely, as my heart pulsated faster in my chest.

"You were in a car accident two days ago," the nurse replied.

I swallowed painfully. "A car accident?" My eyes searched hers for an answer.

No sooner had I asked, than an older man appeared at my bedside. He was tall, with broad shoulders and dark brown hair. His pale, green eyes sparkled in the bright, florescent lights, and he smiled as his eyes locked with mine. Not recognising him, I didn't smile back.

"Hello," he said as the nurse stepped aside to allow him to approach me. "It's good to see you awake. How are you feeling?"

"Sore and confused," I muttered.

The doctor chuckled. "Yes, I imagine you would be. I'm Doctor Wright, and you are in the ICU department of Parker Hospital. Can you tell me what happen?"

I shook my head and winced as pain rippled through me again. "I don't know. The nurse mentioned a car accident?"

Doctor Wright nodded. "That's right. You were in a head-on collision Friday afternoon. You sustained a broken leg and several bruised ribs, as well as a significant knock to your head, which left you in a mild state of unconsciousness. We operated on your leg yesterday morning, and well, were just waiting for you to wake."

I looked up at him, my eyes wide, the groggy veil beginning to clear. "I don't remember being in an accident."

"That's not unusual with head injuries." He smiled, his eyes softening at the corners. "You hit your head on the steering wheel, and you were unconscious upon your arrival," he explained.

"Can you tell me your name?" the nurse asked, stepping back into my vision.

"Yeah, sure. It's um ..." I frowned and then laughed in awkwardness as I came up blank. "I don't remember."

"That's alright. We can get all the details when you feel better. Mild amnesia is common with head injuries, and your memory should return as the swelling goes down." He turned to the nurse. "Let's organise another CT scan for this afternoon."

"A CT scan?" I asked in curiosity.

"Yes." He turned his attention back to me. "A brain scan. We did an initial scan when you arrived, but we'll do a follow-up one now you're awake and compare the swelling."

Despite his kind smile, I didn't feel reassured. In fact, I felt terrified.

Doctor Wright turned his attention back to the nurse. "How are her vitals?"

"Good. Everything is within normal range," she replied, handing him my chart.

"How is your pain level?" the Doctor asked, shifting back to me as he flipped through the pages.

Before I could answer, another jolt of pain ripped through my chest, taking my breath away. "High," I groaned. "Everything hurts."

"Where are you feeling the pain the most?" he asked, withdrawing a penlight from his shirt pocket and shining it in my eyes.

"My chest hurts every time I breathe, and my head is pounding," I replied, trying not to blink.

"Not surprising, your seatbelt saved your life," he said, jotting something in my chart. "I'll get the nurse to give you a top up for the pain, which should help you rest." He turned back to the nurse. "Give her some more morphine. I'll check back in a few hours." With a nod, the nurse left.

"Rest up and try to get some sleep," he instructed. "The worst is over." With a pat on my hand, he placed my chart at the foot of my bed and walked away.

Car accident! Broken leg! Bruised ribs! Amnesia!

Thoughts raced through my aching head, and I felt a surge of panic course through my body. The lights seemed too bright, the room too big, and I wanted nothing more than to leave.

And why can't I remember my name?

As I tried to sit up, another bolt of pain shot through my head and I fell back against the pillow, gasping. Bringing my hand up to my face, I felt a small bandage on the right side of my forehead. Tentatively pressing on it, another stab of pain rippled through my head, sending a wave of nausea through me.

I closed my eyes, focused on my breathing, willing it to slow down, and not vomit. Only vaguely aware the nurse had returned, the exhaustion and shock of that had happened overpowered me. As she injected the morphine into the drip, I fell asleep.

The sound of gentle talking awoke me, and I opened my eyes, once again feeling disoriented.

"Afternoon, I'm Paul. Sorry to wake you but I'm here to take you to get some scans done, okay?"

I nodded, too groggy to speak. Paul seemed friendly enough, and I noted he wore the same pale green coloured scrubs as the nurse who was with me, the last time I woke.

Stepped out of my vision temporarily, Paul unplugged a few cords from the wall behind me, then carefully navigated my bed out of the ICU and through some large doors.

Paul steered us down a few wide corridors before pulling to a stop in front of a large silver door. With the push of a red button on the wall, the door slid behind the wall, revealing a spacious room with an enormous round white machine in the centre.

Seeing the machine, my heart raced, and I clenched my hands together in my lap. There were no windows, nothing to see aside from sterile, white walls, and the only light came from six long globes on the ceiling. On the righthand wall was a smaller, closed door with a window through which I could see a male sitting at a computer. Paul pushed me up to the long tray-like bed, which poked out of the scary-looking round contraption.

"Wait here," he said and left me lying in the bed.

Where else am I going to go? I thought defensively.

He walked to the door, knocking on it once and waited. A few seconds later, an older man walked out, greeting Paul and the two men chatted briefly while they looked over my chart.

"I'll leave you with Nick," Paul said returning to my side. "I'll be back soon," he added, as he patted my shoulder, then disappeared behind me.

"Hi. I'm Nick, the radiologist. How are you doing?" Nick asked.

"Okay, I guess. Bit scared though."

"Don't be. I'll look after you," he reassured me as he eased me off my bed, carefully pulling the tubes attached to me along. I stood on my good leg, gripping his arm as I fought back the surge of dizziness. Nick gently guided me to the machine, allowing me to sit on the scanner tray. Carefully, he swung my legs up and helped me to lie back. Noting my body tense up, he continued to chat to me.

"It won't hurt, although it can be loud. Just lie still and it will be over before you know it. If you get scared, just talk and I'll hear you in the next room. We'll keep you calm, okay?"

"Sure," I uttered nervously.

He carefully positioned my head on a small piece of foam and draped a thin blanket over me. I heard him push my bed to the corner of the room before he slipped back through the silver door. I tried to remain calm and was in the process of telling myself I wasn't scared at all when the machine suddenly turned on.

The scanner whined loudly, and with a small jolt, the tray slowly slid backwards into the large, round hole. I clenched my fists and squeezed my eyes shut, trying to breathe as deeply as my bruised ribs would allow.

"Just lie still and try not to move," Nick's voice echoed around me. "This won't take long."

My heart took off again as the machine thumped around me and sweat beaded across my forehead. I forced my eyes open and focused on my breathing, trying to keep myself composed and still. I waited for what felt like an eternity while the doctor studied the scans. Finally, the machine quietened, and the tray slowly slid out. Within moments, Nick walked into the room and wheeled my bed towards me.

"Okey dokey. Wasn't too bad, was it?" he chuckled as he again helped me to stand and clamber onto my bed.

"No, not too scary," I whispered back, not sure I believed myself.

Chapter 3

Monday, September 11ᵗʰ

Low voices and clanking wheels rolling across the floor drew me back towards consciousness. Turning my head to the left, trying to ignore the consistent dull pain throbbing behind my temples, I realised I wasn't in the same place as before. This room was smaller, and there were only two beds. The second one was empty.

"Hello?" I called out into the quiet room. My voice was soft and croaky, and my dry, sore throat ached. I needed water. "Hello!" I called out again. Nothing happened. The door was closed.

Can no one hear me?

I felt myself break out into a cold sweat and was about to sit up when I noticed a remote on the right side of the bed. Grabbing it, I looked at the buttons, hoping there was something that could call attention. I noticed a small red button with a female symbol on it and pushed it. A single chime sounded outside the room as a light turned on above the door. Pushing the button again, the light flickered, and the chime sounded again. As I was about to push it a third time, I heard movement beyond the door and finally it opened.

A friendly-looking woman burst into the room; her face lined with a few wrinkles and her light brown hair pulled neatly back into a bun. She wore a dark blue uniform and white shoes that were almost soundless on the grey, lino floor. Although I didn't recognise her, the way she smiled gave me the impression that this wasn't the first time she'd seen me. She rushed to my bedside and grabbed my hand.

"Ah, hello my dear," she said, her voice soft as she removed the remote from my hand. "How are you feeling?"

"Where am I?" I choked with relief to see someone.

"You're in the hospital. My name is Tracey. I'm your nurse," she replied as she bustled around me, first turning off the red call button before checking a beeping machine next to my bed and the clear bag of fluid which hung off it, all the while with a cheery smile on her face.

"How did I get here?" I asked, still confused.

"You don't remember?" she replied, stopping by my side.

"No." I shook my head slowly.

"That's alright," she continued to chat, calmly and slowly.

"You were in the ICU, but after you woke up yesterday, they sent you here to my ward. Do you remember being in the ICU?" She had a grandmother-like quality about her, and I found myself at ease in her presence.

"Yes, somewhat." Fuzzy memories popped into my head, but nothing tangible. I scratched at the tube in my nose again.

"That's good." She eased my hand away from my nose. "Leave that there. It's a feeding tube. While you were in and out of consciousness, this is how we kept you fed. Now you're awake again, we'll organise some tests to see if you can eat solids. If you pass, we'll take it out."

I nodded with disappointment. I could feel the tube down my throat every time I swallowed.

"Now, I'm going to get the doctor. He'll be happy to see you awake again," she said with a friendly smile, then before I could say anything, she turned and marched off towards the door. As she was about to leave, she pivoted.

"Oh, how rude of me!" she gasped. "My dear, by any chance, have you remembered your name? We received a handbag and small tote bag that were found in the car with you, but no one could find your ID in your purse. The doctor asked you yesterday in the ICU, but you couldn't remember. So, for now, you've been a Jane Doe!"

"Um," I smiled slightly at her, "it's ..." My smile vanished as my mind drew another blank. I stared back at her, my frown deepening, and my mouth slightly ajar.

My name! What is my name?

I closed my mouth, swallowed, and dropped my eyes to the bed. A million and one thoughts bounced around my head, yet nothing helpful. I exhaled.

"Oh, dear. It's not come back to you yet?" she asked again when I didn't respond.

"No," I shook my head. "I still don't remember." I could hear the panic in my voice.

"That's okay, dear. Do you know what day it is then?" she asked, her gentle smile returning.

"Um ... No, I'm not sure," I replied.

"How about the date? Do you know that?"

"No," I cried, feeling foolish and frustrated that I couldn't answer such simple questions.

"It's alright, it's a common side effect in head trauma patients. I'm sure you will remember soon, but for now, it's Monday, the eleventh of September 2012. I'll be back soon."

She slipped out of the room and took off down the passageway, letting the door swing gently closed behind her.

I lay my head back against the pillow, feeling more afraid than I was when I first woke up yesterday.

How hard did I hit my head? How could I still not remember my name?

I looked at my hands in the hope I might recall something. I wore no rings on my slim fingers, though there were some slight indents on the fourth finger of my left hand.

So, did I wear a wedding ring once? Was I married?

Returning my hands to my lap, I looked around the room. I couldn't see any personal belongings, nor the tote bag the doctor and nurse had mentioned, only the simple, light green hospital gown I wore.

My name!? What on earth is my name? How does one forget their own name?

My hands became clammy, and I felt my heart racing—it was scary being alone in a place I didn't know. About five minutes later, the door opened again, and Tracey and Doctor Wright walked in.

"Good morning," Doctor Wright said as he walked up to the bed, his gentle smile conveying warm and calmness. "How are you feeling today?"

"Still confused about what happened to me."

"Completely understandable. How is the memory going? Anything come to mind?"

I shook my head. "No, everything is still blank."

"Hmmm," he pondered. "I have the results from the CT scan we did yesterday. There is a decrease in swelling, so that's good. As for your memory, I guess time will tell."

"Okay." I glanced at the nurse hesitantly.

"We have time. It's okay," she said with a friendly smile.

"Do I still need this?" I touched the feeding tube.

"I don't see why we should keep it in, but I'll organise a speech pathologist to come and do a swallow assessment first."

"A swallow assessment?"

"Yes, we need to make sure you haven't damaged your throat and can eat without choking. If all goes well, we'll remove the tube and fluid bag and get you on the road to recovery." He hesitated for a moment. "There's a sheriff outside who needs to speak to you. Are you up for a visitor?"

"A sheriff?" I asked worriedly.

"Yes. It's in regard to the car accident. I'm sure he just needs to get a few details from you."

"Um, sure."

Doctor Wright left and a few minutes later, the Sheriff of Parker entered. He was a rather large-bellied man with a round face and a bushy grey moustache. As he entered, he ran his fingers through his sandy hair, the movement highlighted the greying patches at his ears.

He pulled a chair over to my bed and sat down with an audible huff. His light brown uniform pulled tightly over his belly and the sleeves dug into the folds of his arms. With some difficultly, he withdrew a small notebook from his shirt pocket, followed by a pen, and flicked me a tight smile.

"Good morning. I'm Sheriff Simon Hadlock."

"Hi," I replied quietly.

"How are you feeling today?"

"Not so great."

The Sheriff nodded and looked at me carefully. "I need to ask you a few questions about the accident," he said, flipping his notebook open and clicking his pen. "Can you tell me what happened?"

"I don't know, sorry."

"You don't remember the crash?" he looked at me, his eyebrows raised.

I shook my head.

"Okay," he paused. "Well, I attended the crash scene on Friday—you're lucky to be alive. Your car is a total write-off." He stared at me. When I said nothing, he continued. "After you were taken to the hospital, we searched the car. We located a small handbag, but no ID. Can you tell me your name?"

"No, sorry." I shook my head again. "I don't remember."

He glanced at the Doctor who hovered by the door, before looking back at me. "Do you know where you are?"

"A hospital in ... oh, I'm sorry, I've forgotten the name."

"You're in Parker, a small town in Camberton."

"Yes, that's right." I nodded softly.

"Can you tell me where you were heading, or where you were driving from?"

I glanced at Doctor Wright nervously. "I don't know."

Sheriff Hadlock scratched his chin. "Do you remember anything? Your address, date of birth, anything useful?" he asked me, and I could hear the agitation in his voice.

"No, sorry, Sheriff. I don't remember anything about myself or how I got here or where I'm from. I wish I could help you out more, but there is nothing there," I said, pointing to my head as I fought back the tears. His stern expression made me feel like I was wasting his time.

As though sensing my distress, Doctor Wright quickly stepped over. "That will have to be enough for now, I'm afraid, Sheriff. She needs her rest."

Without a word, Sheriff Hadlock stood, grunting with the effort, his eyes fixed on me.

"After the accident, we impounded the car at the police station, where we searched it and entered the registration into the vehicle data registry. We're waiting to see what information comes up."

I stared back at him. I hadn't even thought about the car.

"For now, I'll continue the investigation and contact you when I know more." He pivoted and walked towards the door but stopped a few steps away. "Oh yeah, one more thing. There'll be a reporter coming to see you early Wednesday morning. He'll take a picture or two, put your story in the paper. Seems your accident has made the local news."

The Doctor walked the Sheriff out of my room. In the hallway, I could hear the muffled voice of the two of them talking about me. I felt so alone.

Just before lunch, there was a knock on the door and an older lady walked in carrying a small tray of food. I shuffled myself upright, grimacing as my ribs protested, and smiled shyly at her.

"Good morning. I'm Jennifer, the Speech Pathologist." She placed the tray on the side table.

"Hello."

"Doctor Wright asked me to assess you and see if we can remove that tube. Are you up for having something to eat?"

"Yes, that would be nice," I nodded enthusiastically.

"Right. I've brought a few different foods in varying textures. We will start with the soft food and thick water first. If you can swallow those without issue, we'll move up to the next level, okay?" She pulled the table towards the bed and opened the water first. Bringing it up to my mouth, I took a small sip. The thick fluid was cold and slid down my throat without an issue.

"Good. Let's try the apple puree next." She grabbed the small container, opened the lid, and held it out to me with a spoon. Eagerly, I had a mouthful, again swallowing without difficulty. The sweetness of the apple was delicious.

She nodded in approval. "Any pain or discomfort?"

"No."

After ten minutes of trying the other foods and drinks on the table, Jennifer smiled and pushed the table away from her.

"Fantastic. Thank you for trying everything. I'll have a chat with the doctor, and if he is happy, we can remove the feeding tube. You should be back on a normal diet by tonight."

She left, taking the tray of food scraps with her. Feeling some relief, and with my belly fuller, I settled back and closed my eyes.

Chapter 4

⟫◦⟪

Monday, September 11ᵗʰ

Martin Collins, a detective for the Missing Persons department at Hinterfield Police Station, in Missionly, was deep in thought when a younger co-worker named Brody knocked on his door.

"Dude ... do you ever go home?" he joked as he placed some files on Martin's in-tray.

"Sure," Martin answered without even looking up from his laptop.

"I don't know how your wife puts up with you spending all your time here and never with her."

"She knows the job, Brody, she always has."

Brody shook his head. "You sure are a lucky guy to have her. Don't forget to sign those papers in the blue file ... and go home!" he said with a cheerful grin.

Martin listened to Brody say a few goodbyes to the other late-night workers as he left before he reached over and grabbed the files in his tray and slipped them into his briefcase. Brody was right—Martin spent more time in the office than at home, but his job was not a typical nine-to-five. It was a twenty-four-hour, seven-days-a-week job, and Martin wouldn't have it any other way.

The smooth, matte black leather briefcase was a gift from his wife six years earlier, when Martin first joined the Missing Persons Unit. Working in this department had not been Martin's initial goal when he joined the police force. In fact, if you were to ask him, he would have said he never thought he would end up here.

The street was Martin's first choice after leaving high school. The chance to wear the uniform and chase the bad guys all the way to jail made him happy.

Martin and his best friend, Josh Poretess, joined the police force together after graduating. They both passed the training with high distinctions and even got paired up on the beat. Working together, driving in the squad car each day, the duo became closer than ever. While they'd grown up in different suburbs, they went to the same school where they'd hit it off instantly. Working together was just a natural progression in their friendship.

Martin's transition into the missing persons department occurred after a terrible and heart wrenching seven months, watching Josh go through a nightmare no parent should ever have to endure.

Eight years earlier, on a summers day at the beach, Josh's five-year-old daughter disappeared. Despite searching for her all day and over the next few weeks, no sign of his daughter or any indication of what happened to her eventuated.

Following the case closely, and helping where he could, Martin and two detectives questioned every witness time and time again, chasing whatever leads showed up, but to no avail. Six months after she went missing, another young girl disappeared from the same beach, but this time, thanks to the vigilant co-operation of witnesses, they found her, and the police apprehended the kidnapper. After a few hours of interrogations, he admitted to not only kidnapping that young girl but also Josh's daughter and two others over the previous three years.

The monster had kept each of the girls alive for a week in his brutal care, before he strangled them to death and buried their bodies in the forest. He informed the police of the burial sites and Josh could finally lay his daughter to rest.

Understandably, Josh's life fell apart, destroyed by the hours of searching and then the final, devastating outcome. He left the force to spend time with his wife and young son.

Martin's wife, Colleen, watched her husband spend every waking moment trying to solve the case and find his best mate's daughter. After he solved the case, it was Colleen who recognised a passion in Martin that he'd lost for the beat in recent years. A few months later, she suggested applying for detective training and a transfer. One thing led to another, and Martin was now one of the best missing person detectives in his state.

No case was ever the same. Some took a few weeks, others a few months—some went cold. Yet Martin never gave up on them and kept those files in his office, a reminder to never stop looking. At any given opportunity, Martin picked a cold case from the pile, trying to find closure for the families, links to more recent cases, anything to keep himself busy. In the past four years, Martin solved several cases that others had given up on.

Adding his laptop to his briefcase, along with his wallet and mobile phone, Martin grabbed his car keys and glanced into the oval mirror, which hung next to his office door. Time had been good to Martin. He was forty-three years old, and his chestnut brown hair was just starting to turn grey at the temples and behind his ears. Staring at his reflection, he winked his green eyes and shook his head at the small wrinkles that had formed around them.

At just over six-foot, Martin carried his weight well, spending at least an hour every morning exercising before work. His dark blue linen suit was tailor made, as were all the suits he owned, by a local tailor Martin had once helped. He took pride in his appearance ensuring he looked his best for wherever the day would take him.

Walking out of the office for the night, Martin knew he needed to lighten his load and spend more time with his wife. They'd been married for nine years now. No children, though.

Colleen was also in the police force, and they had both decided not long after they got engaged that work was always busy and time for children was not high on their list of priorities. A decision not looked back upon with sorrow or regret. The rare times they weren't both working was time spent together, just the two of them. They were a happy couple.

Five years ago, they bought a puppy, and to them, this was as close enough to a child as they wanted to get. Perhaps in the back of their minds, watching what Josh went through, and because of the missing person's cases Martin took, they both agreed children would lead to unwanted stress and distraction in their lives—and more emotional grief that Colleen knew she wouldn't be able to handle. Overall, Martin was a content man. Willing to go the extra mile to solve a case, help a family in need, and go to bed each night hoping to find the next missing person.

Chapter 5

Tuesday, September 12th

The routine of hospital life started early and now crept closer to my door. I could hear a trolley being wheeled past my room and a few moments later, my door swung open, and a breakfast tray was brought in by an elderly gentleman wearing a clean, crisp, light blue shirt and pants.

"Good morning, miss. Good to see you're awake," he commented as he lowered the tray onto the small table and pushed it towards me. He shuffled over to the end of my bed and slowly raised the top half, so I was in a better position to eat. "I hope this is okay. The kitchen has organised your meals for the day. There's cereal, milk, and a small selection of fruit—and a menu for tomorrow. Please make sure you fill it out and I will pick it up after you have finished." He smiled and quietly strolled out into the corridor.

Glancing over the menu for the next day, I randomly picked an item for each meal and slipped the menu onto the table. I devoured my cereal and fruit; grateful the feeding tube was gone.

After breakfast, the reporter the sheriff mentioned stopped by. He was nothing memorable to look at. Older man, with short greying hair, neatly trimmed beard, and thick, black-rimmed glasses. He asked the same questions as the sheriff had and got the same answers.

"I don't know who I am. I don't remember anything."

He took a few photos and informed me that my story would be on the local news tonight and an article printed in the newspaper the following day. As quickly as he'd turned up, he was gone, replaced by Tracey.

"I don't understand why I can't remember anything!" I moaned, curling my hands up into fists.

"Relax," she said, placing her hands on mine. "Sometimes the brain blocks out a few things for it to get better and heal faster. Your memories will come back eventually, but for now, just relax. Stressing yourself over it will only make the matter worse."

The rest of the day passed quietly. To entertain myself, I watched television and settled back to see what was happening in the world outside until Tracey returned that afternoon.

"Hello again," she smiled at me as she checked my chart. "I just wanted to check in with you before I head home for the day."

"Thank you. That's very kind."

"Are you doing, okay?"

I shook my head in disappointment.

"I know things are bad now, but they will improve. Your memory loss cannot last forever." She bustled around the room, topping up my water, checking my vitals and making sure I had enough pain medication. "I take it you've had no visitors yet?"

"No, should there be?" I asked, wondering if there was something she knew that I didn't.

"I had hoped so. There was a brief story on the news, the night of your accident. I thought someone would have come in by now to find you."

"No, no one other than the staff, the sheriff, the reporter and you, has been in to see me."

"Ah, not to worry, my dear. It should be soon, I would say. Someone out there is missing you. Now, is there anything I can do before I go?"

"Actually, yes there is," I said. "Would you be able to get me a mirror, please?"

"Sure thing. There's one right here." She came over to the side of the bed and opened the little cupboard under the side table. She lent down and a few seconds later, straightened, holding a small oval mirror.

"Here you go." She handed it to me, and I took it slowly and placed it face down on my leg. "Are you okay?" she asked.

I nodded but still didn't lift the mirror. I didn't tell her, but it had occurred to me earlier, I didn't even remember what I looked like. If I looked at myself, it might jog a memory or two.

"Would you like me to leave the room? Let you be by yourself for a bit?"

I nodded again. I didn't know what to expect, and I wanted to be alone when I looked at myself. "Oh, before you go. You said before I had a small bag and purse. Can I have them, please?"

"Yes, yes, of course." Tracey turned around and walked to a thin cupboard tucked in the corner of the room. Opening the door, she brought out a green tote bag and placed it next to my side.

"No problem, sweetheart. I hope it helps you." She patted the back of my hand gently and left.

Taking a deep breath, I lifted the mirror up towards my face, but I closed my eyes. Fear welled within me.

What if I don't recognise my own face? What if I I see nothing in the reflection that will open the door to my mind?

Holding the mirror directly up, I took another, deeper breath, willing myself to calm down as I opened my eyes. The face in the reflection, was swollen and bruised. On the right side of my temple was a nasty blemish in shades of red, yellow, and blue, surrounding the stitches of my head wound.

This must be where my head hit the steering wheel.

Studying the face in the mirror, I felt nothing. No spark of recognition.

This face could belong to anyone.

Looking past the bruising, the first thing I noticed were two clear, dark blue eyes, framed with black eyelashes. A small turned-up nose sat in the middle of my face and a splatter of freckles spread out across the bridge of my nose, under my eyes, and across my cheeks.

My mouth was small, with slim lips. I smiled, and the reflection smiled back, revealing straight white teeth, which peeked through the gaps between the lips.

A pleasant smile.

Shifting my eyes to the side of my face I took in the bland shade of light, mousey blonde tones of my long hair, which lay limp and messy over my shoulders. It had no style and with small clumps of dried blood around the wound, it certainly needed a wash. Overall, I looked okay—not bad for someone who'd spent the last few days in the hospital, but not pretty enough to be classed as beautiful.

I placed the mirror down on the bed and looked at the tote bag. I didn't recognise it. Pulling it towards me, I placed it on my lap and opened the zip. Inside, I saw a colourful array of clothes, and as I pulled them out one by one, I tried to remember wearing them.

Two pairs of denim shorts, one white, one blue, three cotton t-shirts in various colours, a red singlet, a pair of faded blue jeans, two floral dresses, a black cardigan, and a few articles of underwear ended up in a pile on the bed. A pair of black flat sandals and white slip-on shoes lay at the bottom of the bag.

From the corner of the bag, I pulled out a simple, dark-pink cotton nightie. I stared at the pile yet felt nothing.

Turning the tote bag upside-down, a hairbrush, a small toiletries bag and a black purse fell out.

The toiletry bag held the usual bits and bobs. Soap, toothbrush, and toothpaste, a few hair ties, and a lip gloss and a roll-on deodorant. Popping off the lid, I smelled the strawberry scented lip gloss, then generously applied a small amount to my lips and rubbed them together.

Feeling like I wasn't getting anywhere with the clothes, I shoved them back into the tote and grabbed the purse. With a sigh, I opened the clasp and looked inside, revealing a few notes and coins. Counting the money, I had a few hundred dollars, but nothing else. No bank cards, no driver's licence, nothing with my name on it. To say I felt deflated was an understatement. I'd hoped seeing my belongings would jog my memory. They did not.

They may as well belong to a stranger.

Placing the purse back into the bag, and dropping it to the floor, my eyes drifted towards the small, attached bathroom. Feeling unclean and clammy, I was desperately in need of a shower. I wondered how that would work with my leg in a cast. Something I would have to ask Tracey the next time I saw her.

With the events of the day taking their toll, feeling emotionally and physically exhausted, I fell asleep and woke a few hours later to dinner being served. Hearing a commotion beside me, I noticed the bed next to me was now occupied by a middle-aged female. Turning to her, I smiled politely as she ate her food. Although she did not engage in any conversation with me, I was pleasantly relieved to know I was no longer alone.

A couple more nurses popped into see me throughout the evening to check my vitals, each of them prompting me for any recollections. All of them getting the same response. I still remembered nothing.

To my relief, a nurse removed my catheter, and with some assistance, she got me to the bathroom. Here, I used the toilet and once again, looked into the mirror to see if I recognised the girl in the reflection. I did not.

Settling myself in for the night, laying on my side, I listened to the light, rhythmic breathing of the female besides me.

I wonder if she has anyone coming to visit her tomorrow.

Closing my eyes, I soon drifted off into a dreamless slumber.

Chapter 6

Wednesday, September 13th

"Tony, there is a Sheriff Hadlock on line one for you," the voice called through the speaker, interrupting Tony from his work.

"Thank you, Amanda," he replied.

Tony was an older gentleman who, much to his dislike, had recently turned fifty-six. His once thick, dark-brown hair was now mostly light ash grey and thinning out terribly. Over the past few years, he'd stopped watching what he ate, and the evidence showed around his waist. He put it down to the fact his wife walked out on him six years ago, taking their three children with her, and therefore there was no one at home to cook him healthy meals. Tony resorted to driving through fast-food joints on his way home every night and had stopped going for his nightly walks—something he'd previously done with his wife.

Work was the extent of his social life now because there was no one to go home to. Tony used his job to keep himself busy, working from early in the morning until late at night most days of the week.

Sheriff Hadlock ... Now why does that name sound familiar?

After a few seconds, failing to remember, he leant forward in his chair, grabbed his notepad and pen, picked up the receiver, and pressed the flashing red button.

"Hello, Officer Tony Smitten speaking."

"Good morning, Officer Smitten. This is Sheriff Hadlock from Parker in Camberton. Sorry to bother you so early," said the deep voice on the phone.

A flash of recognition finally passed through Tony's mind. "That's okay, Sheriff, how can I help you today?" he replied, leaning back in his chair.

"I sent you an email on Monday, regarding a number plate I have here. I was wondering if you had any information for me yet."

"Funny you should ask that," Tony said, sitting back up and moving the computer's curser over an email he'd received only a few moments ago. "I received a phone call earlier regarding it." He clicked the left button on the mouse and opened a document he'd created an hour earlier, displaying the information Sheriff Hadlock enquired about.

"The plates are registered to Mr Colin Tanner, who lives in Barrister, about fifteen minutes from here. Apparently, he reported the car missing just over a week ago. Went for a walk early Monday morning and when he returned, the car was gone," he paused, hearing the Sheriff huff on the other end of the line. "You say you have the car there?"

"Yes, I do," he replied in a tone of annoyance. "It's not the news I was hoping for. I assume Mr Tanner wants his car back?"

"I guess so. But didn't your report say it was totalled?" asked Tony.

"It sure is, a right royal mess. Not sure what he'll want to do with it once he gets it though," Sheriff Hadlock grunted into the phone.

"Me neither. I'll inform Mr Tanner you've found his car and pass on your information. That way, the two of you can work out the finer details. What did you mean by the comment, 'It was not the news you were hoping for'?" Tony queried with a slight frown.

"When we got to the accident scene, there was a female in the driver's seat. She had no identification on her, or in the car, and because of a head injury she sustained in the crash, she has no memory of the event, or of anything actually." He sighed heavily. "I was hoping you would have the missing information I needed. We assumed she was the owner of the vehicle. Instead, it looks like we have a crime scene here and she is a possible car thief."

"Ah, I see. What will you do with her now?"

"Well, I can't arrest her yet. She's still in hospital and with no memory, we have no proof she stole it. Plus, it makes it harder to find out what happened and how she's involved. I'll hold her here, though until we sort things out."

"She has no memory of the crash?"

"No, and conveniently, has no memory of anything before the crash, either. Doesn't even know her own name."

Tony raised his eyebrows at the Sheriff's words, as he turned and stared out the window. "Look, I'll get in contact with Mr Tanner now and let him know what's going on. Maybe he knows the girl, and as I said, I'll pass on your details so he can contact you and vice versa. Perhaps it's just his daughter or something like that. A simple misunderstanding."

"Yeah, that sounds fine," the Sheriff replied, sounding a little more relieved.

"In the meantime, are you able to send me any information on the girl? Perhaps I can investigate it from this end, seeing how the whole thing looks like it might have started from near here."

"Sure. It's not much though, seeing how she can't remember anything. I'll send what I have, plus photos of the car. As soon as my reporter returns with the photos of her, I'll send everything through. Hopefully, it will be early this afternoon," he replied.

"Sounds good." Tony didn't have a too many cases on his hands, another local one would keep him busy. "I'll email you the licence and insurance information I received from the owner. That way, if he contacts you, you have the details. I look forward to your email on the girl. Maybe get some fingerprints as well. That might help us figure out who she is. Was there anything else I could help you with?"

"Nothing now. Thanks for the info on the car, detective. Promising idea on the prints. I'll get them tomorrow and put them into the database."

"No worries."

"Okay, well, until next time," responded Sheriff Hadlock before he hung up.

Tony forwarded an email to the sheriff right away and returned to his normal morning routine.

A few hours later, he received the expected email from the sheriff. Opening it, he read through the pages and inspected the pictures of the female and the damaged car.

This might not be as straightforward as I thought.

After printing off the pictures and the relevant information, along with the previous email he'd received on Tuesday, Tony gathered all the papers, slipped them into a file and strolled out his office.

The days passed by like they did in any week of Martin's life. New cases appeared on his desk each morning. He'd distribute them out to his staff, keeping the cases, he deemed to be the most interesting for himself—a challenge, something to work the mind and test his skills.

Sometimes the cases with the least amount of information were the ones which grabbed his attention—more to uncover, more unanswered questions and more heart, sweat and tears to put forward, in the hopes he could solve the case and help a grieving family find closure.

Wednesday morning started out much the same. Arriving at work at eight am sharp, with a strong, tall, black coffee he always bought from the cafe across the road from the Police Department, he greeted his staff as he made his way through the building to his office.

Sitting down at his desk, Martin removing his laptop, phone, and files from his briefcase, he then slid it behind himself against the wall under the window. Having a large window behind Martin was something he didn't take for granted. He worked on the third floor and the view out over the city was not exactly breath taking but was pleasant enough for him to sit back each day and spend a morning or afternoon coffee break watching the world pass by.

Grabbing the new files and mail from his in-tray, he placed them onto the middle of his desk. Switching on his laptop and taking a gentle sip of his still hot coffee, Martin looked through the mail he had received. A few sheets of information on a cold case he was working on. A letter from a family wishing him all the best after closing a missing person case two weeks earlier, and a news article on a missing girl dated from four years ago, sent in by 'Mr Anon.' It amazed Martin how many people sent in information about missing people, useful or not, and never signed their names.

In amongst the mail, Martin found two new cases. One was regarding a young boy, aged fifteen, who didn't come home from school three days ago. The second case was an elderly lady who'd gone missing from her nursing home two days before. Her family was concerned, as Mrs Walsh needed daily medication to help with her Alzheimer's and diabetes.

Taking another sip of his coffee, Martin sent emails to two coworkers regarding the new cases, then continued with his work. When he finally took the time to glance up at the clock,

Martin was stunned to realise five hours had passed, and his half-drunk coffee was now cold, and he was also hungry.

"Afternoon, Collins."

Martin looked up to see Tony standing at the door holding a manilla folder in his right hand. Tony worked in the traffic department and often helped Martin out with information pertaining to some cases he worked on.

"Afternoon, Tony, what you got for me?" replied Martin as his eyes lowered to the file.

Tony walked in and pulled a black leather office chair from the corner of the room towards Martin's desk. Flopping into the chair, he tossed the folder onto Martin's laptop.

"Something rather interesting, actually!" he said, sounding impressed with himself. "This originally came through on Tuesday, with more information about half an hour ago. It appears we have a possible stolen car. Disappeared from over in Barrister just over a week ago."

"Okay, and ..." Martin said, ignoring the file now covering his keyboard.

"The car was found in Parker. Over two thousand, eight hundred kilometres away!"

"That's a long joy ride," Martin laughed.

"Yes, it is," Tony laughed too. "It was involved in a nasty car accident. Run in with a drunk driver. Looking at the pictures, the car's totalled."

Martin opened the file and glanced at four photos, which lay on the top of a stack of papers. Three showed the car and the damage it received, and the fourth was of a female, in a hospital bed, looking rather battered and bruised—and scared.

"And this relates to me, how?" Martin asked—stolen cars were not a part of his job.

Tony smiled and leaned forward in the chair. "Well, if it didn't relate to you, I wouldn't be in here now, would I?" he grinned.

Martin shook his head slightly. Tony loved to play up the drama in cases he thought were going to be tough. Seeing no amusement on his face, Tony continued.

"Fine. According to the email you have in front of you, the young lady in the photo was driving the car." He pointed to the photo. "She's in hospital with a few non-life-threatening injuries, but she can't remember anything. Doesn't help that there was little with her in the car. A small travel bag, but no ID, and no phone."

"Okay ..." his eyebrows arched.

Consider my interest peaked. He thought.

Martin placed the photos to the side and read the email. As he did, Tony leaned back in the chair and continued the conversation.

"Now, using the information the Sheriff of Parker gave me, I spoke to the owner of the car this morning who lives over in Barrister," he grinned. "He was happy to know we'd found his car, but he was rather pissed off to hear it's a write-off and ended up so far from home. Paperwork is at the bottom of the pile." He motioned for Martin to look at them, too.

"I bet. It looks bad. And the female driver only got minor injuries? Lucky girl," Martin said, looking back at the photos.

"Yes. She has a broken leg and was in a coma or something like that after smashing her forehead on the steering wheel, but other than that, she's fine, incredibly lucky. Apparently, she has amnesia. I'm still trying to work out if the memory loss is convenient or real. Anyway, the owner reported the car missing four days ago. This is the first he's heard about it."

"And there's no clue who she is?" Martin asked.

"Nope," Tony smirked, shrugged his shoulders, and raised his hands into the air. "Mystery lady."

"Still not seeing what any of this has to do with me. I don't work grand theft auto cases," Martin said, closing the folder and placing it back on his desk.

Tony straightened in the chair and frowned. "The sheriff is happy we found the owner of the car. He'll work out the finer details to get the car back to him. Not so happy it wasn't the females, though. Regarding the girl, he can't arrest her without evidence she stole it. He wants me to show the photo of her to the owner. Hopefully, he might recognise her. But if he doesn't, would you be interested in looking into who she is?"

Martin ran his hand over his chin. "I can run a quick missing person's check in the database, but try the owner of the car first, okay?"

"Sweet." Tony stood, grabbed the file, and turned to walk out the office. "I know it's not an overly important case for you, Martin. Just thought seeing how you're the best, you might be interested."

"Just talk to the owner first, see what he knows, and if it comes up negative, give me the file and I'll take it from there."

"No worries, mate. Mr Tanner is coming in tomorrow morning at nine. I'll let you know after that." Tony walked out the door and turned right, heading toward the elevators.

Martin shook his head; Tony was a great guy, always putting his heart and soul into his cases. He appreciated his efficiency and work ethic.

The following morning, a little after nine-thirty, Tony returned with the file.

"No luck?" Martin asked as Tony walked up to the desk.

"Nope. Didn't recognise her at all," he replied, shaking his head.

"Thanks," Martin said as he grabbed the file and placed it into his IN tray. "I'll get a profile set up this afternoon. Just got a few things I need to finish first."

Tony nodded and turned to walk out of the room. "Thanks again, mate, I owe you one!" he called out as he walked through the doorway.

Martin shook his head and rolled his eyes. "That means you own me about ten favours now, Tony! And make sure you ring the Sheriff back and let him know too," he called out after him. He heard a faint laugh and a 'will do' from Tony as he disappeared down the corridor.

Not long after lunch, Martin sat at his desk, grabbed the file Tony had dropped off, and opened his computer. The attached paperwork in the file included the finer details of the female in the photo. Martin accessed the missing person's database and entered a new profile case labelled 'Jane Doe'. Perhaps there was a matching profile already in the database, here in the capital of Missionly, which would solve the case.

The rest of Martin's afternoon passed without so much as a second thought to the girl with no memory. Things like this happened often with head trauma and he hoped by the following morning; the missing people's database would have identified her. He could then close the case.

Chapter 8

Wednesday, September 13th

Just before lunch, the Sheriff arrived. As he entered the room, I looked at him, hoping he had some good news for me.

"Hello Sheriff," I said with a smile, straightening the blanket over my legs.

"Hello," he replied, his tone blunt and his expression filled with discontent.

My smile faltered as I watched him approach the bed, a small, black bag in his hands, which he placed on the bedside table.

What is going on here?

"Have you got any good news for me?" I asked, hopefully.

"No, not really. How is that memory of yours going? Do you have any good news for me?" he asked with a sneer, the sarcasm in his voice not lost on me.

I took a moment before answering, wondering why he seemed so hostile. "No, not yet," I replied.

"Convenient," he scoffed, and made his way to the other side of my bed, pulling the curtain closed, to create the illusion of privacy between myself and the other patient. While the sheriff wasn't exactly friendly during our first visit, his attitude today felt far more personal. When I failed to say anything, he moved back to the table and continued. "Let's get to business then. Regarding the car, you were in ..."

"You found something!" I sat up straighter, wincing in pain as my bruised ribs protested the movement.

"We ran a trace on the number plate. Turns out it's registered in Missionly, two thousand, eight hundred kilometres from here ..." He paused, gazing at me before he continued.

"Does the name Colin Tanner sound familiar?" he asked, an eyebrow raised. Frowning, I wracked my brain, hoping the name would unlock a memory, but nothing came. I shook my head. The sheriff's scowl deepened as he continued.

"He reported his car stolen over a week ago, before you totalled it and ended up here—with no recollection, apparently."

The way he looked at me made me feel uneasy, as though he was waiting for me to confess to something, yet I felt as though I was two steps behind him.

What is he getting at?

"Can you explain to me how you ended up in possession of a car that doesn't belong to you, so far from where it's registered?"

My jaw drooped open, and I stared at him with a blank expression.

"I'm sorry ..." I stammered. "I don't know ... I don't ... I can't remember." My hands became clammy, and I started shaking.

"I am very much aware of your memory loss, Ms Doe, and I find it most inconvenient you can't remember anything. I've notified the Missionly police department and forwarded them your photo. They're searching for a match as we speak." He paused, looking at me intently. "They've requested your fingerprints." He opened the bag and pulled out a pile of papers and a small metal tin, before wheeling the table towards me.

My eyes widened and felt my heart skip.

Why does he need my fingerprints? Am I being arrested?

"Are you arresting me, Sheriff?" I asked nervously. My mouth felt like sandpaper, and I struggled to swallow.

"No, I cannot formally charge you—yet, but there's no denying that you were in possession of a stolen vehicle at the time of the accident," he said slowly, though his expression distinctly told me he wished he was. "As we're still trying to identify you, your prints could prove useful if you're in the system. If circumstance change, well, we'll have them on file, won't we?"

Placing his things on the table, he opened the tin, revealing a black ink pad. Glancing at me, he held out his hand.

"Do you think I stole it?" I asked, tears stinging my dry eyes.

"That's why I'm here, to find out. Your left hand, please."

I slowly gave him my hand, and he grabbed it roughly. One by one, he lowered each finger to the pad, rolled it slightly left to right, then moved my finger to the paper, where he repeated the movement. All I could do was watch, my mind racing as he transferred the ink onto the form, revealing clear images of my fingerprints. He repeated the process with my right hand, taking his time, making sure each print was clear.

"It will take a few days to run these through the database. I'll let you know if anything comes up." He slipped my prints into a plastic protective sleeve and packed everything away in the bag. "While the accident was not your fault, I suggest you don't leave Parker anytime soon. The moment you *do* remember anything, you're to come straight to me. Do you understand?" he said, his voice oddly low but firm, leaving no room for argument.

"Yes, sir," I whispered, leaning back against the pillows.

He moved the table back against the wall and walked out of the room, leaving me looking down at the blackened tips of my fingers.

Two thousand, eight hundred kilometres, is a long way to travel. Am I a car thief? No, of course I'm not. Why would I need to steal a car? Why had I driven so far and where was I heading? And who's Mr Colin Tanner? I must know him if I have his car. I couldn't be a thief!

Sitting in bed, I stared at my hands, too embarrassed to look at the curtain dividing the room in half. I knew the female in the bed next to me heard the entire conversation.

Tears of fear, confusion, and anger ran down my cheeks.

When lunch arrived, the porter opened the dividing curtain, spilling the light from the window across my bed. After dropping a tray of food on my table and pushing it close to the bed, he repeated the action for the patient next to me, leaving soon after.

Staring at my stained fingertips, I pushed the tray away from me. This did not go unseen by my roommate. Climbing out of bed, she came to my side, holding a packet of bed wipes.

"For your fingers," she smiled warmly.

"Thank you." My eyes widened.

"You're welcome," she replied and returned to her bed, leaving me to eat in silence.

I cleaned my fingertips as best as I could and nibbled absent-mindedly at the food, paying no attention to what I ate.

The afternoon then dragged slowly, a haze of pain medication, nurse checks, and mundane television shows. I watched the shadows snake across the room as the sun arced through the sky, creeping closer to the horizon.

"Ms. Doe, how are we this evening?" Doctor Wright asked as he entered the room just before dinner.

"About the same," I replied.

"Still no change, hey?" he asked.

"Nope, nothing yet."

Closing the dividing curtain, he ran through a series of tests, checking my reactions and reflexes.

"Let's try a word game. What is this?" he said, holding up an object.

"A pen."

"What is that?" He pointed to the corner of the room.

"A chair."

"Name three days of the week."

"Monday, Tuesday, Wednesday."

"What is five times three?"

"Fifteen."

"Name two types of mammals?"

"Um, dog and bear," I frowned.

He smiled as he nodded. "It looks like you have retrograde amnesia."

"What's that?" I asked, feeling anxious.

"It's a type of amnesia where you can make and retain new memories, but you can't recall memories from before the accident. Your memory recollection of everyday objects and retained knowledge is great. It's just your memory that's blank."

"Is that bad?" I bunched the blanket up in my fists.

"It is common in head trauma cases. It just means your brain is blocking you from remembering something. Perhaps giving you time to heal."

"Blocking me from what?"

"I'm not sure. I would like you to see a friend of mine who helps patients suffering from trauma, amnesia, and the like. Perhaps with their help, you can restore that memory of yours."

"Okay, like a shrink?"

Great, now I'm crazy!

"Sort of. Her name is Doctor Stephanie Wilkins. Her clinic is on the first floor of the hospital. I'll get her to come up and see you tomorrow." With a last smile, he opened the curtain and left, his words echoing, leaving me feeling afraid.

What is my brain be protecting me from?

Glancing sideways, to the bed next to me, the woman gave me a sympathetic smile, before turning her attention back to the book in her hands.

Did the doctors really think drawing the curtain could stop their voices from being overheard?

I shook my head in annoyance. I wasn't sure what was worse; not having anyone come to the hospital to visit me, or identify me, or to have the patient next to me think I'm crazy.

Tracey was my only visitor, and the highlight of my day. She could see when I was struggling and always put a smile on my face.

"Good evening," she said cheerfully, carrying a pair of crutches, which she rested against the wall, then placed a small shopping bag on the bed.

"Hi," I replied, noting the crutches, then looking suspiciously at the packet. "What's that?"

"Well, the crutches are for you, so you can start moving around, and some nurses bought you a few toiletries. They wanted to let you know you're not alone here." She pulled the bag closer to me.

"That's very kind of them, but I have some in my bag." I motioned to the closed cupboard door.

Tracey's smile faulted slightly. "We weren't sure what was in your bag, so we all thought you might like a few things to pamper yourself with."

"Thank you," I reached my hand towards her, grateful for her generosity. "Well, show me what they bought." I beamed.

Tracey grabbed the bag and upended it. A bottle of shampoo, conditioner, and moisturiser fell onto my lap. Two small tubes of lips gloss, a can of deodorant, some hair ties, and a new brush, tumbled out as well.

"Wow, so much stuff." I picked each item up, opening the bottles and smelling their sweet aromas.

"I have some free time now," she said, bagging the toiletries. "So, I thought I could watch the news with you, see what the report is like, then afterwards, get you into a nice warm shower?" Tracey asked.

"Please." I smiled. A sigh of relief escaped me, as I was looking forward to feeling a bit more normal.

Tracey pulled the chair close to my bed, and together we watched the news on the television. I grimaced at the images of me as they flashed onto the screen. I looked like a mess. The bruises on my face were healing but were now horrible shades of yellow and blues.

How could anyone recognise me in this state?

Sensing my discouragement, Tracey got me out of bed and into my first shower since the accident. It felt amazing to feel the hot water run over me, as though it could somehow wash away all the confusion of the past few days. While the nurses had done their best to get the blood out of my hair while I was bedridden, it made such a difference to wash it myself.

Feeling so much better after the shower, I settled down in bed, hopeful the news article would bring someone who knew me. Five days is a long time, for family and friends not to miss me.

The following morning, Doctor Wilkins popped in for her visit, and I was taken aback at how young and elegant she was. For some reason, I'd pictured someone in her late fifties. Instead, her long black hair was stylishly combed back into a high ponytail, and her warm, brown eyes, were elegantly framed by long, black eyelashes. Her perfectly applied red lipstick drew in my gaze.

She wore an elegant, silky lemon-yellow shirt paired with a pair of loose-fitting, navy-blue pants that swished as she walked, and her expensive-looking black heels clicked across the floor as she approached me. Very professional.

"Good morning. I'm Doctor Wilkins, but you may call me Stephanie," said, extending her hand.

"Good morning," I replied, shaking her hand.

As the patient in the bed mine was discharged an hour before, Doctor Wilkins didn't have to close the curtain. She moved the chair from the corner of the room next to the bed, sat, and placed a notepad on her lap. "How are you feeling this morning?"

"Not bad considering," I gestured to my head and leg.

"Yes, I can see that. I've had a chat with Doctor Wright, and he informed me of everything there is to know about you, as little as that is for now."

I laughed at that, surprising myself.

How right she is.

"What I'd like to do today," she continued, "Is have you talk to me about whatever you want, okay? No pressure, no questions from me. I just want you to chat about whatever you need to."

"Um ... Okay." I wasn't sure how this would help me and had no idea what to say. I sat there for a few moments, looking at the bed, avoiding eye contact.

What am I meant to say?

"Doctor Wright said I have retrograde amnesia," I breathed.

"Yes, that is correct. Do you understand what it means?" she asked.

"I can make new memories and keep them, but I can't recall anything from before the accident."

"That's right."

"He said I should get my memories back, but for now, the accident caused a blockage, so to speak, and because of the traumatic event, my brain is perhaps, um, protecting me."

"That's a good way to look at it," she said as she wrote on her notepad. As though sensing my stare, she looked up. "Just taking notes for your file."

"Okay." Realising how nervous I was, I tried my best to relax.

Stephanie watched me, waiting for me to continue.

"How long do you think it will take?" I asked.

"For what?" she responded.

"For my memories to come back. To remember who I am and where I'm from."

"It all depends on you and your brain—the duration is different for each patient. I wouldn't worry about it right now. You're still healing."

"But what happens if it never comes back? Doctor Wright said not to worry, but I *am* worried. I don't want to go on, day after day, without knowing who I am and what's happened."

"I completely understand, and if you're willing, I'd like to help you as much as possible."

"How? What can you do?" I asked tentatively.

"Exactly what we're doing now. Talking. We might try some games and memory tasks. Perhaps hypnotherapy? I have several techniques we can use to try to unlock those memories of yours."

"Hypnotherapy? Is that safe?"

"Yes. I'm trained and I've had success with other patients."

"Okay, well, I'll think about that one. Can we just stick to talking for now?"

"Absolutely. Whatever makes you comfortable."

We chatted for a few more minutes before Stephanie scheduled our next appointment for the following Monday. After she left, I felt positive that for the first time; I had a way to move forward.

"Don't give up yet, love. If you are not from around here, it might take longer for the news article to get out," Tracey had reassured me after the meeting with Doctor Wilkins. "There will be someone out there who misses you."

Worn out from another long and somewhat uneventful day, I welcomed the evening's pain medication and drifted off into another dreamless sleep.

Chapter 9

Thursday, September 14th

Sheriff Hadlock picked up the receiver on the third ring. "Good afternoon, Sheriff Hadlock speaking."

"Afternoon Sheriff, it's Officer Tony Smitten from Hinterfield Police station."

"Good afternoon, Officer Smitten. You have something for me?"

"I do. I spoke to Mr Tanner, the owner of the car in question. He came into the station this morning and looked over the pictures you sent. Unfortunately, he didn't recognise your Jane Doe."

"Hm ... that's a problem then," Sheriff Hadlock said, tapping his pen on the desk.

"Mr Tanner asked what will happen with his car now?" Tony asked.

"Well, for now I'll have to keep it here as evidence, until we ascertain whether she stole it—or at the very least, how she came to be in possession of it," he replied, trying to contain his annoyance.

"And what about your mystery girl? Did you get her prints?"

"Yes. I will forward them to you."

"Thank you."

Sheriff Hadlock hung up the phone and leaned back in his chair. Rubbing his hand down his face, he sighed heavily. He knew he had to return to the hospital and question the woman again.

Within fifteen minutes, he was parking his patrol car in the hospital carpark. Looking up towards the building, he sighed heavily again—he wasn't looking forward to dealing with the mysterious patient again.

As he entered the patient's room, the first thing Sheriff Hadlock noticed was that she was sitting in a chair beside her bed.

"Hello, Sheriff," she greeted him tentatively.

"Morning. Good to see you are out of the bed for a change," he said, a hint of delight in his tone.

She nodded with a cautious smile. "It's nice to move around more."

Despite her smile, he could see she was nervous as he walked towards her and, with an audible grunt, sat at the end of the mattress.

"I've been in contact with an officer in Missionly, who's spoken to the owner of the car. The officer showed him your photo, but unfortunately, he didn't recognise you." He inspected the woman as her face dropped and she turned away from him, looking out towards the window.

"Are you going to arrest me now?" she asked, still looking outside.

"No, not yet."

She whipped around and stared at him, her eyes wide.

"At this point," he continued. "There's still no evidence you stole the car, but you were in possession of a stolen vehicle, so it's complicated."

"So, what happens now?" she asked quietly.

Sheriff Hadlock sighed heavily. "Your details and fingerprints have been entered into the missing person's database. Hopefully, we'll get a hit soon. Until we know who you are, and what happened, it's hard to know what to do with you."

"Do with me?" She sat up a little straighter in the chair.

"You're suspected of car theft. In any other circumstances, I'd arrest you, but we don't have enough evidence yet. Once we do, and if we can prove that you did in fact steal the car, I'll formally charge you and take you to Missionly."

Sheriff Hadlock watched as she lowered her head, a tear running slowly down her cheek. It made him feel uncomfortable, and he turned his head towards the window and focused on the garden outside. After a minute or two, he cleared his throat and stood. "As I've mentioned, I wouldn't plan on leaving."

"Where exactly would I go?" she huffed, still avoiding looking at him as another tear ran down her cheek and dripped off her chin.

"If anything comes up, I'll let you know." Not waiting for a response, Sheriff Hadlock left the room.

Chapter 10

Saturday, September 16th

I was genuinely shocked to realise six days had passed and there was still no sign of my memories returning. Doctor Wright could find no reason to keep me in the hospital, since I was recovering well from my injuries. The physical ones, at least.

"I have to say, you've been the most interesting case I've had in a while," he commented. "This is a small town, and most strangers only pass though."

I stared at him, not sharing his enthusiasm. Clearing his throat, he continued.

"I am aware we've not made any headway with your memory yet, so I'd like you to continue seeing Doctor Wilkins, okay?"

"Sure, I can do that."

"Also, I'd like you to come back next week for another scan, and again in a fortnight, for a checkup on the leg. Sound good?"

"Yes, thank you."

The doctor stared at me for a moment, and I did my best to look braver than I felt. The hospital had become my haven, as though my identity was tied to it. I didn't know who I was outside of it.

"Look," he said softly. "I am well aware that no-one has come to the hospital to identify you, and it's not that we need the bed, but I think it's best for you to continue your recovery, out of the hospital environment." All I could do was look at him, mouth agape. "I know it's daunting, but I've written the name of a nearby hotel, and took the liberty of speaking to the manager regarding your lack of identification."

With as much of a smile as I could muster, I accepted the piece of paper, but I could feel the tremble in my chin. The thought of leaving was overwhelming—I had a few hundred dollars in my bag and little else.

After Doctor Wright left to finalise the discharge papers, Tracey walked in holding a small brown paper bag.

"I hear the Doctor is letting you go," she murmured as she sat on the end of my bed.

"Yes," I replied, feeling the hot sting of tears.

"Oh, don't cry now," she patted me gently on the hand. "It's not so bad ... I've bought you a change of clothes. I know it's not much, and they're not new, but you look to be the same size as my daughter. I'm sure they'll fit you."

"Oh no, you didn't have to do that!" I gasped.

"Nothing to it, my dear. Honestly, doubt she'll notice they're missing. These are just a few of the things she leaves behind for the next time she visits. It's been a while since she has been home, so at least someone will get use out of them." Tracey ducked her head with a sigh before she looked back up at me with a forced smile.

"But I already have some clothes in my bag."

"Yes, which might need a wash. They have been in your bag for a few days now. I wasn't sure when you might have last washed them. I was thinking you could wear something fresh."

She had a point. I didn't have much with me, and who knows how long it had been since I cleaned them. "Thank you so much," I replied gratefully, taking the bag from her hands. She nodded slowly, looking around the room, and I got the feeling there was something wrong.

"Is everything okay?" I asked.

"Everything is fine, dear," she said quickly. "It's just that ... well, I don't want to intrude ..." she paused, flicking me a quick glance before dropping her gaze to the floor.

"No intrusion," I replied. "Please, what is it?"

She took a deep breath and gave me a gentle smile. "Well, it's just no one has come forward to say they know who you are, and I know how much it upsets you that you can't remember. So, I was just wondering where you'd go from here. Where will you stay?"

I sighed. "Doctor Wright told me I could get a room at a nearby motel. I guess I'll head there first."

"What about money?" she asked.

"Yeah, I thought about that. I have some money, not much though. It might pay for a night or two," I replied, unable to stop the tears from streaming down my cheeks.

She jumped off the bed and came to my side, placing her hand on my shoulder. "Now, now, hopefully, I can save the day. I would like to offer you a bedroom at my house. Now, it's not as grand as the motel in town," she chuckled, "but it has a warm bed, a cosy kitchen and it's yours until you can get back on your feet ... and I won't take no for an answer!"

My mouth dropped open; I was so stunned by her generosity. "Why are you being so nice to me? You don't even know me!"

"And you don't know me either, but you need to stay somewhere ... and I have a place. Plus, I heard the sheriff tell you not to leave town. This way, he'll know where you are if he needs to talk to you again."

I had to admit, from the first day Tracey walked into my room, I knew I had found in her a good friend, someone I felt safe and comfortable with.

"What if I'm some crazy lunatic who attacks you in the middle of the night?"

"Then," she said to me with her eyebrows raised. "It will make for an interesting adventure."

I smiled gently in response. "Thank you, Tracey."

"Well then," she chirped, standing up. "I'll give you some privacy to get dressed. When you're done, I'll meet you at the front desk. My shift is over for the day." She beamed at me, turned, and walked out of the room, closing the door behind her.

As I leaned against the bed for balance, I was grateful for Tracey's thoughtfulness and generosity as I pulled the clothes out of the bag. Discarding the hospital gown, I slipped on a dark blue, flowing skirt with an elastic waist—easy for me to pull up over my broken leg, and the soft-woven cream shirt, which fitted me perfectly. Reaching for the tote bag, I pulled out one white shoe and slipped it on.

Once dressed, I glanced around the room one last time.

What's going to become of me? What would happen now?

I gathered the toiletries in the bathroom and placed them in the tote bag and, along with my handbag, slung them over my shoulder. Grabbing the crutches, I tried to ignore the mild ache in my ribs as I made my way to the front desk to wait for Tracey. It was strange knowing a world I didn't remember waited for me outside the hospital doors.

Upon leaving the hospital, Tracey drove me straight to the Sheriff's department—we had to inform him I was staying with her. The last thing I wanted was for him to put out an alert because he thought I had skipped town.

As he came out of his office, Sheriff Hadlock looked surprised to see us standing at the counter.

"Has something changed?" he asked hopefully.

"No," I shook my head and looked tentatively at Tracey. "We just wanted to let you know that I've been discharged from the hospital and will be staying with Tracey. You know, since you told me not to leave town." I leaned nervously on the crutches.

"Right," he paused, eyeing us both. "I'll need your address and phone number, please." He spoke directly to Tracey.

"No problems." Accepting a notepad and pen, she wrote the information down for him.

"What are your plans now?" he asked, inspecting the notepad.

"I'm not sure. Rest and keep up my appointments with the shrink."

He nodded slowly; the growing silence was deafening. "Thanks for the information," he finally said, waving the notepad as though it were a dismissal. Relieved, I awkwardly manoeuvred the crutches, eager to leave. As we turned and made our way to the door, Sheriff Hadlock spoke again. "The car you were in is currently sitting in the impound lot. Maybe we should take a ride to it. Perhaps seeing the car might jog your memory?"

I glanced at Tracey. "That sounds like a good plan," she said to him.

The Sheriff nodded in agreement. "Fantastic. Here is the address." Flipping the page over on the notepad, he jotted down the address, tore the paper free and gave it to Tracey. "I'll meet you there." He stepped back into his office as we headed out the door. It was only a short five-minute drive and once we arrived, the owner of the lot, Mark, came out into the parking lot to meet me.

"The Sheriff said you were coming. We'll just wait till he gets here." No sooner than Mark had finished talking, the Sheriff drove into the carpark. After Sheriff Hadlock climbed out of his car, Mark escorted us all to the back of the lot where the car sat. Looking at it lying in the dirt, nestled between two other wrecked cars, I saw nothing I recognised.

It was a light blue 1989 model sedan with a grey interior. Standing in front of the car, I stared at the front right-hand panel, shocked to see the crushed and twisted metal fender. Closing my eyes briefly, my stomach twisted, matching the vision before me, and my palms began to sweat as a wave of anxiety swept over me. Taking in a small breath, I opened my eyes and allowed them to trail over the bonnet, but they came to a stop when I took in the cracked windscreen and the spiderweb of fractures, spreading across the glass.

Seeing the colour rush away from my face, Tracey stepped forward. "Are you okay?" she asked, placing a hand tenderly on my shoulder. "You're as white as a ghost."

"Ahhmm," I replied quietly, but knew I was not okay. Swallowing down my fear and anxiety, I hobbled to the driver's door, careful not to get the crutches caught in the wreck. I noticed the bent front tyre, rim, and the missing driver's door, and another wave of angst coursed through me. Peering into the car, I tried to overcome the nausea I felt as I searched for something to trigger my memory, but still nothing jumped to my mind.

Seeing the new position of the engine block, and how the accelerator and brake pedals now sat halfway into the leg space, I could see how I broke my leg. As I moved backwards slightly, moving my eyes from the damage, I noticed the steering wheel was covered in blood. Obviously, where my head collided with it.

The wreck of the car was too much—a harsh reminder that I'd almost died, nearly crushed to death, and I still had no memories of the traumatic event. I shuffled backwards, desperate to away from the car, as the nausea intensified.

Feeling lightheaded, I made my way back to the mechanic's shop and leant against the cool concrete wall of the garage, closed my eyes again and sighed. Sheriff Hadlock, who hadn't taken his eyes off me, followed me closely to the building.

"Anything?" he questioned, his voice brimming with desperation.

I shook my head slowly. "Do you know what will happen to the car now?" I asked.

"Because it is a stolen car, it is officially evidence," the sheriff answered. "I'm waiting for the go ahead to send it back to Missionly, where they'll impound it for the forensics team to go through. We don't have the capabilities here."

I stared at the ground.

Did I really steal a car? Where had I gotten it and why would I have taken someone else's car and driven it to another state?

"May I go?" I looked at the Sheriff.

He nodded. "Sure."

I turned around and hobbled away, grateful when Tracey wrapped her arm around my shoulder and guided me slowly back to her car.

"It will all come back to you in time, my dear. Don't worry about it."

She helped me into the car and placed the crutches on the back seat. As though sensing my confusion and worry, Tracey kept silent on the way to her house. I watched the scenery passing by without really taking anything in. So many thoughts raced through my head.

Why would I steal the car? I thought. *Am I a thief? Was I running away from something?*

I shook my head slightly, annoyed at the lack of answers. After ten minutes, we pulled into her driveway, and I waited patiently for Tracey to retrieve my crutches and help me from the car.

Tracey's house was a cute, three-bedroom cottage at the west end of town. The moment I saw the house; I felt the tension of the morning flooding from me. The light-beige, wooden walls topped with a dark-grey, slate roof gave the house a cottage vibe. A large, forest green veranda wrapped around the front of the house, with a small, wrought-iron table with matching chairs.

An array of pot plants adorned the veranda, boasting lush, colourful foliage, and there were a few flower beds outside the front of the house, all in full bloom. It was clear Tracey had a green thumb. The lawn was soft, green, and mowed short with an ornate, round, stone bird bath brimming with water in the centre.

Carrying my bags for me, Tracey led me along the stone path, towards the veranda, assisting me with the two front steps. Unlocking the front door, Tracey invited me into her warm and cosy home.

To the left of the entrance was the lounge room. A large, high-backed couch sat in the centre of the room with a soft-looking brown rug laid out before it. An expensive-looking television hung on the wall in front of it, and stacked bookcases lined the wall to the side.

The wooden floorboards beneath my feet, were a light golden colour which matched nicely with the off-white walls, completing the homey look.

"Right. First things first!" Tracey said as she closed the door behind us. "Let me show you to my daughter's room. I'm sure you'll be very comfortable there."

She headed down the passageway, which ran from the front door through the centre of the house to the back. Halfway down, she turned right and opened a door.

The bedroom was simple and pretty, with cream-coloured walls and a double bed pushed against the right wall. A white wardrobe stood against the far wall opposite the door, and a matching mirrored dressing table nestled against the same wall as the door. Bright sunlight streamed through the delicate white lace curtains of the window which overlooked the backyard.

"There are more clothes in the wardrobe. I'm sure my daughter won't mind you borrowing them," she said as she placed my two bags on the bed.

"Thank you, Tracey. Thank you for your kindness."

"Anytime, my dear. There is a bathroom across the hall here." She pointed to a closed door. "Dinner will be ready at about six." With a smile, she left the room, leaving me alone to take in my new surroundings.

I sat on the bed and glanced at the tote bag containing my meagre possessions. Sighing, I peered through the lace curtains into the backyard that looked like a small tropical garden. I spotted another water fountain centred high on a large stone against the rear wall and smiled as I heard the water trickling over the stone and into the pond.

There was no grass, just a large, paved courtyard with two stone benches which bordered either side of the pond. Miniature palm trees in enormous pots stood at either end of the benches, their fronds swinging gently in the late afternoon breeze. Smaller pots circled the palms, filled with brightly coloured flowers. I could picture myself sitting out there on a warm summer afternoon watching the sunset, relaxing, and caring about very little. I sighed, closed my eyes, and hoped things would be better tomorrow.

After adding my things to the wardrobe, I followed the amazing smells of home-cooked food towards the kitchen, so I could watch Tracey cook.

"Better than the hospital food," I grinned.

She laughed. "Yes, the food there is okay, but nothing ever beats home cooking."

The kitchen was bright and cheerful, and leaning my crutches against the wall, I sat at the small, round wooden and glass table and stared through the large glass door which opened onto the backyard yard.

"Your backyard," I sighed blissfully. "It's beautiful. Did you design it?"

Tracey laughed. "Yes. That was our place. My husband and I used to sit out there almost every afternoon together."

"You don't sit out there anymore?" I asked.

"Well, I do, but my husband doesn't. He passed away three years ago, unfortunately."

"I'm so sorry." I felt awful for my ignorance, and it saddened me I didn't know that about her. My thoughts were so consumed about my own life, and the little I knew about it, that I hadn't thought about the lives of anyone else at the hospital.

"It's okay, dear. His passing was expected, and he's in a better place now. But I still feel him out there in the garden. We built this house right after we got married." A small smile touched her lips. "We had plenty of years together, and I have no regrets."

"Is there anything I can do to help you with dinner?" I asked awkwardly, needing to change the subject.

"And have you knocking me over with those crutches of yours?" she laughed. "No, you stay right where you are."

Tracey served a delicious meal of fried chicken with a garden salad. Cutting open a warm, crunchy bread roll, I smothered it in butter, watching it melt into the bread. After we finished eating, I washed the dishes, much to Tracey's disagreement.

"I didn't help you cook. The least I can do is clean up."

She smiled warmly, and picking up a kitchen towel, started drying. After cleaning the kitchen, we moved to the lounge room to relax and chat.

"That's a very large TV you have," I commented.

"Oh yes, that, a present from my daughter for my last birthday. I can't say I watch it very often and it's surely going to waste sitting up there, but I guess it was the thought that counts."

I didn't know what to say to that, so I just watched as Tracey reached over the side of the chair and pulled a small bag onto her lap. Opening it, she withdrew yarn and needles and commenced knitting.

"What are you making?" I asked.

"Bonnets and booties for the babies at the hospital. A small gift to them from me." She looked at me. "Do you knit?"

"I ... I don't know," I replied with a shrug.

"Sorry, I shouldn't have asked that."

"Don't be, Tracey. It's okay." I shook my head, then laughed. "It's weird to have someone ask such a simple question and not know the answer."

"I guess it would be," she smiled.

"I just wonder if there's anyone missing me, you know? If there's any family out there, somewhere? Someone must know I am gone!"

Tracey stopped knitting and looked at me. "Well, I guess we'll have to make it our mission to find those answers for you. We can start tomorrow. I have a computer. Together, we'll try to find out who you are. I promise."

Chapter 11

Monday, September 18th

The rest of the weekend passed peacefully. After the ceaseless noise of the hospital, I enjoyed the relaxed quiet of Tracey's house. Sunday morning, I slept in and by the time I got up, Tracey was already up and about, doing the daily household chores and gardening. I admit, it made me feel guilty, not helping her. Yet, when I apologised, Tracey just battered me away.

"Think nothing of it. You need to rest if you want to heal."

At lunch on Sunday, we sat at the dining table chatting about, well, mostly Tracey and her life, her daughter, her husband, and her childhood. I loved hearing her stories and watching her eyes light up as she recalled special memories. It helped give me a sense of belonging. Taking advantage of the warm sunshine, I relaxed in the backyard and spent the afternoon reading one of Tracey's books.

Not long after dinner, Tracey and I sat at her computer, but our efforts gave us nothing. There was no one looking for me. Feeling dejected and alone, I excused myself from Tracey's company and retired to my room. Lying in bed, an overwhelming sense of dread came over me.

Waking to a new day, I felt an urge to push through my recovery process. After breakfast, Tracey drove me to the hospital for my appointment with Doctor Wilkins. The drive was quiet—I think Tracey knew I was nervous. Today, we would try hypnosis to see if that would unlock my memories. Doctor Wilkins was more enthusiastic about the next step than I was, but I wanted to try. I needed to. If there was a chance it could work.

Doctor Wilkins' office had a spacious waiting room with a few small plants, a TV hanging from the ceiling, and huge windows looking out towards the town. A reception desk sat in the middle of the room, occupied by two young female staff.

"Will you be okay here, waiting on your own?" Tracey asked.

"Of course," I smiled. "I don't want you to be late for work." As soon as she was out of sight, my smile faltered, and I shoved my hands beneath my legs to stop from fidgeting.

There were three other people in the waiting room, but I avoided looking at them, instead glancing beyond the desk towards a corridor that ran back towards the far end of the hospital. A few closed doors were visible, but little else.

I didn't have to wait long before a door opened, and Doctor Wilkins walked towards the waiting room. As she met my watchful stare, she smiled and called out my name. I hobbled over to her, still not quite used to the crutches yet.

"How have you been since the last time we spoke?" she asked as she showed me through the door and walked me over to a large, comfortable, light green chair.

"Okay, I guess," I replied, laying the crutches on the floor next to me as she sat in a bright blue chair opposite me.

"And how are your memories going? Have you remembered anything yet?"

"No, unfortunately." I shifted a little in the chair, trying not to get upset.

"I know it's distressing, but we'll keep trying. I have a few ideas I would like to run past you today, if that suits you." She grabbed a brown, leather-bound diary from the coffee table between us.

"Sure, whatever you think will help me," I smiled, trying my best to appear confident as she opened the diary and clicked her pen.

"The first thing I would like to try is some gentle hypnotherapy. Something I hope might trigger some of those locked memories."

"Okay," I said nervously, and Doctor Wilkins looked up at the hesitation in my voice.

"You don't have to do it if you're not comfortable with it. We can try other methods first if you like."

I shook my head. "No, I want to do it. I guess I'm just afraid of what I might remember, to be honest."

The reality of what I was about to do suddenly hit me.

What if, once my memories return, I don't like what I find?

I knew Doctor Wilkins had suggested that maybe my brain was blocking memories to protect me. Perhaps of the accident, or maybe something more. Now that there was a possibility of unlocking them, I was anxious.

"We'll do it slowly, and I'll monitor you the entire time. If I see any signs of distress, I'll pull you back out. Basically, we're just going to have a poke around the seal that's holding your memories back."

"Okay," I swallowed thickly. "So, how does it work, anyway?"

"Well, although there is no hard scientific evidence hypnosis works, there is a belief it can help access the subconscious mind and uncover memories or moments from your past, which are currently unobtainable." She looked at me, waiting for me to respond.

"And if it doesn't work? Then what?" I asked quietly.

"Well, then we can try Cognitive Behavioural Therapy."

"How does that work?" I frowned.

"We'd work on any fears you have. It could help us identify any issues which might be contributing to your amnesia. Then, once we have identified them, I would teach you some techniques around breathing and focus that might help in breaking down the walls your brain has put up."

I nodded slowly as I took the information in. "Okay, well, that doesn't sound so scary. Let's give this hypnosis a go, then, shall we?"

Doctor Wilkins smiled reassuringly, and I did my best to smile back.

"All right, then. I would like you to please move over to the lounge and get yourself comfortable. When you're ready, I want you to close your eyes."

As I hobbled over to the lounge, Doctor Wilkins reached over and picked up a small remote from the coffee table. Pointing it at the window, she pressed a button, and the room darkened as thick, black curtains slowly slid across the rails, shutting out the light.

I lay down, heaving my heavy cast onto the couch, before feeling my body nestle into the velvety material. Resting my head on a small cushion, I closed my eyes.

"I want to you to focus on your breathing," Doctor Wilkins said softly. "Inhale through your nose. Exhale through your mouth. That's it. Inhale through your nose. Exhale through your mouth. Keep your breaths soft and rhythmic. Feel your lungs expand and contract."

I relaxed my body and listened carefully to her voice.

"Inhale and hold for two seconds. Exhale and hold for two seconds."

She paused for a few moments, allowing me to find the rhythm and regulate my breathing. "With every breath in, feel your lungs rise. With every breath out, feel yourself relax deeper into the lounge. Breathe in for four seconds. Exhale for four seconds." Her voice became quieter and softer.

Shutting everything else out, I listened to the air rush into my nose. I focused on my lungs expanding and holding my breath, and I started feeling heavier with each breath out. I continued breathing and relaxing, breathing and relaxing, drifting slowly down into a peaceful, dark place.

Chapter 12

Wednesday, September 20th

"Well, what's the verdict?" Tony called out, poking his head into Martin's office.

"Verdict on what?" Martin replied, not bothering to look up from his work.

"Um ... the verdict on the missing girl with the stolen car!"

"Oh, that."

Tony made his way into the office and grabbed the same black office chair as before.

"Well?" he said, looking intently at Martin.

"Nothing, no hits, no matches. I don't know who she is."

"Damn! I'd hoped Mr Tanner would recognise her. This one's a toughie, hey?" Tony grinned.

"Yeah, I guess it is."

"So, you going to find out who she is ... take on the case?"

"I don't know, Tony. It's not like it's an overly important one, if you know what I mean. Mr Tanner has organised the issues with his car. His insurance company is covering the damage, and he's getting a payout. Case closed there. The girl ... she's not in the system. No one is missing her. It's not a high priority."

"Yeah, I know," sighed Tony. "It would be nice to know who she is and why she took the car though, wouldn't it?"

"I guess ... but I kinda have a few cases now, mate, which need my full attention. If something comes up and it matches her file, I'll let you know, okay?"

"Fair enough." Tony got up, replaced the chair in the corner and shuffled out of the office, his shoulders hunched.

Martin tried to regain his focus on his work before Tony had interrupted him. After a few minutes, Martin put down his pen and stared at the empty chair. Tony had a good heart and a great instinct when it came to the cases, he brought him.

What if this case is no different? He asked himself.

"Belinda?" Martin buzzed his receptionist.

"Yes, Detective?" she responded swiftly.

"Can you please get Sheriff Hadlock in Parker on the line for me?"

"Certainly, sir."

Martin didn't see the point of having a receptionist as he was quite happy to do most of the general day-to-day tasks himself; filing and phone calls and administration tasks, but his boss, Brad Swinton, never took no for an answer.

"Martin!" he'd said firmly. "You didn't work your ass off to get to the top of your game, only to be left to do all the crappy office work yourself! You're getting a receptionist whether you like it or not. And I better not hear she's got nothing to do!"

So, he hired Belinda.

Belinda was in her mid-forties, with years of experience within the police force, and had worked for him for the past three years, and although he would still rather do it all himself, some days he was grateful for her help.

"Martin, Sheriff Hadlock is on line two," Belinda buzzed through a few minutes later.

"Thank you, Belinda,"

"You're welcome. Would you like another coffee?" she asked politely.

"Yes, actually, that would be great."

Case in point, he smiled to himself.

Martin waited for Belinda to hang up, and then, leaning back into his chair, he pressed the flashing red button on the second line.

"Sheriff, Detective Martin Collins here, how are you today?"

"Good," replied the Sheriff.

"How's our mystery girl going? Any news on her?" he asked hopefully.

"Not much to tell sorry, she still can't remember anything. I was hoping you might have some better news for me."

"No, nothing came up in the local district. I widened the search to other states, but I don't have a match, sorry," said Martin frankly.

"Well, that's strange, isn't it?" the sheriff replied in a flat tone.

"Yes," replied Martin. "Does she have an accent at all, Sheriff?"

"Nope. Nothing to indicate she is from overseas."

"Okay. Well, the best I can do is keep her file on hand. If anything comes up on your end, she gets her memory back or something, please email me so I can close the case. Likewise, if anything pops up in the system here, I'll let you know."

"No worries, thanks for the call, detective."

"Anytime." Ending the call, Martin leaned his head on his hands, slowly massaging his temples with his thumbs. He took a deep breath, willing the tension from his shoulders in the hopes it would reduce the mild headache which had steadily pulsated behind his eyes all morning.

"Your coffee, Martin," Belinda said softly as she entered with the steaming mug.

"Thanks," he replied, hardly noticing as she exited.

For most cases involving missing young women, they were easy to solve. The majority were runaways, either from a miserable home life or abusive partners, and turned up in a week or two. Martin wasn't too worried about this one. She may not be a local, but she belonged to someone, and that someone would eventually report her missing, and his team would notify him. Feeling confident in his self-reassurance that this case could wait, Martin sipped on his coffee and continued his work on a more pressing case.

Chapter 13

Friday, September 22ⁿᵈ

Before I knew it, a week had passed since I moved in with Tracey. The days and nights blended seamlessly and during that time, nothing interesting changed for me. I visited the hospital for a final CT scan, and the results showed the swelling had disappeared. Doctor Wright was happy and signed me off, stating I no longer needed to visit him again. Personally, I was worried ... two weeks, and I still had no memories, two weeks and there was no indication that anyone was looking for me.

To me, it seemed odd, and I hated the way it played on my mind. To Doctor Wright, he believed the less I worried about it, the less time I spent thinking about it and stressing about something I had no power over, the more likely something positive would happen.

With Doctor Wilkins, things were a little more complicated. While she believed we were making progress, albeit slowly, I felt like we were getting nowhere. The hypnosis did nothing. My mind was like a blank slate during the process. Doctor Wilkins suggested I might not have been deep enough in the hypnosis or not relaxed enough for my mind to open. She hoped to try again soon. Until I had my memories back, there wasn't much I could do, except be patient. If I was the thief, if I had stolen the car, she was sure there was a good reason behind it.

So waiting was what I would do, but I wasn't going to do it sitting around moping. I convinced Tracey that for me to stay with her, I would help with the cooking and cleaning. It wasn't a hotel, and she was not my housekeeper or personnel chef. I helped where I could, and she continued to fuss over me—it was a happy compromise.

Tracey and I got along like we were long-time friends. She even started teaching me how to knit. Although I was terrible at it, my knitting was saggy and full of dropped stitches, but at least I was having some fun.

"Tracey," I commented during dinner one night, "I feel a bit odd about being called 'Jane'. The name doesn't mean anything to me."

"I was thinking the same thing," she replied, nodding in agreement.

"Maybe we could come up with something better."

"Sure." She put her fork down. "How about Sharon?"

"No." I turned up my nose. "Beth?"

She shook her head. "You don't look like a Beth." She propped her chin on her palm. "Lisa or Nicole?"

I giggled. "No."

"This is like picking baby names all over again," she laughed. "How about ... Amber."

Amber, Amber.

"I like the sound of that!" I smiled.

"Me too," she grinned.

So, now I was Amber. A lost girl in a strange place with no past, and only a future to look to. Despite the fact it felt good to have a name other than Jane Doe, I still felt down. It was hard to accept there was no-one in the country looking for me. No one who missed me. No family desperately seeking a missing daughter or sister.

But what else am I meant to do?

I decided sitting around Tracey's house feeling sorry for myself wasn't the answer. Although she repeatedly told me not to worry about paying my way, I knew a sense of purpose would be good for me. So, I decided to find myself a part-time job. Something I could manage with a cast on my leg and crutches at my side.

"I don't want to discourage you, dear," Tracey said. "But it might be difficult to get a job when you have no identification or bank account, and you're not sure of your work history."

"I know, but I must try. I'm going crazy sitting here doing nothing."

"I get that, sweetheart," she commented. "But you're still the stranger in town with no past. While I know you're a good person, all anyone around here knows about you is that you may have stolen a car. It doesn't look good."

"What else am I meant to do?" I asked.

"I don't know. Give it a try I guess," she said after a while. "But have some faith in the Sheriff. I'm sure he'll find something soon. You can't stay a mystery forever. Plus, your work with Doctor Wright will help, too." With a pat on the hand, she walked past me towards the kitchen, leaving me lost in thought.

Chapter 14

Thursday, September 28th - 10:30am

I started the day with a trip to the local shops to ask around for a job. Tracey gave me some money so I could catch the bus and buy myself some lunch. Grateful for her generosity, it only spurred me on to earn my own money and buy the things I needed.

Due to the news coverage of the car accident and my interview with the reporter, I was somewhat a local celebrity. Whenever Tracey and I popped out to do some shopping, people pointed and stared but never approached me.

At first, I'd admit I hated the attention it brought. I was worried people would ask questions I couldn't answer. Whenever I left the sanctuary of Tracey's home, I kept my head down, avoiding eye contact. Gradually, I started blending in more, and while I'd never pass as a local, the curiosity surrounding me seemed to lessen. Though I was still uncomfortable with the looks and stares.

It turned out, walking from shop to shop, asking for work wasn't the best idea. The cast and crutches were a huge barrier to employment prospects and were incessantly slowing me down and wearing me out. When I did have the opportunity to fill out an application form, the only personal information I could provide was an address and Tracey's details for a reference. Not much help, unfortunately.

After I quickly ruled out any prospects of working as a cashier, or a sales assistant in the local retail stores, I also checked off cafes, since I couldn't carry trays for a few more weeks. There seemed to be only one place left in town to try. The post office.

As I entered the building, a nervous shiver swept over me.

Maybe they have something I can do while sitting down? Please let there be a job here.

With the most confident smile I could muster, I approached the counter, hoping for the best.

"Hi, how are you today?" asked the young girl behind the counter.

"Good, thanks. Um, I'm wondering if there is a manager I could speak to, please?"

"Aren't you the person with the memory thing?" she asked, a bit too loudly.

I smiled tightly. "Yes, that's me. I'm Amber."

"Wow, so you remember your name. That's cool. Do you remember everything else too?" she asked, leaning on the counter.

"No, actually, I don't remember my name. Amber is just something I chose, so I'm not a Jane Doe."

"Oh, well, it's a nice name," she said sweetly. "It's such a pity you don't remember who you are. I don't know what I'd do if it happened to me," she commented while picking at the chipped pink polish on her nails.

"Yeah, I don't really know what I'm doing either."

"At least you weren't too badly hurt in the car accident, right? What about your family? Do you think they know where you are? I hope they haven't given up looking for you."

This young girl was talking faster than I could keep up with. No sooner had she asked one question; she followed it with another.

Oh my god, she talks so much!

"I don't know about my family," I mumbled before she rambled on.

"You know you've been the talk of the town for weeks. Everyone wants to know about you, but we don't want to invade your personnel space, you know?" When I didn't answer, she stopped, her eyes widening.

"Oh, look at me. Doing exactly that. I'm sorry. That was a bit rude of me. Um, I'll get Charles for you. He's, our manager. Sorry." Her face turned a bright shade of pink as she spun on her heels and walked out through a door at the rear of the room.

Thanks to the volume of her questions, I could sense eyes on me from around the room. Glancing over my shoulder, I tried to smile at the other people waiting in line to be served. They returned my smile, though I noted apprehension in more than one of them, and they all quickly made a show of having something more interesting to do than eaves-drop.

A few minutes later, the young girl returned and discreetly moved to another counter to serve the waiting customers, but not before glancing sideways at me, a look of apology in her eyes.

Behind her, a rather large man walked into the room and came up to the counter where I waited. He was an older gentleman with receding grey hair and a full grey beard, making me think of a grizzly bear.

"Good morning," he said in a loud, gruff voice, his protruding belly resting against the countertop. "My name is Charles Peterson. How can I help you today?"

"I'm Amber. Is there somewhere a little more private where we could talk?" If I was about to be turned down for another job, I didn't want it to be in front of the locals. He gestured towards the far-left counter. I followed and watched as he leaned over the counter and lowered his voice.

"What can I do for you?"

"Well, I'm sure you know who I am."

"Yes, kind of."

"Well," I looked at him nervously. "I need a job. I know I am not really in a position with a broken leg and no background history and all, but I was hoping you might have something I can do out the back. Something I can do sitting down a few hours a week, like sorting the mail? Please."

Charles smiled, and at first, I thought he was preparing to let me down like everyone else had so far.

"That makes it hard, doesn't it?" Charles said, nodding towards my leg.

"Yes, it does, but I have to stay here in Parker until everything's cleared up and I thought, while I'm here, I'd like to help pay my way."

"You live with Tracey, yes?"

"Yes, that's right." I took it as a good sign that he knew her.

"She's a great woman. Heart of gold," he said, his smile widening.

"Exactly. Which is why I'd like to help pay my way—I don't want to take advantage of her generosity," I pleaded with him.

Charles stared at me, as though pondering something. Then, with a smile, he spoke the words I was hoping to hear.

"Then I guess you are in luck. I do need someone to work out the back. It's only about four hours per day, Monday to Friday. Nine to one. I'll pay you in cash. I hope that will be, okay?"

"Perfect. Thank you very much," I sighed with relief.

"No worries. You can start on Monday if you like."

"Thank you so much, Mr Peterson. You've made my day."

He let out a full belly chuckle. "Firstly, it's Charles to you. No need to be formal with me, Amber."

I grinned at Charles. Past his grizzly bear appearance, he was a very gentle-natured man. I liked him very much. Turning around, I found the post office was quiet and void of customers. With a smile still on my lips, I made my way out to the main road, happy knowing I had a job. I knew Tracey would protest, but I planned on giving her a little money each week for letting me stay with her.

Finally, something has gone right. Perhaps this is my fresh start. Maybe whoever I was in my past life isn't who I'm meant to be now.

Heading away from the post office, I took a left down Main Street and came upon a small café. The bright green door was closed, but a large *open* sign hung on the door. Through the windows, I could see a few people already sitting at the tables inside. Having some time before the next bus arrived, I decided to indulge myself with some lunch. I hobbled my way to the door but then realised, as I was trying to push it open, I couldn't hold the door open and walk through with my crutches.

Noticing my predicament, a young man on the sidewalk rushed over.

"Can I help you?" he smiled as he squeezed past me, pushing the door open, allowing me to step into the café. A small bell hung over the threshold, and it chimed sweetly as the door brushed against it.

"Thank you," I said as he let the door swing slowly behind me and the bell chimed again.

The room inside smelled like freshly baked bread, coffee and other delicious aromas that made my mouth water. Scanning the café, I took in the warm, yellow lights hanging from the ceiling, one above each table, over centrepieces of small bouquets of fresh flowers. The entire room felt cosy and inviting. I smiled to myself.

This place is wonderful.

Navigating my way between the tables, I prayed I wouldn't knock anyone's legs with my crutches as I made my way to the menu board hanging on the wall beside the large, off-white marble counter. I smiled and nodded politely at the customers, who watched me hobble past. When I finally made it to the counter, I ordered a toasted ham and cheese sandwich and a hot chocolate. Paying for my meal, I carefully moved to a small window table at the front of the café.

It was then that I started feeling self-conscious, aware of the sideways glances cast in my direction, as the other customers realised who I was. Trying to ignore them, I turned to watch the hustle and bustle of the people and traffic outside. There were so many people in the café that I began feeling closed in.

Closing my eyes, I worked on my breathing, like Doctor Wilkins taught me. With each breath, I felt the building anxiety ease.

It wasn't long before a waitress brought my food over, and I ate my sandwich as I continued to watch the world beyond the café. Smiling to myself, I made a conscious effort to be brave and focus on the positives. It was three weeks since my accident. I had a part-time job, a cosy, warm house to stay in and a good friend in Tracey. Despite my fears regarding my past, things were looking up.

After my meal and delicious thick hot chocolate, I bought a slice of passionfruit cake to go and made my way back outside. Graciously, an older gentleman about to enter the cafe held the door open for me. I continued down Main Street, passing clothing shops, a newsagent and shoe stores. Taking in the sounds of people chatting, the cars motoring past and the rustle of the breeze as it whipped small leaves across my path, I felt content for the first time in weeks.

All the limping about on my crutches was taking its toll, and I was relieved when I reached the bus stop. Resting on the bench, I held my crutches to the side and gazed across the road. There was a small park, where a few young children played on the equipment, their laughter drifting towards me on the breeze.

They were no more than five or six years old, completely unaware of the hardships they would face upon growing up. Their sweet, innocent laughter and squeals of delight as they played brought a smile to my face. But as I watched them, an awful thought occurred to me, and my smile faded.

What if I have children? What if I'm a mother?

Watching the mothers react to their children's laughter, I felt a sudden, deep ache in my chest. Unwillingly, the ache inched towards anger. Squeezing my eyes shut, I realised I felt jealous of those women. Sighing, I dropped my head in shame. I told myself it wasn't right to be angry with these strangers. It wasn't their fault that I didn't know who I was, that the life I'd lived until three weeks ago was nothing more than a phantom. Dead and gone, a ghost.

Keeping my eyes closed, I reminded myself today had gone well, and I took a big breath in, held it for a few seconds, and slowly let it out, pushing away the negative thoughts.

This is a clean start for me. Whatever got me to this point in my life was for a reason. Maybe this is a second chance to live a better life.

A few minutes later, the bus pulled up, and I manoeuvred my way up the steps to the small counter in front of the driver. I noticed he was the same driver from my bus into town, and I was touched when he greeted me with a warm smile of recognition.

"Did you have a good day?" he asked as I paid for a ticket.

"Yes, thanks."

"That's good to hear. Do you need a hand to get to your seat?"

"No, thanks, I'll be fine." I shuffled my way to a vacant seat a few rows down.

With a hiss of the brakes, the bus took off. The momentum of the ride was soothing, and I rested against my seat as I watched the streets pass by. This was my new town. My new home at present—and I was determined to fit in, just like everyone else.

The bus stopped periodically, and passengers got on and off. As the bus was not big, the only way in or out was at the front, therefore all passengers had to walk past me at some point. Making eye contact with each of them, I nodded a brief hello or gave a small goodbye smile. Most of them returned the greeting, which felt nice. I was starting to feel a little less like an outsider, and a little more welcome.

As I considered the fifteen-minute bus ride, I realised getting to and from work each day would be quick and easy. But as I got off the bus and headed towards Tracey's house, I felt myself rapidly tiring. While I hadn't been out more than a few hours, I'd underestimated my recovery. The cast felt very heavy, and my leg ached from trying to keep it off the ground as I walked. The crutches dug painfully under my arms and trying to avoid any unnecessary weight on them added to the exhaustion.

Resting my back against a small, white, wooden fence a few houses away from Tracey's, I stretched my arms above my head, closing my eyes as the pain crept up to my wrists.

I need to get better—I have a new job to start.

With my eyes still closed, I listened to the breeze stirring the trees overhead and revelled in the warmth of the afternoon sun on my face. Unexpectedly, I heard the soft mewl of a cat. Instinctively, I smiled at the sound, and an image flashed through my mind of a large, ginger tabby with a snow-white chest and small white furry socks on the front paws. The cat mewled again. I opened my eyes and looked over my shoulder, towards the sound.

"Here kitty, kitty, kitty," I called over the fence as I peeked over at the garden. I couldn't see the cat, so, turning around, I propped my hand on the fence and looked towards the house and veranda. Letting my eyes wonder over the cane wicker chair and table which stood on the porch, I couldn't find the feline. I frowned.

I was sure I had heard a cat mewl—and it had sounded like it was right behind me. Leaning over the fence, to peer down into the low garden beds, I squinted my eyes, trying to focus between the plants.

"Can I help you?" a voice called, startling me. My right hand, that was supporting my weight, slipped from the top of the fence, and I slammed my chest against the tips of the wooden palings.

"Ow ..." I groaned as the air whooshed out my lungs, and pain radiated through my ribs, bringing tears to my eyes. I raised my head and glanced at the house, where I saw an elderly man leaning against the door frame, using its solid timber arch as a brace to steady himself. His grey hair was parted over his head in a neat comb over.

Shit, where did he come from?

"Um ... sorry," I muttered through clenched teeth as I righted myself. "I was looking for your cat."

"I don't own a cat," he replied cooly.

"Oh, I thought I heard a cat before and I was looking for it."

"There ain't no cat that lives here or ever did." He paused, looking at me with interest. "Ain't you the young lass that lives with Tracey?" he asked, still leaning on the doorframe.

"Yes. I'm Amber. Nice to meet you, Mr ...?"

He looked at me intently, his expression void of warmth. "There ain't no cat here." He turned his back on me and shuffled into his house, slamming the door behind him. Turning around, trying to ignore the dull ache in my chest, and the puzzling conversation with the gentleman, I grabbed my crutches, pushed the cat from my mind, and staggered home.

Chapter 15

Thursday, September 28th - 2:30pm

Alone in the house, I sat down at the kitchen table with a glass of icy water. I was looking forward to seeing Tracey when she got home from work. I wanted to surprise her with my good news that I could now help with the bills. It meant a lot to me that I could now repay some of her kindness.

During the past week I had honed my ability to move around the house without the crutches, using the walls and furniture to support me and was excited, that in two and a half weeks, I could return to the hospital and have the cast removed. I'd have a final x-ray to ensure the break had healed, and then hopefully that would be the last of it. Lucky for me, my ribs had healed quicker—and aside from today's mishap, they were no longer tender to the touch, and it didn't hurt to breathe. Unfortunately, I now had a sore spot in the middle of my sternum that pulsed and ached if I inhaled too deeply.

Three steps forward, one step back!

Tracey arrived home just after six, and after a quick shower, joined me at the table to share the dinner I'd prepared. Chicken Cacciatore and rice. A flare for cooking was something else I'd discovered about myself since staying with

"

Tracey, and recipes came easily to me. Anything I made Tracey loved. Either that, or she didn't want to disappoint me by telling me it was bad.

"How was work today?" I asked as we ate.

"Good. Not too busy."

"If you don't mind me asking, how did you get into nursing?"

"I don't mind." She put her fork down. "I think I'd always known I wanted to be a nurse. Once I left school, I went to university. My first placement was in a small hospital in the city. After a while, I moved to the emergency department and worked within the trauma unit."

"Sounds terrifying," I stated.

"No, not at all. I always worked better under stressful conditions. There was never a dull day."

"And now?"

"Now, I don't have the stamina to keep up with the trauma cases. I enjoy being on the wards. More peaceful as I get older," she chuckled softly.

"I never asked how you met your husband?"

Her eyes brightened. "Richard was a young intern at the hospital. He'd d started a few months before me. We had a few nervous chats, and a mild flirtation, before he finally found the courage to ask me out on a date."

"I take it the date went well," I grinned.

"Indeed. We started dating that night and the rest is history." She stood up and took our empty plates to the sink. "He proposed six months later, and we started looking for a house in the city. During that time, my mother became ill. My father passed away a few years after I graduated, and I don't think my mother ever got over his death."

"I am so sorry," I said as I followed her and filled the sink with hot water to wash the dishes.

"Thank you. He died from a heart attack. We weren't aware he had a health issue."

I smiled tenderly at her.

"So, since my mum lived here in Parker, Richard and I moved to care for her. Luckily for us, the hospital had been recently upgraded, and they needed new staff."

"Convenient."

"Very. We lived with my mum for about a year, saving everything we could, and then built this house. We married six months later. I was twenty-four and Richard was twenty-six. It was just a small ceremony back in the city. Most of our friends still lived there." She laughed suddenly. "I remember driving back here in Richard's white Ford Thunderbird. He loved that car. Might even have loved it more than me." She giggled again.

It was wonderful to see her face light up as we talked about her life, and once the dishes were done, we made our way to the lounge to relax.

"Where is the car now?" I asked as I sat down.

"Oh, he sold it a few years after our wedding. Said it wasn't suitable for a family." She pulled her basket onto her lap and continued knitting a baby bonnet.

"Tell me more about your daughter."

"She lives in the city with her fiancé. Moved out when she was about twenty-three, to spread her wings. She works in the restaurant her fiancé owns."

"She doesn't mind me staying in her room, does she?" I asked.

"No. She doesn't visit me much anymore. The restaurant takes up a lot of her time. And since Richard died, she visits even less."

"I'm deeply sorry he passed. He sounds like a wonderful man."

"He was. I miss him very much. You know, he spent so much of his time as a doctor, trying to cure different cancers, and ironically, he passed away from prostate cancer. He's been gone for three years, but it feels like yesterday that I said goodbye."

A small shadow of sadness passed briefly across her face as we talked about her more painful memories, and I got a glimpse into her private and lonely world. Wanting to lighten the mood, I decide it was a suitable time to tell her my news.

"Guess what happened to me today?"

"Well, something exciting, I hope," Tracey smiled, glancing up from her knitting.

"I caught the bus into town and went job hunting. After a few friendly knock backs, I got a part-time job at the post office. I start next week."

Tracey's face lit up. "Oh, that's wonderful news! I'm so happy for you."

"Thanks."

"I hope this doesn't mean you're planning on getting a place of your own, are you?" She looked a little disappointed.

"Well, eventually—I hadn't really thought about it. If I could stay a bit longer, I'd really appreciate it."

"Of course, my dear. If anything, I'd rather you never moved out. I'd forgotten how nice it was to have some company around. I'd be incredibly happy to have you stay for however long you need to."

"Thank you."

"You'll like working for Charles. He is a wonderful man. Easy to talk to, even though he looks and sounds like a big grizzly bear."

I laughed aloud at her perfect description. "That's the first thing I thought of when I met him."

"He and Richard were good friends. Charles lost a piece of himself when Richard passed. He pops in every couple of months to check up on me, making sure I'm coping and not too alone," she smiled.

"He did seem kind. I hope we get along well."

I was excited my life was taking shape, and I felt hopeful that I had a bright future, even though I couldn't remember my past.

The following day, Tracey and I went shopping for more appropriate work clothes. After promising her I'd pay her back every cent once I got paid, we had a fantastic day out, shopping, eating lunch at a small trendy café and chatting away like two best friends. We returned home two happy ladies.

Once home, I sat in my room, looking at the smart clothes we'd picked up. A classic black, knee-length, cotton skirt with soft pleats was my favourite item. I'd also bought a simple, navy-blue A-line skirt, also knee-length, with a large, ornate, silver buckle on the belt. To pair with them, I purchased three button-up cotton blouses. A few short dresses and some new flat shoes completed my new wardrobe.

Since I was only working four hours each day, I figured I could match some of the other shirts I had already had, with two other skirts. In time, I would make sure I topped up my clothes, and as soon as the cast came off, I'd be off to the shops again, to buy a few pairs of pants.

While relaxing in the lounge, I asked Tracey to help me with a few minor issues. Because we knew nothing about me, other than my new first name, I needed a surname and at least an age I could pass for. With no idea when my birthday was, I found it difficult to judge my age.

Together, we tossed surnames around like rice at a wedding. Bouncing off the walls, the coffee table, and sofa until finally one got stuck into my head. Cooper. Amber Cooper. My age ... we giggled and laughed about that.

"Well, how old do you feel?" she asked.

I stared at her, my face void of emotions. "With all my aches and pains, I feel old!" I laughed, unable to hold my composure.

"Then you have aged well, my dear," she giggled.

"I have no idea. How old do I look?" I queried, looking at her innocently.

"Mid-twenties?" her brows raised.

"Alright, how about an even twenty-five? Not too old, but not too young."

"Perfect." She nodded in agreement.

I now had three aspects of my life sorted. A first name, a surname, and an age. I felt like I was slowly becoming someone.

"I think it would be a good idea if you inform the Sheriff tomorrow of your new name and your job at the post office," Tracey suggested. She was right. The sheriff had made a point of saying time and time again, to make sure I updated him with any changes. I didn't think he trusted that I wouldn't just disappear. After all, at the end of the day, I was still a suspected car thief.

Chapter 16

Saturday, September 30ʰ

After a hearty breakfast, Tracey drove me to the police department to visit Sheriff Hadlock.

"Good morning, Sheriff," I greeted him, offering my hand.

"Hmm, good morning," he replied bluntly, barely shaking my hand. Dropping my hand onto my lap, I looked at him across the desk.

"How can I help you today?" he asked, leaning forward in his chair. "Do you have something worthwhile to tell me?"

"Actually, I do," I replied, knowing my news wasn't what he wanted.

"Ah, so you have finally remembered something?"

"Um, well, no," I stammered, suddenly feeling nervous.

"Well, what then?" His growing impatience was evident.

"I, um, have a name now. Amber Cooper," I blurted.

"Amber Cooper," he repeated, his eyebrow raised. "Is that your real name?"

I shook my head. "No. I still don't know what it is. I just didn't want to be referred to as Jane Doe anymore," I replied.

He sighed loudly. "You're right, I guess. It's better than that."

"Yes, it is. I also wanted to inform you I've got a job at the post office."

"A job?" His eyebrows raised further, giving him a comical look.

"Yes. I hope that's okay. It's not much, just a few hours a day. I'm not planning on going anywhere, Sheriff Hadlock, but I can't just sit around doing nothing either," I explained.

"You have a point," he said gruffly.

I sighed and leaned back in my chair. Relief spread through me, and I felt my shoulders relax.

"I suppose working will keep you in the area. How are you to be paid, seeing you don't know your own bank details?"

"We'll go to the bank and open up an account for her," Tracey piped up. "I will make sure it's in her name, and I can be the trustee for it. Would that work?" she asked, looking pointedly at the sheriff.

"Hmmm, yes, I guess that will do," he grumbled. "Was there anything else, Amber Cooper?"

"No, Sheriff. That's it for today."

"Well, until next time," he said dismissively, returning his attention to the paperwork lying on the desk. Glancing at Tracey, we got up and left his office.

Heading to the bank, we opened an account, and I felt a sense of pride sweep over me.

I have a name, a job, and now, a bank account.

I was working towards creating a new life in this small town. The past was still a mystery, and hopefully that would change, but for now, I had a future to look forward to.

And I was happy.

Chapter 17

Monday, October 2ⁿᵈ

Arriving for my first day at work, I introduced myself as Amber Cooper. The work was simple, and I was grateful for being able to sit down most of the time. I sorted the mail, both from the customers who came in and from the delivery bags that were dropped off the night before.

I separated the letters and parcels into different postal codes and placed them into large bags. From there, the postal service would deliver them to their relevant addresses the next day. It was not challenging work by any means, and it was slightly repetitive, but it passed the time—and I was earning my own way.

Besides Charlie, there were six other staff members. William Pallington, the senior mailman, was an elderly gent, about sixty-five, and had spent the better part of his life delivering the mail. Everyone in the town knew him, and it took him most of the day to deliver his bags of mail because he tended to stop and chat with those who waited at their letter boxes. I discovered quickly he was a delightful old man with quite a few wonderful stories up his sleeve.

To assist William was Jacob Wilson, a young, twenty-five-year-old. He delivered to the other side of town and usually made it back to the office at least two hours before William. He'd worked at the post office for the past five years, starting with my job and eventually delivering the mail, when his predecessor retired. With his youthful appearance and fit physic, Jacob was also popular with the locals, but he was a hard worker and saving up to buy a new car.

Rebecca Marsh was the young woman I first spoke to when I'd asked for a job. A single mother to a three-year-old boy named Michael. Unfortunately for her, the father of her son had walked out on her a few months into the pregnancy and never came back. At only twenty-two, she lived with her parents and was saving up to buy herself and her son a small home. Lucky for her, her mother doted on her son and looked after him while Rebecca worked.

She talked fast, worked fast, yet still had time to check her makeup every hour to ensure she looked flawless in every way. With her friendly disposition and charm, I hoped we could become good friends.

Adam Hunter was the local postal truck driver and worked two shifts per day. One in the morning, picking up the bags for the larger delivery centre, an hour away, in a larger town, and one in the afternoon, when he drove around Parker, emptying the postal boxes, returning their contents to the post office before closing.

He was a tall, slim-set man, '*fifty-eight years young*' with a bushy, grey beard and thin rimmed glasses. He had a jovial manner about him and walked around everywhere with a big smile. '*Happily married for twenty-seven years,*' he told me with immense pride. I liked him immediately.

The final member of the post office staff was Mrs Grace Murphy. Although she didn't tell me her age, I guessed she was in her early seventies, though her disposition certainly made her seem older. She wore no makeup and had a pair of glasses that she constantly pushed up her nose. Her light grey hair was pulled back tightly, into a neat bun and with a stern, matron-like appearance, she looked like she'd just stepped out of a strict boarding school for girls.

Her clothes did little to diminish the impression, with her white, cotton shirt and knee length dark grey skirt over tan stockings. According to Rebecca, she wore them every day even in summer, and she joked, '*Grace is about ninety years old, as I'm fairly sure she's been living in Parker since the dark ages.*'

After work, I asked Tracey about her, and she informed me that Mrs. Murphy lost her husband in a farming accident with his plough horse over thirty years ago. They never had children, and her ensuring solitude made her a quiet and reserved person who kept very much to herself.

My new routine helped me create a sense of purpose. I worked in the mornings and had my afternoons free to explore the town centre, browse through the many shops, or stop in at the grocers to buy food for dinner.

By the end of my shift on Wednesday, I left work with customers waving and saying hello or goodbye, and a few of them even greeted me by name. I now felt very much at home in Parker.

When I finally remember who I am, will I want to leave this cosy little place and return to my other life? I quite like the life I'm creating for myself here.

Stopping by a small park, I eased myself down onto the soft grass and eagerly ate my ham and salad sandwich. While watching some ducks on the little lake in front of me, I heard a cat meow behind me. I turned around, but there was nothing there. Puzzled, I shuffled around on the grass, adjusting my position so I could see better. I glanced towards a small patch of trees and bushes, searching for the little four-legged fur ball.

I lowered my head to peer deeper into the shadowy spaces under the foliage but had no luck. Slowly, I glanced around to either side of me but still couldn't see a cat. Sighing loudly, and thinking I was going a bit mad, I finished my sandwich and drank the last mouthfuls of juice. I had too many things to do at Tracey's this afternoon to worry about a cat I couldn't find.

Carefully, I got myself back on my feet. I was proud of how well I now moved around with the cast and crutches. Still not gracefully though, but agile enough that I didn't feel like my injuries hindered me too much. Throwing my rubbish in the bin, I headed back towards the bus stop.

Chapter 18

Friday, October 6th

The appointment with Doctor Wilkins went just like the others. We started by running through some breathing techniques, getting me to slow down and concentrate on relaxing my whole body.

Although these exercises made me feel calm and refreshed, I didn't think they helped much with regaining my memories. Though I did let her know that I used them at night and was sleeping much better for it.

We tried the word associated games again. Doctor Wilkins would say a random word, and I would reply with the first thing that came to mind. She wrote down everything we talked about and analysed my answers in the hopes that there might be some relevance in my words.

The hypnosis hadn't produced any positive outcomes. Whatever had happened to me, my mind continued to block it out, even while I was under. Small snippets of childhood images came up, but nothing remained long enough to trigger me to remember everything.

After almost a month of living in Parker, I was no closer to remembering anything about myself. I was still frustrated with the whole situation.

"Has Sheriff Hadlock spoken to you again?" Doctor Wilkins asked as we wrapped up our session for the day.

"No. Not for the past week. It's like he doesn't really care."

"I'm sure that's not true," she replied, sitting forward, and reaching out her hand, resting it on my knee. "I'm sure he's just busy."

"Or maybe there really isn't anyone out there missing me," I said, tears welling. "I mean, it's been nearly four weeks since I got here, and the sheriff said the owner of the car didn't recognise me. How could no one miss me?" I looked out the window, avoiding looking at her for fear of losing the tentative grip I had on my emotions. I knew that if I started crying, I might not stop.

"Amber, I understand how hard this is for you. I can't imagine what it must be like for you to not remember anything. But I promise you, amnesia isn't uncommon with head trauma like you sustained, and your memories will return. I'm sure of it." She patted my knee tenderly. I glanced back at her with a small smile. Not feeling overly positive, I nodded my head.

"I think it will be beneficial to continue our sessions. We just never know. The next session might crack the wall in your brain," she smiled reassuringly. I had to admit; it was nice to have someone other than Tracey who cared about me and had my best interests at heart. "And keep checking in with the Sheriff, remind him you're still here," she added as she stood, signalling the end of our session.

Chapter 19

After work, I grabbed some lunch and quickly ate it as Tracey drove me once again to the hospital for another check-up. Despite the fact Doctor Wright signed me off two weeks earlier, he booked me in to have another head scan, upon hearing I still didn't have my memories back. The new scan showed that everything appeared normal, at least physically, just like the previous one. It didn't make me feel any better. At least my leg had healed well, and I was set to have the cast removed on Monday. That was the best news I'd received regarding my accident.

Leaving Tracey to start her shift, I went outside to catch the bus home. While sitting on the bench, I once again heard a faint cat mewl. I sat up straight and focused my hearing on my left side. Slowly, I turned, hoping to see a cat sitting on the grass near the bus stop, but there was nothing there.

Am I'm losing my mind?

Shaking my head, I scowled as I turned my attention back to the carpark and searched for the bus. Yet, a few minutes later, I heard another distinct, louder meow, and I quickly glanced over my left shoulder. I scanned the surroundings, but I couldn't see any sign of a cat.

This is ridiculous.

Sighing with frustration, I twisted my body around and rested my arm on the back of the bench. There was a garden area behind me, with a few small trees, bushes, and flower beds. I leaned forward, trying to see through the glass of the bus shelter, into the shadows of the plants, for a small pair of eyes. After a few unsuccessful minutes, I swivelled around and pretended I hadn't heard anything.

No more than two minutes later, I heard it again, only this time it was much louder—like the cat was right behind me. I spun around and looked directly behind the bench. There was nothing there. No cat, no kitten, just ... nothing.

I leant over the back of the seat, trying to get a better look in case the cat had ducked under the bench.

"Lost something?" A male's voice broke the silence.

"Ah!" I yelped, spinning back around in fright.

"Sorry. I didn't mean to scare you," he said regretfully.

With my heart pounding, I looked up into the most beautiful, dark blue eyes I had ever seen, framed with long black eyelashes. I was momentarily lost for words.

Shaking my head, I giggled nervously, and I smiled up at him. "Um, no, I haven't lost anything. I just thought I heard a cat meow. I was just looking for it."

"Oh ... Did you need some help?" he asked, his voice deep and masculine.

"Um ... sure. If you can find it. I think it might be under the seat."

The stranger got down onto the ground in front of me, propped his hand on the bench next to me, and looked under the bench. I watched his every move as he looked for the cat. Moving my legs slightly, so they weren't in the way, I admired his wavy, shoulder-length, chocolate brown hair. Unexpectedly, an urge to run my fingers through it flashed in my mind, and as my cheeks flushed, I pushed the thought away.

After having a good look around, he raised his head and sat back on his heels. Still embarrassed by my thoughts, I quickly averted my gaze.

"Sorry. No cat under there. Is it your cat?"

"No."

"You sure you heard a cat?" he frowned a little.

"Yes, and now I feel like a complete idiot, because there is nothing there."

"Maybe it ran away?"

"Maybe."

As he pushed himself back to his feet, I got a better look at him. He was in his late twenties, a good head taller than me, and well-toned judging by his muscular arms, which bulged beneath his T-shirt, as he pushed himself up off the ground. The light blue jeans hugged his long, lean legs, only tormenting my imagination further.

"Mind if I sit?"

"No, go ahead. Are you waiting for the bus too?" I asked.

"No, just heading to my car."

"Okay."

Why does he want to sit next to me?

He stepped forward and sat down, positioning himself close to my leg. He sat at a slight angle, so he could lean back against the bench but still face me. Casually, he propped his right ankle over his left knee and looked at me with a slight smile on his face. I glanced down at my hands in my lap, suddenly feeling nervous, but unable to resist, I raised my eyes back to his face.

His well-formed chin and high cheekbones were covered in a few days' beard growth. It was like looking into a magazine, finding the most handsome model, and placing him right in front of me. I found myself getting lost in his eyes again, and I almost reached out to touch his face, wanting to make sure he was real.

I caught myself just in time, sweeping a stray hair off my forehead instead, hoping he didn't see through me.

"You're her, aren't you?" he asked gently, looking at me with his sultry come-hither eyes.

"Her who?" I mumbled almost tripping over my own tongue.

Get a grip! He's just a guy.

"The mystery girl with no memory!"

I laughed. "Is that what they call me?"

His smile widened, and he lowered his eyes to the ground for a brief second. "Well, no one really knows much about you, and this is a small town, so word travels, unfortunately."

"Right, so people are still talking about me?" I rolled my eyes, feeling a little annoyed. I'd worked so hard to fit in.

"Not so much anymore, but when you were first here, sure, you were the gossip on everyone's lips." He laughed again.

"Awesome," I mumbled, trying not to dwell on it.

"It's okay now, though," he continued. "People have gotten used to you being around, but I'm sure they still want to know all about you."

"Well, they're not the only one!" I snapped, instantly kicking myself.

"I'm sorry. I never meant to upset you," he said, his expression apologetic.

"No ... I'm sorry. I shouldn't have snapped at you. You're just like me and everyone else, wanting to know the truth and unable to get it. I shouldn't have spoken to you like that. It was mean."

"It's fine. I have no idea what it's like to be in your shoes, but I bet it is pretty crap."

"Yes, it is," I said, looking off into the distance.

We sat there in silence for a few minutes, neither of us knowing what to say next.

"I'm Craig Merrla, by the way." He offered his hand.

"Amber. Amber Cooper," I replied, slipping my hand into his, allowing my fingers to wrap around his. I was surprised at how smooth and warm his hand felt in mine. His grasp was firm but gentle as we shook hands.

"Amber Cooper ... Well, it's nice to meet you. Is that your real name?"

"No, but it's a name which will do for now, I guess."

"Well, I like it."

"Thank you."

"Do you mind me asking how you got here? To our small town."

"Well, there's really only one thing I *can* tell you."

"That's fine. It would be interesting to find out something." He sat back, watching me closely.

"Well," I started, not really knowing what to say. "I woke up in hospital a few weeks ago, after being in a car accident, and have no memory of what happened, or who I am. And to make things more complicated, the car I was driving, isn't even mine. Apparently, it's stolen, possibly by me, from a few states away. Or so I've been told."

"Wow, so I'm sitting next to a car thief!" he said with a cheeky grin. "Who doesn't remember she jacked a car?"

"Yeah, tell me about it. Who knows how bad I could be?" I joked, my eyes twinkling with mirth.

He laughed, and my heart skipped a beat at the sound.

"The CT scans have all come up clear, so no brain injuries. The Doctor believes it's just shock preventing me from remembering anything."

"They do say in times of trauma, or at the moment of impact, the brain can sometimes shut down to protect itself. Strange, hey?"

"Clever if you ask me, but also frustrating."

"Yeh, I bet it is," he said. "So, what are your plans now?"

"I don't really know." I sat back, staring out across the carpark. "Here I am now, with a made-up name, living with a nurse who looked after me in the hospital." I shrugged. "I'm working at the post office; to earn some money, and now I'm hearing cats meowing even though I can't see them." I was surprised that I'd admitted that to Craig.

"Them? So, this isn't the first time you've heard it?" he asked.

Now I felt foolish for admitting I had heard the cat before. Ducking my head, I stared at my lap, avoiding eye contact for fear he might see some crazy girl, hearing invisible animals.

"Sorry, I didn't mean to pry," he said after a moment.

"It's okay ... I'm so messed up now. Trying to figure out everything, while also moving on with what I have."

"That's understandable. Well, Ms Amber Cooper, if I cannot help you find the missing cat, I had best be on my way," he said slowly as he stood.

"Oh," I replied, disappointed he was leaving.

"Unless you want me to stay? I can keep you company, or if you like, since you're waiting for the bus, I could drive you home or wherever it is you're heading?"

"Oh, you don't need to do that for me!" I was surprised he offered to drive me home. I knew nothing about this guy and seeing how we'd just met, I was suddenly nervous at the thought of getting into his car. But on the other hand, there was something so calming and genuine about him. I felt like we had an instant connection, and I wanted to say yes. My mind raced with conflicting emotions, and I took a few deep breaths to calm myself down.

"Really, it's no hassle for me. It's not like I'm some crazy guy, kidnapping beautiful girls from bus stops," he said with a wink and a cute, toothy grin. "I promise to behave, and I will take you straight to wherever it is you're going."

"Yes, you seem like a nice guy, and yes, I'm sure you'll drop me home without any problems, but I just don't know you very well. In fact, I don't know you at all."

"That's okay, I understand," he said, with a slight hint of rejection in his voice.

I wanted to say yes—to trust this guy who'd sat and chatted to me, even though he didn't need to. But I was still the stranger in the town.

How can I trust someone I don't know? I hardly know myself.

Glancing at the bus timetable, noting the bus was running late, I struggled to decide whether to take a chance with this good-looking guy and get a lift from him or play it safe and wait.

I realised he was staring at me, his eyebrows raised as he waited for me to answer. "Scouts honour. I promise no harm will come to you!" He put up his right hand with the first two fingers pointing up.

"I'm sorry, I don't think I should," I said, looking down at my hands, trying not to meet his eyes.

"Okay. No worries. Well, some other time then. It was nice to meet you, Amber Cooper," he said, offering his hand again. As I accepted it, his fingers curled around my palm and squeezed softly as we shook. The shake lingered before I let go, and with a small wave and a regretful smile, Craig stepped off the footpath and walked away.

I stared after him, watching the way his hair moved in the light breeze. Not to mention admiring the way his jeans defined his behind and his strong, muscular legs.

Am I crazy for playing it safe?

Maybe I was, but I knew the sensible thing to do was wait for the bus.

"Craig. Wait!" I called out suddenly, surprising even myself.

Craig stopped in his tracks and quickly turned around. "Changed your mind, did you?"

"Yes," I answered meekly.

"Cool, I'm glad. Wait there; I'll come help you get up." He was at my side in seconds, leaning forward with his arm extended for me to grab a hold of. I could have stood perfectly fine with the aid of my crutches, but I found myself wanting to touch him again. As I let him pull me to my feet, I felt the heat in my cheeks, and I ducked my head so that he wouldn't see me blushing. Thankfully, he was busy grabbing my crutches.

"Ready?" he asked, and I nodded. "Excellent. Follow me. My car isn't too far away."

"Okay, lead the way."

We walked the short distance to the carpark and Craig pointed towards a silver four-wheel drive.

"This is mine." He walked ahead to the passenger side door, unlocked the door, and opened it for me. "You sure you're okay with this?" he asked.

"Yes, I think so," I replied.

With a nod, he held the crutches for me as I tried to slide in as elegantly as I could. Once I was settled, he closed the door. Watching him through the side mirror, Craig walked to the back of the car, where he unlocked the boot and placed the crutches inside.

Taking a deep breath, I waited for him to get in while rearranging my skirt, ensuring it covered my legs. As he slid into the driver's seat, he flashed me a cheeky grin and inserted the key into the ignition.

"Where to?"

I looked at him blankly.

"Are you okay?" he asked, the smile falling from his face.

"Yes," I laughed, feeling embarrassed that I looked like a total fool in front of him. "Sorry, it's all good. Fifteen Blackwood Ave please."

"No worries."

Sitting next to this sweet, generous guy, my thoughts drifted, and I wondered what my life had been before now. While I was attracted to Craig, I couldn't help but wonder if there was a guy out there. One who looked like him, someone I was involved with before the accident.

Is Craig my usual type? How do I know?

Within the close confines of the car, I could smell the intoxicating scent of his aftershave—slightly masculine and musky. I knew straight away I liked it. Combined with his looks and physic, my pulse quickened being so close to him.

There was silence between us as he drove, yet it didn't feel uncomfortable. Which was just as well, since I was so distracted by him that I couldn't think of anything to say.

"So, I take it the police are still trying to figure out where you are from?"

"Yes, well, I hope they are. For now, they don't seem to have any leads. The guy who owned the car I was in didn't know me. And there doesn't seem to be any missing persons reports matching my description either."

"That would make it hard for them, I guess," he commented, keeping his eyes on the road. "So, where abouts was the car from?"

"Missionly," I said softly as I stared out the window.

"Wow," he said, his voice rising in surprise. "That is a few states over. Would have taken you a few days to drive here, yeah?"

"I guess."

"And you don't know where you were heading?"

"Nope. No clue."

"That's crazy," he said as he shook his head.

As Craig pulled into Tracey's driveway, he peered through the windscreen at the gardens Tracey loving attended to.

"This looks like a nice place."

"Yes, I'm very lucky to be staying here. Tracey's so generous, letting me stay here as long as I need to. I don't really know what I would do without her."

Craig turned and looked at me, his eyes piercing as he smiled and gently laid his hand on mine. "What if these things that have happened to you, are just meant to be? Perhaps you were destined to end up here. Fate has put you on a new path, and maybe you should follow it."

My mouth dropped open as I stared at him, lost for words, yet he seemed not to notice as he got out of the car.

Did I just hear him right?

The boot opened and closed, but I hardly noticed—my mind raced at his words.

Is he right? Is this where I'm meant to be? Was there some kind of plan in motion for me?

Admittedly, I found it an interesting concept.

Craig tapped on my window, pulling me from my thoughts, and I turned to see him holding my crutches.

"Are you getting out of the car?" he smiled.

Smiling back, I realised how comfortable I felt around him. "Sure thing."

Craig opened the door and offered his hand, proving himself the gentleman. I managed to get out without falling over and making a total fool of myself. Manoeuvring me to the side of the car, he gently closed the door and handed me the crutches, one by one.

"You all good?" he asked as he watched me position myself on them.

"Yes ... I think so."

"See? I got you home in one piece, just as I promised," he grinned, and I felt a flutter in my chest.

"That you did. Thank you," I managed to say.

"You're welcome. Shall I walk you to the door?"

"Um ... sure, I guess." I felt like a schoolgirl coming home after a first date. Nervous, excited, and incredibly happy all at the same time.

Hobbling my way up the path to the front door, I noticed Craig walked slowly to match my pace, staying by my side the whole time. As we reached the two steps on the veranda, Craig stopped and turned to me.

"Well, Ms Amber Cooper, it was genuinely nice to meet you. I'm glad to have a face to the rumours," he chuckled. "And I'm also glad you'll be okay."

"And thank you, Mr Craig Merrla. It was truly kind of you to bring me home. Taking a risk with the crazy, no memory girl."

"Hey, no one said you were crazy!" he laughed.

"Give it time," I chuckled back.

Shuffling from foot to foot, his hands behind his back, Craig smiled, and I thought he looked a little nervous.

"Would it be too much to ask if I could see you again, Amber?"

I raised my eyebrows, feeling my cheeks warm again.

This lovely, gorgeous guy wants to see me again?

I tried to stop the smile from sweeping across my face, but it was impossible. I wanted to shout *yes*, but a part of me had reservations. I'd just met him, and although I was intrigued, I was scared I'd make the wrong choice.

Take another risk! Don't be scared!

I had barely gotten my feet on the ground, after moving in with Tracey, and working at the Post Office, would a new relationship be pushing the limits?

He seems like a gentleman, what could go wrong?

My head and heart battled against one another, and I didn't know which to listen to.

Yes? No? What to do? What to say?

But being with him, chatting to him, made me feel normal, like I mattered to someone.

What the hell, let fate take the reins.

"That would be nice, Craig, thank you," I replied, my voice bordering on a squeak.

"Awesome. How about this Thursday night? I know a wonderful place to have dinner."

"Okay," I nodded slowly.

"Are you sure?" he asked, a slight frown on his face as he looked at me.

I laughed and smiled gently. "Yes, I'm sure."

"Okay. I'll pick you up at six."

"Great. I look forward to it."

He helped me up the two stairs and watched me make my way to the door. "See you on Thursday then."

"Okay."

I watched him walk back to his car, stopping to wave, before he got back in and reversing down the driveway. With another quick wave, he took off down the street, leaving me standing at the front door, grinning like an idiot.

How can a guy I've just met have such an effect on me?

It felt amazing to have something to feel excited about, and I was already eagerly awaiting Thursday, so I could see him again. Opening the door, I wondered what Tracey would say when I told her. There was a good chance that she would reprimand me in her motherly way for getting into the car with a stranger.

Knowing Tracey wouldn't get home from her shift until after nine, I took the opportunity to spend the rest of the afternoon relaxing in the back garden. I figured a little sunshine might give me a nice glow for the date.

I made dinner and popped Tracey's into the fridge for her. Something I'd done quite a few times now—it was the least I could do for her. Settling down into the lounge, I absently watched TV as I thought about Craig, until Tracey arrived home. As I heard her keys in the front door, I was suddenly nervous about relaying the day's events, and I hoped she'd be happy for me. Even if Craig turned out to be just a friend.

"Hi Tracey," I called out.

"Hello, Love. Had a good day?" she asked, stepping into the lounge.

"I did actually." I shifted nervously on the couch. "How was yours?"

"Very busy." She dropped her bag on the coffee table and plopped herself on the couch next to me. "How did your appointment with Doctor Wilkins go?"

"Oh, about the same." I didn't want to talk about the doctor, and thinking of Craig, I grinned. "I met someone today." My heart beat a little faster with excitement.

Tracey's brows lifted, and she stared at me with curiosity. "Someone you know?" she asked hopefully.

"No. His name is Craig Merrla. We met at the bus stop at the hospital. He offered to drive me home after we chatted."

"Craig Merrla, hey?" she smiled. "He's a lovely young man. I know his mother well. We went to school together."

My mouth dropped open. That was not the reaction I'd expected.

"You know him?" My heart slowed down, and I sighed with relief. "He asked me out to dinner on Thursday night."

"Sounds wonderful." She smiled.

"I'm a bit nervous though," I confessed. "I feel like I'm in high school and the hottest guy just asked me out." I chuckled and was surprised by the happy sound that escaped me.

"Yes, he is a good-looking young man, and this could be a good thing," Tracey said.

"You think?"

"Absolutely. It's a chance for you to go out, dress up a bit, have some fun. What could go wrong?"

"But I have no idea when I last went on a date. I'm not sure I even know what to do on a date."

"Just be yourself," she replied, patting me lightly on the knee.

"That's the problem, Tracey. I don't know who I am. What are we meant to talk about?"

She laughed, a twinkle of mirth in her eye. "I guess you just need to go and find out. Clearly, he wants to spend time with you. I bet you will have fun. She stood and grabbed her bag. "Please excuse me, Amber, but I do need to have a shower." I smiled at her as she left the room. She was right, though. It could be fun.

Chapter 20

Wednesday, October 18th

Gavin Stowick was a big guy. Towering at a height of six feet, three inches, he had broad shoulders, thick, muscular arms, and large, trunk-like legs. At twenty-seven years of age, he filled the door frame with his whole body, leaving little room around him.

Sighing heavily, his dark green eyes scanned the lounge room of his three-bedroom house with disgust. Since he'd forgotten to put the rubbish bins out for collection more than once, there was nowhere to dispose of the growing piles of trash in the house. The small coffee table in the middle of the room was covered in newspapers, used coffee mugs, plates, and cutlery. Beer cans and coke bottles littered the carpeted floor, which hadn't been cleaned properly in almost six weeks.

Empty chip packets and chocolate wrappers lay strewn in all directions, while fast food containers, burger wrappers, and drinking cups piled up on the sofa. Gavin wasn't usually a fan of eating junk food, but when push came to shove, and overcome by his anger, frustration, and annoyance, it was the easiest option. He'd rather sit down to a wholesome, home-cooked meal at his dining table, which was looking no better.

As he walked through the rest of the house, the chaos continued. The master bedroom sank of musty air and sweaty socks. He hadn't bothered to make the bed in ages, and what were once crisp, fresh, white sheets had taken on a yellowish hue.

The bathroom fared no better and reeked of sweat, mould, and something else, he could not place, from the damp wet towels draped over the towel rail, the door handles, and over the shower screen.

The toilet bowl was stained and in desperate need of a clean, as was the glass shower door and white marble tiled walls. Toothpaste smeared the countertop, and mirror and scattered over the basin, were small, black hairs from Gavin's shaver, which currently lay in a pool of water next to the tap.

The pungent smell of rotting food and mild decay wafted through the house from the kitchen. Used pots caked with burnt food and mould were piled into the sink, along with plates, glasses, and cutlery that overflowed onto the counter. Rubbish spilled out of the bin, and at the sound of Gavin's heavy footsteps, a few cockroaches scuttle away from the bin to hide under the fridge.

Rich, mahogany floorboards, which ran from the front door through the centre of the house, were covered in dusty boot prints, added to each day when Gavin came home from work. His work boots lay dirty and caked with mud, just inside the laundry door, waiting to be cleaned. A pile of clothes lay in a pile next to the washing machine, stained with sweat and dirt, desperately needing to be washed. In fact, Gavin had no more clean socks, or jocks or work clothes—they were all in the laundry.

Gavin's first effort at washing his clothes led to an overdose in laundry liquid, and the excess bubbles erupted out of the top of the machine like a white frothy lava flow, which then oozed onto the floor, sending Gavin's already bad mood into overdrive. His next two attempts were marginally better, but that didn't mean he has happy he had to do it.

When he'd attempted to vacuum the lounge two weeks ago, all he managed to do, was to block the vacuum cleaner hose with trash. In a rage, he'd thrown the whole thing across the room, smashing it into the wall. Later that night, after his anger subsided, he picked up the vacuum to clean out the blockage and discovered it no longer worked. He didn't replace it.

But this was not how Gavin normally lived! This pigsty was not how his house usually looked. Picking up after himself was not his job! Doing the laundry was not his job! Cooking and cleaning were not his job!

Gavin was too busy working to spend his free time cleaning the house. He owned his own construction company, working as a builder, and it was dirty work. Gavin took over his father's business not long after leaving school, knowing he could run it better than his old man. He enjoyed being out in the weather every day, working hard, building his strength and muscles, and proving to his father a hard day's work never hurt anyone. He ran the business-like clockwork, especially once he'd fired the older blokes who'd worked for his father and employed some of his schoolmates instead.

A young, formidable team of men building houses. Erecting them quickly but flawlessly. There was always another building job waiting in the line, another customer to satisfy, another dollar to earn and another buck to save. That was Gavin's motto.

And save is what he did. Almost all the money he earned went into his bank account. Each week, he put a little aside for food, bills, and petrol for his work Ute. He was an honest worker, a tough boss, and a good mate. That's how he saw himself. Gavin was a well-respected and trusted bloke in the community—a young man everyone looked up to. Well, at least he thought so. Yes, he was a big guy. Yes, he got into the occasional fistfight at the pub, often knocking the other bloke out minutes into the brawl, but overall, he was a decent fellow and a good husband. Wasn't he? After all, he was the man about the house.

The bread winner! The money maker! The provider!

So, where the hell was his wife!

Chapter 21

Thursday, October 19th

It was hard to pay attention at work when all I could think about was tonight's date with Craig. I struggled to focus on the letters I sorted as I imagined what the night could hold. Even the girls noticed I was a little distracted.

By the end of my shift, Rebecca knew about the dinner and even gave me tips on what to do. She seemed more excited than I was. I liked the fact I had a close friendship with her already and could share my excitement.

Not long after I finished work, I popped into one of the few clothing stores Parker had to offer and bought myself a new dress. I wanted to look pretty for my first date with Craig.

By the time I got home, it was just after two, and I still had a few hours to get myself ready. I tried to clean the house a little, to distract myself from my nerves, but it didn't work. By four I'd showered and washed my hair and spent the next hour trying diverse ways to style it. Not happy with any look, I eventually opted for a simple ponytail, held back with a black and silver clasp.

I slipped on my new dark green dress and admired the way the soft cotton clung delicately to me. The dress had small, ruffled sleeves which covered my shoulders, and the waist boasted a cute, wrapped effect which suited my slim frame. The hem of the dress ended just above my knees, and although it did not have a full skirt, the extra material gave the dress a nice flowing motion when I moved. Sliding a simple flat, black slip-on shoe onto my left foot, I stood back to admire my ensemble. I giggled at the reflection in the mirror. All the effort I'd made to look pretty, and yet, my leg was still covered in the cast. Although I had become familiar with my face, it was strange, looking at myself and wondering what things my blue eyes had seen that I couldn't remember. It was frustrating to no end.

Entering the kitchen, where Tracey was preparing her own dinner, I spun around, showing off my outfit. "How do I look?"

"Beautiful," she said, looking me over.

"Pity about the bulky cast," I mused. "Kind of ruins the look." I stuck out my foot.

"I think it looks classy!" Tracey chuckled. "Are you nervous?" she asked, turning back to her cooking.

"Yes, but also excited."

"That's good. I'm happy for you." Before I knew it, there was a knock at the door and Tracey nodded as she walked off to answer it, leaving me standing in the kitchen.

"Hello, Craig." I heard her say politely.

"Hello, Tracey. Nice to see you again." I listened to Craig's voice. The deepness in the tone gave me a small flush of goosebumps, and I closed my eyes to steady my breathing.

I can't believe how nervous I am!

"Please come in," Tracey beckoned. "I hope your mother is well?"

"Thank you, she is."

"Amber is just in the kitchen." Tracey commented, and I heard their footsteps echo down the hall towards me. For a moment, I considered changing my mind, believing this was a silly idea.

What would he really want to know from me? What would we talk about when I don't know who I am?

Yet, before I could talk myself into it, Craig walked into the kitchen.

My breath hitched in my throat as I looked at him. He wore a pair of dark blue pants, and a maroon collared, short-sleeved shirt. His hair framed his face, which I noted was clean shaven. When I looked into his eyes, they widened as he smiled broadly at me.

"Wow, you look lovely," he commented, breaking my trance.

"Um ... Thank you," I replied quietly.

"These are for you." He stepped forward and handed me a bunch of flowers. "I didn't know what flowers you like, so I hope these are okay."

"They're beautiful." I took the bouquet of yellow roses, lifting them to my face. I slowly inhaled the sweet aroma as I smiled at him over them. "Thank you."

"Here," Tracey said, stepping forward. "I'll pop those into a vase for you."

"Well, shall we?" Craig asked once I'd passed the flowers over.

"Sure." I grabbed my purse, which lay on the table, picked up my crutches and tottered towards the door. Like a gentleman, he stepped quickly around me and held the door open for me.

Craig took us to a popular restaurant called The Sapphire Bar on the other side of Parker, high on a hill which overlooked the town. The view was beautiful, and clearly, we were not the only people wanting to enjoy a night out. As the main room was filled with tables, occupied with patrons already eating, we were led to the outside dining deck.

"Popular place this," I said as Craig pulled my chair out for me.

"Very. I hope you like it." He smiled, sitting opposite me.

Picking up the menu, I frowned at the choices. "Everything sounds so good. What are you having?" I asked curiously.

"I'm easy to please, he grinned. "The steak here is amazing."

"Hmm, I thought that, but I think I might order the Carbonara," I replied.

Waiting for our food, we watched the sun set over the town, and I sat in awe as the town lights twinkled on. There was a light warm breeze in the air, and the music playing from inside set the perfect tone for the date.

Sitting outside together, watching the sky darken and the stars come out, I felt more relaxed than ever—all my nerves had faded away.

"How have the past few days been?" Craig asked between mouthfuls.

"Good, although nothing overly exciting has happened. And you?" I responded.

"Not much. Work as usual."

"Ah," I noted and laughed softly. "There is something I want to ask you." I put my knife and fork down and sat back in the chair.

"You want to know something about me?" he asked, mirroring my actions.

"Yes."

"Well, be my guest. Ask anything you want." He smiled at me, waiting for me to talk.

"Okay. To start with, what do you do for a job?"

Craig laughed and leaned forwards, picking up his fork again. "The boring stuff first, hey? Okay." He popped some food in his mouth, chewed quickly and swallowed, all the while keeping his eyes locked on mine. "I work for a computer company. Nothing overly exciting, I'm afraid," he paused, looking at my quizzical expression. "I repair computer software, IT, set up company's computer systems, stuff like that."

"Ah, I see," I nodded. "Have you done that for a while?"

"Yeah, pretty much straight from high school. Went to collage to get my qualifications. Then a few friends and I moved to Colton, a large city about a two-hour drive away. I opened a small business and by the time I was twenty-four, I had four other guys working for me."

"That's impressive. You enjoy it?"

"Yes, I do. I was always a bit of a technology nerd at school. Figured it made sense to get paid to play with computers."

"Do you have family?" I asked, leaning forward as I resumed eating.

"Yeah, I have an older brother and sister. Both have moved away to the city, plus two nephews. One from each of them. My dad died a few years ago, and my mum still lives here in Parker."

"I'm so sorry about your dad." I felt like reaching over the table to grab his hand, but I held back.

"It's okay. He was sick. Lung cancer. He was a heavy smoker. Mum asked him so many times to quit, but he just kept telling her he'd be fine. Then he wasn't."

I looked at him, feeling sorry for what they went through. "The cancer took him quickly. By the time he was diagnosed, it had spread. He passed away three months later."

I reached forward then, gently placing my fingers on the top of his hand. His skin was so warm to my touch, and I felt a slight tingle pulse through my skin. Our eyes locked together for a moment.

With a sheepish grin, he pulled his hand away, picking up the fork again. "Tell me about your job at the Post-office," Craig asked, changing the subject.

"Not much to say, really." I finished my glass of wine. "I sort through the mail customers drop off or put into the mailboxes. Separate the letters and parcels that head to the city, or local delivery. Fairly easy work."

"Might be easy, but it's still important."

"Yes, I guess it is."

"And the staff you work with, friendly enough?" He sat forward in his chair, awaiting my response.

"They're all wonderful. Very friendly and have accepted me as one of the team. Well, at least I hope they have. Early days still."

"I'm sure they have. You're an easy person to chat to."

"Even with my mysterious past?" I said, with a hint of amusement.

"Absolutely. Who doesn't like to solve mysteries?" he joked.

I couldn't help but smile. Craig looked past the fact I was a stranger in town with an odd story. He genuinely wanted to chat with me, like we were already friends.

It was only once we noticed the staff cleaning up around us, did we get up to leave. Back at Tracey's house, Craig escorted me along the path to the veranda, where he paused at the base of the stairs, looking at me with those deep blue eyes.

"I had a wonderful time," I said, trying not to lose myself in his gaze.

"Me too." He placed his hand on my forearm, and I felt a warmth spread through me at his touch. It was intoxicating, and in that moment, I wished he would step closer and embrace me. Instead, he smiled, chuckling softly. "I think I should go. It's late, and we both have work tomorrow."

I nodded in agreement, even though internally I was screaming at him to stay longer. Then Craig stepped closer and wrapped his muscular arms around my waist in a gentle hug. As I hugged him back, I breathed in his musky scent. My heart quickened, and I felt myself melt against him. Craig must have noticed it and squeezed me a little tighter. He sighed deeply, and the heat of his breath against my neck sent a chill of desire through me. Yet, the moment ended as he planted a gentle kiss on my cheek and stepped back.

I was grateful for the darkness as I felt my face flush.

Blushing like a schoolgirl. How ridiculous.

"I'd love to see you again, Amber."

A grin spread across my face. I felt overwhelmingly happy that this gorgeous guy wanted to spend more time with me.

"I'd like that very much." I took a step back from him, so I could see his face better.

"How about lunch and a movie on Sunday? We have a decent cinema complex, and there is a nice café not far from there?"

"A movie?" I asked, my eyebrows raised.

"You do like movies? Don't you?"

"Well, I think I do." I laughed at his concerned expression. "Although I'm not sure what types of movies I like."

"That's alright. I'll pick something ... not scary," he laughed. The sound sent a warm ripple through me. There was something so calming about his tone and his laugh, like a young boy playing in the park. Upbeat and happy.

"Okay. A movie and lunch would be nice."

"Fantastic. I'll pick you up at about twelve. We can buy the tickets first and then enjoy lunch."

"I look forward to it."

"Great. I'll see you Sunday." He gave me a small wave and took a few steps backwards, before turning around and walking to his car. Too nervous to keep watching him, I turned quickly and entered the house. Following the sound of the TV, I found Tracey curled up on the lounge.

"How did your date go?" she asked, looking up from the screen.

"Very nice. He took me out to dinner to a place called The Sapphire Bar."

"Oh, I like it there, such beautiful views."

"Yes. The sunset was gorgeous. And the food ..." I lowered myself onto a lounge chair and carefully propped my crutches up beside me. "It was so good."

"Richard and I went there all the time. He used to joke that he wanted to be buried on the hill, so every time I went to visit him, I would have that view to look out on. Of course, that didn't happen. I haven't been back to the restaurant in years." She turned back to the TV.

Sensing her grief, I changed the subject. "Craig asked me out on another date."

Tracey turned back to me with a smile. "Oh, where to this time?"

"Lunch and a movie on Sunday."

"That will be nice. He is a lovely young man."

I nodded in agreement.

Yes, he certainly seems like a lovely guy.

Chapter 22

Friday, October 20th

The front door slammed shut, the abrupt sound startled me, and I dropped the kitchen knife; it clattered loudly to the benchtop, giving me another fright. Within seconds, a male's voice screamed at me, his terrifying voice booming through the house.

"You fucking bitch! You fucking whore! Did you think you were going to get away with it? Did you think I would never find out?"

Heavy footsteps on the wooden floorboards, echoed towards the kitchen, where I stood frozen, my heart racing, my eyes wide, my breath hitched.

Panic and fear overwhelmed me, and my fingertips began to tingle in apprehension. Regaining my sensors and willing my body to move, I quickly scanned the room, wanting to find a place to hide. As the footsteps got louder, and seeing no way out, other than heading towards the angry voice, I grabbed the knife I had dropped and held out my arm, the tip of the blade pointing towards the kitchen door.

If I was not able to escape the room, I would defend myself as best I could. Breathing in deeply, I watched as a shadow crossed the kitchen threshold. The muscles in my legs were so tightly coiled, I thought they might snap.

I woke suddenly, my heart beating so hard, I swear it almost burst through my chest. My pyjamas were damp with perspiration, and my hands were clenched tight; the sheets wound tightly within their grasp. Panic set in as I peered around the darkened room, and the nightmare that had woken me, began to fade.

Slowing down my breathing, I tried to recall what I had been dreaming about, but by the time my rhythm was back to normal, the dream was gone.

Swinging my bare legs over the edge of the bed, I allowed my toes to caress the carpet and sighed in relief as my sensors grounded me back to reality.

Shaking my head in frustration, I reached for the water bottle beside my bed and took a long deep drink, relaxing more as the cool water slid down my throat.

This was the second time this week I'd woken in the middle of the night, scared. Returning the bottle to the nightstand, I lay back, swung my legs back on the bed and rolled on to my side, trying to get into a more comfortable position. Despite the nightmare waking me, and sending my heart racing, I closed my eyes, pushing the incident into the back of my mind. It didn't take long before I drifted off to sleep again.

When I opened my eyes again, the sun was creeping its way through the curtains. A mild headache throbbed behind my eyes, and I felt a little dizzy as I sat up. Walking slowly into the kitchen, I found Tracey at the table, finishing her breakfast.

"Good morning, love," she said, placing her teacup down. As she turned and looked at me, the smile dropped from her face as her brows furrowed. "Are you okay?" she asked, quickly standing up.

"Hmm ... I'm okay. Bit of a headache though," I mumbled as I sat in a chair at the end of the table.

"Oh, I'll get you some Paracetamol then." She hurried to a cupboard above the bench and brought down a large basket full of medications and bandages. Taking two tablets out of a box, she placed them in front of me and poured a glass of cold water from the tap. "These will help. Do I need to take you to the hospital for another check-up?"

"No. I don't think so. I didn't sleep very well, but I'm sure it will pass." Popping the tablets in my mouth, I swallowed them with a mouthful of water.

"Will you be okay to get to work? I have the day off. If you need to stay home, I can call the Post Office."

"No. Please don't. I'll just have a shower and get ready. I can catch the bus like normal." Grabbing an apple from the fruit bowl in the middle of the table, I took a large bite.

Tracey bustled around me, cleaning up her dishes and took herself off to sit in the lounge. After finishing the apple, I went to the bathroom for a warm shower. Needing to get ready for work, I tried to push my night terror from my mind. I couldn't remember if it was a bad dream which had awoken me, or something else.

The rest of the morning passed without issues, and I made my way to the bus stop. By the time I arrived at work, all the thoughts of the night were gone, and all I could think about was my date with Craig.

It went better than I had hoped for. He was a perfect gentleman the entire night, and I was looking forward to our next date. Sitting beside him in a darkened cinema sounded exciting. When I walked into the Post office, I was once again grinning like a young teenager.

"Well, you look like the mouse who got the cheese," Adam called out to me. "What are you all smiles about?"

"She went on her date last night," Rebecca called back from behind the counter as she smiled at me. "You must have had a good night."

I laughed. "Yes, actually. I had a wonderful time."

"Tell me all about it," she said, hurrying over to me.

"Please save it for morning teatime, ladies. We need to open the shop," Mrs. Murphy pipped up.

Rebecca rolled her eyes and walked back to the counter with her shoulders hunched over. I laughed quietly and made my way into the back room where bags of letters awaited sorting.

Over the past two weeks, I'd developed a steady flow. It was easy work, and everyone was always so friendly. Customers had stopped gossiping about me, and thanks to Mrs Murphy's zero tolerance for idle chitchat, the staff had stopped questioning me as well.

As soon as Rebecca's tea-brake arrived, she rushed to my side, sitting down quickly, and grabbing both my hands. "Quick, we only have fifteen minutes. Tell me everything."

Laughing at how easy it was to talk to her, I gave her a recap of the date, leaving out very little. I watched in awe at how delighted she was. She squealed like a schoolgirl, and bounced excitedly, when I told her Craig wanted to take me to the movies and lunch on Sunday.

"I'm so jealous. I haven't been on a date in ages," she said once I finished talking.

"And you aren't likely to, if you keep screeching like that," Mrs. Murphy commented as she walked past us on her way to the tearoom. "And your time is up, Rebecca. Back to work, please."

Rebecca rolled her eyes again and giggled. "We'll talk again on Monday." She walked back to the counter, and I got back to work, finishing the bags just before one.

I caught the bus home and prepared a few things for dinner. Tracey was working the late shift, so I was on my own. I plodded around the house for a bit before settling down on the front porch with my dinner and a book. Losing myself in the novel, it was well after sunset when I finally went inside.

Chapter 23

Sunday, October 22nd

Bolting upright, my heart thumping loudly in my chest again, I struggled to breathe, as a wave of frustration and fear washed over me. A slick layer of sweat coated the base of my neck and around my hairline and the air in the room felt thick and warm. Sunlight already filtered through my room, but it didn't help to chase away the scared feeling in my chest.

I couldn't recall the dream that woke me, or why I was fearful, but I had the overwhelming feeling I was being watched. Tentatively I looked around the room, expecting to find someone else with me, but I was alone.

Feeling on edge, I slowly eased myself off my bed and quietly placed my feet onto the carpet. Swallowing thickly, I crept towards the closed bedroom door and rested my ear against it. An eery silence enveloped me, heightening my already overwhelmed emotions.

Tracey had the day off today, but I couldn't hear her moving around the house. Usually, by this time, she was up and making breakfast. Carefully, I opened my door and peered into the hallway. The house was quiet. Too quiet.

Gingerly stepping out onto the floorboards of the passageway, I inched my way down to the kitchen, using the wall to support me. As I passed the bathroom and laundry, I peered into them, making sure no one was hiding inside. Not that I would have known what to do if there was, as I had no weapons other than my fists.

Edging into the kitchen, panic coursed through me, when I noticed the back door was wide open and I froze, the cast on my leg suddenly weighing me down. Abruptly, I heard a noise outside and my stomach twisted in fear.

"Tracey!" I called out in fear, my voice more a squeak.

"Out here!" she called back.

Relief rushed through me, and my heart skipped a beat. I leant against the wall to stop myself from sinking to the floor. Laughing lightly to myself and shaking my head for being so pathetic, I hobbled to the open door.

"You're up early," I said as casually as I could, leaning against the door frame as I looked out at Tracey watering the pot plants on the back porch.

"I couldn't sleep this morning; thought I would get in a bit of gardening before it got too warm." She turned to me and fell quiet when she saw my face. "Are you okay? You look pale?" Tracey came over to me and placed her hand on my forehead. "You're sweating, and where are your crutches?"

"They're in the bedroom and I'm fine. Bad dream, I think," I smiled weakly, pushing back off the frame and limping my way to the fridge.

"Are you sure?" She followed me into the kitchen.

"Yeah. I think I just got spooked. I'll be fine."

"This is the second morning in a row you've come out looking like death. If you're feeling unwell ..."

"No, honestly. I'm fine. I might have a shower, freshen up. After all, I have a movie to go to soon." I poured myself a small glass of orange juice, gulped it down and rinsed the glass before placing it onto the drying rack.

"Do you want me to get your crutches? I know the cast comes off tomorrow, but I don't want you to fall," she asked.

"No, it's not that far," I said as I ambled my way to my room.

"I'll just be outside if you need me dear," Tracey said, watching me, before walking back outside to her plants.

I showered and dressed. Brushing my damp hair back into a tight ponytail, I looked at my reflection in the mirror.

Who am I? Why is this happening to me?

Realising I was ready far too early, I sat in the lounge and tried to relax my nerves with a book. Yet, with the overwhelming emotions this morning, I couldn't sit still.

Remembering Doctor Wilkins' breathing exercises, I closed my eyes and focused. I inhaled through my nose, feeling the air flood my lungs, before exhaling through my mouth. Instantly, I felt some of the tension leave my shoulders, and I relaxed.

"I've made us some morning tea," Tracey said, walking into the lounge, carrying a tray, ladened with drinks and biscuits.

"Perfect." I placed the book down next to me.

"Feeling better?" she asked, handing me a cup of tea.

"Yes, although I won't lie. These bad dreams, or whatever they are, are annoying me."

"I think you should talk to Doctor Wilkins about them next time you see her." She sat with her tea, a concerned look in her eyes.

"Yes, perhaps I should." I took a biscuit, dunked it into my tea, and enjoyed the sweet taste. Just before twelve, I heard a car pull into the driveway. Without wanting to look too eager, I asked Tracey to open the door when Craig knocked.

"You're an adult, and I'm not here," she teased before rushing back through to the kitchen, taking the tray of empty cups and plate with her. Taking a deep breath, I opened the door where Craig greeted me with his handsome smile.

"Ready Ms Cooper?"

"Yes, I am." I grabbed my handbag off the hall table, called out a farewell to Tracey, and followed Craig to his car.

"Are you looking forward to getting your cast off?" he asked, as he took the crutches and placed them on the back seat.

"You have no idea. I can't wait to wear a pair of pants."

He laughed as he got into the car. "I bet you are."

"So, did you pick a good movie?" I joked.

"I hope so. It's a comedy. Got some good actors in it. It's rated high on the charts."

"Well, let's hope so."

We chatted about trivial things on the way into town. Craig parked in front of the cinema and let me wait in the car while he popped inside to buy the tickets. Within a few minutes, we were heading down the road to a small café. Even though I informed him I was happy to walk the short distance, he reassured me he had no issue driving the short distance.

The café was a beautiful little corner restaurant, with soft, pastel-coloured walls and simple wooden tables and chairs. A waitress directed us to a small table next to the window, with an easy route for me to navigate with the crutches.

My small plate of nachos and Craig's hamburger and chips arrived shortly after ordering, and the food was delicious. Still feeling nervous, and not knowing what to talk about, we ate our food with small chatter.

"How's your mum?" I asked.

"Good. My brother will be visiting her soon. She's looking forward to seeing her grandson."

"That sounds wonderful."

"She'll be thrilled to see him. How's Tracey?" he asked.

"A blessing. I don't know what I would have done without her help."

"That was yummy." I wiped my mouth with a napkin once I finished.

"Indeed, it was," Craig replied, pushing his plate aside. "Shall we go?" He looked at me with those intense eyes.

"Please. And can we walk? It's so nice outside. Gotta get my vitamin D," I giggled.

"You sure it's not too far?"

I shook my head. "No."

The walk to the cinema complex was slow, but I didn't mind. Craig matched my pace as we passed shop windows adorned with sale items and joked about the crazy things people spent their money on.

"These porcelain dolls are scary." Craig motioned to a few in a children's toy shop display.

"Oh, I think they are pretty," I commented, pausing to admire their frilly dresses and tightly curled hair.

"You like these?" Craig asked, his brow lifting with surprise.

"Sure." I turned to him and smiled.

He turned to me and spoke with a serious tone. "If you get your memory back and tell me you have a room full of dolls like this, our friendship is over!" He tried to hide the smile as he turned back to the window.

"Oh, so they are a deal breaker?" I asked, trying not to laugh. He nodded enthusiastically. "Duly noted." I giggled.

Thankfully, the cinema had a lift; we headed up to the second floor to find our seats in the theatre. Craig sat me next to the aisle and placed my crutches under our seat. We settled back, and a sudden rush of nerves and excitement came over me as the lights dimmed.

This is it. I can't believe I'm in the dark with Craig.

I nestled back further in the seat, unable to suppress the girlish smile, as I felt his presence next to me. Halfway through the movie, Craig slipped his hand over the armrest and gently took my hand in his. Even in the darkness, I could not hold back my smile, and when I turned to glance at him, he was already looking at me with a sheepish grin.

"Is this, okay?" he asked, leaning in to whisper.

"Yes," I nodded. His hand was warm and his grasp on my fingers was firm yet gentle. He never let go until the movie ended.

If this is what I went through as a teenager, then I would've been one happy young girl.

True to his word, the movie was hilarious. It was nice to laugh, to forget about every negative thought that rambled through my mind each day. By the end of the movie, I had tears of joy streaming down my face. As the credits rolled, I felt regret knowing our date was ending. Walking out of the dark cinema, we squinted against the bright sunlight.

"I really enjoyed that. Thank you," I said as we started walking back to the car.

"Me too. Honestly, it was better than I expected."

"The movie, or the date?" I laughed.

"Both," he laughed back.

The drive back home went too quickly, and before I knew it, Craig pulled into the driveway.

"I had a great time today," he said, as he cradled my arm in his and helped me walk up to the veranda without the crutches.

"Me too." We stopped at the stairs, and I leant against the handrail for support, resting my heavy cast on the ground. He lowered his hand, casually letting it slip into the pocket of his jeans.

"I would like to make this a three for three, if that's okay."

"Meaning?" I asked coyly, knowing exactly what he meant, but wanting to hear him say it.

His eyes glinted playfully as he cocked his head to the side. "Can I take you out again?"

I smiled widely at him. "I'd love that."

"How does a picnic by the lake sound? It's lovely and green, and all the flowers are in bloom. Say, next Sunday?"

"Sounds wonderful, and with my cast coming off tomorrow, hopefully I'll be less of a burden to walk with."

"You're not a burden, slow, yes, but not a burden." He joked, putting his hand back on my arm.

"You're a funny guy." I laughed.

"So, I've been told." He squeezed my arm gently. "Well, how does ten-thirty Sunday morning sound?"

"Good."

"Fantastic." He took a step closer to me, lent forward and kissed me gently on the forehead. I felt my knees weaken as I inhaled his musky scent, the aroma beginning to feel familiar. The warm pressure of his lips against my skin was irresistible. I tilted my head up slightly, but he pulled back, and with a smile, he slowly turned and walked back to his car. I watched from the porch steps until he disappeared down the road. Stepping into the house, I couldn't wipe off the huge teenager grin on my face.

Chapter 24

After finishing my shift, Tracey dropped me off at the hospital to have my cast removed. The procedure was quick and simple, and I was over the moon to finally be free of it—although I wasn't happy to see the hairy state of my leg. After weeks of not being able to scratch, it felt good to drag my nails over the dry skin. Pleased with the doctor's check over, I left and made my way to Doctor Wilkins' office.

"Good afternoon, Amber. So, the cast came off without any issues?" she asked as I sat down.

"Yes, apparently everything is fine. The doctor is happy with how it looks."

"Fantastic. How does it feel?"

"Lighter," I laughed.

"I bet it does," she smiled. "But that wasn't quite what I meant."

"Yeah, I know," I said, feeling a little embarrassed at my poor sense of humour.

"Well. How do you feel now that the last of your physical injuries have healed?"

"To be honest, it feels good, but it still doesn't change the fact I still can't remember anything. I don't know how much longer I can take this uncertainty."

"What do you mean by that?" she asked with a slight frown.

Realising she might have interpreted the comment the wrong way, I quickly expanded. "Oh, I didn't mean anything like that. I'm not going to run away or do something silly. I just want to move on with my life without this ... stuff hanging over me." Turning my head, I glanced out the window, sighing deeply.

"I understand how hard this must be for you," Tracey said, and I could feel her gaze on me, but I didn't respond. "I still believe your memory will return. With the work you've put in over the past few sessions, I can see the progress you've made, even if you can't."

"And if they don't come back?" I asked, turning back to face her.

"Then you have to find, or I should say, *we* have to find a way for you to cope with it."

I laughed. "Cope with it! How do I just cope with it? I have a whole life somewhere out there." I gestured at the window. "It's not like I just came out of nowhere!" I could hear the anger in my voice, and I forced myself to stop talking. It wasn't Doctor Wilkins I was angry at, just the situation.

"Okay. Here's a thought," she said, noting my growing irritation. "Next week, I would like to try hypnosis again on you. I know it hasn't worked overly well the last two times we tried, but the possibility of it helping you outranks the way you currently feel. What do you think?"

I looked at her with uncertainty. I wasn't overly confident about it trying it again when I'd had no success with it so far. "No. I don't want to do hypnosis anymore."

"You don't?" she asked, her eyebrows raised.

"No. I don't feel like it's doing anything. We've tried twice, other than leaving here feeling very relaxed. I'm no closer to getting my memories back than I was weeks ago!"

"Amber, I understand your frustrations. I really do," she replied, her voice filled with sympathy. "Is there anything you would like to discuss in today's session?" she asked, trying to redirect the conversation.

"Well," I swallowed slowly. "I met someone last week."

"Someone you think you know?"

"No. A guy." I small smile tugged at the corners of my mouth, and I felt my face warm at the thought of him.

"Oh, really?" she asked, leaning forward slightly in her chair. "Where did you meet?"

A small laugh escaped me. "At a bus stop, actually." My smile widened, thinking back to the moment I first looked up into Craig's eyes.

"A bus stop, interesting. Was he catching the bus too?"

"No, he was walking past but saw me looking for a cat ... well, he didn't know I was looking for a cat until I told him. He was helpful enough to look with me."

"Ah, so you met over a cat. That's nice."

"No, not really. We never found the cat. It must have run off or something." I waved dismissively.

Doctor Wilkins smiled. "Well, it was a good way to start a conversation, I suppose."

"I guess it was. It was strange, though, hearing the cat. I'd heard another one a few days before and couldn't find that one either. In fact, it's happened three times now," I commented with a frown.

"You're hearing cat sounds. But not actually seeing a cat?" she asked earnestly.

"Yeah. Weird, isn't it?" I replied flippantly.

"Well, that could be a good thing, you know," she said as she made some notes in her book.

"I'm hearing a cat meow, and you think this could be a good thing?" I mused. "It sounds more like I hit my head and broke my brain. I can't remember who I am, but I can hear cat sounds!"

"Maybe your brain is trying to push something forward. What if, during our next session, we give hypnosis another attempt?" She held her hands up to stop me from protesting. "This time, we focus on cats. You never know what might happen."

I stared at her. Even though I had just stated I didn't want to try hypnosis again, maybe she had a point. We had something new we could focus on. I sighed. "Okay, we'll try one more time."

"Great. How about ..." she leant over to the small table and grabbed her diary. Turning to the following week and scanning the pages, she picked up her pen. "Next week on Friday at two-thirty? Does that give you enough time after work?"

"Yes. That will be fine."

"Fantastic. Well, I'll see you then." She stood up as I did and shook my hand.

Chapter 25

Saturday, October 28th

Having the day to myself, I made my way into town to get a haircut. Knowing I had a date with Craig tomorrow, I wanted to look my best, and had booked an appointment, earlier last week.

Walking without the crutches certainly made life easier. As I entered the hair salon, I was greeted with friendly smiles and a few congratulations from the staff and customers when they noticed the cast was gone. The last seven weeks of my new life had been better than I had ever thought. I no longer seemed to be the object of their suspicion, and I felt extremely comfortable in Parker.

"Good morning, Amber," called out a young blonde behind the counter. "Welcome to Megan's Cut and Colour. Nathan is ready for you."

"Morning, Amber!" I looked beyond the counter and saw one of the post office regulars, Martha, sitting under a hair dryer, her hair packed solidly with curlers.

"Hey, you got your cast off. That's great news. Bet your leg feels lighter!" said another customer. I didn't recognise her, but she seemed to know who I was.

"Hey sweetheart, come sit here." I looked up at the sound of a male's voice as he gestured at the chair before him.

I smiled as I walked towards him, greeting the locals as I passed.

"Hi."

"How are you going?"

"Thanks, the leg feels better."

"Hi, how are you?"

It was humorous and mildly scary to have all these people in one room happy to see me, and for a small town, it sure was busy in here.

"Hi, I'm Nathan. Take a seat," Nathan said, as he grabbed his hair trolley and wheeled it over behind me. Dressed in all black, his youthful face was framed with dark brown hair, streaked with blond highlights. "So, what are we doing for you today?" He started running his fingers through my hair.

"Um, just a trim please, I guess."

"Okay," he smiled politely, and picking up a brush, he started running it gently through my hair.

I stared at my reflection, watching his hands move. Glancing around the room through the mirror, I realised my hair was bland compared to the other ladies in the salon. Just as Nathan was separating my hair, preparing to cut, I stopped him.

"Wait." I held up my hand.

"Is everything okay?" He looked at me through the mirror.

"Do you think you could ..." I paused. "Add some life to it?"

"Your hair?"

I nodded.

"Absolutely. I could cut in a few layers and add some colour or highlights. Freshen it up a bit."

As I turned slightly to look at Nathan, my eyes rested on a young girl sitting to the right of me. She smiled and offered her hand.

"Hi, I'm Shelly. You can trust Nathan. He's been doing my hair for years."

"Hi," I said, shaking her hand quickly. "I guess my hair does look a little boring, doesn't it?" I laughed, running my own fingers through it as I examined my dull blonde colour.

"Thank you, Shelly." Nathan beamed. "Well?" he rested his hands on my shoulders.

"Alright. Not too many layers, though. I do like it long. And maybe some light blonde highlights?"

"I can do that. May I suggest some white/blonde highlights and some cranberry red highlights? It will look amazing."

I glanced back to Shelly. She nodded her head enthusiastically.

"Sure," I said bravely.

Nathan grinned. "Let me go whip up some colours. Be back soon." I watched him saunter towards the back of the salon.

Within a few minutes, Nathan returned with two bowls, brushes, and aluminium foil. I felt apprehensive, yet excited, as he placed them on the tray. He smiled at me and grabbed his comb.

"Right. Let get this creation started, shall we?"

"You're the boss, go for it, just be kind," I joked.

"You'll be fine. Just sit back and relax."

The next three hours passed faster than I expected. Nathan was very gentle and pampered me. Offering me coffee, giving me a head massage as he washed the colour out and chatted to me the whole time, like I was a regular customer. I felt so at peace there. I found myself chatting openly to him about the last seven weeks, and he listened without judging or criticising. In fact, all the staff and customers were happy to chat, and I felt like this was a place I could come back to.

After trimming my hair and adding a few layers to frame my face, Nathan passed a smaller mirror around behind me. "In the sun, darling, your hair will shine with a hint of gold."

I was amazed to see how much better it looked and wondered why I didn't already style my hair like this before.

Was I not a very adventurous girl in my past? Did I not bother about fashion and looking good before I ended up in Parker?

With my previous lack of style, I wondered if perhaps I'd never had time to go to the hairdressers. Maybe I was too busy with work or something.

Concentrating on my new hairdo, I admired my reflection in the mirror. Staring back at me was the same face I was recognising as mine, but now with a fresher, lighter twist. A smile spread across my face as I turned my head from side to side.

Simple but elegant.

The length remained past my shoulders, but with the added colour and shape, my hair looked amazing.

"Beautiful!"

"Lovely!"

"Gorgeous!"

A round of kind words and smiles greeted me as I made my way to the counter to pay.

"Thank you so much for what you have done, Nathan," I commented. "I love it."

"You're welcome, sweetheart. Make sure you come back in about eight weeks for a trim. Any other issues, just ring," he said, passing me a business card.

I paid the bill, said goodbye, and walked out of the salon with my head held high. I felt like a movie star, walking down the red-carpet, and I couldn't wait to get home and show Tracey. Thinking about my date the next day, I couldn't stop grinning from ear to ear. Although I had a few small doubts and fears about my new friendship with Craig, Tracey had assured me he really was a nice guy.

Walking down the main street, surrounded by fashion boutiques, shoe stores and cafes, I decided since the cast was off, I would buy a new pair of shorts and some summer shoes for the picnic tomorrow. The thought of being able to try on shorts made me smile. Wearing nothing but skirts and short dresses, I'd felt extremely limited.

I entered a lady's boutique and browsed through the racks of colourful clothing. Finding a few pairs of shorts and pants, I took them to the change room and tried them on. Deciding on two pairs of shorts, one a cotton blend in an olive-green colour and another pair in dark blue denim, I returned the rest of the shorts and pants to the racks.

As I browsed through another rack of jeans, I heard a sound which made me stop in my tracks.

"Meow."

I froze, holding my breath. This was now the fourth time I'd heard a cat meow. Glancing around the store, I tried to determine if anyone else had heard it, but the other patrons appeared engrossed in their shopping. Taking a deep breath, I shook my head, pushing the sound into the back of my mind and continued shopping. Taking a few steps forward towards the next rack of jeans, I heard the sound again.

"Meow."

I spun around and looked at the ground. There was nothing there. No cat, no kitten. Nothing! Again, I looked around the store at the other customers, and while I'd drawn a couple of curious stares, I seemed to be the only one losing it.

Carefully, I parted the pants on the racks, pretending I was looking at the clothes, but didn't find any mysterious cat hiding or sheltering within the darkness. This was starting to feel like someone was playing a prank on me—and it wasn't the least bit funny.

Shaking my head in frustration, I dashed to the shoe department and busied myself among the vast variety of footwear on display. Trying on a few different styles, I eventually decided on a pretty pair of white summer wedges with a light green trim. Something I could wear with my new shorts. I also grabbed a simple pair of blue and white runners. I thought to myself it would be nice to go for walks after work, just before dinner, as the day wound down. So, feeling on top of the world, and with my new hair and clothes, I headed to the bus stop, eager to show my hair off to Tracey.

Chapter 26

The sounds of the outside world drifted towards me as I woke slowly, feeling rested and content. I opened my eyes and smiled. The morning sun shone through the window; I noted the day was perfect for a picnic. I sat up and swung my legs over the bed. The feeling of being able to move without the cast felt wonderful.

Standing tall, I stretched my arms over my head; I sighed loudly as I felt all the muscles in my body loosen and relax. I grabbed my robe and made my way towards the bathroom. Tracey had already left for the day, so I had plenty of time to get myself ready. Fastening my newly coloured hair up into a tight bun to prevent it from getting wet, I jumped in the shower and washed away the night's sweat and grime.

Ten glorious minutes later, I rinsed off, turned off the taps, and stepped out of the shower. Grabbing the towel off the rail, I froze as heavy footsteps sounded outside the bathroom. My eyes widened as I stared at the door.

Tracey's left for work, so who's inside the house?

I straightened slowly and wrapped the towel around my body, constantly keeping an eye on the door and an ear out for more steps. My body trembled as my fear and apprehension intensified, anticipating something bad was about to happen. Holding my breath, I stared at the doorhandle, expecting it to open. Nothing happened.

I remained motionless for a few moments and tried to calm myself enough to avoid a panic attack. Edging towards the door, I pressed my ear against it, but when I didn't hear any other noises, I dropped the towel and wrapped myself in my bathrobe. Stepping back to the door, I tentatively placed my hand on the doorknob and turned it carefully.

I inched the door open a fraction and cautiously peaked through the gap. I couldn't see anyone on the other side. Taking a deep breath, I swung the door open and boldly stepped into the hallway. Looking up and down, I was relieved to see I was alone.

"Hello?" I called out quietly, still feeling a little nervous. "Is someone there?" No one responded. Yet the silence in the house was eerie. Frowning, I moved as silently as I could towards the kitchen, looking into the bedrooms as I passed them. They were all empty.

Creeping into the kitchen, an overwhelming feeling crashed through me, and my breath hitched. I looked over at the kitchen table, half-expecting to see a man sitting there. To my relief, the chairs around the table were empty. I closed my eyes, my hand resting on my beating chest.

Still feeling uneasy, I hurried to the backdoor, finding it locked. If someone was still in the house, they must be in the front area. Resisting the urge to unlock the backdoor and run outside, I closed my eyes again and concentrated on the surrounding silence. The fact that I still felt on edge frustrated me. There didn't seem to be any reason to feel so afraid, but no matter how I tried to remove the fear, it still lingered with me.

Gathering up what courage I could muster; I made my way out of the kitchen and back down the hall towards the front of the house.

"Hello?" I called out again, a little louder, trying to sound confident.

Moving into the lounge, I quickly scanned the room and was thankful to find no one in it. The front door was the last thing to check—at least it was closed. I walked over to it and grasped the handle; I couldn't turn it. It was locked. It made no sense to me at all.

Pressing my back against the door, I looked back at the empty house and sighed heavily.

For crying out loud, this is ridiculous! I chastised myself. *There's no one here and there never was. It's just my mind playing tricks on me again—like the cat sounds.*

Releasing a frustrated sigh, I eyes fell on the clock and I noticed the time. I gasped in shock and dashed to my room to finish getting ready. I wanted to make sure I looked my best for the date.

Before long, there was a knock on the door. Craig had arrived. Taking a last glance in the mirror, I ran my hand over my top, smoothing it down. I'd gone with my new olive shorts and paired them with a crisp, white, cotton singlet. Slipping on my new wedges, I spun on my heels and walked confidently to greet my date.

"Wow, look at you!" Craig gasped after I opened the door.

"Is that a good look or a bad look?" I asked with a hint of a smile.

"Good, all good, and, hey! Your cast is off!" he exclaimed, looking down at my legs.

"Yes, and I'm loving it. Feels so much better."

"Looks better too," he laughed, and a twinkle of desire flashed briefly in his eyes.

Our small talk made me smile and his flirting certainly had a way of relaxing me. All the nerves I felt after this morning's weird incident had simply fluttered away as soon as I opened the door and saw his face. Today he wore denim shorts and a dark green, buttoned-up shirt. The colour of his shirt made his eyes look an even darker blue than I remembered. They seemed to sparkle as he looked at me. His hair was down and the urge to run my fingers through it returned.

"Come on in," I said, pushing the thoughts from my mind as I led him into the kitchen to grab the picnic basket I'd prepared earlier.

"Sandwiches, drinks, some fruit, and an apple slice for dessert. Does that sound okay?" I asked as I reached the counter.

"Sounds great." Craig was not far behind me, and when he spoke, I jumped with fright. "Are you alright?" he asked, stepping forward and placing his hand on my shoulder.

"Yes," I gasped. "Sorry, you were just closer than I expected." I turned slightly around to face him, feeling the weight of his hand as I moved. It was not as heavy as I was expecting, and the warmth of it helped to soothe me.

Wow, perhaps I'm not quite as over the morning's episode as I'd thought.

With Craig standing so close to me, I could smell his aftershave. A hint of musk mixed with a spice, a masculine smell. I could not recognise the brand but overall, I liked it. I breathed it in and felt my pulse race. This guy had such an effect on me. It was slightly overwhelming, but I didn't want it to stop.

"Are you sure you're, okay?" he asked again, this time running his hand down my arm to my hand and gently wrapping his fingers around mine. His touch sent tingles through me, and I smiled up at him.

"Yes, just nervous, I guess."

"Nothing to be nervous about," he assured me, a hint of laughter in his eyes. "Shall we get going, then?"

I nodded, and he grabbed the basket with his free hand, spun on his heels and, gripping my hand a little harder, pulled me along behind him towards the door. The sun was shining brightly, with only a few wispy clouds in the sky.

Today's going to be great. I said to myself, as I pushed the event from this morning out my mind.

Watching Craig drive, I studied his face, taking in the shape of his nose and chin. The way he blinked and moved his eyes as he concentrated on the road. There was something intriguing about him, and I found it hard to turn away.

"It's rude to stare, you know," he said, catching me out.

"Oh sorry, I didn't mean to," I stuttered, turning a light shade of pink, and turning away from him to look out my window.

"It's okay, and I didn't say you should stop," he teased.

I laughed and glanced back at him. He was watching me with a huge grin on his face. "I'll take it as a compliment." I turned my head, grinning like a fool, and watched the traffic before us.

"So, where are we going exactly?" I asked, trying to chance the subject.

"A small park with a lake not far from here. It's nice there. I hope you like it."

"I'm sure I will."

True to his word, the park was beautiful.

A large deep blue lake spread out before us, edged with clumps of reeds and water grasses. Tall Birch trees thrived amongst the lush green grass that grew to the edge of the sandy shoreline. A few ducks swam effortlessly across the smooth surface of the water, leaving small wakes behind them.

Picnic benches and tables were scattered through-out the park, with free barbeque facilities available to use. All were in use and the smell of cooking meat and onions drifting our way on the breeze made my stomach rumbled. We picked a shaded area under a large tree a few meters from the lake's edge. Laying out a large picnic blanket Craig brought with, we settled down.

"Popular place, this," I commented as I retrieved the plates and glasses from the basket.

"Yes, it's a delightful place to come. Do you like it?" he asked.

"Yes, very much. Very relaxing. A lot of families here!" I noted.

"And a few couples," he responded with a mischievous undertone I was beginning to recognise.

I spread the food onto the picnic rug, and we started eating. Sitting next to Craig felt so normal, like we'd known each other for years. I was surprised at how easy it felt to be around him. However, it was never far from my mind that I'd had another life before Parker. The fact was that after all this time, there was no news of anyone looking for me. I was a long way from home, and no one missed me.

What does that say about me?

"Earth to Amber?" Craig nudged me, pulling me from my thoughts.

"Sorry, just enjoying the view," I apologised as I turned to him. His eyes brimmed with curiosity, and I smiled at him reassuringly.

"Hmm ... me too!" he smiled back, desire replacing the curiosity in his expression. "By the way, I love your hair!"

"Thank you," I said, ducking my head as I felt myself blush, and I tried to hide it by running my fingers through it.

"It suits you and looks amazing in the sun." He trailed his fingers through the ends of my hair, slightly brushing his fingertips along my back. Shivers of pleasure rippled through me, and I closed my eyes slightly. Craig dropped his hand and turned to look out at the lake.

The atmosphere in the park was amazing. There were kids laughing, a dog barking, birds chirping in the trees and the gentle lapping of the water at the lake's edge was mesmerising. With full stomachs, we lay down on the rug.

"Thank you for bringing me here, Craig. It's a beautiful place."

"You are more than welcome. Anytime you want to come back, we will."

"You say that like you are expecting another date?" I teased.

Craig chuckled as I lay there looking at him. His smile was intoxicating, and I suddenly felt the urge to lean forward and kiss him. His eye locked onto mine, and the feeling, I realised, was mutual. Suddenly nervous, I cleared my throat and turned to look up through the branches and leaves towards the blue sky.

"Do you want to go for a walk around the lake?" Craig asked as he slowly sat up.

"Sure, that would be great," I responded, thankful he had taken no offence to me turning away from him. Together, we packed up the picnic things, and, leaving the basket and blanket under the tree, strolled down to the lake.

"Can you walk all the way around it?" I asked.

"You can, but it takes a long time. There's a path leading around to the western edge to a small jetty where people fish off." He pointed out towards the left. "I thought maybe we could walk there and back. Take about half an hour each way. Is that okay with you? Will your leg be alright?"

"Only one way to find out. Let's go," I urged, walking toward the pathway.

Walking along the wide pathway, the cool breeze brew softly through my hair. Summer was on its way, and I was content.

"Tell me more about your life," I urged him.

"I bought my first house when I was twenty-five in the city, but I moved back to Parker just under a year ago. My mum's not doing too well."

"I'm sorry to hear that." I placed my hand on his arm as we walked.

"Thanks. Misses my dad I think." He glanced at me, giving me a small smile. "So, I sold my house and bought another one, a few streets away from her."

"And your business?"

"I still own it, but I have one of the other guys running it while I work out what I want to do. In the meantime, I work for a small company here, as Assistant Manager."

"And your siblings, do they visit your mum?"

"Yes, they come aver a few times a year. She livens up more when she sees her grandkids."

I let him do most of the talking on the way to the jetty. As we walked along, my mind began to wonder, and I imagined what it would be like to live with him. To snuggle up to him every night on the couch, share meals together and make love at night. These images and thoughts passed into my brain so quickly I barely had time to censor myself.

I have no business thinking about a future with this guy when I don't know who I've left in my past.

With Craig, everything felt so natural. I was so comfortable around him, and I didn't really want those images to go away. Yet, talking to him, like anyone else since the accident, felt very one sided. Craig shared so much about himself as we walked that I felt odd that I had nothing to say in return.

"A penny for your thoughts," he said.

"I feel bad you've been doing all the talking today, and I don't really have much to tell you about me," I sighed.

"It's okay."

"No, it's not." I stopped walking and turned myself away from him, looking out over the water. "It doesn't seem very fair." I glanced back over my shoulder to look at him.

"Okay, I'd be lying if I said I didn't want to know more about you," he smiled, stepping up beside me. "But I know you can't share anything until your memories come back, and I'm okay with that." He placed his hand on my arm to reassure me. Once again, his touch sent a shiver up to my shoulder and down my back. It was a good shiver. Craig gently slid his hand down my arm towards my hand, slowly clasping his fingers around my wrist. My skin reacted to his soft touch and a warm ripple spread up my arm again. I didn't pull away.

"Is this, okay?" he asked.

I welcomed the motion and glanced up into his blue eyes. Smiling, he slowly released my wrist and lowered his hand, sliding his fingers between mine. I tightened my grip around his and allowed him to move closer to me.

It was strange. Despite the fact we had only recently met, it felt so right. Like we'd known each other for years. This stranger, who wanted to spend time with me, who wanted to hold my hand. I was nervous, scared, excited, happy, feeling everything all at once, yet I also felt safe.

Walking hand in hand, we made our way to the end of the jetty. A few people were there fishing and drinking, enjoying the day like we were.

"Does it bother you that you still don't have your memory back?" he asked tenderly.

"It does. Chatting to Doctor Wilkins has helped a little, trying to understand where my memory loss comes from. She's happy I retain my new memories, so there isn't any brain injury, so to speak."

"Do you think she can help you remember everything about who you are?" he asked, turning his body to face mine.

"I hope so. There's got to be so much more to who I am and where I came from," I replied, looking up at him.

"I'm sure she'll be able to help. Keep positive. If there is anything I can do to help you, let me know."

"Thank you."

"I am sorry for bringing it up. It just worries me that no one has come looking for you since the accident."

"It worries me, too," I laughed bitterly. "How is there no one who misses me?"

Moving his free hand around my waist, he pulled me closer and gently wrapped his arm tighter around me. I stepped into him, cradling myself against his chest. Standing so close to him felt like home. His warmth soothed me. Relaxed me. I breathed in his sweet aroma, feeling like I was at home, like I was exactly where I was supposed to be. Forgetting about the fact I had a past, and that there could be a guy out there from my past, or even a family, I melted deeper into Craig's chest and closed my eyes.

His arms tightened around me, and he rested his cheek on the top of my head. I could feel his chest rising and falling with each breath, and I listened to his heart race. No fear, no uneasiness, no reason to worry about anything. We stood like that for a few minutes, enjoying the moment. No pressure, no expectations.

"Time to go back, I think," Craig finally said, breaking the silence and bringing me back to reality. I pulled back and looked up at him.

"Yes, I think you might be right."

"It's not like I want to leave, but I have a few other things I need to do today," he said, stroking my back slowly as he spoke. "I'd much rather stay with you but, you know ..."

"It's okay, I understand. I've had an enjoyable day, though. Thank you so much for getting me out of the house."

"You are more than welcome." He lent forward and gently pressed his lips to my forehead. Kissing it softly. Again, I breathed him in, wanting to melt into his skin. The feeling was intoxicating, and it was getting harder and harder to find the need or want to push myself out of his embrace. I sighed loudly, and he chuckled softly.

Is he feeling the same way as I am?

Gently, he removed his arms from around my back and moved them up onto my elbows. He tilted his head down and locked his eyes with mine.

I stared into those beautiful eyes and again got lost in the moment. His gaze locked with mine, not wanting to blink or turn away either.

"Come on, Amber," he laughed again, his whole face lighting up, as he finally blinked. Stepping back, he held me at arm's length before releasing me.

"Yep, let's go."

"I promise to take you out again, if you like."

"I would love that."

"Great. Dinner again? I know of a nice Chinese place, and I'm happy to pick you up again."

I couldn't wipe the smile from my face, knowing he wanted to spend more time with me. "Sounds perfect." Taking his hand back in mine, I turned around and pulled him next to me. Together, we walked back to the picnic rug, gathered everything up, and made our way to the car.

We'd had such a wonderful day that the morning's fear was well and truly gone from my mind. Craig and I got on so well that I could think of nothing else but the coming days and our next date.

Before I knew it, we'd arrived back at the house. Once again, he escorted me down the path, up the steps, and stopped at the door. Craig wrapped his arms around me, pulling me back into his embrace, and kissed me again on the forehead.

"Thank you for coming with me today. I had a wonderful time," he murmured in my ear.

"Me too," I said, looking up at him. Slowly, he lowered his head so that our noses almost touched. The intense desire to grab him around the neck and pull him closer was indescribable. Feeling my heart race, I pushed myself up onto the balls of my feet to close the gap between our lips. He looked down at me with such an intense gaze, I had to blink and break the connection between us.

Craig withdrew his head slowly, widening the gap as he smiled sheepishly. "Sorry, I want to. I really do, but I don't want to force you to do anything you're not ready for."

"What makes you think I'm not ready for this?" I asked him, frowning in confusion.

"Just with everything you're going through, I don't want you to ... you know, get too involved with someone when you still don't have your memories."

Feeling a little rejected, I pushed myself away from him and, turning my back on him, walked quickly to toward the veranda railing. I stood there for a few moments, looking out into the garden, my hands resting on the wooden banister. Closing my eyes, I wondered why things had taken a sudden turn.

I shouldn't have wished for thing to go so well.

Frustration welled within my chest and my fingers tightened on the rail.

I don't know how to get my memory back. How long will this last? How long am I meant to live a life when I knew absolutely nothing about myself?

As though sensing I was upset. Craig walked up behind me, wrapping his arms around my waist and pulling me back against his chest. I dropped my hands to my sides, allowing him to cradle me.

"I'm sorry. I didn't mean to upset you," he whispered, placing his cheek close to mine.

"It's okay," I said quietly. "I just ... I don't know. The day was going so well. I thought you liked me. I guess I didn't think about the possibility of my past coming into it."

Craig slid his hands to my hips and slowly turned me around. Raising his hand, he tenderly cradled my chin and tilted my face up to look at him. "Trust me, I do like you. And I want to kiss you very much, but let's just work on finding out everything about you before we take that step. I want it to be right, and I don't want to end up possibly being ... the other guy in your life."

"I understand."

Still feeling a little put out, I leant back into him, feeling the warmth of his body relax me as I rested my head on his shoulder. Deep down, I knew he was right. There could be another guy who I was involved with. What would I do if I fell in love with Craig, got my memories back and found out I had a partner?

Chapter 27

Wednesday, November 1ˢᵗ

It was mid-way through another week, and a half and Gavin was still home alone. He knew it wasn't his job to do all the housework, and look after himself when he worked all day, yet Gavin couldn't stand to live this way any longer, and casting his stubbornness aside, he'd knew he had to do it himself.

There was no one else.

Gavin slowly sorted through the trash that had accumulated in his house for almost two months and finally put out the overflowing bins to be emptied by the rubbish trucks, only to fill to the brim once more.

With a smug sense of pride, Gavin finally managed to do a few loads of washing without overflowing the machine with suds and even hung the clothes out to dry. His efforts to clean the kitchen, though, were still poor. No matter how many times he walked into that room, the pile in the sink never seemed to get smaller.

With the broken vacuum cleaner in the garage, Gavin bought a new one and ran it over the carpets, but the results were not how his wife would do it, but at least for now, Gavins's house started looking somewhat presentable again and the aroma of sweat, rotting food and damp clothes were now gone.

Returning home after a long day at work, Gavin showered, dressed in a pair of clean black jeans and a casual shirt. Slipping on his black boots, Gavin left the house to once again head to the pub for dinner. Although he'd fixed most of the issues in the house, cooking was something Gavin had truly little experience with, and the unclean pile of burnt pots and pans proved his point.

His mother had made his family dinner every night. And once he got married, his wife took over that role and cooked for him. He'd never needed to make a meal, ever. Even after all these weeks of looking after himself, the kitchen was still an area he just could not navigate.

Gavin was a regular at Holeman's Pub, a local place only ten minutes' drive from home. He had been going there for years. Usually, three or four times a week, in fact. It was a good place to wind down with the lads after a long day at work. Finish work at five, get home to eat a well-cooked dinner at six and then go to the pub by six-thirty. A few drinks with the boys, then home by nine for some intimate time with his lovely wife before he fell asleep.

Wednesday was his favourite night. He never knew why, maybe because it was the middle of the week. He knew the weekend was approaching, where he would spend most of Saturday and Sunday night with his good mates, enjoying the entertainment provided by local bands.

Plus, Sunday nights he brought his wife along, and they would enjoy a meal, and she could catch up with a few of the other wives. Although she was friends with most of them, she didn't see them much during the week. It did, however, give her the chance to socialize while the men drank.

But since his wife had gone missing, Gavin had avoided the pub on Sunday nights. He didn't t want his mates to know something was wrong–and he certainly did not want the other wives poking around in his personal business. After all, Gavin was a great guy and had a wonderful marriage to a beautiful woman. His high school sweetheart.

Walking into the pub, Gavin went straight to the bar and ordered a meal. Peppered steak with chips and salad. Buying a beer, he steered his way to a table against the far wall. Because he was there earlier than the usual time, he wanted to eat his meal before the boys arrived. The last thing he wanted to do was explain why he was eating dinner at the pub, in the first place, and not at home with his wife.

Sitting at the table, waiting for his food to arrive, Gavin watched other couples in the pub, and sighed heavily in frustration. He didn't believe anything sinister had happened to her, but he couldn't understand why she would have left. Despite appearances, Gavin knew they didn't have the best relationship. Like all couples, they had their good and tough times. A few arguments here and there, but certainly nothing that would make her leave him. But the more he thought about the last morning he saw her, the more he was forced to realise there was an incredibly good chance she'd walked out on him.

Yes, they'd had a bigger fight than normal a few days before she disappeared. Yes, he yelled a few things at her that maybe he shouldn't have. It wasn't the first time, and she always took him back—she was always at home when he finished work, ready to forgive him for losing control of his anger.

Gavin had checked the places he thought she might have gone to but found no evidence she'd been there. Though he'd refused to tell her family and raise their suspicions, he'd taken to frequently watching their house—just in case she'd run to them. After all, none of them really liked him anyway, and he knew for a fact her mother had tried to convince her not to marry him so young.

Thankfully, Gavin didn't need to wait long before his meal arrived, delivered to his table by a young, buxom blonde girl.

She was one of the regular staff members, and by the way she always battered her eyes at Gavin, he knew, if push came to shove, she'd be open to a little fun in the bedroom. For now, even with his wife missing, Gavin told himself he was not the cheating kind.

As she placed the food and cutlery on the table, he thanked her, quickly lowering his head to break their eye contact. Out of the corner of his eye, though, he watched her backside sway from side to side as she walked back to the kitchen. A rather dirty thought entered his mind. He smiled smugly to himself, and a small laughing huff escaped his throat.

Unlike the other nights he'd come to Holeman's for dinner, this night did not go as planned. Halfway through his meal, one of the boys turned up early and saw Gavin sitting at the table on his own. Frowning, he made his way over, pulled out a chair and sat down opposite Gavin.

Gavin, startled by seeing his friend so soon, stopped mid chew and stared back silently.

"Hey Gav, what brings you here for dinner on a Wednesday night? Miss's not feeling well?" he asked.

Gavin swallowed his mouthful slowly and picked up his almost empty glass. "Yeah, something like that," he replied curtly, before finishing the rest of his beer.

"Hope it's nothing too serious, mate?"

"Na, she'll be right soon." Gavin continued eating his steak. "How come you're here already?" He asked between mouthfuls.

"Ah, just felt like coming in early. Beats sitting at home doing nothing," his mate replied.

"Guess it's better than nothing since you live alone," he snapped back, feeling irritated by the interruption.

"What the fuck is wrong with you?" His co-worker asked, leaning back a little in his chair. "You've been testy for weeks now."

"Nothing, just mind your own business, Andrew!" Gavin stood up suddenly, grabbing the now empty plate and glass before storming off towards the bar.

Andrew sat in the chair, looking rather surprised, as he watched Gavin order another drink.

Gavin stood at the bar, his back facing Andrew. He was aware his moods had become apparent to the boys at work—he'd heard their whispers. Yet, they also knew he had a temper, and he assumed none of them would want to tempt their luck by pushing his buttons. Andrew, it seemed, may have finally pushed the wrong one.

Within fifteen minutes, the rest of the boys filed into the pub and Gavin returned to the table with a big smile, acting like nothing had just happened but being careful to avoid eye contact with Andrew. Before long, they were all drinking and chatting loudly to each other, as the alcohol flowed, and more drinks were consumed than normal.

Normally, Gavin didn't drink too much—well, except on Saturday nights when he got drunk, but on a weekday, he always controlled how much he had. Tonight, however, was different. Tonight, he just did not care. He flirted with the young blonde waitress when she brought over an order of hot chips, and he raised his voice louder than normal as he talked over everyone.

Without meaning to, Gavin turned to Charlie, his young electrician, and blurted out that his wife was missing.

"I haven't seen her in weeks. Do you know where she is?" he slurred his words.

"Sorry mate. I don't know." Charlie glanced slideways towards Andrew.

"She hasn't cooked me a meal in ages or washed my clothes." His head lolled backwards as his eyes closes. "And she hasn't tended to my needs at all!" he exclaimed, snapping his head forward.

Most of them looked at Gavin with shock and raised eyebrows. This was a side of Gavin they never saw.

"Why the hell would she leave me, hey? Ain't I a good guy? Don't I provide her with everything she needs?" he muttered, pushing his face up close to Andrew's.

"Sure, you are mate," Andrew said with a reassuring pat on the back.

"Then why ain't she home?" Gavin asked, looking at one of the other guys, as he slammed his half-drunken beer onto the table, spilling it.

"No idea, Gav. Have you told the police yet?" Another guy asked.

"Ah, fuck the police. What would they do?" Gavin said, throwing his hand into the air. "Those fools couldn't find their noses in front of their faces," he laughed, spilling his beer on the table again.

"Are you sure she's missing?" Charlie asked.

Gavin spun his head towards him, slapping his hand on the table. "What are you implying, Charlie? Do ya think I've done something bad to her?" His voice boomed across the table.

Charlie stammered. "No. I wasn't implying anything." He sat back, putting some distance between himself and Gavin.

"Yeah, whatever!" Gavin drowned the rest of his beer. "Right, who's shout next?" He called out, wanting another drink. Finally, after a finishing another two beers, Andrew and one of the other boys, Trent, helped Gavin stagger outside. Despite his loud protests that he was fine to drive, they ignored him, pushing him into Andrew's car, with Trent following behind in Gavin's Ute. They both helped him into the house, manoeuvring him carefully down the passageway and into the bedroom.

With assistance, Andrew and Trent toppled Gavin onto the bed, rolling him onto his side, and before Andrew could remove his boots, Gavin passed out. After placing his boots on the floor, Trent covered him with a blanket. Leaving him to sleep, both men hurried through the house to the front door.

"What do you think happened to Rachel?" Trent asked, glancing around the lounge.

"I don't know." Andrew muttered as he pushed Trent out the front door.

"You don't think Gav did something to her, do you? We all know he can get a bit hands-on when he's angry."

"I don't know Trent. I'd like to think he hasn't hurt her."

"Should we call the cops? Put in a missing person's report?" Trent asked hesitantly.

"No. Not if you want to suffer the consequences. I'm sure Gavin knows what he's doing!"

Closing the door and heading back to the car, Andrew knew better than to stick his nose into Gavin's business. Missing wife or not, he wasn't getting involved.

Chapter 28

—⟫◦⟪—

Thursday, November 2nd

The weeks flew by for Detective Martin, each day flowing into the next. New cases landed on his desk—Missing persons, kidnappings and a murder case involving an elderly gentleman. Martin looked over each of these and allocated them to his team.

The meeting with Mr Tanner was not as successful as Martin had hoped. Upon looking at the photo of the alleged female who took his car and crashed it nearly three thousand kilometres away, he hadn't recognised her at all. After answering a few other standard questions, Martin felt no need to take up any more of Mr Tanner's time and let him go home. Though he stressed that he was to contact the station should he remember anything, even remotely weird, or unusual.

The day Martin received the photo of the mysterious lady in Parker; he'd scanned it and ran it through the department's facial recognition system to look for a match. Perhaps she had a prior record of vehicle theft or burglary, although looking at her picture, Martin thought she looked more scared than anything. While his instincts told him the search would come up empty, he was still disappointed—he was back at square one. What did surprise him was that there was no match in the missing person's database, either. It dawned on Martin that this case would be tougher to crack than he thought.

As the end of another day drew closer, Martin routinely checked his emails, hoping to see some new information. Browsing through them, he came upon one from Tony.

Hey Martin,

I have some interesting information which might have something to do with the mystery girl of ours. Last night I was at Holeman's Pub with some of my mates. Overheard some guy complaining he hadn't seen his wife in, like, seven weeks or something. Thought she'd done some kind of runner on him and hasn't seen or heard from her since. Sounded real pissed off. Not sure if this is related or not but might be worth looking into. I'll be at work tomorrow if you want more info.

Tony.

Martin reread the message, his mind racing at the possibility of a potential lead. He was eager to chat to Tony the next day and find out more about what he'd overheard. Domestic issues often ended up in police stations, so this might be nothing new. Perhaps the guy's wife had done it before, or maybe she ran off with another guy, or he scared her off—either way, Martin decided it warranted further investigation. At this stage in the case, anything was better than nothing.

Checking the remaining emails, Martin noting anything relevant to his other cases, then closed his email.

The pub Tony mentioned was not one he was familiar with, as Martin wasn't a big drinker. When he was younger, he got stuck into it a few times with his buddies, but overall, he never had the need for it. Tony, on the other hand, was someone who often went out for a drink or two with friends after work and on the weekends.

Running a quick search on the computer for "Holeman Pub," Martin found it was about twenty minutes' drive from work and about thirty-five mins from his house. He jotted down the address and shut his computer down. Grabbing his jacket, he placed his wallet and mobile in his pocket and snatched his keys off the desk. Just before he walked out the door, his receptionist paged him.

"Martin, your wife is on line one."

Walking back to his desk, Martin leaned over his desk and pushed the glowing button as he picked up the phone.

"Well, hello, my lovely wife. What can I do for you on this quiet Thursday afternoon?"

"Hey, I was just seeing what time you planned to leave work."

"Actually, I was just about to walk out the door."

"I have great timing, then. I thought maybe we could get Chinese for dinner. What do you think?" she asked.

"Sounds good. Would you like me to pick it up on the way home?"

"Yes, please," she responded with a hint of humour in her voice.

"Well, order me the usual, and I'll see you in about twenty minutes."

"Yes, sir," she giggled. "Thanks, hon. Drive safe. I'll see you soon."

"Okay bye." He hung up the phone with a smile, said goodbye to Belinda, and told her not to work back too late as he left.

The drive to the Chinese restaurant didn't take long, and before he knew it, Martin was safely home, eating his favourite meal with his wife. They chatted about the day's events—his day at the station and hers at the office, their nightly routine. Not that Martin was complaining, it's just nothing changed from one day to the next.

Dinner was followed by their normal routine—washing the dishes, sitting in front of the television for a few hours and eventually going to bed, to read a book or sleep, depending how long their day dragged out. They still had a romantic relationship, enjoying the intimacy, even after twenty years of marriage. Martin and his wife had a happy, content marriage filled with love, respect, and honest communication.

Chapter 29

Friday, November 3ʳᵈ

Finishing off another day at work, I caught the bus to the hospital to meet with Doctor Wilkins again. I felt confident that the appointment would go well, and I quickened my pace to her office. I had a good feeling about today. The week had been perfect, and I was looking forward to sharing what had happened since the last time we spoke.

"Welcome," Doctor Wilkins said, as she opened the door for me. "How have you been? It feels like it's been a long time since we last spoke." She led me to the chairs.

"Yes, it has been a while." I settled myself down and looked outside through the large window again. The view of the well-manicured gardens always relaxed me.

"How's your leg feeling?"

"Good, actually. It's so much easier to walk without the weight of the cast. Also makes wearing clothes more exciting. I can wear pants and shorts," I laughed, and Doctor Wilkins joined in.

"How are things going with the guy you spoke about last week? Have you seen him again?" She picked up her notebook, with a pen in hand, ready to jot down our discussions.

"Great," I smiled at her. "He took me to the lake for a picnic on the weekend."

"Oh, I like it there. It's a peaceful place to visit," she nodded and quickly wrote something onto the paper.

"It was beautiful."

"So, do you think there is potential for a relationship with him?"

I felt the heat rush to my face, and Doctor Wilkins grinned when she noticed my cheeks flushed. "I hope there is." I couldn't help the smile twitching at the corners of my lips.

"I like seeing you so happy, Amber. It's a positive step you've taken."

"I feel happy when I'm with him."

"I like what you have done with your hair as well."

"Thank you. I wanted to do something to feel a little prettier."

"You don't think you're pretty?" Doctor Wilkins questioned as she continued jotting something down in her notebook.

"Well, after the accident, and all the bruising on my face, no, I can't say I've felt pretty. Plus, I guess I wanted to look good for Craig."

"Is it important for you to look good for a man?"

I shrugged my shoulders. "I'm not sure." Suddenly, I felt foolish for putting effort into my looks.

"Please don't take it the wrong way. We all like to feel about our appearance. I go to the hairdresser and get my hair done. I like to feel pretty, too," she smiled, and I sensed she was trying to ease the tension which was now in the room. Changing the subject, she brought up the cat noises. "Have you heard any more cats recently?"

"Yes, two other times in the past week."

"Where did you hear them?"

"Both times I was in the backyard. Once, while watering the flowers for Tracey and the other, I was just stilling out the back, enjoying the sun."

"And did you find a cat?"

"No. Just like the other times, hearing sounds but not finding anything."

"Okay, then. Let's get you to lay down and we'll try to jog your memory."

Following Doctor Wilkins' directions, I moved over to the long cream couch and lay down, propping my head up on the small cushion. As Doctor Wilkins closed the curtains, I placed my hands on my stomach, and with a deep sigh, I closed my eyes.

Talking in a low, soft voice, Doctor Wilkins helped me to relax my muscles and slow my breathing, counting down from ten to zero. Soon I drifted into a calm, hypnotic state of mind.

"I want you to focus on cats now, Amber," she prompted me.

My mind swam with images of all sorts of cats. Large black cats, small tabby's, ginger cats, fluffy grey cats, and short-haired white kittens.

"Can you see a cat?" Doctor Wilkins asked.

I nodded.

"I want you to focus on one you feel drawn to." Her voice sounded so far away. I searched through the images rushing through my mind, but nothing seemed to stick. "Look for a cat who calls to you. A cat that seems familiar."

So many cats flickered by, but none stayed long enough for my mind to sufficiently connect to any memories. "Nothing."

"I want you to look back to a time when you were younger, when you may have had a cat." Her voice was quiet, yet soothing.

My mind was like a large window, only with thick, black curtains drawn across it—a barrier separating me from what lay just behind them. Unable to focus on just one cat, I felt like I was being pulling into a deep black void. My breathing quickened, and I could feel myself getting lost in the moment.

"I want you to focus on your breathing, Amber. Inhale slowly through your nose and exhale slowly through your mouth," Doctor Wilkins' voice echoed towards me in the darkness. "Nothing can harm you. You are safe in my office."

I felt myself pull back as I slowed my breathing down. My hands, which were clenched into tight fists, relaxed and opened.

"I want you to count backwards from ten to zero again for me, Amber, and with each number, I want to you to feel yourself waking up and returning to me. Ten, nine, eight ... feel the weight of your legs return to you. Seven, six, five ... feel your arms and slowly move your fingers. Four, three ... feel your body grow heavier as you wake up. Two, one. When you are ready, open your eyes, Amber."

I opened my eyes slowly, allowing them to adjust to the darkness of the room. "That didn't go very well, did it?" I asked, sitting up slowly.

"No. Not as well as I'd hoped, unfortunately," she spoke. Gradually the room brightened as the curtains rolled back, and sunlight spilled through the office.

I smiled weakly and placed my feet back on the floor. Feeling deflated, I wanted to walk out and forget about the experience.

"Please don't give up on this just yet," Doctor Wilkins said, her tone encouraging. "I know this is hard for you, but I still believe we'll break through this blockage."

"I'm trying," I replied quietly.

Chapter 30

At the end of another workday, and after a helpful conversation with Tony that morning, Martin drove to Holeman Pub, in the hopes he might find the guy with the missing wife. Perhaps his luck was about to change. Or maybe this would be another dead end.

The pub itself was nothing to look at from the outside. An older style building, it was two stories with a wooden balcony running the length of the front wall, and an old, battered sign hung above the door, gently swinging in the cool night breeze. A few motorbikes were parked out the front on the verge, and two rough-looking men in leather jackets, holding their bike helmets in their hands, watched Martin as he approached.

Loud music drifted through the air as he passed the bikers. He nodded at them before turning to face the large, ornate wooden doors. Martin was surprised that Tony would come here, as he appeared nothing like the rough-looking bikers. Pushing the left door, Martin stepped over the stoop and entered a large, brightly lit room, abuzz with men and women sitting at booths, tables, and hovering around the long mahogany bar, in the centre of the room.

Surprisingly, Martin found the inside of the pub friendly and inviting, and he felt a little guilty for assuming it was a rough place to have a drink. On the contrary, Martin was quite wrong. He walked across the room towards the right-hand side of the bar, where he spotted an empty stool. Ordering a light beer from the bartender, Martin sat back and glanced around the room, scanning the faces of the other patrons.

As far as he could see, there was no one present who matched the description Tony gave him. After finishing his beer, he ordered a coke with no ice. Sitting alone at the bar, watching the patrons come and go for another hour, Martin realised perhaps the mystery guy wouldn't show. After hanging around for another half an hour, Martin had finished his second coke, so he got up and went home.

The following night, he returned to the pub, but this time he brought his wife along on the promise that it looked like a lovely place to eat. Although the night before, Martin hadn't eaten, the food going out to the tables smelled amazing, making his mouth water. So, in essence, he killed two birds with one stone. A night out to dinner with his lovely wife, enjoying a delicious meal and another chance to look the place over, and hopefully see someone worth chatting to.

The meals tasted better than Martin anticipated, and the two of them enjoyed a semi-romantic night together. Yet, during the two and a half hours they spent there, there was no sign of the mystery guy.

On the following Tuesday, Martin visited the pub for the third time with the plan to chat to some patrons about the regular customers who frequented the pub. He was careful to keep his conversations light and simple to avoid any suspicion.

The last thing Martin wanted was for anyone to know he was a detective. Snooping was understandably looked down upon, and in a pub atmosphere, it would not go down too well. Not that it mattered much, no one he spoke to talked about anyone who matched his suspect.

Perhaps there was nothing in this, after all.

Feeling desperate, Martin took a photo out of his jacket pocket and asked three men sitting next to him if they knew the female.

"By any chance, do you recognise this lady?"

They all shook their heads. None of them did. Moving to a table behind him, he quietly showed the photo to a couple enjoying a meal.

"Sorry to interrupt your meal but do you recognise this young lady?" They looked at the photo, showing a young girl with bruising and cuts on her face, both then shaking their heads.

"No, sorry," they informed Martin. "We don't know her."

After showing the picture to a few more people, Martin approached some of the bar staff, who each shook their head, lowered their eyes, and quickly went back to work, Martin decided maybe this lead was a dead end, and nothing to do with his case. Disappointed, he headed home.

The bartender, on the other hand, watched Martin closely as he left. He knew almost everyone in the pub, and a new face often stood out. Especially one who looked like he was poking around. When he saw the stranger showing a photograph around, the bartender got the distinct feeling the guy was not who he pretended to be.

Chapter 31

Saturday, November 4th

Bustling around the kitchen, organising lunch, I couldn't wipe the smile off my face. Craig called the night before and asked me out for another dinner and movie date. Of course, I said yes.

This feeling of falling in love was intoxicating, and no matter how hard I tried, I couldn't ignore the intensity of my feelings for him. Even after the last time I saw him, I knew I wanted to spend more time with him, regardless of what might be hiding in my past.

Right now, while my mind remained blank to the life I used to live, I'd decided that until things changed, I would live my new life. I wondered if deep down, I was supposed to forget about my past and maybe, just maybe, this was where I was meant to be.

Since Tracey was working, I had the house to myself, and I knew I needed to keep myself busy, to distract myself from the long wait until Craig arrived at five. It felt like a lifetime away. Finishing with lunch, I washed and dried the dishes, tidied the already clean kitchen, and swept the floor. All just to stop myself from going crazy.

By three o'clock, I'd showered and stood in my room trying on multiple outfits, wanting to find the right one for the date. Summer was settling in, and the nights were becoming warm. Parading in front of the mirror, I must have tried on at least seven different outfits, before finally choosing the first one I put on—a black, knee-length dress adorned with small orange flowers embossed across the material. The full skirt hung in soft pleats and swished gracefully around my thighs as I moved, while the modest V-neck showed off my ample bust. I paired the dress with some low-heeled black summer shoes.

After brushing out my hair, I pulled the sides into a small bun and secured it at the back of my head, allowing the rest of my hair to fall loosely down my back. Applying mascara and lipstick, I stared at my reflexion in the mirror and was pleasantly surprised by the vision staring back at me.

I wouldn't say I was a beautiful, even though Doctor Wilkins had said so, for the most part, I thought I looked rather average. But today, after the fussing and preening, I liked what I saw in the mirror. Trailing my eyes from my feet to my head, I hoped Craig would like what he saw, too.

A few minutes later, I heard the front door close, quickly followed by footsteps coming down the hallway.

"Crap," I said to myself quietly. Craig had arrived sooner than he'd said. "I'll be out in a minute!" I called out, as I quickly grabbed a bottle of perfume and placed a few sprays of the sweet vanilla and musk scent onto my neck and wrist.

Craig didn't reply, yet the footsteps grew louder as they neared my bedroom. I moved swiftly to the doorway and stepped out, hoping I would surprise him before he made it to my room. To my surprise, the hallway was empty.

Craig was not there.

In fact, there was no one in the hallway. Immediately, my heart raced.

"Hello!" I called out. "Is anyone here?"

Silence followed. I glanced to the end of the hall—the front door was closed. Turning slowly, I looked behind me and towards the kitchen. There was no movement or noise.

"Hello? I heard your footsteps!" I called out, hoping I sounded braver than I felt. Again, the only sound was my rapid breathing.

Unable to shake the feeling that I wasn't alone, I ducked back into my room, grabbed my handbag, and rushed down the hall to the front door. Moving swiftly, and refusing to look back, I slipped through the door and closed it tightly behind me. Knowing Craig would arrive shortly; I waited at the bottom of the stairs. No more than a few minutes passed when Craig drove into the driveway.

"Wow, you look beautiful," he exclaimed as he got out of his car.

"Thank you." I almost ran up to him, eager to get some distance from the house and myself.

"What's the rush?" he asked, looking a bit puzzled as I approached.

"No rush, just happy to see you." I put my hands on his arms, leant in, and kissed him gently on the cheek. His skin was soft and recently shaved, and I could smell his musky cologne. Breathing him in, I felt myself calm down, and I instantly felt safe standing next to him.

"Well, if that's how you're going to greet me every time I come over, I won't be complaining," he laughed and wrapped his arms around my waist, pulling me into a tight hug. "Hmm, you smell beautiful, too." His nose touched the side of my neck, and I felt a warm rush of pleasure pulse through me.

Pulling back, I looked into his blue eyes. I couldn't help the smile which spread across my face. "I think I could handle greeting you like this every time, as well."

He tilted his head towards my face but paused just a few inches from mine. Staring intensely into my eyes, I felt his breath quicken. Slowly, not breaking eye contact, he moved his face closer before finally pressing his lips to mine.

The moment our lips connected, I closed my eyes and sighed. Every inch of my body wanted to pull him in and kiss him harder, but I held back, remembering what he'd said earlier.

The kiss only lasted a few seconds, and when he pulled back, I could see a change in his eyes. They'd softened, and he seemed to stare deep into mine. For our first kiss, it was better than I'd fantasised, and I hoped he would kiss me again soon.

"Dang," he laughed. "Well, that was nice."

"Yes, it was." My face blushed as I laughed with him.

"Okay, let's get to dinner, because suddenly, I'm starving." His eyes twinkled with mischief as he walked me to the other side of the car and opened the door.

"Milady." He smirked as I sat down.

"Sir," I teased back as he closed the door. While Craig made his way back to the driver's side, I glanced back towards the house, half-expecting to see someone standing on the porch, or at least, peering out the lounge window. Thankfully, no one was there.

"Ready?" Craig's voice caught my attention, and I turned to look at him.

"Sure. So, where are we going for dinner?"

"A nice little Italian place. I hope you like Italian," he said, as though it just occurred to him that I didn't know.

"Well, there's only one way to find out."

I risked another glance towards the house as we reversed down the driveway. Although I couldn't see anyone, the odd feeling someone watched me lingered.

I discovered, much to my satisfaction, I rather liked Italian food. Dinner with Craig was wonderful. The chicken alfredo I picked was delicious, and the bacon carbonara Craig ate was just as yummy.

Halfway through our meal, a flower vender walked through the restaurant, selling his roses and carnations. Approaching our table, he stopped.

"A pretty flower for the lady?" he asked, bringing his basket forward.

I smiled nervously at Craig, not sure what to expect in the moment. Without a second thought, Craig pulled out his wallet and offered the vender some cash.

"I'll have a yellow rose, please," he smiled at the vender, accepting the rose before he turned to me. "For you." He passed the rose across the table, tenderly brushing his fingers along mine.

"You really didn't need to do that," I replied, blushing.

"Yes, I did," he replied casually. "I am going to make it my mission, to find out what your favourite flower is." He smiled at me. "Starting with a yellow rose."

"You are crazy," I said, looking at him in awe. The sweet scent filled the air, and I lifted the rose, inhaling deeply, all the while never taking my eyes off his.

The way Craig spoke and looked at me, even though neither of us knew much about me, held me in awe. This man, so willing to stand by my side, desperately wanted to help me remember who I was. I felt so touched and lucky.

After our meal, we walked the few blocks to the cinema, my yellow rose clasped tightly in my left hand. Craig held my right hand the whole way, tenderly caressed my skin with his thumb. Light waves of sensation danced through my hand, and I never wanted to let go.

Arriving at the cinema, Craig let me pick the movie this time, and of course, I picked the sappiest, most romantic movie they had showing. Craig sat through it without complaining, holding my hand, or placing his hand on my leg, ever so gently stroking my thigh. He certainly knew how to distract me from the movie.

On the way back to the car, we stopped at the same café he took me to two weeks earlier and bought us ice-creams, happily sharing his choc-mint scoop with my strawberry passion scoop.

"Is this the standard I should expect on all our dates?" I teased, as he let go of my hand to unlock his car.

"What makes you think we're going to have another date?" he taunted back.

I looked at him, my eyes wide with mock disappointment. "Do you mean all this ..." I motioned to my outfit and hair, "was for nothing?" I tried desperately not to giggle.

"You could have made a better effort," he laughed at me, and before I could retaliate, he wrapped his arms around me and pulled me into a tight hug.

"You're very cheeky, you know," I said into his chest.

"I could say the same about you," he whispered in my ear. "Plus, there are a lot more flowers I need to buy, in order to find your favourite!"

His breath on my neck sent shivers down my spine, and I sighed. Craig pulled back a little and aligned his face with mine. Looking deeply into my eyes, he shook his head slightly, smiled gently and leaned in, again pressing his lips to mine.

Melting into the kiss, I closed my eyes and pressed my body against his. In doing so, Craig wrapped his arms tighter around me and cradled the back of my head with his hand. My legs weakened with the sensations of our lips moving.

Slowly, he parted my lips with his and allowed his tongue to slip into my mouth. This only caused me to pull him closer, wrapping my arms around his neck. Gently wrapping his muscular arms around my waist, he lifted me off the ground.

After what felt like an eternity, he gently lowered me and released me from the kiss. "Wow," he smiled at me. "You're killing me."

"Sorry," I blushed again, trying to retain the lingering feeling of his lips on mine.

"I know I said I wanted to wait until you knew more about yourself, but I don't think I can stay away from you." He cupped my face in his hands.

"I know the feeling."

He pulled me back in and kissed me again.

Craig made me feel secure, and young. Ending the kiss, he gently pushed me back.

"I think I need to take you home. I don't want something to happen here, which might cause us to get in trouble with the law."

"Don't you like to live on the edge?" I teased, tickling his side.

"I do like to take the odd risk here and there, but getting arrested for lewd behaviour in public, I'd like to keep that record clean, thanks," he smirked.

I laughed at this and knew exactly what he was referring to. Best to play it safe.

He opened the door for me before hurrying around to the other side. The trip back to Tracey's house was filled with small talk and plans to catch up again during the week.

I invited him for dinner on Wednesday night, knowing Tracey would be at work on the late shift. The house would be all ours, and maybe we wouldn't have to play it so safe.

Thoughts of what had happened at the house earlier were well and truly out of my mind. Even after Craig dropped me off, I was preoccupied with only him. Curling myself up in bed, I beamed into the dark. I loved the fact I was constantly grinning like a little girl who'd received the best present in the world. I drifted off to sleep, peaceful, rested, content.

Chapter 32

Wednesday, November 8th

Another miserable week passed and there was still no sign of Gavin's wife. Not wanting to alert her family that he'd 'lost' Rachel, he sent his long-time mate, Brett, over to scout their house and see if she was hiding out there. After a few nights of surveillance, Brett reported back to Gavin. His wife was not there.

Feeling frustrated, Gavin then sent Brett to watch what few friends his wife had, knowing it would be a waste of time, as most of her friends were married to his mates, but he needed to be sure. Brett, expectantly, came back with the same answers. His wife was not hiding out with anyone who Gavin knew.

There was no indication anything bad had happened to her. No ransom notes, no calls from strangers demanding money for her release. Nothing. When he'd come home from work eight weeks ago, the house, although unlocked, was not in disarray. Nothing was out of place or missing. It was as though she'd vanished into the thin air.

For the second time that week, Gavin headed to Holeman Pub to drink away his frustrations. Normally, he'd have one or two social drinks with his workmates, followed by another two or three at home, but over the last few weeks, he'd spent far more time at the pub than at home.

Tonight was no different, and as per what had become the norm, he had no intention of going home sober. When Gavin arrived at the pub, he marched straight to the bar and ordered a beer from the young blonde girl behind the counter. Joining his mates at their table, he tried to follow the conversation, but his mind kept drifting off to his quiet and empty house.

He couldn't understand why Rachel would leave him. He hadn't *done* anything wrong. Only provided her with a pleasant house to live in and money to buy the things she needed. Not to mention a satisfying lover and avid protector to keep her safe. He loved her, and she loved him.

It made no sense to him that she would leave without a trace. What could make her walk away, abandoning him to fend for himself, when she should be home with him?

Heading up to the counter to refill his glass, the bartender waved to Gavin and motioned for him to move over to the end of the bar. Glancing back at the table where his friends sat, noting they were busy talking to each other, Gavin ambled slowly to the far end of the bar and leant against it.

"How've you been, Gavin?" the bartender asked, leaning over the counter to keep the conversation away from eaves dropping customers.

"Been better, I guess, Max," Gavin answered, looking at the balding, overweight man.

"Haven't seen your wife in here for a while. Is everything okay?"

Gavin froze for a second, shocked the bartender would ask such a personal question.

"Why are you asking, Max?" Gavin's back tensed and he shifted his position at the counter, slightly turning his body towards the man. His attention was now solely on someone who might know the whereabouts of Rachel.

"You know you're one of my regular patrons, and I know how much that little lady of yours means to you. I don't want to seem like I'm putting my big, fat, nose into business that isn't mine, but ... well ... see," he paused, his eyes darting nervously over the room.

"Spit it out, Max. If you have something to say ... say it!" Gavin stood tall, glaring at Max, feeling his temper rising. If Max knew where she was, he was a dead man!

"Okay, okay," Max motioned for him to keep his voice down. "I noticed over the last few weeks your wife hasn't been in here, and then ... well, the other night, there was this guy nosing around ... I think he was a cop. Anyway, he came in a few times, innocent like, but then started chatting to the customers, asking questions about a missing friend of his." In a matter of seconds, Gavin sobered up and fixed his attention on Max like a hawk circling its prey.

"What guy? What questions?" he asked, straining to keep his voice to a low whisper.

"Not a guy I've seen before. In fact, he was in here looking like he was trying to blend in ... you know, didn't want to look like a cop, but you know me, I can pick them out of a crowd any day." Max said with a hint of pride. "Anyway, he kinda scoped the place out first before he started talking to the patrons and showing a picture around. He came up to me, asked me if I knew her. I told him no. Never seen her before. I got the impression that's what everyone had told him."

"And what does this have to do with Rachel?"

"The girl in the picture. She looked like her."

"Like Rachel? My Rachel?"

"Yeah. Bit bruised and beaten up, though." Max noticed Gavin's face redden as it grew hot in frustration. As though realising what he'd said, Max took a stepped back from the bar. "I didn't mean it like that."

"Like what?" Gavin asked, leaning across the bar to close the gap, putting Max under pressure.

"Like you'd done it or anything," Max stammered, as small beads of perspiration formed along his receding hairline. Max knew Gavin had a reputation as a tough guy and wasn't shy when it came to throwing a fist or two in his pub. That often resulted in a brawl. He knew he was *not* a guy to cross.

"So how *did* you mean it, then?" Gavin asked, glaring at the bartender.

"Like she'd been hurt, that's all," Max said, backing away from Gavin until he hit the shelves behind him. "She looked like she was in hospital."

Gavin closed his eyes and forced himself to take a deep breath, calming himself down. He held still for a moment, his silence making Max breath faster.

"You sure it was Rachael?" Gavin asked Max.

"Yeah, I'm pretty sure it was her." Max cautiously flicked his eyes along the bar, making sure no-one was watching.

Gavin's hands gripped the edge of the bar so tightly that he heard his knuckles crack.

"Why would Rachael be in hospital, Max? Who would want to hurt her?" he asked, releasing the tension in his fingers.

"I don't know." Max tentatively stepped forward, easing his back off the shelves.

"This cop, did he say if he was going to come back here?"

"No. Didn't say much. I think he's hit a dead end." He took a step closer to Gavin, noticing his mood was calming down.

"Did he give you, his name? Say what cop shop he's from?" he asked, trying to lower his voice again.

"Nope, like I said, he was trying to blend in. Acted like he was just a friend of the girl, looking for her."

"Right. Thanks for the heads up. If he shows his face here again and I'm not here, you call me straight away ... got it?" Gavin let go of the bar and stepped back.

"Sure, Gavin, no worries," Max said, shuffling from one foot to the other as he made a show of looking anywhere but at Gavin.

Gavin turned away from Max and stormed off, leaving his mates behind as he returned to his car, shaking his head in frustration. He wanted nothing more than to find out who hurt his wife and break the stranger's spine. But first, he needed to know more about the cop who'd come in and asked questions about an injured lady that apparently looked like Rachel.

As there were a few police departments in the city, and the surrounding suburbs, and the cop hadn't passed on any contact details, a smirk crossed Gavin's face as he unlocked his car. Getting behind the wheel, Gavin pulled his mobile out of his jacket pocket, scrolled down to a number saved in his contacts, and pressed the call button. Staring out into the carpark, he waited for his call to be answered. On the fifth ring, the call connected, and Gavin heard a male's voice on the other end.

"Brian, it's me. Meet me at my place in fifteen minutes ... Yeah, it's important ... I have a job for you ... Yes ... Good. See you soon."

Ending the call and sliding the phone back into his pocket, Gavin started the car and headed home, grinning like a Cheshire cat, Gavin was happy for the first time in weeks.

Chapter 33

Thursday, November 9[h]

Sitting outside Doctor Wilkins' office, I wondered if things were ever going to change. Two months had passed since the accident which brought me to Parker. Although my life was moving along a pleasant path, it was never far from my mind that perhaps one day, my past would catch up with me.

I was also concerned after all these weeks; the Sheriff still had no lead on my identity. I'd visited him a few weeks earlier, and he'd informed me the owner of the car wasn't pressing charges. It still didn't sit well with me, knowing I could have stolen the car. What type of person was I if I was capable of car theft? Doctor Wilkins called out to me from her office, pulling me from my thoughts.

"Amber."

I stood and made my way to her room. Another sunny day meant the room was brightly lit and warm. I walked over to the empty chair opposite the doctor.

"Today, I don't want to do any exercises. This session I would just like to talk to you about anything you feel you want to discuss." She sat patiently, with her hands in her lap, waiting for me to talk.

"Um ... okay." I looked at her with a slight frown on my face. "I'm not sure what you want me to say."

"How have you been sleeping lately?"

"Fine."

"Are you sure?" she asked, raising her eyebrows.

I frowned back at her. "Why do you ask?"

Doctor Wilkins sighed and looked at me with sympathetic eyes. "Tracey came to see me yesterday." She paused, gauging my reaction. When I said nothing, she continued. "She's worried about you. Tracey told me you sometimes wake up at night, crying out. And there have been times she noticed when you've seemed jumpy."

"Oh." I looked outside, trying to hide my embarrassment.

"Would you like to talk to me about what's going on?"

I sat silent for a moment, trying to work out what to say. With everything I'd gone through, hearing noises wasn't something I wanted people to know about. Admittedly, there were plenty of nights where I'd woken up terrified, but with no idea why.

"Amber?" she pushed a little. "Please don't be angry with Tracey. She's worried about you."

"I'm not," I replied curtly. "Well, maybe a little annoyed, but I know she would have said something, because she cares about me." I turned my gaze to Doctor Wilkins.

"Yes, she does."

I squared my shoulders, letting out an audible sign. "You know I've been hearing cat meows, right?" I whispered.

"Yes."

"Well, there have been times when I've heard other noises in the house, and a few times, I've woken in the middle of the night, scared, and shaking. I don't know what's happening to me, but there have been moments when ... I just don't feel safe."

"What types of noises?" She opened her diary, and with pen ready, waited for me to talk.

"Footsteps," I replied, my fingers fidgeting nervously in my lap. "And heavy breathing."

"Okay. And how are those noises making you feel?"

"Terrified." I looked down at my hands as my eyes welled.

"How many times has this happened?"

"About three."

"And you say you were alone in the house at those times?"

"Yes."

"Okay," she replied, a flash of concern brushed over her face as she wrote in her notebook. "Why didn't you mention the noises in our other sessions?" she asked cooly, a hint of annoyance in her tone.

"I wasn't sure if it was all in my head, or if it was something real. The cat thing is all in my head, isn't it? I mean, I hear a cat, but I never find it. The hypnosis didn't work. Maybe there really is something broken deep down in my brain that the doctors can't see." Tears fell down my cheeks and Doctor Wilkins leaned over, passing me a box of tissues.

"Anything you are going through could help in the healing process, and I think it's a good idea if you tell me," she said, her voice filled with concern.

"I'm sorry," I sniffled into a tissue. "I just feel like such a fool when these things happen, like I'm going crazy."

"You're not crazy, Amber. Still recovering, but not crazy. But anything new, especially something to do with the brain and the mind, I would like to know about. Okay?" Her tone finally softening.

I nodded. "So, what do we do with this information?"

"I can book another MRI and see if anything has changed from the last scans."

"I guess."

"Or we could try the hypnosis again, perhaps focus on the footsteps, or the breathing, see if it triggers any responses."

I looked up at her and shrugged my shoulders, knowing deep down, nothing would happen during the next sitting. I'd lost faith in hypnosis, but didn't want to tell Doctor Wilkins, as she seemed so positive about trying it again.

"Is there anything else you've heard or seen that was out of the ordinary?" she prompted.

"Seeing things?" I questioned.

"Yes. I thought perhaps, if you were hearing things, then you might have seen things too."

"No. I haven't seen things, and I really hope I don't, either. I already feel like I'm going nuts. I don't think I'd be able to handle seeing things!" I stammered. My heart raced at the thought, and my palms became sweaty.

"That's okay. This could be very normal behaviour, as your brain is still healing." Doctor Wilkins said, reassuring me. She placed her notebook down on the table, sensing my change of emotions. "These very much could be remnants or fragments of your memories locked away and are now trying to break through."

"Really?"

"Yes. Maybe this is the start of your healing process and the beginning of your memories returning. I think we might stop for the day then. Maybe we can poke a bit more in our next session. Okay?"

"So, you think maybe I owned a cat?"

"Maybe," she smiled.

"And the footsteps? Maybe I was with someone?"

"Sure. That could be the case."

"Then why haven't they put out a missing report for me?"

"I don't know. Maybe for now, we just let this ... these fragments reveal themselves to you in time. We shouldn't rush things too much."

"So, I shouldn't be worried?" I questioned, still feeling like I wanted the sounds to go away.

"I don't think so. Not yet. Maybe, when you hear them, focus on the sounds, and try to relate them to a memory. Maybe try visualising someone there."

The thought of this horrified me, but I wasn't going to tell her. When I heard those footsteps, and never found anyone in the house, I felt fear and terror, and if they were memory related, maybe I didn't want to remember them, at least not now.

"I'll try."

"Good. We'll book another session for next week and see what has happened from here." Doctor Wilkins stood. "And Amber, I think you should talk to Tracey about the things you are hearing. It might help her to understand what you are going through."

"Sure, okay," I replied. After we booked another appointment in her diary, I left the doctor's office, feeling overwhelmed at how much I'd revealed. Letting her know I'd heard more than just a cat set my nerves on edge.

I made my way to the bus stop and sat on the same bench where I'd met Craig. Closing my eyes, I felt so alone.

I wish you were here, Craig. I need you.

Thinking back over my session with Doctor Wilkins, I thought about her reaction to the footsteps I'd heard. I was glad I hadn't told her that two nights ago, when I was lying in bed alone, I swear I felt a warm breath on the back of my neck.

Chapter 34

Friday, November 10th

Gavin's day finished at four pm. He received a phone call earlier that morning from Brian, who wanted to see him as soon as possible. By the sound of excitement in Brian's voice, Gavin was eager to hear what information he'd found.

After meeting with Brian on Wednesday night, Gavin informed him of the situation with his missing wife, and how there had been a detective or cop poking around the pub. Brian was more than eager to help investigate and, knowing a few people who worked at the police station, confidently told Gavin he'd have something for him within a few days.

As soon as he got home, Gavin jumped into the shower, washing away the day's dirt and grime. He then quickly dried himself and dressed in a clean pair of black jeans and a dark blue shirt. Combing his wet, black hair back, he looked at his reflection in the mirror. Running his hand over his clean-shaven chin, Gavin smiled at his reflection.

"Not long now, Rachael," he spoke aloud. "Not long."

Just after five, there was a sharp knock at the door, and Gavin eagerly opened it.

"Brian," he said as he stepped aside so his friend could enter. "Come in," he gestured to the lounge room, and after closing the door, followed Brian to the large room.

Brian sat in one of the comfortable, clean, pale green chairs, while Gavin sat opposite him on the matching double sofa. Eager to find out what Brian knew; Gavin wasted no time in questioning him.

"So, what do you have for me? Did you find out who the guy was?"

"Yes, I did. His name is Detective Martin Collins, and he works for the police department over in Hinterfield."

"Detective?" He raised his eyebrows. "What does he know about my wife?" Gavin sat forward, looking at Brian closely.

"Well, from what I found, the girl in the photo he showed to patrons at the pub, was in fact your wife, or at least, looks very similar to her."

Gavin's back stiffened and leaned back in the chair. His eyes darkened as he felt a surge of anger well inside his chest. "Go on."

As Brian continued, he spoke faster. "I was told the woman was in a hospital in Parker, Camberton and ..."

"Camberton!" Gavin exclaimed; his voice raised.

"Yeh, I know, quite far from here, I'm afraid," Brian said, pausing for Gavin to process the information. When Gavin said nothing, he continued. "She was apparently involved in a car accident that put her in a coma of sorts, and she regained consciousness in the hospital ..."

"She was in a car accident?" Gavin's interrupted, his voice strained, and he sighed heavily. Unable to sit still, he started pacing the room.

"Yeah, she was hit by a drunk driver. He's been fined."

"A drunk driver hit my wife!" he bellowed, stopping in his tracks.

"Apparently," Brian replied, rubbing his chin.

"Well, that would explain why she looked beaten up and bruised in the photograph." He paused. "What else?" he asked, his dark green eyes flickering back to Brian.

"Apparently, she has amnesia," Brian said matter of factually.

Gavin stared at him in shock. "Amnesia!" he laughed. "Fuck off, Brian, she doesn't have amnesia!" He started pacing again.

"That's the information I was given," Brian said confidently.

"And where is she now?" Gavin asked, stopping to lean against the fireplace.

"Living in Parker with some nurse."

"Living with a nurse?" Gavin looked confused. "She doesn't know any nurses." He paused, looking into the distance.

"I don't know what else to tell you," Brian said, leaning back.

"Even if she had amnesia, which I'm sure she doesn't, why would she be living with a nurse?"

"Maybe that's why she's staying with a nurse, because of the amnesia."

Gavin looked sternly at Brian. "Are you sure this woman is my wife? Camberton is a long way away. How would she even get there?"

"I'm fairly sure it's Rachael. Everything about her description is a match." Brian scratched his chin again.

"Does this nurse have a name?"

"All I know is her first name. Tracey."

Gavin looked off towards the kitchen, deep in thought. Absently, he ran his hand over his face for a few minutes. Suddenly he stopped and looked back to Brian, as he took a deep breath and squared his shoulders.

"Thank you. You've been an immense help, mate." Gavin strode over to Brian and extended his hand for him to shake.

"I don't think I need your assistance anymore, but make sure you keep this information just between the two of us."

"No worries, mate." Brian stood and shook Gavin's hand.

Gavin was confident that Brian would keep this information to himself. He had used Brian a few times before to outsource information and never had a reason not to trust him.

Escorting Brian to the front door, Gavin waved goodbye, then returning to the lounge room, he continued pacing back and forth, eventually sitting back on the couch.

"Amnesia my arse!" Gavin said aloud. "What the hell is this bitch up to?" Gavin ran his fingers through his damp hair as he spoke to the empty room. The longer he sat on the couch, the faster his rage boiled.

Anger coursed through him, and Gavin jumped to his feet, picked up Rachel's favourite vase and flung it at the fireplace. Clenching his fists at his side, he screamed.

"Fuck!"

Standing in the middle of the room, his face buried deep in his hands, he willed himself to calm down. With a sigh of contempt, Gavin marched to the kitchen, grabbed the dustpan and broom, and returned to the lounge to sweep up the shattered vase.

Throwing the porcelain shards in the bin, Gavin knew the next step was to retrieve his wife. Despite the distance to Parker, Gavin was going to do whatever was necessary to bring Rachel home.

Chapter 35

Saturday, November 11th

Craig listened to the ring tone as he waited patiently for someone to answer the phone. After the sixth or seventh ring, the call connected.

"Hello, Tracey speaking." Craig heard.

"Hey Tracey, it's Craig," he said politely.

"Hello Craig, how are you?" Tracey replied, her voice rang out in delight.

"Good thanks, is Amber there please?"

"Yes, I'll just get her for you."

Craig relaxed on the lounge as he heard Tracey's footsteps on her wooden floorboards, echo through the phone.

"Hang on Craig, I'm looking for her," Tracey said after a few minutes.

"Have you lost her?" he laughed, running his hand through his hair.

"No, I thought she was in her room, but she's not there, nor in the lounge," Tracey replied, and Craig heard a slight hint of concern in her voice.

"Oh, did she pop out?" Craig questioned.

"Not that I'm aware of. I've been in the kitchen all morning and she hasn't come past me."

"Um, do I need to come over with a search party?" Craig joked, trying to hide his own concern.

"Oh, I found her. She's outside on the front veranda. Hang on a minute." Craig heard Tracey's voice brighten and her footsteps quicken as the sound of the front door opened.

"Amber, phone for you."

Craig listened to Tracey call out, and pushing the phone closer to his ear, frowned when he didn't hear Amber reply.

"Amber?" he heard Tracey say, her voice thick with worry and now sounding far away. "Craig's on the phone for you."

Craig's heart thumped loudly; his eyes widened as he absently scanned his loungeroom while listening to the odd interaction on the other end of the line.

"Are you okay?" Tracey questioned.

"Yes. Sorry. Off in my own world for a moment there," he heard Amber reply, her voice quiet.

"Hello, Craig." Ambers sweet voice came through the phone after a few seconds.

"Hey, how are you?" he asked, hoping nothing was wrong.

"I'm okay, and you?" Amber replied quietly.

"I'm good. I was ringing to see if you were busy today?" Craig asked hopefully but still felt like something was wrong.

"I'm free," Amber's voice perked up. "What did you have in mind?"

"Well, I thought, since it's such a nice day, you might like to go to the beach," he said tentatively.

"The beach? Oh, that would be awesome!" Amber replied excitedly as Craig heard her readjust her position in a chair.

"Fantastic. I could be at your place in half an hour if you can be ready by then." He stood and began to walk to his room.

"I could be ... oh, no wait," she paused, halting Craigs steps.

"Um ... do you have other plans?" Craig asked, his brow creasing.

"No." She paused again, the moment seeming to last forever. "I don't own a pair of bathers," she giggled softly, her voice like music through the receiver.

"That's okay," Craig said. "I'd be more than happy to take you shopping for a pair." He picked up his feet and continued to his room.

"I bet you would," Amber laughed again.

"No, seriously. There are a few beachy-type shops down by the ocean. You should find a lovely pair of bikinis there."

"That's very presumptuous of you, thinking I want a pair of bikinis and not a one piece." Her voice sang out in mirth.

"Well, I won't complain either way. In fact, you could wear nothing if you wanted," he laughed, teasing her.

"Are you taking me to a beach where people wear nothing?" Amber asked, her voice suddenly changing and Craig thought he heard a hint of worry in it.

"Good grief, no!" Craig replied, hoping to calm her. "I don't even know where the closest nudist beach is."

"Well, that's a relief," she sighed.

Craig smiled as her tone picked up again.

"Hey," Craig said quickly, "there is nothing wrong with your body. In fact, I rather like it," he added as he pulled his boardshorts from the drawer.

Craig knew Amber's face would have reddened at his comment. Thinking back to Wednesday night, he recalled the events. Dinner was a nice, casual meal with Amber, but what happened afterwards, in her room, sent his head spinning just thinking about it. He was sure the same images were now rushing through hers.

"Behave," she giggled, and Craig's smile widened as her laughter confirmed his suspicions.

"I'm trying," he laughed back. "So, I'll see you in thirty minutes?"

"I'll be waiting."

Hanging up, Craig smiled to himself as images flashed in his mind of Amber, taking his shirt off, removing her shirt. Thoughts of how he had kissed her neck and stomach and, well, other places, brought on an overwhelming sense of desire. Shaking the thoughts from his head, Craig changed his clothes and got ready for the beach.

"Everything alright?" Tracey piped up from the kitchen, as Amber headed her way.

"Yes. Craig wants to take me to the beach," she responded as she walked in.

"Oh, that sounds wonderful. It's a good day for it," Tracey added, returning her attention to her baking.

"It is, although he will have to take me to the shops once we get down there. I don't own any bathers," Amber smiled as she put the phone back into the cradle.

"Well, it would help to own a pair," Tracey smiled, glancing at Amber.

As Amber made her way back to her room, Tracey discretely followed, as her concern for her strange state earlier still lingered on her mind. Tracey stood hesitantly in the doorway as Amber brushed her hair.

"I don't want to intrude, my dear, but were you okay earlier? You seemed a bit ... vacant."

Amber's arm stopped mid brush, and she flicked a glance at Tracey through the mirror.

"I'm alright," she replied, but Tracey could sense something wasn't right.

"If you ever need to talk to me about anything, please don't hesitate."

Amber placed the brush down on the small table and turned to face Tracey. "Doctor Wilkins told me you'd spoken to her and were worried about me."

"Oh," Tracey's face dropped, and she turned her gaze away. "I'm sorry if I intruded. I never meant any harm." She looked back at Amber, her eyes pleading for forgiveness.

"It's okay. I was shocked and annoyed at first, to be honest, but I can understand why you did it." Amber moved over to the bed and sat down. She motioned for Tracey to do the same.

"I haven't been sleeping overly well. I keep having weird dreams, where I wake up scared, feeling like I'm not alone, but I can never remember what I dreamt of," Amber explained, as she nervously wrung her hands.

"Yes, I'd worked out something wasn't right at night but didn't know how to say anything to you." Tracey smiled as her, trying to ease the tension.

"That's okay. I've been avoiding talking to Doctor Wilkins about it too, but now she knows she hopes we can use this to our advantage."

"I hope so. I don't like to see you worrying." Tracey placed her hand on Amber's arm, hoping the skin-to-skin contact, would relax her.

Amber sighed. "Me neither. Well, I'd better get ready. Craig will be here soon."

With another reassuring squeeze, Tracey stood and went back to the kitchen, leaving Amber to continue getting ready.

The drive to the coast took just over an hour, and Craig sat in awe, watching Amber take in the landscape as it changed from the small town they lived in, to a vast, open area, where the trees changed from bushy, large oaks to tall, skinny pines and vast open green fields, spread out as far as the eye could see.

Lush fields of cattle and sheep passed by as they both took it all in, reminding Craig how peaceful the drive was. The cloudless, deep blue sky and flat black asphalt beckoned the car forward towards their destination. Before long, the ocean appeared on the horizon, as they crested a small hill and Craig could see Amber fidgeting.

"Relax, we're almost there," Craig chuckled, watching Amber wriggle in her seat.

"It's so blue!" she exclaimed as she stared out the windscreen.

"It looks great today," he nodded in agreement.

Before long, Craig pulled into a carpark and stopped in an empty bay. Amber immediately jumped out and ran to the edge of the pavement, where the white sand from the small dune in front of the carpark, had blown its way over.

Laughing, Craig came up behind her and wrapped his arms around her waist, pulling her back to his chest.

"You look happy. Like a little girl seeing something for the first time."

"I don't know if I've seen the beach before!" she said, leaning her head back onto Craig's shoulder.

"Well, before we actually head onto the beach, let's go get you a little red bikini, to celebrate the day."

"Red!" she exclaimed and twisted herself around to face him.

"Why not? You looked mighty fine in your red lingerie the other night!"

"Ah, quiet!" Amber giggled and slapped him slightly on the arm. "Someone might hear you."

"And if they do?" He grinned at her.

"I don't need strangers knowing what colour underwear I wear!"

Craig's smile widened as Amber's cheeks blushed. "Fair enough. We'll keep it just between you and me," he said, tilting her chin slightly, then kissing her gently on the lips before pulling away and grabbing her bag from the car. "Let's go shopping!"

Grabbing Amber's hand, Craig led them through the carpark to a row of shops on the other side of the road. The main street ran parallel to the beach, and was filled with clothing stores, café's, restaurants, and gift shops.

There were people sitting outside along the walkway, eating ice-creams and hamburgers, laughing in groups and pairs, enjoying the warm summer weather. The shops were full of customers browsing through clothes, shoes, and summer hats. Amber walked eagerly down the esplanade, pulling Craig along, as she took in everything going on around them.

"Oh, let's go in here!" she said as she suddenly tugged Craig through a large open door and into a brightly lit ladies' fashion shop. In the shop window, three mannequins were dressed in pairs of bright bathers, and one pair had apparently caught Amber's eye.

"Good morning," a young shop assistant greeted them.

"Morning," Amber replied as she left Craigs side and glanced around the shop.

"Is there anything I can help you with?" the young girl asked.

"Yes, actually," replied Amber. "I'm looking for those blue bathers in the window." She pointed past Craig and back towards the window.

"Ah, yes. Just here." The assistant guided Craig and Amber to a rack of bathers on the far wall of the shop. "There you go."

"Thank you." Craig watched as Amber selected a pair in her size and turned to him. "Do you like these?"

"Anything on you will look awesome," he teased and winked playfully. She grinned back at him.

"I think I might go try them on."

"Sure, I'll keep looking for a nice red set!" he joked and turned away from Amber before she could reach out and slap him.

A few minutes later, still hovering by the changeroom Craig waited patiently before Amber finally stepped out of the cubicle, wearing a sapphire blue, two-piece bikini—the colour almost matched her eyes, and when Craig saw her, his own blue eyes widened, and a large smile spread across his face.

"Damn! You look stunning," he said, wanting to reach forward and touch her.

Amber blushed and turned to look at herself in the mirror. The bathers weren't a skimpy pair, but they certainly showed off her slim figure.

"I like them. I think they will do," she remarked, turning herself around to see the bikini from behind.

"Yes, they will." Craig turned away, to stop himself from staring too much. Never in his dreams did he think he'd find someone who he cared about so much. The way he felt when he was around Amber was exhilarating. He felt at ease with her. Like he had known her an exceptionally long time. There was never a moment he felt uncomfortable, or like he wanted to leave. Just being with her made him happy.

Amber returned to the cubicle and changed back into her summer dress, and joining Craig a few minutes later, purchased the bathers. With her shopping done, Amber grabbed Craig's hand and eagerly pulled him out of the store.

"I think it's time to hit the beach," she said, giving Craig a quick kiss on the lips, her eyes twinkling at him.

"Let's go," Craig replied, giving her hand a tender squeeze.

They walked hand in hand back down the main street and returned to the car. Craig retrieved their towels, a beach blanket, and a large cooler bag before they made their way to a small set of toilets, allowing Amber to change into her new swim wear.

Stepping onto the beach, Craig was surprised at how flat and wide it was, and how far the tide was out. The soft, silky white sand slipped between their toes as they walked along the shore until Craig spied a shaded area where some trees hung over the beach.

"I think this is a good spot to sit." Craig placed the towels and cooler bag down and spread open the beach blanket for them to sit on, as Amber stood and looked out over the ocean. The horizon line was dark blue, in contrast to the lighter, bright blue tones of the sky. There was not a cloud in sight. A few sailboats dotted the horizon, and closer to the shore, a young man paddled past on his canoe.

The beach was a mirage of scattered colours with people sunbathing, kids playing games on the sand and splashing around in the water. The day seemed perfect. Tapping Amber on the shoulder, Craig moved the cooler bag to the blanket and sat down.

"Would you like a drink?" he asked as he opened the bag and pulled out two bottles of juice.

"Ooh, thank you." Amber sat on the blanket, stretching out her legs in front of her. "This place is beautiful. Thank you for bringing me here." She looked at Craig, who leaned in, kissed her tenderly, and placed a hand on her thigh.

"I very much approve of the bathers," he said, a cheeky smile crossing his face.

"Again, thank you." She took the drink, opened the lid, and took a sip of the cold, refreshing liquid. "I could get used to coming here all the time."

"It would be nice to live close to the beach." Craig stretched himself out on the blanket, propped his head up with his hands, and admired the view over the ocean.

Amber lay down next to Craig and looked at him tenderly. "So ... are we like ... a couple now?" She asked with a hint of amusement in her voice.

Craig turned and looked at her. "Do you want us to be a couple?" Amber enthusiastically nodded her head. Craig smiled and rolled onto his side to face her. "What about your past?"

"Right now, there is nothing I can do about it. All I want to do is focus on what I have in front of me." She brought her hand up and placed it on Craig's cheek.

"I like the sound of that." He turned his face slightly into her hand and kissed her palm.

Craig watched as Amber closed her eyes and sighed. Before she could open them, he pulled her over, cradled her head, and kissed her deeply. As he felt Amber melt into his embrace, he knew he'd never felt so happy. Pushing every other thought out of his mind, he focused only on how much he never wanted this moment to end.

Breaking the kiss, Craig smiled at Amber with a twinkle in his eye. "I need to cool off." he said, as the kiss began to stir feelings of desire in him. Jumping up, he stretched out his hand. "Come on. I didn't bring you here just to look at the ocean. Time to go swimming!"

Returning the smile, Amber reached up and took his hand. With a little skip, they ran off towards the cool water.

Chapter 36

Monday, November 13th

With all the information Brian gave him, Gavin used the weekend to do some investigating. His priority was to find out where in Parker this woman, who could quite possibly be his wife, was living.

Not wanting to alert the police, he knew his best bet would be to go to Parker and look for himself. Having worked out how long the drive would take, Gavin realised he needed to obtain a car that couldn't be traced back to him. Lucky for Gavin he worked with a few good mates, who in any type of situation, were more than willing to help him out.

And there was one he knew that would be extremely helpful indeed.

Arriving at work, Gavin scanned the building site, looking for a guy he'd known since high school. When he couldn't find him, he approached one of the other builders.

"Paul, have you seen Joe?"

"Ah, no, not yet."

"He's running late!" a voice called out from behind Paul. Gavin looked over Paul's shoulder to see Scott bending down over some bags of cement.

"Do you know when he'll be here?" he asked as he walked over to him.

"Said he had to run a few errands this morning and would be here about eleven."

"Thanks." Gavin walked back to his car and retrieved his work belt. As it was only eight thirty in the morning, Gavin had plenty of time to get more construction work done on the house before Joe turned up. Either way, work would hopefully distract him from thinking about what he'd do if he found Rachel living in Parker.

Gavin knew deep down his marriage wasn't perfect, but then, whose marriage was. Sure, there were times he didn't treat his wife the way a good husband should, but it *was* important to him to have a good wife, a wife who listened and knew her place. Unfortunately, sometimes Rachel needed a small reminder of where her place was in their relationship.

Gavin also knew he was the type of guy who always got what he wanted in life, because he worked hard for it, and his marriage wouldn't fall apart on Rachel's terms. She needed to be home with him, where she belonged. There was no way he would allow a female to dictate his life. Not again.

Growing up, Gavin saw his father as a weak man, and it was his mother who ran the house and was strict with Gavin and his brother. Scolding them if they stepped out of line, severely punishing them for any wrongdoing or behaviour she deemed inappropriate. His mother had a strong hand and a powerful voice, which she was never afraid to use, belittling Gavin, his brother, and his father, and making them feel worthless and unloved.

Gavin was more like his grandfather. Proud, strong, and a force to be reckoned with. He certainly never allowed his grandmother to tell him what to do! When Gavin moved in with Rachel, he vowed never to be weak like his old man.

After Gavin took over his father's building company, his grandfather praised him and put him up high on the list of family members he tolerated. His own son, Gavin's father, was certainly not one of those people. Even when he created the building company, his own father had truly little hope he would run it successfully.

With Rachel missing, Gavin felt like he would lose his stature and reputation in the town. Not that many people even knew she was missing, as Gavin had only told a few of his mates. He still didn't want other people to find out she may have walked out on him.

Shortly after eleven, Gavin saw Joe drive into the building site, and he put down his tools and strode over to him.

"Joe, do you have a minute, mate?"

"Yeah, sorry I'm late, issues with the kids," Joe said as he climbed out of his car.

"Yeah, no worries. I just need to ask you a favour."

"Sure, what do you need?" Joe lent up against his car, looking at Gavin with peaked interest.

"I need to go away for about a week or two, and I was wondering if I could borrow your van?"

"Ah? This van?" He motioned to the vehicle he was leaning against.

"Yep." Gavin put his hand on the roof and patted it.

Joe looked at him with a puzzled expression before a realisation seemed to dawn on him.

"Have you found her?" He looked Gavin squarely in the eyes.

Gavin nodded. "Yeah, I think so."

Joe was one of the few people who knew Gavin's wife had been missing for the past two months. And as one of Gavin's long-time friends, he would do anything for him.

"Sure mate, whatever you need."

"Thanks. I won't need it until next week. There are still a few things I need to organise, but I'll let you know when. You can use my ute while I'm gone."

"Sure."

"Thanks," Gavin smiled and patted Joe on the shoulder before he went back to work. If all went to plan, Gavin would find his beloved Rachel and bring her home soon.

Chapter 37

———⇒❂⇐———

Monday, November 13ᵗʰ

Back at work Monday morning, I walked around the back of the post office, unable to wipe the grin from my face.

"Tell me everything!" Rebecca pipped up as she came in to retrieve a customer's package.

"What makes you think I have something to share with you?" I teased her.

"Because your ridiculously large smile is giving it away," she stated, matching it with her own.

"Come find me at morning tea." I replied and shooed her away before I sat at my desk to sort through the three bags of mail Josh had dropped off that morning.

The moment I stopped smiling, another thought about Saturday afternoon would return, once again bringing the corners of my lips up again, and I shook my head with frustration.

Concentrate, Amber!

The rest of Saturday, at the beach, was wonderful. We swam in the cool water, ate the simple picnic Craig brought, and lay in the glorious sun, soaking in the warmth and turning my pale skin, a light shade of red. Craig made sure I didn't burn too much and took great pains to reapply the sun cream on me a few times.

We left the beach around three, heading back to the esplanade for a stroll around, and wandered through the many small shops. I ended up buying another pair of bathers, a beach towel, a pretty sun hat and another pair of summer sandals with the full intention of returning to the beach in the next few weeks.

True to his word, Craig bought me another flower. Walking past a flower boutique, he stopped and purchased a single orange carnation. Bringing to flower to my nose and inhaling, I smile at him.

"It's nice."

"Better than the rose?" he asked, his brows raising in curiosity.

"Hmmm, I think I prefer the rose."

"Duley noted." He grinned and took my hand as we returned to the car.

Driving home, I felt like I didn't want the day to end and invited Caig to stay for dinner. It was the least I could do to thank him for the outing.

We watched TV with Tracey afterwards, cuddling on the couch, and he finally left about eleven thirty that night. It was a perfect day—I couldn't have asked for a better way to spend my Saturday.

Climbing into bed, I was so relaxed and fell into a dreamless sleep until around three in the morning, when I woke up suddenly, feeling a heavy weight behind me. Too scared to move, I lay silently on my side, hoping for the sensation that someone was behind me, would go away.

Laying still, trying to work out what to do next, I again felt a warm breath tickle the back of my neck. Panic took over, and I spun around, only to find the other side of the bed completely empty. As my heart thundered against my chest, I knew I had no choice but to bring this up in our next session.

Doctor Wilkins said in our last session that seeing and hearing things could be signs of my memories returning, but feeling an actual breath on my neck, this was something else entirely.

Still feeling shaky, I got out of bed and made my way to the lounge room. Picking up a small blanket, I curled up on the sofa and stared out into the dark room, unable to sleep. I was still there when Tracey found me the next morning.

Sunday, I stayed home and pottered in the garden with Tracey. I knew she could see I wasn't the happiest, and she went out of her way to get me to talk about what Craig and I had done the day before, trying to distract me from my thoughts. She was clever, and to her joy, it worked. By lunch time, all thoughts about the events during the night were all but gone.

Right at ten thirty, Rebecca rushed to my desk and pulled me up, and we made our way to the small tearoom at the back of the Post Office.

"We have fifteen minutes. Don't waste a single one!" She said, as she made herself a cup of coffee, grabbed two biscuits from the large cookie jar and sat next to me, eagerly waiting for me to talk.

"He took me to the beach on Saturday," I said, as I opened the small bottle of juice I'd grabbed from the fridge as we walked in.

"Murtal Beach?" She asked, passing the biscuits to me.
"Yes."

"Oh, I love that beach. It's a bit far to drive my little boy there, but when I was younger, my family used to go there all the time in summer."

"It was nice. I could live out there," I said, thinking back to the beach, the sand, and the water.

"That would be nice. Maybe one day, you could."

"Who knows?"

"Did anything else exciting happen?" She winked at me as she dunked her biscuit into her coffee.

"I don't think Amber is going to tell you anything about her sex life!" Charlie commented as he walked into the tearoom.

"That's not what I was asking!" she blurted out and quickly turned a light shade of red.

"It's okay," I smiled and winked at her. Her face lit up as she smiled back at me.

"I'm super happy for you," she said, leaning forward and placing her hand on my arm. "It's hard to find good men here in Parker."

Charlie stood at the coffee machine, shaking his head. "Have you got nothing better to talk about?" He asked, looking at the two of us.

"No, not really!" Rebecca said to him casually.

He looked at me and shook his head. "Women!" he exclaimed with a wink and a smile as he walked past me, taking his coffee back out to the counter where a few more customers had come in.

"I don't mean to pry, but it's been a while since I've had someone even close to my age to talk to here. Everyone is so much older than me."

"I totally understand." I patted her arm.

"Amber, I really am happy for you. I hope I find someone, too, who makes me smile as much as you do." She ate the last of her biscuit and sipped her coffee.

"I don't smile that much ..." I said after taking a sip of my juice. She just laughed at me.

"Oh, yes, you do."

"Really?" I put the bottle down onto the table.

"All the time. Well, much more than the first week or two you started here."

"Well, a lot has changed since then." I finished my biscuit and drank the last of my juice.

"Yes, it has."

We chatted for a few more minutes about how her little boy was going and she told me about the new words he had learnt.

"Teatime's over," I said as I glanced up at the clock above the doorway.

"Dang." Rebecca got up quickly, went to the sink and washed her cup. "Do you think," she paused for a moment, looking back at me. "Maybe one weekend, we could, maybe hangout. At the park or something. You could meet my son?"

"I would like that very much," I said, smiling at her.

"Cool," she smiled and skipped past me to go back to work. I got up and made my way over to the sink to wash out my bottle.

"That girl has some growing up to do!" Mrs. Murphy said as she walked past me.

"We were all young once," I commented and then stopped in my tracks. "Well, I don't remember what I was like, but ..."

Mrs Murphy looked at me with alarm, as though realising what she had said may have touched a nerve. "Oh, I'm sorry dear, I didn't mean to offend you."

"No, it's all good. Maybe I was just like her at that age."

"It must still be hard for you," she said as she came closer. "We've hardly spoken since you started working there. How are you coping with your memory loss?"

I could see she was trying to be nice, but I could also see it was making her uncomfortable, asking such personal questions.

"There are good and bad days. I'm still hoping someone will come looking for me." I laughed nervously.

It was true, though. Even after all this time, I couldn't figure out why the Sheriff still hadn't matched me to any missing persons alerts.

I made a mental note to pop back to the police station after work and see if the sheriff had found anything else out which might be of use to me.

The rest of my shift passed by quickly and I even helped behind the counter, with Charlie teaching me how to use the register and weigh the parcels customers dropped off. It felt good learning new skills and having Charlie trust in me gave me a new sense of pride. Finally, I felt like I was part of the team.

Arriving at the police station, I was greeted by Justin, a young officer, who'd only joined the police force two years ago. At twenty-six, he was engaged to a pretty, brunette girl who he'd met four years earlier while on holiday at a ski resort. I knew this, as he happily told me all about her the last time I'd paid a visit to the Sheriff.

"Nice to see you again," Justin said, standing as he saw me walk in.

"Thanks, you too," I replied and approached the counter.

"Do you have an appointment to see the Sheriff?" he asked, as he looked down at the computer screen.

"No. I don't, but I was hoping he was in," I replied tentatively.

"He is in. I'll see if he has time to see you." Justin picked up the phone and dialled the extension number. "Sheriff, Amber Cooper is here to see you ... Yes, she is ... No, she didn't say ... Yes, sir, I will." He hung up the phone and looked at me with a small smile. "He'll be out shortly. In the meantime, please have a seat."

I returned his smile and moved to the chairs that lined the far wall and sat in one close to the window.

Justin sat down and went back to looking at his computer screen as I tried to ignore the feeling that the Sheriff was trying to brush me off. The clock above the counter showed one fifteen pm.

I sat in the chair looking outside the window, watching the traffic passing by. The reception room was empty and quiet.

The only sounds came from the melodic tapping of Justin typing on his computer, and the odd phone call somewhere behind the counter. Glancing back at the clock, it felt like the past ten minutes had passed by so slowly. I contemplated how long I would wait for the sheriff.

Another seven minutes passed, and just as I was about to get up to talk to Justin, a door on the other end of the room opened, and Sheriff Hadlock walked through.

"Amber," he called out and motioned for me to join him.

"Sheriff Hadlock," I responded, and hurried towards him.

"Please, come in." He waved me through the doorway and directed me to a small room just down the corridor. Indicating for me to sit in one of the chairs at a small round table, he pulled out a second chair for himself.

"I know why you're here, and I'm sorry to tell you. Nothing has changed since the last time we spoke." He looked at me earnestly.

"There's been no missing reports matching my description at all?" I queried.

"No. Nothing here. I have just been in contact with the detective in Barrister, hence the delay in speaking to you, and he had nothing come up on his end either."

"So, what does this mean for me?" My shoulders dropped, and I felt disheartened.

"We can just keep looking, I suppose," he said, looking a little bored. "The detective said we might widen the search. You may not have even come from anywhere in Missionly."

"But the car?"

"Yes. The car came from there, but you could have lived elsewhere. Petersberg is just over the boarder of Missionly. It's a big city. Brampton and Richards Field are only a few hours away as well. You could have lived there," he advised, clasping his hands on the table.

"So, the mystery of me remains!" I joked, but I could hear the bitterness in my voice.

"So, it seems. I take it you still don't remember anything?" His expression was stern and emotionless.

I shook my head slightly. "No. Nothings come back."

He sighed loudly—we both knew I was wasting his time. "Was there anything else I could help you with?" He asked, unclasping his hands.

"No. Thank you for seeing me," I said and stood up. "I really do appreciate what you trying to help me."

As he stood, his face softened a bit, and he exhaled deeply. "Sorry, I haven't been of more use."

I extended my hand for him to shake. "Thank you again, Sheriff." He took my hand in his. I could feel the warmth of his calloused skin as he wrapped his large fingers around my small hand.

"I'll make sure I contact you if anything changes. Are you still staying with Tracey?" He asked, letting my hand go.

"Yes, I am."

He nodded and walked to the door, opened it, and waited for me to pass through. Leading me back out to the second door, he held this one open for me as well.

"Until next time," he said as I walked past him. He closed the door before I could respond. Instead, I said goodbye to Justin.

Heading back to the bus stop, I felt like my life was one big unsolved mystery. How could someone disappear for eight weeks without anyone missing them?

Chapter 38

Having swapped cars at work yesterday, Gavin set off for Parker at nine-thirty in the morning. He'd spent the past two days looking over maps, working out the best route to drive the two thousand, seven hundred kilometres to reach his destination—and hopefully his beloved wife. Although he was in a hurry to get there and, Gavin didn't drive faster than necessary. Last thing he wanted was for the police to pull him over and delay his task.

He had no real plans for when he arrived in Parker, other than to seek out the nurse who was apparently assisting in his wife's disappearance. Since he'd taken over his father's business, Gavin hadn't once taken holidays, so he knew he would take as long as needed to find her. He'd left the management of the business to one of his good mates, so he could focus on locating his wife and bringing her home where she belonged. That was, if the woman in the photo truly was Rachel.

Turning up the radio, Gavin relaxed into the driver's seat and smiled to himself. He felt like he was at the start of a game of cat and mouse. And when the cat finally caught his mouse, he'd make sure she was sorry for leaving him.

He drove for a few hours, only stopping to relieve himself and stretch his legs. By six o'clock, he pulled into the lot of a small motel complex, a few hours away from the border. The bright neon signs out the front showed there was a vacancy. Parking the car at the front of the building, he got out, walked to reception, and rang a small silver bell sitting on the countertop.

"Good evening, sir," said an overweight, older man, as he arrived from a room behind the counter. "What can I do for you?"

"Just looking for a room for the night, please," Gavin responded politely.

"Just for yourself?" The man turned to the computer and started typing on the keyboard.

"Yes. Just me."

"And just one night?"

"Yes." Gavin looked at the large man, wishing he would hurry up.

"We have a room at the back of the motel. Sixty dollars a night," the man said, his expression apprehensive.

"That will do." Gavin pulled out his wallet and handed the man seventy dollars in cash. "Is there somewhere I can get a meal?"

"Yep. There're a few take-away places just down the road. You can't miss them." He motioned with his hand, pointing in the opposite direction Gavin came from.

"Anything a bit healthier?" Gavin asked. He didn't want to eat anymore junk food. With his wife potentially only a few days away, Gavin couldn't wait to enjoy some real, home-cooked meals.

"There's The Ranch, a steak house about two blocks from here."

"Perfect!" Gavin retrieved his change and slipped his wallet back into his jeans pocket.

"Room twenty-seven. Check out is at ten-thirty tomorrow morning." He passed Gavin a silver key, attached to a large plastic card, with the hotel's name and phone number on it. Nodding politely, Gavin turned on his heels and walked outside.

Slipping back behind the wheel, he drove through the large gate to the left of the main building and onto a long driveway. After passing a few units, Gavin finally found the carport for number twenty-seven and pulled in. Grabbing a small bag from the passenger seat, he exited the car and walked to the bright green door.

Looking around the complex, Gavin could see there were many vacant carports.

Unlocking the door, Gavin walked into a small but clean unit. A double bed sat in the middle of the room and there was a small table with two chairs on the far end of the room, under the curtained window. Next to the door was a small, but bright, bathroom and toilet.

Gavin placed his bag on a thin counter under the television. Placed neatly on a tray, sat a kettle, a set of teacups, and an assortment of teas, coffees, and sugar sachets. Hot beverages on the house. Not giving himself anytime to relax, he slipped back out the room, locked the door and returned to the car. A few minutes later, Gavin found the steak house and pulled in.

Entering the busy, cowboy-themed restaurant, a young, buxom blonde girl greeted him. Upon setting eyes on Gavin, she broke into a huge smile and jutted her large breasts forward. The movement didn't go unnoticed by Gavin. His dark green eyes looked down and, as he smirked, thoughts of burying his face between them ran through his mind.

"Hello, welcome to The Ranch. My name is Tiffany, and I'll be your waitress tonight," she said, battering her eyelashes at him. "Do you have a booking?"

Upon hearing her talk, Gavin brought his eyes up to her pretty face. Not prettier than his wife's, but her young features held his attention. Her brown eyes, defined by long black eyelashes, gazed back at him, though he noticed that her dark brown eyebrows didn't match her ash-blonde hair.

"No, no booking," he finally said, fixated on her bold, red lips.

"Dinner for one or are you waiting on a friend?" she smiled sweetly at him.

"Just myself, thanks," he smiled politely. Gavin was aware of the attention he got from other women. Being tall and muscular, he knew young girls and older women flirted with him. With his deep voice and handsome features, Gavin relished in the attention but never acted on the flirtatious advancements.

Not once had he been unfaithful during his marriage. When his wife was home, they had an active sex life. Even if his wife wasn't in the mood, she certainly appeared to enjoy herself.

Despite being married, his wife wasn't the only woman he'd been with. Gavin had lost his virginity when he was sixteen years old to a girl two years older than him. Although they didn't date, he had learnt a few things from her during the three months they'd slept together. A year later, he'd met another girl, who was a year older than him, and they dated for a few months. When he finally started dating Rachel, he did so, feeling very much the experienced man. His wife, on the other hand, lost her virginity to him a few months into their relationship.

"Okay, I have a table just over here." Tiffany perked up her chest again and grabbed a menu as she looked up at him through her long lashes.

Walking past him to direct him to the table, Gavin, against his better morals, lowered his eyes to watch the young girl's pert bottom as she swayed in front of him. More thoughts quickly entered his mind, and he sneered to himself.

Tiffany led Gavin to a small table near the bar. Setting down the menu, she removed the second setting and waited for him to sit.

"Would you like to see the specials?"

Gavin shook his head. "No, thanks."

"No worries. I'll give you a few minutes to look at the menu," she purred and smiled again, lowering her eyes to blink at him slowly, before turning away and sashaying back to the front desk. Again, Gavin watched her backside swish from side to side, putting more explicit images into his head.

It had been too long for Gavin. All these weeks without his wife was taking a mental and sexual toll on him. Not having anyone to relieve him, he was tired of having to pleasure himself. Being on his own had other drawbacks. Random thoughts ran through his head. One he couldn't shake was that maybe his wife hadn't just left him but had perhaps met someone else.

If she is, in fact, living in Parker, what if she isn't alone?

If that was the case, then she'd likely been unfaithful to him and maybe he should return the favour. Watching Tiffany, with her flirting smile, her big perky breasts, and red lips he already envisaged kissing, he considered she just might be what he needed.

After waiting a few minutes, Tiffany returned to the table and Gavin noticed she had re-applied her lip gloss, making her red lips look shiny and almost wet.

"Ready for your order?" she cooed at him, bending slightly forward so that her breasts took centre stage. Again, Gavin's eyes trailed to her low-cut shirt, and he watched her breasts rise and fall with each breath.

"Just the prime steak with chips and salad, thanks," he said, finally looking up and meeting her gaze.

"Anything to drink, cowboy?" She pursed her lips together, rubbing them slightly with the aid of the gloss.

"Just a coke," he replied, his gaze locked on her mouth as he watched her lips move. Gavin smiled slightly, feeling masculine and desired.

"Sure." Tiffany wrote his order down on her little notepad. "Is there anything else I can do for you?" she asked, putting her hand on the table to lean down a bit further.

Gavin looked back at her and held her gaze. She returned the stare and let the tip of her tongue peek through her lips. "What time do you get off?" he asked quietly as he lent in and looked deep into her eyes.

"My shift finishes at nine," she replied just as quietly before she smiled at him tenderly. Gavin placed his hand on hers briefly. "I'm staying at the Bluemont Motel, room twenty-seven."

She nodded in acknowledgement, gave him a sultry look, let her tongue sweep slowly over her lips, and straightened.

"Your food will be ready shortly, sir." She turned and walked away to the kitchen. Gavin was already visualising what he wanted to do to her when she arrived at his hotel. So involved were his images that Gavin was grateful he was sitting at a table. He had an erection so hard it was pushing into the seams of his jeans. Nine o'clock couldn't come fast enough.

Chapter 39

Friday, November 17th

Craig nervously approached the large, white, frosted glass front door. He knew he shouldn't be worried, but this was a big step for him. Amber lent in closely and gave his warm hand a gentle squeeze.

"Are you ready?" she whispered to him.

"I don't think so," he said quietly, as his breath quickened.

She laughed tenderly. "I'm not that scary ... am I?"

He looked at her, studying her features, getting lost in her blue eyes.

"How did I get to be this lucky? How did I find someone who makes me feel so happy?"

"No idea, but I could ask you the same thing." Amber replied.

Smiling, Craig leaned over, kissed Amber's nose, and puffed up his chest. "Okay, let's do this!"

Reaching forward, Craig pressed the small white button next to the door. From inside, they heard the sweet chimes of a doorbell and moments later; the door opened to reveal a slender, and attractive, older, grey-haired lady.

"Craig!" she exclaimed with a warm smile.

"Hey, Mum." Craig opened his arm and stepped forward to embrace his mother.

"Oh, it's good to see you. You don't visit enough." She looked at Amber and winked.

"Mum, this is Amber." He stepped back from his mother's embrace and, letting go of Amber's hand, placed it gently on Amber's lower back.

"Lovely to meet you," Craig's mum said and offered her hand.

"And Amber, this is my Mum, Linda."

"Nice to meet you, too." Amber took Linda's small hand in hers. Her skin was tough and calloused, but warm and gentle.

"Please come in. Dinner won't be too long." She stepped aside, allowing Amber and Craig to enter the house.

The doorway opened into a long passageway. A thick, worn carpet runner, decorated in blue, white, with small green flowers, ran the full length over the chestnut brown wooden floor. All along the cream walls hung bright paintings of landscapes. A small, white, semi-circle table nestled against the wall beside the door with a large, blue, and white vase of fresh flowers at its centre.

Linda directed them both through a doorway on the right of the passageway and into a cosy lounge room. The room was lit by a large hanging crystal chandelier, and the light bounced off the crystals, creating bright sparkles across the cream walls.

Craig pulled Amber along and watched her reaction to the room, as it was like walking onto an old movie set. An enormous fireplace, stood against the far wall and many framed photos of family members adorned the white and grey marbled mantle.

"Make yourself at home. I just need to finish a few things," Linda said and then rushed off down the passageway.

Amber's eyes widen, as she looked around the room, taking in the upright piano in the right corner with more framed photos displayed on top. Craig smiled in bemusement.

"It takes a bit of getting used to," Craig said.

Amber's eyes twinkled as she ran her fingers over the thick, soft pink curtains, and made her way across a fluffy cream rug laying on the wooden floor, towards two huge bookcases, that stood either side of the fireplace.

"So many books!" Amber exclaimed, browsing over the titles.

"Mum loves to read." Craig crept up behind her, wrapped his arms around her waist, gently pulling her towards his chest. Turning her around, Craig edged her towards the sofa.

"Oh, these flowers smell wonderful," Amber said, bending over a vase on the coffee table, and inhaled their sweet aroma.

"Yes, mum loves her flowers." Craig paused. "Is there one in particular you feel drawn to?"

Amber laughed, understanding his implications. "No, they all look and smell wonderful."

"And the house?" he queried nervously.

"I love it," Amber said honestly, running her hand slowly over the plush, velvety material, before she sat down onto the low set, dusky pink lounge suite three-seater sofa, that looked like it had come straight from the fifties.

"Yeah?" Craig asked, his eyebrows raised.

"It's so cosy in here."

"I don't think anything has changed in here for years," he said, glancing around the room.

"Is this the house you grew up in?" Amber looked at him with a mischievous smile.

"Yep. The very one."

"Oh. Will I get to see your room?" She giggled.

Craig looked at her and laughed back. "Not while my mother is here," he whispered, and Amber laughed louder.

"Sorry about that," commented Linda, as she walked into the lounge via the dining room.

"That's okay, Mum."

"Dinner smells wonderful," Amber said as Linda sat down in one of the single sofa chairs.

"Thank you. I do hope you like it. It's not often Craig brings a lovely girl home to meet his mother," she teased, looking at Craig with a slight smile and a twinkle in her eye.

Craig rolled his eyes and leaned into Amber. "And this is why I don't," he said, mocking his mum.

"Hmph, enough about you, Craig. Amber, tell me more about yourself."

Amber froze. "Um ..." She didn't know what to say.

"Oh, no," Linda gasped and brought her hand up to her face. "I didn't mean to put you on the spot. Craig told me you can't remember anything before your accident."

Amber breathed a little. "That's okay."

"Forgive me."

"Honestly, it's fine. I'm still getting used to not knowing who I am, but I am loving getting to know who I'm becoming," Amber said, looking sideways at Craig.

"Well, I like the sound of that," Linda said, letting her hand drop back to her lap.

"So am I," Craig added, placing a hand gentle on Amber's knee. Amber blushed a little. She was on a road of discovery, and Craig had the pleasure of watching her travel through the highs and the lows.

"How have you been, Mum?" he asked, changing the subject.

"Not too bad. The eyes are getting worse. I might need to get new glasses. The perks of getting old," she said to Amber. "Other than that. Not much else has changed. Oh, but your sister has news," she paused, looking at Craig to see if he already knew. When he raised his eyebrows, she continued. "She pregnant again," she said, beaming with joy.

"Oh, that's wonderful!" Amber stated.

"Yes, another grandchild. That will make three."

"Do you get to see your other two often?" Amber asked, happy the conversation had changed.

"Oh, yes. A few times a year. I'm hoping we might have Christmas here this year. It's about time we all got together again."

Before Craig could comment, a bell chimed from another room and Linda promptly got up. "Ahh, dinner is ready."

"Can I help with anything?" Amber asked, standing up as well.

"Sure. The table's set, but you could help bring out the vegetables. Craig can organise the drinks," she nodded at Craig and beckoned Amber to follow her. Moving through into the dining room, Amber's eyes widened with surprise as she took in the full set out of the lavish space.

The same cream paint extended into the dining room and another crystal chandelier hung in the centre of the ceiling, casting more sparkles across the walls.

The large, dark, wooden, rectangular table was set for three people, with round, baby blue cotton placemats, topped with a white dinner plate, a small side plate, silver cutlery and two glasses. Matching baby blue napkins rolled into silver ring holders, lay across the plate.

"This room is exquisite," Amber said in awe.

"Thank you. I do like to entertain well," Linda replied proudly.

In the centre of the table, a round placemat lay under another blue and white vase, with more fresh flowers. Along the side wall stood a wooden sideboard, matching the table and was adorned with lit candles and two smaller vases with dried flower arrangements. Matching pink curtains, as the ones in the lounge, hung at the two small windows at the end of the room.

Craig, upon seeing Amber's expression, rolled his eyes, shook his head, and tried not to laugh. His mother was a little old-fashioned in her decorative tastes, and growing up, he'd always felt like he lived in an opulent house, even though it was just a normal house, in a normal suburb.

The kitchen was no different. There were very few modern appliances in the room. A huge black and green iron stove, which looked like it was from the nineteen fifties, took centre stage. Bright white rectangular tiles formed a splashback across the wall, leading up to the air vent. A centre island with a black marble top took up most of the space in the middle of the room, which was now covered with bowls and plates of food.

A small sink sat under a medium-sized window, and light green cupboards lined the walls on both sides. An older style fridge stood just inside the room to the right, and Craig headed straight for it, grabbing a bottle of wine and a pitcher of orange juice, and took them to the table.

"Make sure you put them on the placemats," Linda called out as he left the kitchen.

"Yes, Mum," he replied, happy to know she couldn't see him roll his eyes again.

Within a few minutes, the table was laid out with bowls of roast potatoes, beans, honey-roasted carrots, cheesy broccoli and cauliflower, and a juicy roast beef with gravy. The food looked and smelt delicious.

"You didn't need to go to all this effort, Mum," Craig said after they sat down.

"Well, I know it's not Sunday, but I thought it would be nice to have a proper home cooked meal," Linda replied, as she reached for the bottle of wine.

"Well, it looks amazing. I can't wait to eat it," Amber commented and waited politely.

"Well then, dig in." Linda reached forward and took food from the bowls. Craig followed soon after and Amber hesitantly dove in. She couldn't remember ever sitting down to such a large spread of food and honestly didn't know where to begin.

Between mouthfuls, Craig, Linda, and Amber chatted away, with Linda, more than happy to indulge Amber's curiosity by talking about Craig's childhood.

"He was great at athletics in school. His favourite thing was the sport carnivals. Craig was a natural. Fast runner, good jumper. Won a few trophies and ribbons."

"Wow, I wouldn't mind seeing those," Amber teased Craig.

"Sure, they should all still be in Craig's bedroom," Linda smiled at Craig, whose face was turning a slight shade of red.

"You still have my stuff?" he questioned.

"Absolutely. It is not every day a mother gets to watch her children excel at school. They are a reminder of the young children who used to live here."

Craig shook his head slightly and smiled at his mum. "Thanks, Mum."

"Plus, I would like to think one day you'll have kids of your own, and you could display them for your children to admire. Perhaps even inspire them to do well at school."

"Maybe one day," he said softly, his eyes darting quickly to Amber's, to find her looking at him with a sly smile.

As dinner finished, and Amber and Linda chatted continuously, neither seemed to notice Craig had cleared the table and started washing the dishes. He smiled to himself in the kitchen as he listened to both ladies' chat about fashion and gardening, Amber's work at the post office, and his mother's friendship with Tracey.

Craig had brought a few women home to meet his mum over the years, but none of the relationships had lasted exceedingly long, and most of the women never connected so well with his mum. Amber, on the other hand, seemed to fit right in.

The conversation finally migrated back to the lounge, and Linda served a dessert of trifle and ice-cream.

"Oh, Craig," his mum said after placing her empty bowl on the coffee table. "You should take Amber to the Summer Carnival."

"The Summer Carnival. What's that?" Amber asked, as she placed her bowl in her lap, and looked at Linda with peaked interest.

"Each year, on the first weekend of December, we have a Summer Carnival, to celebrate ... well ... the beginning of summer. It's a wonderful day out," Linda replied.

"Yeah. Rides, games, show bags, and a fireworks display at the end of the night," Craig added between mouthfuls of dessert.

"Sounds like fun."

"It is. I'll take you if you want to go." Craig looked at Amber and watched her face light up at the thought of going to the carnival.

"I'd love to," she beamed.

Before long, an hour passed, and Craig noticed his mother was tiring. "Thanks for dinner, mum, but I think it's time we get going."

"It was wonderful to meet you," He watched as Amber stood. "And dinner was divine."

"The pleasure was all mine." Linda stepped forward and gave Amber a tight hug. "This one's a keeper," she said to Craig over Amber's shoulder.

"Thanks, Mum. Not embarrassing at all," he laughed. Amber giggled as she stepped back beside Craig.

"Well, my door is always open, next time you two want to visit." Craig smirked. His mum certainly wasn't shy about voicing her opinions.

"Thanks again. Maybe we will take you up on that offer soon." Craig hugged his mum, and they made their way to the front door.

"Thank you again." Amber squeezed Linda's hand and smiled.

Within a few minutes, Craig and Amber were back in the car and heading back to Tracey's house.

"That wasn't so bad, was it?" Amber teased.

"It went better than I expected."

"What were you so nervous about?"

Craig glanced at her quickly. "Mum, as you can see, doesn't have much of a filter and when she doesn't like someone, she'll make a point of not talking to them, or when she does, her responses are usually short and to the point." He glanced back at Amber. "It seems you may have passed and won her approval."

"I hope so. I did rather like her." Amber lay her hand on Craig's knee.

"Well, that's good, because I rather like you too," he replied, resting his hand on hers.

Chapter 40

━━━━━━━◇━━━━━━━

Monday, November 20th

It took two more days before Gavin arrived in Parker. He stopped at two motels along the way and found a few decent places to dine. Unlike the first restaurant, Gavin didn't flirt with any of the waitresses. Although they certainly showed him a lot of interest, he controlled his needs.

Back at the Bluemont, Tiffany arrived not long after nine and Gavin didn't hold back or waste any time in stripping her of her clothes and pushing her onto the bed. Thinking back to the things he'd imagined doing to her while at the restaurant, he was quick to turn them into action, and Tiffany was a willing participant.

A few hours passed before she left the motel, leaving Gavin satisfied, yet still annoyed. He couldn't dispute the fact Tiffany was certainly attractive, and once naked, he had little control over his sexual responses.

Gavin lay in bed, hating the fact he just slept with someone who was not his wife, yet it still turned him on. Tiffany was a lot more adventurous and eager to play than Rachel. Thinking back to what he had just done with the waitress, and visualising doing these things to his wife, got Gavin all worked up again and he ended up having a shower and relieving himself, before climbing back into bed.

Although he could have easily reciprocated the advancements, he received from two young waitresses at the last places he dined, he maintained his composure, opting to go to bed alone. Gavin decided that when he got his lovely wife home, he had a few more things to teach her in the bedroom.

Arriving in Parker in the late morning, Gavin used the maps he obtained during his investigations to locate the hospital his potential wife had stayed at. Cruising into the carpark, he found a spot under the shade of a large tree. As he got out of the car and looked around the area, Gavin was unimpressed. It was a small place compared to his hometown. Not entirely sure what to do next, he walked to the main entrance, passing through the glass doors and approached the receptionist to enquire about how to find the medical ward.

After the young man behind the counter gave him directions, Gavin made his way through the corridors and down towards the Medical Unit. Standing in front of the double doors, Gavin took a moment before he walked through, still not a hundred percent sure of his plan. Hesitating, he turned around and walked straight into a nurse.

"Ouch!" the nurse exclaimed, as Gavin slammed into her.

"Crap. I'm sorry." He grabbed her upper arms to stop her from falling. "I didn't see you." He helped steady the nurse before letting go of her.

"Well, that was surprising!" she laughed.

"Are you okay?" he asked, peering down into the face of an older lady.

"I'll be alright," she said as she smoothed down her light green shirt and tugged down at her hem.

Gavin glanced at the name on her badge. A sudden rush of anger flew through him, but he suppressed the feeling.

"Ah, Tracey, is it?" He pointed to the badge on her shirt.

"Yes, that's right," she smiled back at him.

"Well, Tracey, I'm sorry to have run into you. I didn't see you behind me," he spoke cooly.

"That's okay. These things happen."

"Yes, I guess they do."

"You looked like you were going in. Are you visiting someone?" Tracey questioned him.

"Oh, I was going to but ... I thought I might ... get something to eat first," he blurted out the first thing that came to mind. "Can you tell me where the canteen is, please?"

"Sure." Tracey turned and faced the same direction as Gavin. "Just head back through this corridor and take the first left. Follow that until you see a sign hanging from the ceiling. You'll turn right at the doors."

"Thank you. Again, sorry." Gavin walked off quickly and headed down the corridor. As he approached the turnoff on the left, he glanced back and watched Tracey walk through the double doors and disappear into the unit.

Instead of turning left, Gavin walked back through to the entrance and returned to the van, smiling to himself. He'd arrived at the hospital wanting to locate the nurse but hadn't expected to find her so quickly. Instead of climbing into the front of the van, Gavin opted to sit in the back, deciding the next step was to watch Tracey and wait for her to leave the hospital. Settling himself down with the small supply of snacks and drinks he'd purchased at a petrol station on the way, Gavin prepared to wait patiently for as long as needed. Step one of his plan happened faster than he expected and he could now allow himself time to relax while he waited for step two to unfold.

Shortly after three pm, Gavin's attention heightened when he spotted Tracey slip out through the glass entrance doors. His eyes trailed her walk past the main carpark, and into a separate one to the side of the hospital. As she walked between the parked cars, he briefly lost sight of her, and Gavin moved into the front seat, starting the engine. Slowly backing the van out, he steered towards the car park where Tracey had gone.

Before he arrived, a small green car exited the carpark and turned onto the entrance road. Seeing Tracey behind the wheel, Gavin discreetly followed her. He was careful to keep a relative distance behind her car, as he tailed her to a small shopping centre in town. Parking a few rows away from her, he stayed in the van and watched her disappear into the complex. Remaining in the van, Gavin moved into the back to keep out of sight.

Forty-five minutes later, Gavin's attention shifted when Tracey returned to her car, with a shopping trolley full of bags, and watched as she loaded her shopping into the boot. While Tracey returned the trolley, Gavin eased himself back into the driver's seat and started the van.

For ten minutes, Gavin followed Tracey's green car, weaving through side roads and small suburbs until it finally pulled into a long driveway. Passing the house slowly, Gavin did a U-turn further down the street and parked the van two houses down. Silently, he stared at Tracey's house. After a few minutes of surveying the quiet street, he got out of the van, crossed the road, and casually walked past the house, glancing sideways as he looked down the driveway to see Tracey's car. He couldn't see anyone else at the house and continued to walk past.

Taking in the surroundings, Gavin finally turned around and walked back to the van. Climbing back into the vehicle, he slowly drove off. Part two of his plan was complete. Needing to find a place to stay for the night, Gavin headed back towards town. Things were going along smoothly, and Gavin had a good feeling he'd find the woman in the photo sooner rather than later.

Chapter 41

Tuesday, November 21ˢᵗ

"Did I hear you say Craig was taking you to the Summer Carnival?" Charlie asked as he came into the tearoom.

"Yes, he is."

"Oh, you are going to love it. My wife and I go every year."

"I'm really looking forward to going—who knows if I've been to a carnival before?" I looked at Rebecca and smiled.

"I'm sure you have. I'll be taking my boy too. He loves the horses and farm animals," added Rebecca.

"You seemed to have settled in very well here, Amber," continued Charlie, as he made himself a cup of coffee.

"I feel welcome here in Parker. Now that I am no longer the circus attraction, everyone is so nice," I joked.

Charlie came over and sat next to me at the table. He looked at Rebecca and nodded towards the front counter, yet she failed to take the hint he wanted her to leave.

"Could you attend the counter please, Rebecca? Don't leave Mrs. Murphy out there alone."

"Oh, sure." She finally got the point, and quickly jumped up, placed her mug in the sink, and returned to the counter.

"I know you don't have much time in your coffee break, but I was wondering if you had a moment to chat?" Charlie asked me.

"Is everything okay?"

"Yes, all is good. In fact, I was hoping you might want to increase your hours here." He looked at me hesitantly.

"Really?"

"Well, you've proven you're a quicker learner, and you've done a few hours at the front counter and look like you've taken to it without any issues. I thought maybe you'd like to pick up a few more hours each day."

"Oh, Charlie! That would be wonderful," I said, beaming.

"Well, I can't keep you cooped up in the back all the time. Our customers seem to like you, so I think it would be great to have you at the front counter."

"I enjoy the front. Helps mix up the day a bit," I confessed.

"Excellent. How about as of tomorrow, I'll get you to stay an extra three hours, work the counter from twelve-thirty to four? That will give you a half-hour lunch break at twelve. Sound good?"

"Yes. That could work."

"Great. I'll let you get back to it." He stood up, finished his coffee in one big gulp, washed his mug and walked out of the tearoom.

I sat back in the chair, wondering what had just happened. It all seemed to happen so fast. With the extend hours Charlie had offered, I would earn more, and maybe I could save enough money to buy myself a car—and eventually a place to rent.

Two months had passed since I'd arrived in Parker, and so many wonderful things had happened to me. Everyone I'd met was super friendly and kind. As much as I hated to admit it, I kept expecting something bad to happen and shatter my new life.

As much as I was loving the life I now lived, I could never quite shake the feeling that my life before the accident was different. Regardless of my therapy sessions with Doctor Wilkins, which I'd now stopped, I felt like my good luck would soon run out.

Yet, I was determined to focus on the positives. So, I finished work, said my goodbyes to everyone, and headed out to the bus stop. I was eager to get home and tell Tracey and Craig my good news.

"Tracey!" I called out as soon as I walked into the house.

"In the kitchen," she called out with her sweet voice.

"I have the best news ever." I hurried down the passageway, tossing my bag into my room as I passed.

"Did you remember something?" She stopped kneading the pastry on the countertop.

"No. Although, that would be good news." I pulled out a stool and sat at the counter. "Charlie asked if I wanted to extend my hours at work."

"Really? That's great!" she smiled and returned to kneading the pastry, pushing the dough back and forth under her palms.

"Yes, and he wants me to start the extra hours tomorrow, so I'll be home a bit later, as I'll finish at four."

"That's good. I finish at three, so if you like, I can come into town, do some shopping, and pick you up."

"That would be great, thanks." I paused for a moment. "I thought with the extra money, maybe I could get myself a car. Make it easier to get around."

Tracey stopped kneading and grabbed her rolling pin and the sieve of flour. Sprinkling the counter with the flour, she placed the dough in the centre and rolled it out in a large circle.

"That probably would make things easier for you," she smiled.

"Then I'll start putting money aside and find a small place to rent."

Tracey stopped rolling and looked up. "You want to move out?" She looked up, the smile falling from her face.

"No. No, it's not like that," I replied quickly. I could see I'd upset her, which was the last thing I wanted. "Please, I'm sorry. That came out wrong." I reached my hand out and placed it on hers. "I'm so incredibly grateful for everything you have done for me. When I was in the hospital, I could never have hoped to meet someone like you, and you've helped me out for so long. You looked after me when I was broken and bruised and gave me a place to stay—you have no idea how much I appreciate all of it." Tears welled in my eyes.

"We both know I can't live here forever. Your daughter will visit again, and she'll have nowhere to stay. I need to be independent. I don't want to move out—As much as I love it here ..." I shook my head slowly.

"I understand," she said, wiping away a tear with her free hand. "This day was bound to come, but it's like having my daughter move out all over again, and my dear Richard leaving me. I'll be on my own again. I guess I got used to having someone here every day."

"You don't have to worry. I'll always visit, and it's not like I'm moving out next week. It will be months away, I'm sure." I smiled weakly at her.

"I know. I guess I just wasn't ready to hear it." She went back to rolling.

"Can I help you with the pie?" I asked, trying to change the subject.

"Sure, grab a can of peaches and apples from the pantry, please."

"Drain them as well?"

"Please, into a bowl, I'll need to use the juice."

I loved Tracey's cooking. Old school, delicious meals, and deserts with loads of flavour. Recipes handed down from her grandmother to her mother, and then to her. Roasts, stews, meat pies and casseroles, pasta dishes, salads, fruit pies, cheesecakes and so much more.

"I'm going to have to make sure you teach me how to make all these desserts. I do love your pies."

"Well, no time like the present."

"And all your other recipes."

"You are nothing like my daughter," she laughed.

"How so?" I asked as I drained the fruit into a large glass bowl.

"She never wanted to learn how to cook. Everything she makes is quite simple, or out of a box or jar," she sighed with a shake of her head.

"Well, I'm more than happy to learn." Rinsing out the tins and putting them aside, I moved back to the counter.

"Time to bake the base." Tracey transferred the pastry into the dish and pressed it down, fluting the edges with a fork.

"Why do you do that?"

"To make it look pretty," she laughed as she placed the tin into the oven. "Now, let's cook up the fruit and make the sauce."

I followed Tracey's instructions, step by step, eager to learn more. Not knowing if my own mother had taught me to cook, I cherished these moments with Tracey and was grateful to have found a wonderful mother figure.

Chapter 42

Wednesday, November 22nd

After watching Tracey's house on Monday, Gavin found a small motel on the outskirts of town. Freshening up, Gavin felt relaxed and pleased with himself as he headed to a restaurant close to the town. As he waited for nightfall, he enjoyed a hot meal before returning to watch Tracey's house. Yet, as he sat in the back of the van and the hours passed without any sign of his wife, Gavin's good mood rapidly faded. Feeling dejected, he went back to the motel.

Getting up early the next morning, he returned to Tracey's house, but noting her car was not in the driveway, he drove back to town, familiarizing himself with the layout. Keeping himself occupied, Gavin bought lunch at a small cafe and watched the locals meander through their day. After dinner that night, he drove slowly down Tracey's street, but seeing her empty driveway, he returned to the motel.

Returning the next morning, Gavin noted Tracey's car was in the driveway.

Well, this is a good sign, he thought to himself.

Parking the van opposite the house, he settled in for the wait, hoping an opportunity would arise where he could follow her again. Or, if he were lucky, his lovely wife would come out of the house. That was, if she was living there.

He didn't have to wait long.

While cleaning his nails, Gavin glanced up towards the house just as the front door opened and Rachel stepped out onto the porch. His fingers paused, and his eyes widened in surprise. In all honesty, as much as he'd hoped to see her, he hadn't expected it to happen so soon.

"Well, how about that?" he exclaimed quietly.

Unable to take his eyes off her, he watched as his wife skipped gracefully down the porch steps and onto the driveway. His heart thumped loudly in his chest, and he fidgeted nervously in his seat as he watched her head straight towards him.

Swallowing hard, hoping to control the sense of panic building in his chest, he lowered his head quickly, adjusting his cap and turned to face the other direction.

Oh shit, goddamn it! He thought to himself, hoping she had not seen him.

He waited a minute or two, and when she did not approach the van, he looked back up. Rachel was no longer in sight. Turning his head towards the rear of the van, he saw her walking down the side of the road, away from him.

With his panic and surprise subsiding, anger welled in him as he watched her. It took every ounce of his willpower to stay in the van and not chase after her. Griping the steering wheel hard, he closed his eyes briefly.

"Chill out, dude! Don't chase her yet," he muttered under his breath. "She might cause a scene."

Turning his head forward and staring at her through the rear-view mirror, he noticed her long, mousey-blonde hair was different. She'd pulled it back into a high ponytail and with the morning sun hitting the blonde and red highlights, her hair shone like gold. Gavin realised how much he wanted to run his fingers through it again.

Unable to take his eyes off her, he climbed into the back of the van, and moved to the rear, to watch her through the window. Gavin's eyes narrowed as he took in her light green dress and simple flat black shoes. He couldn't remember the last time he'd seen her wear a dress like that. The hem finished above her knees and swayed with every step.

God, she looks sexy, he thought to himself.

Gavin continued to observe her as she made her way to a bus stop a few houses away and sat down on the bench. Watching his wife, Gavin's anger dulled. He hadn't realised how much he'd missed her. The top of the dress was well fitted and showed off her breasts perfectly. Gazing at her, a slight breeze teased her ponytail and the hem of her dress, and Gavin suddenly felt turned on.

Resisting the urge to touch himself in the van, Gavin averted his eyes and stared down the road in front of him, clenching his fists against the door, until the desire passed. Once he had calmed himself down, his eyes trailed back to her.

Before long, a bus arrived behind the van and paused at the bus stop, obscuring Gavins' sight of his wife. After the bus drove off and passed Gavin, he noted Rachel was no longer on the bench. Scrambling back to the seat, Gavin turned the engine on, and trailed slowly behind, keeping his distance, waiting to see where she got off. Finally, in the middle of town, he saw her disembark, and he pulled into a parking spot a few meters away.

Staying in the van and pulling the cap low over his dark sunglasses, Gavin studied his wife as she crossed the street and walked a few meters down the sidewalk before entering a large building. The sign out the front said, 'Post Office.' Gavin sat in the van for more than thirty minutes, expecting Rachel to walk back out of the building.

Becoming agitated, when she didn't re-appear, Gavin got out, locked the van, and crossed the street. Casually walking past the windows to the Post Office, he peered into the shop but could not see his wife anywhere.

Frustrated, he scoured the street, wondering if he might have missed her leaving. Glancing down the road on the opposite side, Gavin noticed a small café and his stomach growled. Unsure of where his wife was, he decided a full breakfast might help distract him from his anger.

Gavin ordered his meal and sat out the front, placing himself in a position where he could observe the busy street. The never-ending traffic rumbled by, and Gavin peered into every car, searching for his wife. Every female he saw walking the street, he scanned quickly, looking for her green dress.

An hour later, without another sighting of his wife, and feeling dejected, Gavin returned to the van and drove back to the motel. Laying on the bed, in his room, he wasn't overly worried about losing her—he knew where she lived. Closing his eyes, Gavin thought about his wife. In his mind, he recalled her walking to the bus stop, remembering how the sun shone off her golden hair, and how badly he had wanted to run his fingers through it.

Visualising how the breeze had teased the hem of her dress, and how sexy she had looked, in her new green dress, the urge to touch himself returned. Allowing the desire to take over, Gavin removed his jeans and underwear and, in the privacy of his room, had no need to control himself.

Later that afternoon, satisfied and fed, he returned to Tracey's house, parked on the other side of the street, and waited patiently.

Eventually, the sun faded over the horizon and, as night took over, Gavin hadn't seen anyone come or go. Watching the house, a few lights turned on, sending a golden glow from the windows, but nothing out of the ordinary happened. Tracey's car hadn't even moved from its position this morning. At eleven pm, Gavin gave up and returned to the motel.

Early the next morning, he returned once again, parked the van a few houses in the opposite direction, and watched the house. He was grateful it wasn't a busy road, and no-one had questioned the van returning each day.

Just after six-thirty, Tracey exited the house, climbed into her car, and left. Gavin ducked as she passed, wanting to remain invisible for as long as he could. Sitting back up, he focused his attention on the front door. At eight-thirty, the same time as yesterday, the front door opened again and Rachel walked out, skipped again down the stairs and along the driveway, narrowing Gavin's attention.

While her fashion choices back home weren't exactly ugly or unsexy, her clothing choices now were similar to what she used to wear when they were first dating, and when she worked. What she wore now annoyed Gavin—it made him question what she was up to, and what was she doing in Parker.

Does she have a job? Is she dressing like this because she's in a relationship with someone else? These thoughts bounced through his mind.

Unable to take his eyes off her, he scrutinised her black, slim, knee-length skirt and pale blue, fitted shirt. Her hair, this time, was mostly down, with only the sides at her temple pulled back. His heart skipped in his chest, as a deep yearning to touch her took over and he once again, he struggled to restrain himself, and not rush out of the van, and grab her.

Against his will, anger and resentment built up, but the bus's arrival averted his attention back to Rachel, and calmly, refocusing his breathing, he started the engine. Once again, following the bus into town and noting her get off at the same stop, Gavin parked the van in a small carpark, near to the Post Office. Watching her through the rearview mirror, he saw her enter the same building again.

"So, you do you have a job, Rachel! Did you leave me so you could work?" Gavin growled, shaking his head in frustration.

Heading back to the same café, he ordered breakfast and sat outside, watching the morning people amble about. Keeping an eye on the Post Office as he ate, his confidence grew when he didn't see his wife exit. After an hour, with his stomach full, and his frustration forgotten, Gavin strutted boldly towards the building.

He wasn't sure what he'd do once he got inside, but something had taken a hold of him, as though he moved on autopilot. Letting things play out, he opened the door and stepped into the brightly lit building.

A few customers were already lined up, ladened with large parcels, boxes, and envelopes. Others stood at a small desk, filling out addresses on envelopes and small packages. A few customers browsed the wall shelves for gifts and other items. It was a surprisingly busy place.

Walking around the room, pretending he was shopping, Gavin carefully glanced towards to the counter. He observed two females serving customers, but neither of them was his wife. Frowning slightly, he moved himself into a position where he could see through a back door and into a large area behind the counter.

After waiting a few minutes, his wife suddenly walked past the doorway carrying a few small parcels. His heart skipped a beat, and abruptly, the anger returned. Hastily, Gavin spun on his heels and stormed out the front door and exited the building before he created a scene. He didn't want to explain.

Making it back to the van, Gavin almost dropped the keys, trying to start the engine. With so much rage in him, his hand wouldn't stop shaking. Finally, getting the key in the slot, and revving the engine, Gavin took off faster than he should.

Driving away from the post office, he started smashing his hands on the steering wheel.

"You fucking bitch! You God-damn fucking bitch!" he screamed.

Fuelled by his rage, Gavin drove faster, needing to put as much distance between him and Rachel as he could.

How could she leave me? Why would she create a new life? His thoughts screamed at him.

Gavin shook his head and continued driving until his anger and confusion subsided, eventually pulling off the main road half an hour later. Sliding out the van, Gavin paced across the small rest-stop, his boots crunching on the gravel.

"Think dude, think. What the fuck do I do now?" he muttered, as he ran his hand across his jaw.

Things had changed, despite the fact, he'd arrived in Parker with few plans. Knowing he was more than likely going to wing it, he now realised he needed to think smarter.

Returning to his seat, Gavin turned the van around and heading back into town, making a quick stop at the grocery store to buy food and something to drink, before returning to the motel.

Sitting at the small table, inside his room, he needed to plan exactly how he would confront her, what he would say to her, and he needed to do it soon—before the rage in him took over, and he did something to her, he might regret.

Chapter 43

I woke with a frighting jolt, my breathing rapid and deep. Beads of sweat moistening my hairline and in the hollow of my neck. Feeling clammy, I looked around the dimly lit room, my heart pounding, believing once again that I wasn't alone. I couldn't see anyone, but that wasn't to say, I was alone.

Hesitantly, I turned my head slowly, peeking over my shoulder, fully expecting to see someone lying behind me. There was no one there. I closed my eyes for a moment, trying to relax. Holding my breath, and mustering all the courage I had, I gently pulled the covers off and sat up. Trying not to make any noise, I inched my way to the edge of the bed, and looked over the side, to the floor. No dark shadows loomed down there, other than my slippers.

I sat still, listening for any sounds in the darkness, but the house was quiet. There wasn't even a breeze coming through the window. My heart would not stop racing, and my breathing echoed in my ears. I was tempted to get up and sprint for the closed bedroom door, but I felt too fearful to move off the bed.

Instead, I focused on controlling my breathing, slowing it down. Staring at the blank, dark wall on the opposite of my bed, I tried to recall what I'd dreamt about. Small images flashed through my mind, but nothing substantial enough for me to hold on to and piece together. Voices, noises, and snippets of sounds echoed in my memory, but nothing I could retain.

Doctor Wilkins had said seeing things could be a sign of my memory returning. If this over-whelming feeling of fear was a recollection of my past, I didn't think I wanted to recall it.

After about ten minutes of sitting on my bed, I finally accepted I was alone, yet I still couldn't shake the fear away. What was so terrifying about my dream that it left me feeling so scared?

Slowly, I laid back and pulled the covers back over me. I rolled onto my side and rugged myself up, despite the fact the night was not chilly. It was at that moment; I regretted Craig's offer to stay the night. Although Tracey made it clear if Craig wished to stay the night, she was fine with it. As she said,

'*We are all adults here, and if you're happy, I'm happy.*'

Still, it was her place and not mine, and I felt awkward at the thought of letting him stay. When I'd told him at dinner, I'd be looking for my own place in a few months, his response was, '*You could always stay at my place!*' When I told Tracey, she'd giggled and raised her eyebrows in amusement.

Now, all I could think of was how I wished Craig were by my side. Instead, I grabbed the spare pillow and hugged it tight. Although I felt calmer, and my heart no longer felt like it was going to beat right out of my chest, I was now wide awake.

I closed my eyes and willed myself to fall asleep. Counting backwards from a hundred, I tried to relax my body, but it didn't work. By the time I counted down to one, I was still conscious. I tried to sing a song in my head, something slow, but found myself moving in rhythm to the tune.

With a groan, I let go of the pillow, rolled onto my back, staring at the ceiling. Admitting defeat, I reached over to my phone and looked at the time; three-thirty am. I sat back up, threw the cover off, and swung my legs over the bed as I sighed.

My feet found the slippers, and within a matter of seconds, I was walking down the hallway to the kitchen. Reaching for a carton of milk in the fridge, I heard Tracey's bedroom door open. I glanced down the passageway and, by the light of the fridge, watched her walk towards me.

"Can't sleep either?" she asked.

I shook my head.

"Another bad dream?" She reached for two mugs in the cupboard.

"Yeh." I poured milk into each mug and returned the carton to the fridge and closed the door, plunging us back into semi-darkness.

"Do you remember what it was about?" Tracey asked as she placed the mugs in the microwave, heating them up for a minute.

"No, not really. I think they're all the same, though." I moved over to the table and sat down.

"In what sense?"

"I always feel like I'm not alone."

Tracey retrieved the hot mugs from the microwave, brought them over to the table, and sat next to me.

"What do you mean?"

Taking a sip of the warm milk, I finally talked freely to Tracey. Even though she knew I wasn't sleeping well, and she was aware of some of my experiences since the accident, this was the first time I found the courage to tell her everything.

"I sometimes feel like someone is behind me when I'm in bed. Like I'm not alone."

She looked at me over the top of her mug. Even though our eyes had adjusted to the darkness, I couldn't read her expression.

"There have been times I have felt like ... there is a breath on my neck, or I can hear someone breathing." I continued.

"Well, that would wake me up too, I'm sure," she said, trying to reassure me.

"It's not pleasant."

"What else do you see, or feel?"

"Footsteps in the house ... Could your house be haunted?" I gave her a slight smile.

"Well, not that I know of." We sat in silence for a minute or two before I spoke again.

"Sometimes I think I'm losing my mind."

"What does Doctor Wilkins think?" she asked, sipping her milk.

"She said maybe my mind is trying to recall memories." I took another sip of milk.

"Do you think maybe ..." Tracey paused and looked at me intently as though she was trying to think of the right words. "Maybe you were with someone else before, and these are memories of your relationship?"

"That thought has crossed my mind, but I never feel safe after these encounters, or feelings ... or whatever you want to call them."

"Have you spoken to Craig about any of this?"

"No!" I blurted.

"Is this why you won't let him stay the night?"

"No," I shook my head slowly and placed my half-drunk mug on the table. "I haven't let him stay because this is your house, and I ..." I blushed and was grateful she couldn't see it. "I don't want you to ... you know ... hear us." My blush deepened and I turn my head, despite sitting in the dark.

She laughed softly. "That wouldn't bother me love, at least someone in this house would be having some fun."

"Tracey!" I was shocked but a huge smile spread across my face.

She laughed again and drank more of her milk. We sat in the dim moonlight for a few more minutes, neither one of us talking. Gently, she reached out and put her hand on mine.

"Maybe you should share this with him. Perhaps he could help."

"Or maybe he might think I've lost the plot and leave," I replied dryly.

"Oh, I don't think that would happen."

"Really?"

"Yes, really. He's been by your side this whole time. I don't think anything would scare him away."

"Yeah, maybe not. I don't know." I picked up my mug again and took another gulp. My milk was already cooling.

"I think you should be open with him. Let him know what you're going through. You can never have too many people to lean on." She pattered my hand. "He cares very much for you. I think you'll be surprised."

"I'll think about it." Glancing over at the clock on the microwave, I sighed. "I need to get back to bed."

"Me too." She stood up, grabbed my mug, and walked to the sink.

"Thank you, Tracey."

"For what?" she asked over her shoulder.

"For just being here with me. I really do appreciate everything you've done for me."

"Anytime." She walked over, kissed me on the forehead, and gave me a small hug. "Good night, my dear. I hope you get back to sleep."

Following her back down the passageway, I watched her disappear into her room. "Good night, Tracey," I said, as she closed her door.

As I climbed back into bed, I pulled the cover up to my neck and once again cuddled up into the spare pillow and closed my eyes. Images of Craig's face floated in my mind, relaxing me, and before long, I slipped back to sleep.

Chapter 44

Saturday, November 25th

As I showered, lathering up my body, and washing away the stale sweat from my skin, I thought about what Tracey said. Talking to Craig about what I was going through might help, but I was worried about how he'd react, and that he'd want nothing to do with me.

Drying and then wrapping myself up in the towel, I sat on my bed and mustered all the courage I had. Picking up my phone, I sent Craig a message.

'Good morning, stranger.' I typed, before putting the phone on the bed, and tried not to look at it.

'Good morning,' he replied, a few minutes later.

Sighing with apprehension, I read his message, then typed nervously. *'Are you busy today?'*

'Not at all. Did you want to hang out?'

I replied, *'Yes please,'* and waited anxiously for a minute, my heart beating with excitement and trepidation.

'Sure, what time?'

'*About ten*. That *will give me time to get dressed and have something to eat.*'

An eager '*Yes!*' was sent followed by a '*See you soon x.*' I smiled at the kiss.

I was not oblivious to the fact he had feelings for me—I'd known for a few weeks now, and I hadn't hidden my feeling for him. I just knew this could be *the* moment which would either make or break our relationship.

True to his word, Craig knocked on the door at ten on the dot. Tracey greeted him and politely invited him inside.

"It's okay, we're not staying," I called out from my room. "I'll be there in a minute."

"Okay, I'll just wait outside," I heard Craig reply.

A few seconds later, Tracey popped her head around the bedroom door. "Are you okay?"

"Yeah." I finished brushing my hair and picked up my handbag. "I'm not sure how long I'll be."

She stopped me at in the doorway, frowning. "Amber?"

"It's okay, I promise. I'm taking your advice, and I'm going to tell him what's going on."

"Oh. You could stay here—I can make myself scarce."

"Thank you, but no, I need to be somewhere ... outside."

"Okay. Well, I'll be here when you get home if you need me."

"Thank you." I kissed her quickly on the cheek and walked past her, towards the front door. With my hand on the doorknob, I paused, forcing myself to take a deep breath. I held it for a moment and exhaled, bringing a calmness over myself.

Opening the door, I looked straight into Craig's beautiful blue eyes.

"Good morning, beautiful," he said, stepping forward to hug me.

I fell into his embrace and took another large breath, this time inhaling his sweet, familiar aroma. Closing my eyes, I stood there for a moment, not wanting to let him go.

"Someone's happy to see me," he murmured into my hair. I pulled back and looked into his eyes again, before stretching up and kissing him fiercely. Taken aback, he hesitated for a split second, and then pulled me in closer, returning the deep kiss. Finally, breaking free from my lips, he looked lovingly down at me, his green eyes drinking me in.

"Hi."

"Hi." I smiled back and laughed lightly.

"You wanted to see me?"

"Yes. Care to take a walk around the lake with me?"

"Absolutely, but first." He unwrapped his arms from my waist, and as his smile widened, he brought his hand up to my face. In his fingers, he held a beautiful pink flower. "For you."

I laughed. "You really don't need to do this, Craig." I took the flower, breathing in its perfume.

"Yes, I do. I promised I would help you find out your favourite flower, and I intend to keep trying." He stared at me, his blue eyes holding my gaze. "Well?"

"What is it?" I asked, staring at the delicate petals.

"It's an Azalea."

"It's better than the rose!" I laughed.

"Winning!" he joked, kissing me tenderly on the forehead.

I grabbed his hand, shaking my head in amazement, and pulled him towards his car. I took a moment before I climbed in and turned my face towards the cloudless, bright blue sky. Letting my senses take over, I listened to a few birds chirping in the trees and quivered as a light breeze teased my hair, flicking loose strands across my face.

"Amber?" Craig asked cautiously.

"I'm good," I replied, bring my gaze back down.

I felt relaxed. Hoping the feeling would last, I climbed into the car and Craig drove us towards the lake where we'd had our picnic.

"Other than the lake, did you have anything else in mind?" he queried, but I could hear it in his voice. He knew something wasn't quite right.

"No, not yet. Let's just see how the day plays out."

"I'm good with that," he commented uneasily.

For the rest of the trip, we listened to music on the radio and chatted about the usual events of our week. Finally reaching the park, the nerves built within me. As I got out of the car, I closed my eyes and turned my face back up to the sun, inhaling deeply.

"Is everything alright?" Craig stood in front of me. "You seem ... a bit ... different today."

I opened my eyes and smiled at him. "I need to talk to you about something."

"Oh. Sounds scary," he replied, his brows furrowed.

"I hope it's not." I tried to laugh, but the sound stuck in my throat.

"Amber?" He took a step backwards, his eyes darkened as he looked at me. "Are you ending this?"

"No! No, I just need to share something with you. But ... I'm worried about how you're going to react."

His eyes lit up. "Have you gotten your memory back?"

"Can we maybe find somewhere to sit first?" I asked, taking his hands in mine. He nodded, but I could see he was still worried.

We walked into the park and found a bench underneath a large oak tree. Sitting down, the view from the bench was breathtaking. Although it was the same lake, we had our picnic at, it looked even better than I remembered. The deep navy-blue water spread out before us, the surface covered in ripples as ducks and swans swam casually around the lily pads.

The grass looked greener, and the trees seemed taller, and the air, fresher. Dotted around the lake, people sat on blankets with picnics, and children played along the water's edge, laughing, and squealing with delight. A profound sense of calmness came over me.

Craig turned his body to face mine and placed his hand tenderly on my knee. "What do you need to tell me?"

I took his hand in mine and starred lovingly into his blue eyes.

"Do you remember the day we first met?"

"Yes," he nodded.

"Do you remember how I was looking for a cat?"

He smiled. "I do."

"Well, obviously, I never found it, but that was not the first or last time I've heard a cat meowing."

"Okay," he drawled, watching me closely.

"And ... it's not the only thing I hear." I lowered my eyes but never let go of his hand.

"I'm listening." His voice was quiet.

Swallowing thickly, I sighed. "I hear footsteps when I'm alone in the house and sounds like someone is breathing next to me when I'm in bed." I looked up at him slowly, my eyes searching his face, reading his concerned expression.

"I ... sometimes feel ... a warm breath on my neck at night. Like someone is lying right up behind me."

I felt Craig's hand tighten around mine. "How?" He swallowed hard; I could see he was trying to find the right words. "How long have you been experiencing this?"

"Roughly six or seven weeks."

His eyes widened in shock. "Have you told anyone else about this?" he asked tentatively.

"Doctor Wilkins knows some things, and Tracey now knows. I told her this morning, well, incredibly early this morning. We both couldn't sleep."

"And what does the Doctor think?" he asked, carefully stroking his thumb across the back of my hand.

"She thinks maybe it's fragments of my memories trying to push through."

"And does that scare you?"

"Yes. Yes, it does."

"Is there anything I can do to help?"

"I don't know."

"How do you feel when you hear the footsteps and the breathing?" he asked hesitantly.

"Scared. Like I'm not alone, and I don't feel safe."

He turned his knees sidewards and suddenly pulled me up close to him, wrapping his arms around me.

"I'm sorry. So sorry." He stroked my hair. "I wish you'd told me earlier."

"I didn't want to scare you away and make you think I was some crazy girl, hearing things."

"I don't think you're crazy." He pulled back and placed his hand under my chin, lifting it up slightly. "You've been through something traumatic. Honestly, I've been wondering when something would happen. Your memory must come back, eventually."

"And when it does? What happens if I remember I was with another guy? If that's whose footsteps I hear, or whose breath is on the back of my neck at night? What if he's not a nice person?"

"Then we deal with it. Together."

I lowered my head against his shoulder as the tears fell. As though knowing my sorrow and pain, Craig wrapped his arms around me again, holding me until the tears stopped.

Chapter 45

Saturday, November 25ᵗʰ 10:45am

Gavin sat in the van; his eyes turned a shade of black, as watched his wife sit next to a male he didn't know. A man shorter than him, which wasn't hard, being he was over six feet, with longer brown hair, and a muscular build.

It was the same man Gavin had observed, arriving at the house on Thursday and Friday night, but both times he'd left before eleven pm. From Gavin's positions on the roadside, he couldn't see the front door and had no way to know if the visitor was there as a friend, or something more.

But watching them now, hugging on a park bench, confirmed Gavin's suspicions. Rachel was dating someone else. The new clothes, the fancy hair colour and style—It wasn't just to make herself look good, it was for another man's pleasure and that did *not* sit well with Gavin.

When the couple finally stood up, their hands intertwined as they walked towards the lake, Gavin got out of the van. Pulling his cap down low, he slipped on his sunglasses and followed them. He needed to know what was going on and find out who the hell was this man his wife was having an affair with. Walking slowly behind them, Gavin matched their pace, keeping enough distance between them so it wasn't obvious he was trailing them.

When they turned onto the long wooden pier which ran out into the middle of the lake, Gavin followed. A few other people walked the pier as well, some throwing out food for the ducks, other sitting on small benches enjoying the sunshine.

When his wife and the stranger stopped and lent against the railing, their attention focused out over the water; Gavin walked casually past. Stopping a few meters away, he kept his back to them as he stood, listening to them chat. He exhaled, as the sound of his wife's honeyed voice brought back a thousand memories, and he struggled against wanting to turn around and confront them both, right there and then.

Gavin had always loved the sweet tone of her voice. Harmonic and feminine. Hearing it now, he didn't realise how much he'd missed it.

Maintaining his composure, while eavesdropping on their conversation, the most wonderful thing happened, and Gavin's dark green eyes lit up in excitement. The plan which he'd struggled to create for the past few days, on how he was going to confront his wife, suddenly clicked into place.

Honing his hearing in, and holding his breath, Gavin made sure he didn't miss a single thing they said.

"So, if I pick you and Tracey up at one-thirty, we should be at the carnival by two. That will give us plenty of time to walk around and see everything," the male said, his deep voice grating Gavins's teeth.

"I can't wait. Will we play some games and go on some rides?" her voice sang out.

"Absolutely. I plan to beat you at everything. Winning all the big prizes and making you carry them for me," he teased her.

"Not likely. You never know, I might be brilliant at all the games. Maybe you'll have to carry all of Tracey's and my prizes," she giggled back.

Gavins's heart sang at her laugh, and a feeling of ecstasy rushed through him, but to his horror, his groin reacted to that emotion, and he gripped the rail hard, turning his knuckles white.

Control! he yelled to himself in his head. *Not the time or place!*

He breathed hard and forced himself to walk away from his wife.

When he finally reached the end of the pier, he turned and peering over his shoulder, looking back at the couple. Glaring at the way the stranger held his wife in his arms, Gavin felt his groin slacken, but an overbearing rage welled within him instead. He turned back around and looked out over the water. The man seemed far too comfortable and familiar with his wife, and Gavin knew things had to change.

But not here. Not in public, with so many people around, and especially not in broad daylight.

With a newfound clarity, Gavin finally worked out his plan. All he needed to do was find out where and when the carnival was, and make sure he was there. Thanks to the new guy in Rachel's life, he'd provided Gavin the perfect opportunity to take back his wife, and when he did, all hell would rain down.

Chapter 46

Thursday, 30th November - Morning

Early in the morning, after Martin settled into work, his phone buzzed, and his receptionist's voice came through the speaker.

"Martin, you have a phone call on line one."

"Who is it?" he asked, pressing down on the speaker button.

"I'm not sure. A female. She didn't want to give me her name but said it was important."

"Okay. Thank you, Belinda." Martin reached for his hot cup of coffee and took a tentative sip. After placing the cup back down, Martin picked up the receiver and pressed the flashing button for line one. "Good morning, Detective Martin Collins speaking."

"Um, hello," a female's voice answered.

"Hello, how can I help you?" Martin picked up his pen with his left hand and started absently tapping it on the desk.

"Um, I hope I have the right person. Were you at a pub in Barrister a few weeks ago?"

Martin straightened, his hand stopping mid-tap. "Which pub are you referring to, please?"

"Holeman's Pub," she replied, the nervousness evident in her voice.

"I did. May I ask who I am speaking to?" He dropped the pen, swapped the phone to his left hand, and pulled a notepad over.

"I'd rather stay anonymous, if that's okay?" the voice replied.

"That's okay with me." Martin was used to receiving calls from people with information on cases he was investigating who didn't want to be identified.

"Thank you."

"May I ask what this phone call is regarding?" He grabbed the pen again, ready to write down everything she said.

"You were showing around a photo of a female who'd been in an accident."

"Yes, I was! Do you know the female?" Martins back straightened a little more.

"Yes, I do. Or I'm hoping I know who it might be."

Martin's face lit up. Three weeks had passed since he'd last visited the pub, and Martin was a little surprised someone called. He hadn't left behind his business card or any other identifying information, so he was intrigued how this woman had found him.

"Whatever you can tell me about her, I'm listening."

"Okay, well, if it's the girl I'm thinking of, I haven't seen her in about two months, which is unusual. She tends to come here at least once a week to have dinner with her husband."

"Okay. And you think the girl in the photo might be the same one you haven't seen at the pub in a while?"

"Maybe. It was hard to tell with the bruising on her face."

"Thank you. Are you able to give me her name, and her husband's name as well?"

"I believe her name is Rachel and her husband is ..." she paused for a moment. "Gavin. Gavin Stowick."

"Again, thank you. This is extremely helpful information." He printed the names quickly on the paper. "Do you know them? Are they friends of yours?"

"Not really, just customers who come in."

Martin quickly deduced he was talking to one of the bar girls who worked at the pub. He noted this information down.

"Are you able to tell me anything about their relationship?"

"As in?"

"Did they look like a happy couple?"

"I guess so. It's a bit hard to tell these things in a pub. She seemed happy with him."

"Can I ask why called me now, and not when I visited?" Martin kept his voice calm and even.

"Well, it seems that ..." she fell silent for so long Martin wondered if she'd hung up.

"Ma'am?" Martin waited patiently on the line.

"I haven't seen Gavin at the pub for the last week and a bit."

"Is this unusual for him?"

"Yes. He's a regular."

"Okay. Do you think something has happened to him as well?" He made notes as he spoke.

"Maybe. I'm just not sure but was visiting a lot more than usual in recent few weeks. And his behaviour ..." Another long pause.

"What about his behaviour?" Martin's detective senses were on high alert now.

"Detective, if the female in the photo you showed me is Rachel, do you think Gavin might have been the one who hurt her?" she asked with a slight tremor in her voice, changing the subject.

Martin sighed heavily. "I'm not sure at the moment." He added two ticks to the comment he'd written about the possibility he was taking to a staff member. Jogging back his memory, he only saw two females working behind the bar on the nights he visited.

"You made a comment about his behaviour. Is there a reason you brought it up?" Silence once again greeted Martin. "Ma'am, is there something you need to tell me?"

"Gavin ... Gavin can be quite ..." she paused, as though trying to find the right words. "Well, when he gets drunk, he can get a bit violent."

Martin scowled. "Has he been violent towards Rachel?" he asked.

"No, not that I have seen. He doesn't really get drunk on the nights she has dinner with him, and well ... after Rachel stopped coming, Gavin visited more ... he's been drinking more, and he leaves ... well, angry."

"And this is not the norm for him?"

"No. He would come to the pub a few days a week with his mates, but it was always after six thirty or closer to seven. He'd have a few beers, then leave. But lately, he'd turn up a lot earlier and have dinner too.

Martin took a deep breath. "Is there anything else you can tell me about Rachel or Gavin? Like, where they live, or work?" He pushed a little, hoping she would have this information.

"I don't know, sorry, but I do know Gavin works in the construction business. He's always here with the guys he works with."

"Thank you. This is helpful information." Martin added the evidence to the notebook. With his mind racing, Martin knew he had to keep the woman on the line. "Did you at any time enquire as to where his wife was once you noticed her absence?"

"I didn't, but I have overheard him telling his mates she'd been unwell for a while and was staying home to rest."

Martin sat back in his chair and rubbed his chin. "Ma'am. Can I ask how you found out who I was?" The phone went quiet. Although the call hadn't disconnected, the female on the other end didn't respond to his question. "Ma'am, it's okay. You don't need to answer that."

The voice sighed on the other end. "I overheard a conversation at the pub, between Gavin and the bar owner a few days after you visited. I tried not to worry about it, but as I have a friend in the police system, I went to him a few days ago when I noticed Gavin stopped coming in."

"And he gave *you,* my details?"

"Sort of. He gave me a few names. You're the third detective I've rung," she confessed.

Martins' eyebrows raised. He wasn't sure what to say. Martin scratched his head and looked down at all the notes he'd written, uncertain how Gavin Stowick might be involved in the investigation. Or if this missing female, Rachel Stowick, was the same missing woman as Amber Cooper.

"Sir," the caller paused again, but when she spoke, her voice quivered as though she were crying. "Is the woman in the photo still alive?"

This time, it was Martin who paused. He couldn't give out the information. Not when the caller didn't want to identify herself and obviously knew the husband. Martin had no idea how involved this female could be.

"I am not at liberty to comment on that, I'm afraid, but I'm grateful you called me. The information you have provided will help me to work out if something has happened to Rachel Stowick, and if she could be the female from the accident."

"I hope I have been of some use."

"You have. Again, thank you. If you ..." The call ended abruptly with a loud click, as the female caller hung up. Martin hung up his phone and leaned back in his chair, his mind spinning with the current information.

Looking at his notes, Martin picked up the phone again and called Tony. Within a minute, Tony rushed into Martin's office.

"So? What's the urgency?" He pulled up a chair and brought it to the table.

"Well, I just had a remarkably interesting phone conversation with a staff member at Holeman's Pub. Well, I believe she works there." He tapped the notepad in front of him.

"And ...?" Tony queried, his eyes squinting.

"You know the mystery female in Parker, the one with no memory?" he said, glancing at his colleague. Tony nodded.

"I think I might know who she is!"

Chapter 47

The last few days flew by quickly for Craig and Amber. They'd spent the rest of Saturday together, with Craig holding her, comforting her and just being there for her.

After she'd confided in him and told him of the things she was experiencing, his heart broke a little and all he wanted to do was hold her forever. To tell her everything would be okay. It saddened him that she thought he'd abandon her if he found out she was seeing things. Instead, he promised to stick by her until she wanted him to leave. In all honesty, he hoped that never happened.

In the back of his mind, he knew one day Amber's memory would return, and he hated to admit it worried him. Although he tried not to show it, he was apprehensive and anxious he'd lose her to her former life. Loving her came easily, and being with Amber was the best thing that had happened to him. Craig treasured spending time with her and wanted to tell her just how much she meant to him. He just wasn't sure when the right time would be.

After dinner at Tracey's house on Saturday, Craig suggested he stay the night with her and help her sleep. Tracey agreed and discreetly excused herself, giving them some privacy. This made Craig laugh, and Amber blush, causing him to laugh even more.

"Careful, or I'll change my mind!" she said, her stern expression silencing his laughter.

"Yes, ma'am," he teased, unable to help himself.

An hour later, as he climbed into bed with her, he wrapped his arms around Amber and held her tight. When she kissed him, he hesitated.

"We don't need to do this. Especially if you're not completely comfortable with Tracey just down the hall." He glanced across the darkened room.

"You don't want me?" she questioned, pulling her head back and looking at Craig with a puzzled frown.

"Oh yes, I want you!"

"Then don't stop!" She leaned back in and kissed him. Instinct took over, and he returned the kiss with passion. All apprehensions disappeared as they caressed each other, removing their clothes and entangling themselves together.

There was no rush that night. Their love making was slow and passionate. Each of them took their time to explore and pleasure each other, only stopping once they were both exhausted.

Sweaty and relaxed, Amber curled her back into Craig and drifted off into a deep sleep. He held her for a long time, stroking her arm and listened to the gentle rhythm of her breathing. He fell asleep to the sound, and they both slept soundly, till late morning.

Sunday brought a day of relaxing, and another trip to the beach. They stayed and watched the sunset, finally getting home after nine. Kissing her goodnight, Craig wanted to say the words rushing around in his head, but he held back again.

"Dinner sometime this week?" she asked.

"How about Thursday? I'll cook."

"Sounds good to me." She kissed him one more time before getting out of the car, waved goodbye, and walked off towards the house. He watched her until she closed the door behind her, then he left, a smile on his face.

Picking Amber up on the way home from work, and presenting her with a beautiful purple Iris, he noticed she'd brought a bag with her, with the full intention of staying the night. A sheepish grin crossed his face; happy she felt comfortable to stay with him.

Dinner was a casual affair, and Craig cooked a simple meal of grilled steak and steamed vegetables, the aroma filling his small kitchen and making Amber's mouth water.

They relaxed after dinner, enjoying a movie and a glass of wine. With little encouragement, the night moved to the bedroom, and once again, the passion took over. Intimacy with Amber was more than just a pleasurable way to pass the time. Holding her, kissing her—Craig couldn't get enough. Amber didn't hold back and happily responded to anything Craig did. She was so beautiful that he kept stopping just to look at her.

"Do I have something on my face?" she questioned.

"No, I just want to look at you."

She laughed, and the sound excited Craig. The sweet melody of her giggle reached through his chest and pulled at his heartstrings. Her smile was intoxicating, and he never wanted her to stop. Her lips were tender, and her skin, warm and slightly fragranced with her vanilla and musk moisturiser, felt soft to his touch.

Craig knew he'd fallen for her hard. Moving as one, their hips pressing together, he rose to match her rhythm repeatedly until she climaxed. Sweat mingled with her wetness, drove him towards his own climax before he collapsed beside her.

"You didn't offer me any dessert?" she said as they lay together, breathing heavily.

"Are you hungry?" he asked, raising his eyebrows at her. "Wasn't I your dessert?" he teased, as she giggled at him.

"You are good enough to eat. I will admit that." She rolled over and kissed him again.

"I can get you something if you like," he said, nuzzling her neck.

"What do you have?" she asked, softly running her hand down Craig's sweaty back, leaving goosebumps in their wake.

"Ice-cream, or chocolate mousse," his voice became low and husky.

"Oh, chocolate mousse, please," she purred back, letting her hand run over his backside and down his thigh.

"Keep doing that, and you might miss out on dessert, because I may not be able to make it to the kitchen."

Amber quickly drew her hand back, and with a mischievous smile, placed it on his chest. "What if you get the mousse and I eat it off you—as my dessert?"

Craig's eyes widened and before she could say anything, he jumped out of the bed and ran to the kitchen. Yanking the fridge door open, he grabbed two pots of mousse, a can of whipped cream, and two spoons before running back to the room. An enormous grin spread across his face when he found Amber sitting up in bed with a sultry twinkle in her eyes and her legs wide open.

Tonight's dessert took a different turn to what Craig had originally planned, but he had no complaints. In fact, he was certain it was the best dessert he'd ever had.

Chapter 48

Friday, November 31st

Within hours of talking to Tony the day before, Martin and Tony conducted a brief investigation and found out where Gavin Stowick worked. Jumping in Martin's car, the two of them drove to the work site, hoping to find him there. If the female in the photo was indeed his wife, Rachel, Martin could put the pieces together and inform Gavin about his wife's whereabouts.

Arriving at the work site, Martin and Tony chatted casually to the men working, and after receiving some vague answers and a lot of awkward silences when they asked after Gavin, Martin finally got his address. He'd also confirmed the mysterious caller's story that Gavin's wife's absence was because of illness. As for Gavin himself, his workmates seemed under the impression that their boss had taken time off work to look after her. The theory didn't sit well with Martin, and he thought there was something more than just a '*sick wife at home*' situation—and he wanted to find the underlying truth.

Early that morning, Martin headed to Gavin's house to meet him and see if everything was okay. The fact that no one had seen either Gavin or his wife in a while heightened Martin's interest. Pulling up into the driveway, Martin noticed the grass in the front yard was unkept and weeds grew in small patches. As he got out of the car, he saw two bags of rubbish sitting on the front porch and the once lush green pot plants had withered and died.

The house had a quiet feel about it, and Martin had the distinct feeling if he knocked on the door, no one would answer. He drummed his knuckles twice on the solid, brown wooden door. Silence echoed in return. Martin moved to the window next to the door and tried to peer into the house. Although the curtains were open, the house appeared dark and empty. Either no one was home, or Gavin was inside hiding.

Martin knocked one more time and after patiently waiting a few minutes, he left and headed back to the office. With the information Martin had gathered, he was ready to declare Gavin as a person of interest. With Tony's assistance, Martin set up a small surveillance team at his house.

Chapter 49

Saturday, December 1ˢᵗ - Morning

It had been a slow week for Gavin, but not an uneventful one.

By Tuesday, he'd found out about the Summer Carnival, where it was, and what time it started. Relaxing a bit, he spent most of his time at the motel, planning what he would do on the day. Knowing where his wife was each day, and although it bothered him that she was involved with another man, he kept his distance. It was no use getting himself all worked up if it meant he risked her seeing him before he was ready. Something could go wrong, and Gavin wouldn't risk it.

Each morning, he took a quick trip into town to watch her walk to work, admiring her from a distance, all the while counting down the days until the carnival. There was only one day she didn't get off the bus, and clenching the steering wheel so hard, he heard it creak, was all he could do not to punch the windscreen, when he saw her get out of the other man's car. Closing his eyes and counting to ten, he forced himself to relax, knowing there were only a few days left before she would be back in his arms.

This morning, after a hearty breakfast, Gavin headed to the hardware shop, purchased a few items, making sure to pay with cash, and tossed the shopping bag into the van. Returning to the motel room, he packed his bag, returned to the van, and tossed it onto the floor in front of the passenger seat. Not wanting to risk leaving any traces of DNA, Gavin grabbed the shopping bag and went back into the motel room.

Emptying the contents onto the bed, Gavin set to work. Grabbing a pair of disposable gloves, Gavin slipped them on and, using a fresh packet of wipes, methodically wiped down any surface he had touched in the room, the bathroom, even the sheets and pillowcase, chastising himself, for not doing this at the other motels he stayed in. He placed the key, which he also wiped down, on the small table.

Discarding the used wipes, the gloves, and the half-empty pack of wipes back into the shopping bag, he glanced around the room one last time, satisfied with his effort. A huge step up from a few months ago when cleaning for him was disastrous.

Shutting the motel door behind him, being sure to cover his hand with his shirt, Gavin transferred the cleaning products to the van, tucking it next to his travel bag. Settling himself into the driver's seat, he drove off. It was time to head off to the carnival.

Entering the Carnival carpark at one-thirty, Gavin parked away from the main entrance, but in a position where he could see who was coming and going. He needed to watch for when his wife's arrival.

Patiently sitting in the van, he waited for the mystery man's car. Just before two o'clock, the dark blue sedan finally arrived and parked close to him. Gavin watched his wife climb out of the passenger side and stand at the rear passenger door to assist Tracey.

Rachel was close enough that he could see the short skirt she wore, and how it fluttered loosely in the warm breeze. Her perfectly tanned legs beckoned him, and he felt himself harden. Placing his hand on his groin, over his jeans, he fantasised about lifting her skirt up and grabbing her bottom to pull her towards him.

Knowing his plan to bring her home was about to unfold, Gavin undid his fly, placed his hand into his jeans and began pleasuring himself, only stopping when his wife was no longer in his line of sight. Quickly withdrawing his hand, he fixed his jeans and exited the van.

He followed the line of people passing through the main gate and out into the large carnival arena. The place was enormous. Scanning the many faces, Gavin couldn't see where his wife had gone and for a fleeting moment, he panicked, thinking his plan had failed.

Pushing past throngs of people, he stomped to the right towards two large alleyways of games. Within a few minutes, he heard the sweet sound of his wife's laughter over the carnival music. Turning towards the first alley way, using his height to his advantage, he saw her golden hair shining like a beacon. A calmness came over Gavin, and a shrewd smile crept back onto his lips.

The game of cat and mouse was now on. It was just a matter of time before he would catch his little mouse and take her home, where she belonged.

Chapter 50

Saturday, December 1ˢᵗ - 3pm

There was so much to look at, I didn't know what to focus on first. We'd been at the carnival for about an hour, and I had already seen so much. The music drifting through the air was loud and lively. Songs overlapped each other as we passed one amusement ride after another. Everything was so bright and colourful; I couldn't stop smiling.

With so many games to play, I didn't know where to go. We started off with Ring Toss and Balloon Pop, where Craig won prizes on both. Further down the alley, Craig challenged me to a game of Laughing Clowns. I loved it and beamed with pride when I won a prize larger than Craig and Tracey. We played Ball and Bucket Toss, where all three of us lost, but we had a good laugh and finally Skee-Ball, which I enjoyed, and played twice, winning small prizes each time.

"Are you having fun?" Craig wrapped his arm around me, as we stood and watched a large rollercoaster zoom across the rails high above us.

"This is incredible!" I replied, over the loud screams that echoed from the riders as they rushed by overhead.

"Do you want to get on?" Craig motioned to the line of people waiting for the ride. I watched the rollercoaster cars racing around the track, twisting, and jolting the people inside.

"Oh, I don't think so," I said anxiously. "Why do people like this? It looks terrifying." I turned and looked into Craig's eyes as he laughed at me.

"I guess it's all a part of the thrill."

"But it goes so fast, and it's so high up."

"Yes," he winked at me.

"Do *you* want to go on it?" I asked hesitantly. He nodded his head enthusiastically, and a smile crept onto his lips. "Well, you'll have to go on your own. I don't think I could do it."

"Smart move," Tracey said, as she came up beside me.

"You don't ride these either?" I asked.

"Absolutely not. I'm too old for that, plus I have a fear of heights, and I'd rather keep my feet on the ground."

Smiling, I nodded—I liked her thinking.

"Well, if you don't want to go then, that's fine." Craig kissed my neck and released me.

"Oh, don't let us stop you," Tracey said quickly.

"Yes, if you want to ride, we'll wait right here for you," I commented, grabbing his hand.

"Really?" His face lit up.

"Really. Go line up." I pushed him towards the queue.

"Thanks." He kissed me quickly on the lips and took off, like a little schoolboy. Tracey and I glanced at each other, laughing at his eagerness. Watching him stand alone in the line, a pang of guilt hit me. Craig brought me here to enjoy the day, and I left him to ride the rollercoaster on his own.

"Here, hold this," I said to Tracey and passed her my bag and a large plastic bag of prizes. "I think I'm crazy." I laughed and ran towards the line, squeezing past other people to find my way to Craig's side. He spun around when he felt me grab his hand.

"You're here," he smiled widely.

"Yep. I'm here."

He grabbed me firmly and kissed me hard on the mouth. Five minutes later, Craig and I inched our way to the ticket box, bought our tickets, and took a seat in the car at the front of the track. After all the seats filled, and the safety bars lowered, I stared nervously as the cars inched forwards towards a large incline.

My heart raced, and I gripped the safety bar tightly. Watching the hill creep higher and higher, I wanted to turn away from the blue sky, straight in front of us, but couldn't. Finally, the cars reached the apex and then quickly rocketed down the other side, and a new chorus of screams filled the air, including mine.

The cars jostled and vibrated across the tracks, throwing me left and right, as we raced around the many turns, dips, inclines, and loops. My adrenaline kicked in and I screamed with both fear and excitement. Looking sideways at Craig, I saw how excited he was, and how much he was enjoying the crazy ride.

Before long, the cars slowed down before stopping completely. With my hair blown into a colossal mess, I climbed out of the car, my cheeks in agony from smiling so much.

"Again?" Craig teased, attempting to smooth my unruly hair.

"No." I clutched my hands to my chest, my heart threating to leap out. "As fun as that was, I don't need to do it again."

He laughed at me once more. "Well, I'm glad you came with me."

We got back to Tracey, who just shook her head in amusement. Handing me back my bags, we moved onto the next row of loud, bright rides. Bumper cars were the next thing we rode. I laughed so hard driving the car, I thought I would pee my pants. Having the chance to slam into Craig brought me too much enjoyment, and I was sorry when the time ended.

"Come on, I can't wait for you to see this." Craig grabbed my hand and lead us to a new area. "This is called Showbag Alley."

I stared in wonder at the two, long, straight stretches of caravans running parallel to each other. Bags and bags of toys, chocolates, and lollies filled the insides of each van. So many people were there that it was hard to make our way to the vans to see what to buy.

"This is amazing!" I honestly didn't know where to go first. Finally, after twenty minutes of bumping and squeezing between other patrons, I bought myself a large chocolate showbag, a small lolly bag filled with soft, jelly sweets, candies and other delicious treats and a big beach bag, with a new towel, sun hat, sunglasses, sun cream and water bottle. This day was turning out to be the most exciting day of my life. Being here with Craig and Tracey, I felt like this was where I belonged.

Moving towards another gaming alley, Craig bought me a large stick of blue and pink fairy floss. The sweet-tasting candy melted in my mouth, and I struggled not to shove the entire thing into my mouth.

"Oh my, this is good!" I said, licking my lips.

Craig smiled at me. "It's like watching a kid in a candy store, trying things for the first time."

Tracey agreed with him and took a small amount of candy floss for herself.

"Well, considering I don't remember if I *have* done any of this before, I guess I am trying things for the first time."

"What do you want to see next?" he asked, taking my show bags from me so I could eat the rest of the candy floss.

"The animals, please," I replied with sticky teeth.

Craig grinned. "Come on, then." He led the way, while I continued to stare in awe at everything around us.

Chapter 51

Saturday December 1ˢᵗ - 5pm

Gavin kept his distance. Wearing a cap to cover most of his face and dark sunglasses, his green eyes never strayed far from his wife. Making sure he blended in with the crowd, he played a few games, throwing balls into buckets and at tin cans, making it look like he was there for the entertainment, but all the time, keeping his dear, beloved wife, only a stone's throw away.

Plans and ideas constantly ran through his head as he tried to determine how he'd approach her. The time for waiting and watching was over—it was time his wife came home to him. He just needed the right timing, but she never was alone.

Gavin struggled as he watched the other man consistently touch her. Every moment between them made him sick to the stomach.

How could she betray me like this? Running around in public with a lover at her side, acting like two teenagers, he thought. *She's a married woman; she's breaking her vows!*

His fingers clenched into fists when he saw them sit next to each other on the roller coaster. When they finally got off, he relaxed and opened his hands. Sudden pain flicked through his hand and when he looked down, he saw how deeply he'd pressed his nails into his palm. Not deep enough to draw blood, but four small crescent-shaped indents were visible in each palm.

His anger rose again as he watched her smile and laugh while driving the bumper cars. Gavin couldn't remember the last time he'd seen her have so much fun.

It's like she's another person, he said to himself. *She's acting like the young girl he first fell in love with.*

The interactions between Rachel and this man were nauseating to watch. In large part, because he couldn't recall the last time, she'd looked at him that way. It had been years since she'd held his hand in public. Pangs of jealousy hit Gavin in waves, and he took out his frustration on a large hammer-hitting game, hitting it so hard that he won a teddy bear.

During the past week, while Gavin watched Rachel, he never bothered trying to find out who the other guy was. He wasn't relevant to his mission, but in saying that, whatever happened today, the man would pay a nasty price for putting his grubby hands, on Gavin's possession.

He continued to follow her through an outdoor farm animal display, watching as she cooed and petted baby goats, lambs, and chickens. Gavin continued following her as she passed the cake decorating and vegetable competitions, all the while picturing how he would punish her when they got home.

Trailing the three of them to the large, central arena, he closed his eyed briefly as Rachel once again sat close to that man, eliminating any space between them. He slipped up to a row of seats behind her to the right, sat down, and spent most of the time watching the back of her head instead of the horse display below.

But timing and patience are what Gavin needed now. He knew, when the right time came, he would approach her. Maybe say something funny to her, to make her laugh, so she'd be happy to see him again.

Yet Gavin's patience was running out.

Chapter 52

Saturday, December 1ˢᵗ - 5.30pm

"That horse show was fantastic," Tracey said as we stood and shuffled our way to the stairs.

"Some of those horses are very clever," I added, gripping my show bags tightly as I navigated the metal steps down to the ground.

"It was a good show. I think some of those cowboys were talented too." Craig stepped aside to allow us to walk past him.

"Do you want to be a cowboy?" I teased.

"Ah, No. But I can ride horses."

"You can ride?" my eyes widened.

"Yeah. Learnt to ride when I was a kid. My Grandfather used to work on a farm when he was young. He taught me and my siblings."

"Would you teach me one day?"

"Sure. If you want."

I grinned wildly. "Yay! So, where shall we go next?" I asked, bouncing up and down like a jackrabbit.

"Well, I have an idea," Tracey pipped up. "How about I take all the bags back to the car, so we don't need to keep carrying them around, and you take Amber to the Ferris Wheel," she said to Craig. "The sun is setting, and the view will be wonderful up there."

"Oh, no, you don't need to do that!" I looked at Tracey with a small frown.

"No, it's fine. Here, give me your bags." Tracey gathered our bags, clearly refusing to take no for an answer. "After you two ride the wheel, we'll get dinner and find somewhere to sit for the fireworks."

"Are you sure? I could help you out!" Craig offered.

"No. I've got it. Plus, it will give me a chance to grab our jumpers. The temperature will drop a bit after the sun disappears."

"Thank you," Craig said as she took off, walking back toward the main entrance.

"Well, that wasn't very subtle!" I giggled.

Craig laughed and wrapped his arms around me, bringing me in, and kissing me gently on the lips.

"I think it was very nice of her," he whispered. "And I think we shouldn't waste the opportunity to fulfil her wishes."

"Well, then ... lead the way, sir." I grabbed Craig's hand and turned to look for the Ferris Wheel. "That way?" I pointed off to the right. Craig nodded and the two of us ambled slowly through the alleys and rides until we finally reached the enormous, brightly lit wheel.

I stood in awe, listening to the pop music that boomed out from two large speakers and watched the bright neon lights pulsed up and down the frame of the wheel as it turned. The entire day had been a magical event, and I couldn't wait for our turn. Inching forwards, Craig kept a tight hold around my waist and lost in the moment, brought his lips to the base of my neck.

"I think this has been one of the best Summer Carnival's I have ever been to."

"You know what, I think this is my best one too!" I giggled, leaning my head back onto his shoulder.

"You're so cute." He whispered in my ear.

"As are you!"

Craig sighed deeply and pulled me closer against his chest. "Have you had a good a day?" he asked, nuzzling his nose into my hair.

"Yes, I certainly have."

Five minutes later, we climbed into a gondola and closed the small gate. Slowly, the wheel turned, stopping every few moments, to let people off and new riders on, continuing until all the gondolas were full, and the wheel rotated without stopping.

The view from the top was breathtaking. We could see the entire carnival below, across the town, and out towards the hills which loomed up into the darkening sky. As the sun sank slowly behind the horizon, the scattered clouds turn beautiful shades of yellow, orange, pink and finally red. I don't think I blinked once. I couldn't take my eyes off the beautiful view.

After the sun faded, the lights from all the rides below lit up the grounds into a kaleidoscope of colour. Bright yellow string lights flickered on along the lengths of the alleys, making the whole carnival shine and twinkle.

"I think I could live up here," I said, gazing at Craig with affection.

"Well, it might be hard to sleep in these gondolas!"

"Funny, funny." I slapped him playfully on the leg.

The ride slowed down and periodically stopped again, letting people off and on. Soon, our gondola returned to the bottom, and we disembarked. Spying Tracey waiting close to the wheel, I skipped over to her.

"That was so amazing. Did you see the sunset?"

"Yes, I did. Although, my view from down here wasn't as good as yours."

"Well, I'm getting rather hungry," Craig interrupted. "What do you ladies say to heading off to the food vans and grabbing some dinner?"

"Yes, please," I responded enthusiastically.

"Good, but I need to stop at the toilets first," Craig said, looking at us.

"I saw some near the Food Alley." Tracey walked off in the direction she pointed. Grabbing my hand, Craig and I followed close behind.

"Any thoughts on what to eat?" Craig asked as we stopped in the middle of the alley, looking around at the many vans, offering delicious meals. Mouth-watering aromas filled the air. Burgers, chips, spices, and fried chicken caused my stomach to grumble.

"Well, I can see a Mexican van over there. I think I'd like some beef nachos." I looked at Craig and smiled.

"Oh, that sounds good," Craig said as he took his wallet out of his back pocket.

"No, my shout, you've paid for all the rides and games today," I said, pushing his hand back down. "Tracey?"

"There's a Fish and Chips van, back at the top. I'll go and get some, and I'll pay for my own." She left before I could stop her.

"Okay, what do you want?" I asked Craig, spinning back to face him.

"You sure about paying?" he asked, his wallet still in his hand.

"Yes, now hurry up. I thought you needed the toilet!"

"Yes. I do. Right. Can I please have beef nachos and a can of Coke?"

"Coming right up." I kissed him on the lips. "Meet me next to the van, okay?" I said, pushing him away slightly. I stood for a moment and watched him disappear into the crowd as he made his way over to the row of public toilets at the end of the alley.

After watching him leave, I pushed my way through the throngs of hungry carnival patrons to the Mexican van and stood patiently in line.

"Two beef nachos, and two cans of coke please," I asked, finally getting to the front of the line.

"That will be sixteen dollars, please," a young girl replied, adding my order to the list.

After paying and putting my purse back into my bag, I stepped towards a gap between the Mexican van and a burger van and waited eagerly for Craig and our food order.

Chapter 53

Saturday, December 1ˢᵗ - 6.15pm

"Hi," Gavin said casually, as he stepped up beside Amber. He watched tentatively, a hint of nerves pulsating through him, as she turned her head and smiled politely at him.

"Hello," Amber replied politely to the stranger, then turned back to face the vending van.

Feeling bolder, he leant towards her, inhaling slightly, catching a light scent of her vanilla perfume.

"Enjoying the Carnival?" he asked.

"Yes, and you?" Amber replied, turning back to face the man by her side.

Gavin stared deep into her dark blue eyes with both wonder and disbelief.

What the hell! he thought. *Why is she talking to me, like I'm a stranger?*

Gavin tilted his head slightly and studied her face.

Why is she not looking at me, like a wife should look at her husband? Especially one who'd just been caught! he thought.

When Amber said nothing further, he frowned, his green eyes darkened. He could see he was making her feel a little uncomfortable. Amber raised her eyebrows a fraction, gave him a weak smile, and took a small step away from him.

"Are you going to say something?" he asked, becoming annoyed.

"Um, am I meant to?" Amber replied. The puzzled look in her eyes deepened.

Gavin laughed and shook his head. "This isn't funny, Rachel!" His brow furrowed further. As he stared at her, watching her own brow crease in curiosity, he realised she didn't know who he was.

"Don't you recognise me?" his voice deepened, and he closed the gap between them. He watched as Amber inspected his face. She looked into his green eyes, trailed her gaze over the strong shape of his jaw, then up to his hairline. Gradually, she glanced down to his shoulders and chest before slowly looked back into his face, frowning in confusion the whole time.

"Should I?" she asked hesitantly.

Gavin snorted in frustration. "Seriously, Rachel!" he hissed at her, trying to keep his voice quiet.

Amber looked at this man, perplexed. "Do I ... know you?" she asked, her voice filled with desperation.

"Are you saying you don't remember me?" Gavin's face turned a deep shade of red as his anger boiled.

"No, I'm sorry, I don't," she said, her hands visibly shaking as she took another step back from him.

In that moment, Gavin snapped. The rage he'd felt over the past few months, the agony he'd endured during the week, watching her live a new life, cheating on him with another man, and working in a job, he did not approve, boiled over and fractured his final nerve.

Suddenly, before anyone noticed what was happening, his left hand shot out, grabbed her arm, and he pulled Amber backwards between the two food vans. In the same momentum, he covered her mouth with his right hand before she could scream. Releasing her arm, he wrapped a strong, muscular arm around her waist and lifted her off the ground. Despite her struggling and writhing in his grip, Gavin stomped through the darkness, behind the vans and out towards the carpark.

Trudging at least thirty meters away from the carnival, Gavin carried Amber, as she squirmed desperately in his grip, before roughly standing her back on the ground, keeping his arm wrapped around her waist, and his hand still across her mouth, pinning her lips together.

"Shut up and walk or I'll hurt you," he growled in her ear, his breath hot against her delicate neck.

Amber shuddered in his grip as Gavin grabbed her arm again, pulling her close to his side to prevent her from running away. She tripped slightly as he walked next to her, keeping his body between the carpark and the carnival, so no one could see her leave.

Struggling against him, trying desperately to free herself of his grip, Amber pleaded, "Let me go. You're hurting me!"

"Enough, Rachel! You're coming home with me!" Gavin growled.

"I ... I don't know who you are!" she sobbed. Gavin could see the terror in her eyes.

"Shut up, Rachel!" he said, yanking her forwards, ensuring his grip was tight enough to hurt her. It seemed to do the trick as he steered them away.

Back at the food area, Craig glanced around, trying to find Amber. Looking up at the Mexican food van, he knew he was in the right spot where they'd planned to meet. Yet, there was no sign of her. Searching further, he spotted Tracey, at the Fish and Chip van, a few meters away, still waiting for her food, but Amber was not by her side.

Feeling a little confused and apprehensive, he walked over to the edge of the vans to get a clearer look at the area when he distinctly heard his name called. Glancing around to find where the call came from, he heard his name again. This time, he could hear the high-pitched fear in the voice, which sounded like it came from the carpark. As he peered across the dimly lit area beyond the food vans, Craig's eyes widened when he observed a tall, stocky man dragging Amber away.

Without hesitation, Craig took off running.

"Amber!" he yelled as loudly as he could. Hearing her name, Amber turned her head back towards the carnival.

"Craig! Help me!" she called out before Gavin violently slapped her across the face and pushed her forward between the cars.

"Amber!" Craig called out again, running faster to close the gap between them. As he reached the two of them, he could see the guy had a powerful hold on Amber's arm.

"Shut up or you'll get another one," the man growled as Craig got within earshot.

Reaching out, Craig grabbed the back of Gavin's shoulder, spinning him around and wrenched his grasp from Amber. Unfortunately for Craig, this allowed Gavin an opportunity to retaliate, and without hesitating, Gavin punched Craig squarely in the jaw, knocking his head sideways.

"Leave him alone!" Amber yelled, trying to step around Gavin, towards Craig.

Gavin shoved her backwards and turned to face Craig. "You need to fuck off!" he growled, and before Craig could recover from the first hit, Gavin slammed his fist into Craig's stomach.

The impact dropped Craig to his knees, knocking the wind out of him. Doubling over in pain, clutching his waist, Craig collapsed onto the grass, his focus blurring.

"Craig ... No!" Amber screamed, her eyes wide in fear, as she tried to get to him.

Gavin spun around quickly, his face reddening even more, as the veins in his neck and arms pulsed. Taking two large strides, he closed the gap between them.

"You fucking bitch!" he bellowed at Amber as he shoved her backwards, sending her to the ground. "How dare you leave me! How dare you make me look for you!"

Amber fell back hard, her backside slamming painfully on the gravel. Looking past the man that had just shoved her down, she flicked her eyes from him to Craig, pleading for help.

"Don't you look at him!" Gavin lent over and yanked Amber's head back by her hair, forcing her to look up at him. "You fucking whore! Did you fuck him? Hey! Did you fucking cheat on me!" He twisted her hair tighter in his hand.

"Please," Amber sobbed desperately. "I don't know you!" Gavin growled at her, when she grabbed at his wrist and tried to turn her face away.

"You're going to pay for this stunt, Rachel! Do you hear me?" he hissed.

Amber stared at this man, desperately trying to recognise him. Clearly, he seemed to know her, but her memories were still veiled.

"I don't know you!" she pleaded again, her voice shaking with fear.

Gavin's face reddened even more, and he slapped her across her face again. Amber's head reeled sideways from the impact, bouncing painfully against the door of a parked car, temporarily stunning her.

"Do *not* play these childish games with me, Rachel! It's time you came home!" Gavin snarled, as he grabbed her arm, yanking her to her feet, and dragged her towards a white van.

"Let me go!" Amber yelled, trying to pull herself free. Getting desperate, Gavin raised his other hand towards Amber's face.

"No!" Craig screamed in fear, as he saw a flash of something shiny flick towards Amber's neck,

No sooner had Craig seen it, Amber noticed the switch blade in Gavin's left hand. She also saw the bright red, glistening, wet stain on the tip of the blade. Realising what it meant, her eyes widened and flicked back to Craig.

Following his wife's gaze, Gavin observed Craig's face, as he, too, saw what was in his hand and what it signified. A slight, bemused grin crossed Gavin's face as he watched Craig pull his hand forward from his waist. It was covered in blood.

Amber screamed, her heart beating wilding in her chest, but Gavin quickly covered her mouth. Pushing the tip of the blade against her throat, she abruptly stopped struggling.

"Make another sound, and this blade will split you open as well!" Gavin whispered, his mouth against her ear. "Anyway, it's not like anyone is going to hear you!" He nodded towards the carnival. "No-one can hear your screams, Rachel. No-one else is coming to save you!"

With a bitter laugh, he pulled her further away. Amber's shoulders sagged in defeat when she realised, he was right. With the sounds of the loud music, the cheers, laughter, and the screams of fun, emitting from the brightly lit carnival, no-one would think twice about her calls.

Reaching the van, Gavin opened the sliding door and pushed his wife in, amazed at how she continued to fight back, desperately trying to avoid the tip of the blade.

"Get in the fucking van, Rachel!" he snarled.

"Please, I'm begging you! I was in a car accident, and I have amnesia. If I'm supposed to know you, I don't remember!" Amber pleaded, trying to hold him off.

"Nice try, my love, but your bullshit excuses won't work on me." He shoved her shoulders down. As Amber's knees buckled against the edge of the open-door frame, he forced her to sit on the dirty van floor.

"Stop pretending you don't know me!" He promptly slapped her again. Tears sprang into Amber's eyes and roll quickly down her stinging and reddened cheek.

Gritting his teeth through the pain, never taking his eyes off Amber, Craig finally managed to sit up, but the movement caused such intense pain that he doubled over again, fresh blood squirting through his fingers. Watching this man abuse Amber, the girl he was falling in love with, was breaking him as he lay on the grass, struggling to breathe.

"Don't touch her!" he called out desperately, his jaw still throbbing from the punch.

Hearing a scuffle and a feeble plea behind him, Gavin looked over his shoulder at Craig, and, knowing he was in no danger, ignored him. Instead, turning back to Amber, he placed the switchblade on the roof of the van. Gavin dug his hand deep into the pocket of his black jeans and withdrew something shiny. Grabbing her left hand, he pushed two rings onto Amber's fourth finger.

"I think these belong to you!" he growled. "Never take these off again!"

Amber glanced down at her finger, but before she had time to understand the relevance, a sharp pain cracked across her left cheek. Amber's right temple smacked into the car door frame, and within seconds, she was unconscious.

Gavin swiftly pushed her backwards, so she lay on the dirty, carpeted floor of the van. Sweeping up her legs, he folded them in after her and slammed the door shut before collecting his blade. Turning back to Craig, he strode towards him, sneering, as Craig began desperately trying to drag himself away, the movement causing more blood to flow freely from his wound.

With the blade in hand, Gavin crouched down, peering into Craig's eyes.

"I don't know who you are ... *Craig*!" he said, emphasizing his name with amusement. "But whatever relationship you had with *my wife*, it's over. Do you understand?" He waved the bloody blade back and forward across Craig's vision.

"Whatever *lies* she told you, don't believe them." He leaned in a little closer, pushing his warm breath into Craig's face. "If you come after her, I will kill you!" With a malicious laugh, Gavin stood and walked off.

"Let her go, you arsehole!" Craig yelled after him, again trying to get up.

Gavin turned abruptly and marched swiftly back. The last thing Craig saw was a black boot heading straight towards his face.

Chapter 54

Saturday, December 1ˢᵗ – 6.45pm

"Someone call the police!" a voice called in the distance.

Craig's eyelids flickered as the words lured him back to consciousness.

"It's going to be alright, mate. Just lay still. We've got the first aid team on the way." Craig could feel pressure against his stomach and when reached up, he felt someone's hand pushing down on his belly.

"Keep still, buddy. You're still bleeding badly."

Craig finally opened his eyes to see several faces staring down at him. He tried to turn his head to look towards the car park, but the movement sent a bolt of pain searing from his jaw up into his head and he was overcome by a wave of nausea.

"Amber ..." he murmured through gritted teeth, too weak to call out any louder.

"Easy does it, Craig." He heard Tracey's voice as she placed her hand on his shoulder, trying to keep him from moving around too much.

"Where is she? Where's Amber!" Craig asked painfully, looking desperately to Tracey for an answer.

"I don't know, love; I can't find her," she replied, looking around her. "What happened to you? Do you know who did this?" she asked as two paramedics hurried over, carrying a first aid bag.

"I don't know, some guy, he took her." he grimaced, as waves of pain rippled through his face. "He punched me, stabbed me. I saw him drag her away. He was hurting her!" With a painful gasp, he tried to get up again, but one of the medic's promptly pushed him back, and told him to keep still.

"You saw someone take her away?" Tracey's eyes widened with shock.

"Yeah, big guy. I think he knew her, kept calling her Rachel, said she was his wife, but Amber didn't seem to recognise him." Craig winced as the medic pulled up his shirt to inspect the stab wound.

"Mate, I'm gonna give you a green whistle, okay? You know how to use it?" the younger medic asked, as he placed the Penthrox inhaler into Craig's hand.

"Yeah. I do," he replied through gritted teeth.

"Nice. Just remember, take slow, deep breaths, okay? Your pain will ease in a minute or two."

Craig placed the inhaler carefully between his lips and drew in a slow breath, full of pain medication. After a few more inhalations, he felt his pain lessened, and he could move a little more without feeling the throbs and aches in his body.

As the medics were attending to Craig, Sheriff Hadlock arrived, and seeing Tracey kneeling in the grass, next to a bleeding male, beckoned her over. Tracey stood quickly and approached him.

"Sheriff Hadlock," she said, grateful he had arrived.

"Do you know what happened here?" Sheriff Hadlock inquired.

"Yes, Craig was beaten and stabbed. I found him here bleeding," she replied, a light tremor in her voice.

"Do you know who stabbed him?" he asked.

"No ... but ..."

"Does he know who stabbed him?" Sheriff Hadlock pointed in Craig's direction.

"No, he said he didn't recognise him, but Sheriff, the man who hurt Craig, took Amber!"

"What!" Sheriff Hadlock's eyes widened. He looked down at Craig, his brows furrowed. "Let me get this straight. Amber was taken by some guy who beat him up?" Again, pointing to Craig.

"Yes, you need to find her," Tracey pleaded desperately.

Sheriff Hadlock moved towards Craig and crouched beside him. "Can you tell me what happened?" he asked, but before Craig could say a word, the medic jumped in.

"Your questions will have to wait, sir. We need to get him to the hospital immediately."

Craig opened his mouth to speak, but his brain felt fuzzy from the painkillers. All he could do was watch the growing crowd of people, lured by the commotion as the medics transferred him to a gurney bed. Feeling overwhelmingly exhausted, his eyelids fluttered as he listened to the Sheriff, order the crowd away.

As the crowd dispersed, the Sheriff turned back to Tracey. "Can you please head to the station with me? I will need to formally get your statement. After that, you can head to the hospital. I'll wait till he's out of surgery before I question him."

Tracey nodded quietly, and as the medics wheeled Craig towards the awaiting ambulance, she slipped her hand slip into his.

"I have to go to the station first, but then I'll drive straight to the hospital, okay?" she said, squeezing his hand gently.

"Thank you, Tracey. I don't know what I'm going to do. We need to find her!" he replied, his voice groggy.

"We will Craig, don't worry, we will!"

Chapter 55

Saturday, December 1ˢᵗ - 10.20pm

I slowly regained conciseness to a painful, pulsating throb in my head. My shoulders ached, and as I tried to move my arms to ease the discomfort, I found my wrists were tightly bound behind me.

Moaning in pain, I stretched out my legs, only to realise they, too, were bound at the ankle. The cold, solid surface I lay upon sent chills through my aching body as I rocked back and forward in a hypnotic rhythm. It was then I noticed the sound of the engine and realised I was in a moving vehicle.

Cautiously, I tried to open my eyes, but the combination of the motion and the pain in my head made my stomach turn and I felt the acidic burn of bile rise into my throat. I squeezed my eyes shut, swallowing the bile down. Yet, the pain in my head intensified and before I could do anything, I passed out again.

The abrupt motion of the vehicle stopping woke me. I opened my eyes but found I could only see from my left eye. My right eye was swollen, blurring my vision. Although the light was dim, I could see I was in the back of a van. Confusion ran through me.

Where am I? How did I get here? Why can't I move properly?

I went to call out but as I moved my jaw; I felt a soft cotton piece of material pressed tightly across my mouth, preventing me from talking. Trying not to panic, I twisted myself around so I could sit up, but without the use of my arms, I couldn't move much.

"Hello?" I called out, my voice muffled against the cloth. "Hello?" I cried out louder. A pain scratched at the back of my throat. I needed something to drink. Hearing footsteps crunching outside, the van rocked slightly to one side as someone climbed into the driver's seat.

"Hello?" I mumbled, hoping the driver would hear me.

"Oh, you're awake," a male voice responded. "Don't worry. We'll be home soon."

"Please, help me!" I muttered.

"Relax, Rachel, I *am* helping you. Now go back to sleep. We still have a long way to go."

The engine sprang into life, sending vibrations through the floor, and within seconds, the van moved once more. Without wanting to, tears welled, and I started crying. Feeling defeated, I closed my eyes and allowed the pain, fear, and headache to take over. Before long, I was asleep.

"Wake up, Rachel." The movement of someone gently rocking my shoulders woke me, sending a spasm of pain shooting from my shoulders down to my wrists.

"If you wake up, you can sit up. Then maybe, if you behave, I might untie your wrists, okay?" The male's voice spoke calmly.

I nodded slowly, wincing against the pounding in my head. Opening my eyes, I could see little other than it was still nighttime. The man, my kidnapper, stood in the open doorway of the van, shrouded by the darkness, hiding his features from me. He lent into the van and grabbing my legs, shifting, and pulling them forward until he'd positioned them so that they hung outside the door. Then, grasping my shoulders, he pulled me up into a seated position.

"Do you need to go to the toilet?"

I gently shook my head. Strange as it was, I couldn't remember the last time I went "No," I muttered into the rag.

"I'm going to take off the gag. Okay? Give you some something to drink. Don't bother screaming for help. We're in the middle of nowhere," he sighed loudly. "Do you understand?"

I nodded my head slightly, looking sideways, past him into the darkness.

"Don't try to run either. You won't get far with your legs still tied up."

He placed his hands on either side of my head and roughly untied the material, painfully pulling strands of hair out and allowing the gag to fall into my lap. Thoughts of yelling out crossed my mind, as I opened and closed my mouth, relieved to move my jaw, as did bitting him if I'd been quick enough to turn my head, but I didn't. I was too scared.

Staring at him in the darkness, taking in his height, his broad shoulders, and thick neck, I knew any opportunity I took to run would be foiled, he would grab me in seconds, and judging by how many times he had already hit me, I knew he would not hesitate to do it again.

Lifting a bottle of juice and cracking open the lid, he brought it up to my mouth, resting it lightly on my dry lips and tilted it slightly, allowing the cool liquid to flow slowly into my mouth. As soon as I swallowed the first mouth full, an overwhelming thirst came over me. I tilted my head back, trying to drink more, but he only allowed me to have a few gulps before he took the bottle away. The fresh orange juice was delicious, but there was a hint of something bitter, which left an odd after taste.

"Do you think you can eat?" he asked, his voice deep. I felt a hazy sense of recognition, as though it was familiar, yet couldn't quite place it.

"Please," I answered quietly. I hadn't realised how hungry I was until he asked me.

Moving his hand slowly and deliberately to a paper bag I hadn't noticed sitting next to me, he withdrew a plastic container, which I could see in the low light, contained a sandwich.

"Nothing special. Just a ham and cheese sandwich." He opened the small triangular container. It looked like the ones you buy at the petrol station. Picking up a half, he brought it to my mouth. "Don't bite me either. I'm not in the mood, Rachel, for any more of your games."

I took a small bite from the corner of the sandwich, chewing slowly before swallowing. "Thank you," I said. He continued to feed me, allowing me to eat the rest of the sandwich before he placed the other half back into the bag.

"Juice?" he asked, picking up the bottle again.

I nodded, and he brought the bottle back to my lips. Again, I tried to swallow as much as I could without choking, and again, a bitter aftertaste remained in my mouth once he took the bottle away. Screwing the lid back on, he placed the bottle back into the bag and lifted the rag up from my lap.

"You don't need to put that back on," I whispered, trying to look into his eyes, but I was unable to read his expression in the shadows.

Silently, he moved closer to me and placed the rag back across my mouth, painfully wedging it between my lips and wrapping it around my head, tying it tightly. Hesitating, he lingered next to my right ear, his breath soft. The sensation of it touching my skin sent a chill of repulsion down my back. Moving his lips closer to my cheek, he inhaled deeply. I cringed, and I tried to move away from him. Suddenly, he grabbed my right arm.

"Too long, have you been gone from my bed, Rachel!" he growled into my ear. His voice had changed. It was deeper, angrier. Abruptly, he pushed me backwards into the van. Without my arms to stop the momentum, my head slammed back against the hard floor. Pain coursed through my skull as my vision blurred.

Unexpectantly, I felt his hands grasp my knees, and he pulled me forwards; the movement hitching my skirt up, exposing my underwear. Without hesitating, he raised my legs, slipping my bound ankles over his head, my bottom no longer on the van floor. Running his hands down my legs, he placed them on either side of my hips, and his strong fingers caressed my waist.

A wave of goosebumps rushed across my skin, as my body reacted to his touch. I tried to move away from his fingertips, as a moment of disgust washing through me.

A small groan of pleasure escaped his lips, and staring at his darkened face, I was aware of what was about to happen. In desperation, I tried to wriggle myself away from him, but it was impossible with my ankles around his neck and my arms pinned painfully under me. My movements only caused him to grasp my hips harder.

"No ... no!" I muttered through the rag, shaking my head, causing a wave of nausea to twist through my stomach.

To my horror, he clutched my underwear and pulled them up quickly, over my bottom, up my thighs, over my knees, to my calves, exposing me to the cool air. In the darkness, I saw him tilt his head, press my underwear to his nose and heard him inhale. Realising what he had done, the bile in my stomach rose again.

I tried to scream out for him to stop again, pleading with him to let me go. But he just ignored me. Helplessly, I watched as he undid his jeans and allowed them to fall to his ankles.

Grabbing my hips again, he pulled me up towards his groin. I could feel his hard erection against my inner thigh.

Without saying a word, he pushed himself into me, another groan of desire escaping him. I cried out in pain and wriggled as much as I could to pull away from him, but it only seemed to turn him on and make him more aroused. My screams and pleas for him to stop were useless.

I don't know how much time passed before I stopped fighting. It could have been a few minutes, or for an eternity. My body and mind had gone numb. Eventually, he stopped thrusting and pushed my hips away from his. Feeling humiliated and ashamed, I hoped it was over, but he roughly spun me over, curling my knees under me, causing my bottom to stick out the van door. Without my hands to support me, my face hit the filthy carpeted floor, the smell of dirt entering my nostrils.

Within seconds, he slammed himself forcefully back into me, over and over, his grunts of pleasure mocking me as I wept silently with shame.

With a final guttural roar, like a wild animal, and his movements finally coming to an end, he stood behind me, panting loudly, my bottom pressed tight against his groin. Slowing down his breathing, he ran his hand across my lower back.

"God, I've missed you!" he exclaimed, a sick hint of satisfaction in his voice, before pulling himself out of me and abruptly shoving my hips aside, causing me to fall over into the van. Laughing sadistically, he stepped back and slammed the door closed. A minute or two passed before I heard his footsteps move away from the door. Moments later, the van rocked as I felt his weight slide into the driver's seat. With a rev of the engine, and a crunch of the gear, I rocked sideways, as the van lurched forward.

Feeling emotionally and physically drained, I closed my eyes against the tears and allowed the rhythm of the van to rock me into merciful sleep.

Chapter 56

Monday, December 3rd

Martin was busy reviewing the surveillance Tony had provided him on Gavin's house. Nothing interesting happened over the weekend, it seemed. No movement from the house. No sign of Gavin anywhere. Just as he closed the file, his phone beeped, and Belinda spoke through the intercom.

"Martin, Sheriff Hadlock on line two."

"Thank you, Belinda." Raising his eyebrows, Martin smiled at the timing of the sheriff's call. He'd meant to call the Sheriff and inform him of the conversation he'd had last week with the bartender, and of the recent investigation he'd started. Although he wasn't one hundred percent certain he was on the right track, Martin's gut told him it would lead to some answers about the mystery girl, 'Amber Cooper' but he'd wanted to find out as much as he could, before making the call.

"Sheriff Hadlock, what can I do for you this early in the morning?" he said after picking up the phone.

"Detective, remember our mysterious lady, Amber Cooper?"

"Yes, I do."

"Well, I'm ringing to inform you she was kidnapped from a carnival here in Parker on Saturday night."

Martin sat up straight, his mouth agape as he grabbed for his notepad. "What happened?"

"A gentleman by the name of Craig Merrla, who is dating Amber, saw a large male pulling Amber away from the carnival. He gave chase and was unfortunately stabbed in an altercation with the other man. Inevitably, he saw Amber being pushed into a white van. Mr Merrla noticed the van had Missionly plates and saw advertising for 'Joe's Pluming' on the side."

"You don't say!" Martin hastily wrote down the two names.

"I was hoping, since the van was registered in your area, you could pinpoint the owner," the Sheriff asked confidently.

"Well, your timing couldn't be any more perfect, actually," Martin said, his voice full of relief.

"What do you mean?" The Sheriff's voice was filled with curiosity.

"I was planning on calling you today. A few weeks ago, I visited a bar in Barrister, after I received a tip off about a guy whose wife was missing. When I went to the bar, with the photo you gave me of your mystery girl, no one recognised her. I went twice, but had no luck, so didn't investigate further," he paused. "Well, last Thursday afternoon, I received a call from an anonymous lady. The woman, who I am fairly sure works at the pub, thought maybe the girl in the photo could be a customer she hasn't seen in a few weeks, named Rachel. Even more interesting, the customer's husband, Gavin Stowick, has now gone AWOL. The caller commented she noticed Mr Stowick's behaviour changed just before he abruptly stopping going to the pub."

"Changed in what way?"

"Visited more than normal and drank more, too. Became progressively volatile towards other patrons."

The sheriff was silent on the other end of the line for a moment. "Do you think Amber is Rachel, the missing wife from Barrister, then?"

"I can't confirm it, but it certainly looks that way. Rachel Stowick hasn't been seen in a few months, and Gavin Stowick stopped going to the pub a week and a half ago. You told me she had no identification on her. What are the chances she left him, but he never reported her absence? Noone seems to know where he is. What if he found out where she was and headed to Parker to *collect* her?"

"Well, that would be an interesting turn of events, for sure."

"Yes, it would. Sheriff, do you have a more recent photo of Amber?"

"I do. I can email it to you."

"Please. You also said the van was identified as Joe's Plumbing, yes?"

"That is correct."

"Okay. Leave this with me. I will investigate the van and get back to you as soon as I have some further information. I've already got a surveillance team watching Gavin Stowick's house. Mr Stowick owns a construction business. I can bet you anything, he knows who Joe the Plumber is and Joe knows the suspect."

After speaking to the Sheriff, he reopened the file and called Tony, requesting he see him as fast as possible. It was moments like this that Martin loved his job. When a case runs out of leads, then suddenly something new comes in weeks, months, sometimes even years later, spurring him on to solve the puzzle.

Today was one of those days. Martin could feel it. While waiting for Tony, he rang his wife, leaving her a message to say he would be home late. A few minutes later, Tony rushed through the door.

"What's up mate? What's the emergency?"

"You remember the case you brought to me a few months ago? The one involving a female who'd stolen a car, crashed it, and ended up in Parker with no memory?"

"Oh, yeah." Tony pulled up a chair. "Has something come up in the ID search?"

"Even worse, actually." Martin spun the laptop around, showing the photo of Amber Cooper in the hospital. "Well, apparently this young lady was kidnapped on Saturday night."

Tony's eyes it up. "You don't say!" A flicker of shock brushed over his face. "Do you know who did it?"

"No confirmation on the perpetrator, but I have a feeling we already know who did it. As per the witness to her kidnapping, the van is registered to Missionly, and we have a business name."

Tony leaned forward and listened closely as Martin relayed everything, including that he was waiting for the Sheriff to email him a more recent picture of Amber, along with the witness reports. After chatting for a few more minutes, Tony left with the name of the van to investigate, and Martin got to work.

This was going to be *a terribly busy day*, indeed.

Chapter 57

Wednesday, December 5ᵗʰ

My head thumped painfully.

What did we do last night?

Hazy images flashed through my mind, but nothing I could completely hold on to. The lights, rides, and music came to me, and I remembered going to the carnival. The day had been so wonderful, though the night seemed hazy.

Struggling to open my eyes, I opened my lips, but they cracked like dry sandpaper. Attempting to moisten them with my tongue was just as useless, my mouth dry. Swallowing, I tried to moisten my throat with what little saliva I had, my throat bobbing painfully.

I was hurting all over, though I struggled to recall why. I brought my hand up to my head and winced at how sensitive my temple was. Carefully, I tried to open my eyes, but struggled, as my left one was almost swollen shut. The pale light made it hard to take in my surroundings, and I sensed that it was still night. Moving my legs, feeling soft, cotton sheets beneath me, I realised I was in bed. Frowning, I didn't remember going home, and I certainly didn't remember climbing into bed.

What on earth had happened?

"Tracey?" I called out, my voice barely a whisper.

There was no reply. Taking a slow, deep breath, I tried to focus on my surroundings. As my eyes adjusted to the dim light shining into the room via the doorway, I noticed I wasn't in my room, yet there was a familiarity to it. Straining my ears, I heard voices coming from another room. Not voices of people talking, more like a television.

"Tracey!" I called out again, slightly louder. I managed to sit up, even though it caused a wave of nausea to rush through me. Gripping the blanket covering me, I slowed my breathing and waited for the pain and sick feeling to subside. My head pulsed painfully, and as I tightened my grip on the blanket, I felt something cold dig into the crease of my fourth finger on my left hand.

Opening my fist, I raised my hand to my face, with my palm facing me. I ran my thumb over the base of my finger and could feel bands of metal. I turned my hand over and in the dim light, saw two rings. Frowning, I tried to remember where they came from. They weren't there this morning.

Images flickered into my mind as I tried to piece them together.

A man pushed these rings on my finger! He yelled at me! Told me never to take them off!

It was weird. I never recognised the man, yet he seemed to know who I was. Other images returned, too ... I was waiting for my food when a stranger started talking to me. I remembered being pulled behind the food van, the stranger so strong, telling me not to yell out. The nausea returned as I saw visions of Craig laying on the grass, bleeding, yelling at the man to leave me alone. The noise of the carnival, the music, snippets of images flashing between the pain. My memory was foggy, which only added to my confusion.

But the more I recalled the events, the more memories returned, of the back of a van, of the man striking me. Being violated and raped. I knew now that the pain in my arms and shoulders was a result of the man binding my hands behind me.

So, where was I? How long had I been gone for?

The room suddenly darkened as a figure appeared in the doorframe.

"Craig, is that you?" I asked, trying to see his face in the dark. He didn't respond. "Hello, Craig?" Instinctively, I knew it wasn't him, and I tried not to t cry, as I stared at the ominous silhouette.

"Oh, please, Rachel!" The man scoffed. "Enough of these games!"

Abruptly, the room lit up, momentarily blinding me. I squinted until eyes focused, and I found myself looking at the face of the man who'd pushed me into a van.

An intense rush of fear pulsated through me as I took in his features, and my jaw dropped open. In less than a second, all my forgotten memories snapped back into place.

Standing in the doorway was the man I had escaped from. The man I had so desperately wanted to be free of. My breath caught in my throat as fear and anxiety buzzed through my body.

He's found me! He's brought me back home.

My best friend, my high school sweetheart. My lover. My abuser. My rapist.

My husband, Gavin Stowick.

Chapter 58

Wednesday, December 5th

"Gavin!" I exclaimed, looking at him with wide eyes.

"Ah, you finally remember me!" he said, as he casually slid his left hand into his jeans pocket. "Hello, Rachel. Welcome home!"

I stared at him, not knowing what to say as he remained in the doorway, staring back. Feeling frightened, I rubbed my thumb against the base of the rings on my finger.

"You found my rings!" I said, trying desperately to sound calm.

"You never lost them, Rachel." He scratched at his cheek and sighed as he glared at me. "I just didn't think you deserved to wear them before."

"And now?" I asked nervously, glancing back to the engagement and wedding ring I thought I'd lost a few years ago.

"Well, it seems you need to be reminded of why you live with me." He took a few steps into the room but stopped as I instinctively tried to shift away from him.

"You need to stop being afraid of me, Rachel. I'm your husband." He took two more strides—he was less than a meter from me now.

I closed my eyes and turned my face away, waiting for the blow. My face was still sore and swollen from the punches and slaps I'd received from him at the Carnival and in the van. When nothing happened, I tentatively opened my eyes and looked back at him.

"You deserved those hits before, but I'm not here to hit you again. You know I don't like having to use my hands, but ... sometimes, Rachel ... you just don't seem to appreciate what you have," he said, pointing his finger at me.

I heard the anger in his words. I dropped my gaze, knowing they were nothing but lies.

"Look at me, Rachel!" he snapped. I lifted my head and shifted my gaze back to Gavin's face, forcing myself to stare into the eyes of the man I once loved a long time ago.

"You left me! You were gone for months. Why did you leave?" he asked, glaring at me. I lowered my eyes, not wanting him to see the anger and pain in them. "Answer me, Rachel!" As he took a step closer to the bed, I once again pulled away from him and closed my eyes, waiting for him to hurt me again.

Although I tried hard not to cry, a single tear rolled down my cheek and Gavin took two steps backwards. Still not wanting to look at him, I sat in silence. What could I say to him? He was a bad husband. Abusive. And I didn't want to live this way anymore. It wouldn't matter what I had said, Gavin would never forgive me for leaving, and he certainly wouldn't let me leave again.

"You need to get up now," Gavin said, breaking the silence. "It's getting late and I'm hungry. It's been a while since I had a nice, hot, home-cooked meal."

Without waiting for a response, Gavin turned and started walking out of the room, but before he left, he paused and looked over his shoulder, his hand resting on the door frame.

"As for your friend Craig," he taunted. "You can forget about him. I doubt you'll ever see him again!"

He stormed off, thankfully out of my sight. I let out a breath I didn't realise I'd held and closed my eyes. Images of Craig rushed to the forefront of my mind. Fighting the tears and clenching my hands, all I could do was pray he was okay.

Did anyone help him? Did he survive the stabbing? Was he even alive?

I forced myself to calm my rapid breathing, slowly inhaling through my nose and exhaling through my mouth, counting to three each time.

I escaped before. I could get away again. I need to get back to Parker, to get in contact with Tracey and find out if Craig is okay.

I felt torn between wanting to stay in bed and hide and wanting to get up and make a run for it. Yet, I knew it wouldn't be worth the aggravation. Gavin would be waiting for me to try it, and he used to warn me not to push his buttons. I knew the consequences if I did. If I was to escape him again, I had to time it perfectly, like I did so many months ago. For now, I had no choice but to play the game once more, except this time, I'd play by my own rules.

Ha! Play by my own rules!

My thoughts mocked me as I moved slightly, wincing against the muscular aches in my body. Who was I to defend myself? I'd run away and look where it got me. I got caught. Gavin found me and if he'd done it once, he would do it again.

Feeling defeated, I threw back the blanket and slowly swung my bare legs over the edge of the bed. Glancing down, Gavin had dressed me in one of my black silk nighties.

Bloody creep! The nerve of him.

Shaking my head in disbelief, I gently stood, slowly stretching out my limbs.

How long had we been on the road? Had I been in the back of the van, hog-tied the whole time?

Avoiding the mirror on the wall, as I really didn't want to see what he'd done to my face, I wrapped myself up in the matching black silk dressing gown, Gavin had deliberately hung on the hook near the closet door and walked slowly out of the bedroom towards the kitchen.

This was my life, apparently. I'd taught myself to keep my head down. Ensured the house was always clean, laundry done. Dinners cooked every night, and a healthy lunch prepared for Gavin, for the next day.

I fulfilled my wifely duties each night, whether I was in the mood for it or not, because knowing if I didn't, he'd take what he wanted anyway, with an extra bit of pain to remind me, he ruled the house.

Padding barefoot down the familiar wooden floorboards and into the kitchen, I stopped and stared in awe at the mess which awaited me. I could see there'd been some attempt made to clean the kitchen, but dirty pots and plates sat piled in the sink, and a thin layer of grime covered the countertop. Sighing with defeat, I approached the fridge first.

I dug through the freezer, finding some mince and popped it into the microwave to thaw out. Filling the sink with hot, soapy water, I cleaned a pot and placed it onto the stove and filled with water to boil some pasta. While waiting for the meat to thaw, I scrubbed everything that had been in the sink, dried it all, put everything away and cleaned the counter tops.

Glancing through the dining room towards the lounge room, I stared the black hair on Gavin's head and at his shoulders, as he lent back on the couch. Although he was watching TV, I had no doubt, he was, in fact, listening intently to what I was doing.

I'd been gone for almost four months. What had he done during that time? I thought. *How did he find me? If I was a few states away, how did he track me down?* My brow creased with curiosity.

"Gavin?" I spoke carefully.

"Yeah?" his deep voice responded.

"What day it is?"

"Why?" He turned his head and looked towards me, his brow creasing.

"Just trying to figure out where we are in the week," I replied, hoping to keep him calm.

"It's Wednesday," he replied, sounding bored.

"Oh, thanks." My brow creased deeper. The Summer carnival had been four days ago. I'd not remembered most of the drive home.

Without fail, he picked up on my facial expression. "I had to drug you. You were making things ... difficult," he said, giving me a look of irritation, before turning back to face the television, as though it were nothing. Memories of the bitter aftertaste in the orange juice swam into my memory. Not only had he kidnapped me, beat me, tied me up, and raped me, he'd drugged me as well.

Just when I thought he couldn't get any worse!

Thinking on the amnesia, which had fogged my memories over the past few months. I realised my mind had shut off for a reason—to prevent me from remembering the horrible life I'd lived. The amnesia had given me the opportunity to see there was a better life for me.

There was a guy out there who didn't abuse his power, his strength or take advantage of his 'manly duties'. There were people who cared about me, who liked me and wanted to spend time with me. I realised as I started cooking dinner just how lonely my life over the past ten years really was. Staring at the back of Gavin's head, I thought about how much I hated him.

Of course, it hadn't always been so bad. Gavin and I met at high school in our senior year. I wouldn't say it was love at first sight, but I found him attractive, and he was one of the popular boys in school. We started dating towards the end of the year, and by the time we finished school and graduated, we were very much in love.

Then Gavin told me he wanted us to be together forever, and I was the happiest girl in the world.

Our life together started off happy and normal. I got a job at the local supermarket, and Gavin attended Trade school and worked hard, completing a trade certificate in four years. I progressed to another job, working for a daycare centre, four days a week.

On my twenty-second birthday, Gavin proposed, and I said yes, against my mother's wishes.

"You're too young, and I'm not sure he's right for you."

But I believed I knew better than her, and we married six months later. How little I knew then. But how much more I know now.

It wasn't long after we married, Gavin bought our house. As a builder, he'd taken over his father's business, employed a few of his close mates, and built up a rather impressive company, which earned him a large amount of money. Plus, since the house was on the small side and a little run down, Gavin renovated it at a cheaper price.

Now it was a nice three-bedroom, two-bathroom house, with a large, open-plan kitchen, dining room and lounge. Perfect for entertaining. Pity we never had anyone over.

My family stopped coming to visit a few years after we got married. I hadn't seen my mum in about two years. Gavin made most of my family feel unwelcome in our house, and over the course of our marriage, they visited less and less. This also included most of my childhood girlfriends. Although a few of my friends married some of Gavin's mates, we never got the time to see each other anymore, except for our weekly dinners at Holman's Pub each Sunday night.

We were three years into the marriage, when Gavin hit me for the first time. We had gone out to dinner with friends, and he'd been drinking. When we got home, we got into a small argument. Gavin took offence to a comment I made about one of his friends, and for that, he slapped me across the face, hard enough to rattle my teeth. The next morning, a large bruise shone across my cheek.

Although he muttered a weak apology the next day, seeing the bruise, it was the last time he did. It was also the moment our marriage took a turn for the worst. The hits, slaps and punches happened after Gavin drank heavily, which at first, wasn't often. But as the years passed, the abuse became more frequent.

Gavin, without fail, never blamed himself, or the alcohol, for his behaviour. Instead, he made sure I knew it was my fault. Gaslighting me and making me feel like I would not be able to survive in this world without him.

'*If you just did what I asked, I wouldn't have hit you.*' He would say casually, or '*God, you are so pathetic. Can't you do anything right?*' The most common reason for hitting me was, '*Sometimes, Rachel, you just need to learn to shut your fucking mouth!*'

My husband crushed my self-esteem, made me feel worthless, and over time, I believed him.

During our marriage, I lost three babies. Each time, it was at the hands of my *loving* husband. The first two times, we'd just found out I was pregnant, but in a fit of rage and anger, accusing me of cheating on him, he beat me, and, like most times, he punched or kicked me in my stomach, inevitably causing the miscarriages.

The third loss I hadn't told him about. I remained pregnant until I was almost three months, a few weeks longer than the others, but in another fight, in another moment, where he blamed me for forgetting to buy a few things, Gavin pushed me, and I fell hard against our square dining table. My stomach slammed into the corner. I knew then that pregnancy wouldn't last either.

That was my wake-up call. That was the moment I knew I needed to get away from him.

Chapter 59

Saturday, December 8th

I hated to admit it to myself, but life with Gavin quickly fell back into the same routine as it was before. Gavin punished me a few more times, punching and hitting me across my back, my stomach, and my thighs. All the places he knew the bruising wouldn't be visible to anyone else. Not that he let me out of the house. Or let anyone else in either.

He took another week off work, telling everyone I'd gone to visit my family, but came home *unwell* and he wanted to *look after me.*

It seemed his favourite thing now was to show me *just how much he loved me.* And *how much he had missed me* by forcing himself on me any chance he got. I couldn't even bathe on my own, without Gavin coming into the bathroom, joining me in the shower, and pushing me up against the wall, spreading my legs apart and thrusting himself into me.

It didn't matter if I tried to push him away. In fact, the harder I fought, the more it seemed to encourage him. This morning, I gave up fighting. I didn't bother to push him away. I just lay in the bed; face turned to the window and willed my mind to drift away to the pond where I'd enjoyed a beautiful picnic with the man, I now believed I would never see again.

As I stood in the kitchen half an hour later, preparing breakfast, my resilience broke. My will to keep fighting completely shattered as silent tears ran down my face.

Feeling deflated and run-down, washing the dishes, I heard a sound which ignited a memory as bright as sunshine. A single sound. A simple sound. The familiar noise triggered a fresh onslaught of emotions. My eyes widened as I desperately peered through the kitchen window into the backyard.

Sitting on the lawn only a few meters from the back veranda, sat a large, ginger tabby with a snow-white chest and small, white, furry socks on its front paws. Not my cat, but I knew him well. He belonged to the neighbour who lived behind us, but he visited me almost every day.

He was a very smart cat. A very brave cat. He learned quickly to stay hidden when Gavin was around. He'd been kicked before by him, just for being in his yard. But the cat loved me as much as I loved him.

Gavin wouldn't allow me to have any pets, saying '*They're too expensive, and I don't have the time to clean up after them!*' Not that he would have looked after them. I would have done all the work—feeding them, cleaning up after them. He would have ignored the pet, anyway.

This cat, who I called Mr Floofy, started visiting me about three years ago. He'd jumped over the fence, and eventually, as I gained his trust, would sit in my lap while I enjoyed my daily cups of tea. Each time he turned up in the garden, he would meow, announcing his arrival.

Looking up at me through the window, he meowed again. I grinned, unable to hide my joy in connecting the details of the mysterious cat meows I'd heard while I was in Parker. Doctor Wilkins was right. My memory had tried to trigger something deep within me. The cat meows were memories of Mr Floofy.

Casually, I turned around to see what Gavin was doing and saw him sitting on the couch watching the television. I glanced around the kitchen, trying to find a reason to go outside, knowing he tracked my every movement throughout the house. Yet, I needed to go outside and greet the wonderful cat, who must have missed our daily catchups.

My eyes fell on the rubbish bin, and I stepped over to it, opened the lid and took out the bag, making enough noise so Gavin would know what I was doing.

"Just taking the rubbish out," I called as I walked over to the glass sliding door, which lead outside.

"Yeah," he replied, not moving from the couch.

As soon as Mr Floofy saw me, he ran over and followed me to the main rubbish bin at the side of the garage. No sooner had I thrown the bag into the bin, Mr Floofy was rubbing his face and body across my legs, mewling softly, letting me know how much he had missed me. I picked him up gently, burying my face into his warm fur and kissed his little face.

"Ah kitty, I've missed you. You have no idea what I've been through. Did you come visit me every day?" I asked, giving the back of his head a good scratch. Mr Floofy responded with more mewls and started purring loudly. "I can't sit with you today, sorry, and maybe not even tomorrow, but soon kitty, soon." I bent down and placed him back on the grass and made my way back to the porch. He watched me walk away but didn't follow. It was like he knew something wasn't right. I returned to the kitchen and resumed washing the dishes, unable to remove a large grin.

Thinking back to those months I was away; I was surprised Mr Floofy returned after my long absence. It was nice to see him again, and it brought me comfort, knowing he never gave up on me.

Finishing the dishes, I moved to the laundry still smiling to myself as I loaded the washer and turned it on.

Maybe this is a sign that things might get better. Maybe this is the nudge I need to get away from this house again.

Knowing Gavin had a tighter leash on me now only inspired me to push harder to break away again. But this time, I refused to go silently.

This time, when I left, I'd go straight to the police. *This time*, Gavin would be the one who suffered. There was no way in hell that I'd spend the rest of my life as his property to control and abuse!

Chapter 60

Monday, December 10ᵗʰ - 11.30am

After talking to Sheriff Hadlock again, Martin was eager to find Amber—or Rachel.

The information the Sheriff passed on the previous week gave him a good place to jump back into his search. With the updated photo he received, along with the witness report, he'd rung Tony, to see if he'd investigated the white van logo 'Joe's Plumbing'.

As things were, Tony had located the address of the van the next day. Within the hour, Martin set up a surveillance team at the house of the van owner and discovered he was a colleague of Gavin's. During the surveillance, Tony discovered that the co-worker was also driving Gavin's work ute. Martin nodded his head in confirmation. Gavin Stowick was now the prime suspect in this case.

Martin's team, who were already watching Gavin's house, informed him when Gavin arrived home late Wednesday afternoon, but noted he was alone in his Ute. He was seen a few times at the house but only briefly, taking the bin out for collection, or answering the door when a driver dropped off food grocery bags. Though not once did he leave the premises.

Now, five days later, Martin planned to confront the man, to see if he was in any way involved with the kidnapping of Amber. Although no-one by Amber's description had arrived or left the house in the past few days, Martin could not wait any longer.

Gathering his coat, keys, wallet and phone, Martin got into his car and drove to the side street, where Tony and two other police officers were already waiting. Hoping this would be a straightforward situation, Martin pulled up behind Tony's car and walked calmly towards the other officers.

"How is it looking?" Martin asked, as he approached the car Tony was hiding behind.

"Quiet," Tony replied, watching Martin crouch down beside him. "No-one has left the house at all today, nor yesterday. He's definitely in there."

"Okay, that's good." Martin nodded his head and peered through the car window towards the house.

"What's your plan?" Tony asked.

"I was thinking I might just knock on the door and chat to Gavin. Find out if his wife is home. Hopefully without too much drama," Martin said confidently.

"Okay. Whenever you're ready." Tony checked his weapon, unclipped the holster strap, and moved towards the front of the car.

Although the street was quiet, there were additional police officers positioned at either ends of the road, closing it off to any local traffic, as well as a second team, composed of three other officers, waiting a few houses away. There was no way Martin wanted things to go wrong and a general member of the public to get caught up in the crossfire. It wouldn't go down well. Better to play it safe.

On Martin's signal, both his, and the second team slowly made their way towards Gavin's house, hiding behind cars, trees, and bushes.

Martin was not a fan of violent confrontations, but in his line of work, these moments kept him on edge. Even planning things to the finest detail, something could go wrong. Breathing slowly, Martin confidently walked up the driveway, towards the house. Behind him, Tony and the other officers waited patiently. Hopefully, Martin would have the issue resolved in a few minutes.

As he walked towards the door, Martin glanced at the window but couldn't see into the house. The curtains were drawn. He thought it odd, seeing how it was a nice, sunny day, and instinctively, his senses heightened. Listening carefully, Martin noted there were no sounds coming from inside the house as he reached the door.

Glancing back down the road one last time, Martin stepped up to the door, squared his shoulders, took a deep breath, and knocked twice. He waited a few moments and knocked again. Looking back down the road towards the car Tony hid behind, Martin shrugged. Tony motioned back to try one more time.

This time, as Martin knocked on the door, he also called out. "Gavin Stowick! My name is Detective Martin Collins, and I just want to chat with you, please."

Silence was all Martin got in response. He knocked one more time. "Gavin, I know you're home. I just want to talk."

Suddenly, from inside the house, Martin heard a loud commotion. A female's voice screamed out, pleading for help, followed by a loud crash and a male's voice, yelling at the female to shut up. Without a second thought, Martin tried to open the front door, only to find it locked. Feeling an adrenaline rush kick in, he slammed his shoulder against the secured door, desperately trying to force it open.

Within seconds, Tony and the other officers sprinted towards the house, their weapons drawn, and back-up called.

Chapter 61

Monday, December 10th - 11:40am

"Help me!" I screamed hoping, to alert the detective at the door.

Gavin lunged over the dining table, charged towards me in the kitchen, and pushed me against the fridge, slamming my back into the handle.

"Shut up!" he growled, firmly clasping his hand over my mouth.

I fought against his grip, twisting and turning my face until I managed to open my mouth a little. I felt one of Gavin's fingers slip in and, using this opportunity, I clamped down and bit hard. Gavin screamed out in pain and shock and yanked his middle finger out from between my teeth.

"You bitch!" He slapped me hard across the face. My vision darkened as the hot sting radiated across my cheek. Gavin grabbed me again, pulling me away from the fridge, twisting me around, and rammed me face first against the kitchen counter. He pushed my face down against the countertop, crushing my cheek, as my knees smashed into the cupboard doors, causing my legs to buckle.

"Keep your goddamn mouth shut!" he snarled close to my ear, his hand holding my head still.

As I lay against the counter, the pain in my cheek extending to my jaw, Gavin lay down on my back, preventing me from moving. The weight of his body against mine restricted my breath, and I couldn't get enough air in my lungs.

Help me, please help me. I screamed over and over in my head. I needed to get out from under him, but I was too scared to move. Fear had set in, and my body froze under Gavin's.

With my heart beating faster and the sound of each beat resonating in my ears, the banging at the front door became louder and more insistent.

"Fuck!" he growled as he lifted his head slightly, and I could feel his body shift as he began looking around the room.

"Gavin Stowick! Open the door!" the detective's voice called out, followed by another loud bang. I didn't know how much longer the door would hold.

"Let go of me!" I screamed as I tried to free myself from under Gavin's weight. Shifting his body back, he pushed his legs into the back of mine, pinning them against the cupboards. With his hand still pushing my head down onto the countertop, he moved slightly off me, as his other hand reached out,

"Come on!" he yelled before I heard the distinct sound of metal scrapping across the counter.

Oh my god, he has a knife!

My eyes widened as my heart skipped. A sudden rush of adrenaline pulsed through my muscles, and I snapped, knowing this was the moment I needed to fight for my life. This would be the last time I was ever going to let my husband hurt me!

Having felt Gavin ease off my back when he reached over for the knife block, I slipped my hands under my hips and gripped the edge of the counter. Feeling me wiggle beneath him, he pushed me back down.

"Don't move!" he whispered, his voice trembling in desperation.

Waiting a few seconds and feigning surrender, I let my body slacken until I felt Gavin relax his grip on my head and move slightly off me again. Then, with an almighty push, I forced my arms and legs to straighten, throwing him off me, and causing him to lose his footing. It was enough motion that I could twist sideways, out of his grasp and away from the counter. At that same moment, the front door burst open with a deafening crack, and a thundering of footsteps charged into the house.

"Rachel Stowick?" a different male called out.

"In the kitchen!" I called back before Gavin grabbed me once more, twisting me around and pulling me back against his chest.

"Don't you move!" Gavin called out as two officers ran into the lounge. They halted abruptly in the dining room, as they saw the large carving knife Gavin pressed against my throat.

"Put it down, Gavin," the taller of the two officers said, his gun aimed at Gavin. I stared at his business suit and tie; *this must have been the detective who first called out.*

"You first!" Gavin spat back, spittle wetting my cheek, as he pushed the blade harder against my neck. I winced at the unexpected sting of pain as the tip of the blade pierced my skin. I stopped squirming.

"Let her go, Gavin," the second officer pleaded, similarly dressed in a business suit, his gun also aimed at Gavin.

"Fuck you. Get out of my house!" he screamed, his chest rising and falling faster against my back.

I stared at both men, my wide eyes pleading for them to help me. Within seconds, three more officers, dressed in police uniforms, entered the house, stopping abruptly behind the first two as they assessed the situation.

Gavin shuffled sideways, pulling me along, trying to move out of the kitchen and into the passageway, which lead down to the back of the house.

"You need to let her go, Gavin," the first man said, slowly tracking Gavin with his gun.

"You need to leave! This is none of your business." Gavin dragged me backwards, moving away from the kitchen entrance. My feet stumbled on the tiles as my eyes flicked to the police officers, silently pleading as I tried to convey my desperation. The detective moved forward; his eyes shifting from mine to Gavin.

"Take another step and I'll cut her throat!" he barked, pulling me closer to him and readjusting the knife.

"Okay, okay!" the first man said, stopping in his tracks and slowly raising his hands in the air, removing his aim off Gavin. "We'll do this your way." He straightened and stared at Gavin, as though trying to gain Gavin's trust. Seeing Gavin pause, slightly loosening his grip on the knife, the man hesitantly shifted his gaze back to me, his green eyes looking at me with warmth, trying to re-assure me.

But the momentary calmness shattered as the back door was thrown open and the sounds of more heavy footsteps echoed through the laundry. Jumping with fright and tightening his grip on me again, Gavin swung me around to find three more police offices facing us in the passageway.

"Get back!" he screamed, his voice booming above my ear. They halted, guns raised, waiting for a command.

"Stay where you are!" Gavin pressed the knife harder into me, the blade slicing deeper into my skin, and I screamed as I felt the thick, warm blood trickle down my neck.

Gavin spun us back around to face the men and officers standing in the lounge and dining room. "Tell them all to get out!" he ordered, his voice quivering slightly, as he dragged me back into the kitchen and out of the view of the men in the passageway.

"Gavin ..." the second man said, his voice calm but stern. "She's bleeding."

There was a moment's pause as Gavin slightly released the pressure of the knife against my skin before he swore under his breath. I felt him tense, and he pulled me closer to his body, his arm painfully digging across my waist.

"Gavin," pleaded the detective. "I know you don't want to hurt her, so you need to let her go. She needs help now. And while my men look after her, you and I, we can just talk."

The atmosphere in the room was intense, and the silence became overwhelming. I could feel Gavin's heart thumping rapidly against my upper back, almost matching the rhythm of my own pounding heart. His breath whirred across the top of my hair, his breathing speeding up, almost hyperventilating, as I felt him look wildly around the room at the five intruders standing in the front of our house.

Adding to the tension, I could hear sirens wailing in the distance, and I felt him trembling against me.

"I said, tell them all to get out!" he groaned, and I heard the quiver again in his voice. Abruptly, Gavin raised his left hand from my waist and cupped it around my throat, press his fingers against the wound on my neck. Moving his other arm down, Gavin pressed the knife against my abdomen.

"Gavin, please," I begged. "Let me go." I tried placed my hand around his wrist, to pull his arm and the knife away from me, but I had little strength to move it.

"This is all your fault!" he lowered his head and growled into my ear. "None of this would have happened if you hadn't left me!"

"And now I'm back. I won't leave you again," I said softly, trying to convince him. "Everything will be okay." I tilted my head back, trying to make eye contact with him.

"Liar!" he screamed at me. "You are nothing but a lying whore!" His grip on my throat tightened, crushing my neck, and stopping my breath.

Feeling like this was the moment I was going to die, another rush of adrenaline buzzed through me, and I knew I had to get away. In one swift motion, I twisted and pulled my head away, loosening my neck from his grasp, and thrust my hips against Gavin, turning sideways. Suddenly, I felt a sharp, unusual pain in my right side and my breath caught in my lungs. Unsure what had happened, I stared at the officers with wide eyes, as the entire room seemed to slow down.

Instinctively, yet feeling like I was moving through water, I brought my hands to my waist, and as my legs gave out, a deafening *bang* echoed through the kitchen, followed by a loud clatter, as something heavy hit the ground. As I collapsed to my knees on the kitchen floor, I felt Gavin slip away from behind me. Dropping my head and glancing at my hands, I watched as my pretty yellow dress turned a dark shade of crimson.

"It's okay now, Rachel, you're going to be fine." I heard a voice say close to me. I looked up through hazy vision into the green eyes of the man who first ran into the house. He knelt in front of me. "My name is Detective Martin Collins, and I need you to take nice slow breaths, okay" He pushed his hand on top of mine, putting pressure on my stomach. A sudden bolt of pain ran through my body, and I gasped aloud.

"It's all right, it's all okay. There's an ambulance on the way." He kept his hand on mine, while the other man, who first entered with the detective, came and placed his hand gently on my throat.

"Is your name Rachel Stowick?" the second man asked. I nodded slowly. "Have you even been known as Amber Cooper?" he inquired, talking calmly to me.

"Yes," I whispered back.

"It's nice to meet you, Rachel. My name is Detective Tony Smitten. You're going to be fine, ma'am." He smiled at me, his blue eyes softening.

I tried to move, but both men held me down. "Try to keep still. You're bleeding heavily and we need you to stay where you are," Detective Collins said calmly, placing a soft hand on my knee. I nodded towards him, feeling lightheaded but incredibly grateful.

"Thank you," I whispered, my voice sounding far away.

"You are very welcome," the tone of Detective Collin's voice soothed me, relaxed me, as the adrenaline slowly left my body.

Trying not to think about the blood seeping out of me, the sounds of scuttling and grunting redirected my focus. I turned my head towards the other side of the kitchen. Writhing and twisting on the floor, I watched Gavin fight against two police officers as a dark pool of blood spread across the clean, white tiles beneath him.

My eyes blinked heavily as the room tilted. There was too much noise. Too many voices were shouting; the light was too bright; the floor was too cold; and my body, too heavy. I closed my eyes, wishing it would all go away.

"Open your eyes, Rachel. Come on, stay with us!" The Detective's voice sounded distorted and far away. The pain in my body intensified, and it felt harder to breathe. My legs felt numb, and although I could see my feet, they felt so light. I was tired, so tired.

I closed my eyes one last time, as my consciousness finally gave out. Faintly, in the distance, I heard a man scream my name.

Chapter 62

Tuesday, December 11th - 10:15am

On the fourth ring, Tracey answered her mobile phone. "Hello, Tracey speaking."

"Tracey, Sheriff Hadlock here."

Tracey's heart raced when she heard his name. "Hello Sheriff. have you heard anything?" she asked hesitantly, her palms beginning to sweat.

"Indeed, I have."

Tracey listened intently to the sheriff as he explained everything that had happened since the last time they had spoken. By the end of the conversation, Tracey could no longer hold back the tears as she hung up the phone. Needing to breathe and calm herself down, she sat in the chair at the table for five minutes, her hands filled with moist tissues.

Once she regained her composure and dried her eyes, Tracey picked up her phone and quickly scrolled through her small red phone book, searching for Craig's name. Locating his number, she dialled and waited patiently for him to answer. It didn't take long before she heard his voice on the other end.

"Tracey!" he blurted.

"Yes, it's me."

"Have you heard anything?" His voice filled with concern.

"I think you'd better come over. I'd rather talk to you face to face than over the phone."

"Oh God, no!" his voice dropped to a whisper. "Tell me she's okay!"

"Just come on over. I'll be waiting for you on the front porch."

Craig hung up the phone and Tracey sat at the table, wondering how she'd explain the situation to him. After a few minutes, she got up quickly and started fussing about the kitchen, humming to distract herself from her thoughts. Opening the fridge, she grabbed a few items, then a plate from the cupboard. Anything to keep her hands and her mind busy. Within a few minutes, she was outside, standing on the porch, waiting for Craig.

Arriving ten minutes later, Craig jumped out of his car and ran up the path to the porch where Tracey waited. He hugged her tightly, his heart racing faster than ever, and didn't let go, until she pushed him back slightly, and motioned for him to sit in one of the cane chairs. Walking beside her, he noticed as he sat down, set up on the small outdoor coffee table, was a jug of orange juice, two glasses and a plate full of assorted biscuits.

He turned tentatively to Tracey, trying his best to read her expression. "Please, Tracey." he pleaded, his eyes searching her face for the unwelcome news. "Please tell me she's okay!"

"Sit," she told him, taking a seat herself.

Craig watched her face, trying to read her expression, as she poured the juice into the glasses.

"They found her," she said, her voice calm as she passed him a glass.

Craig sighed deeply, desperate to ease his nerves and with shaking hands, took the glass and rested it on his knee.

"Now, I want you to listen carefully." Tracey looked at him, waiting for him to nod before she continued. "She's okay, but she was hurt and is currently in hospital."

"No." Craig's eyes widened, and he almost spilt his drink, his hands shaking in fear.

"It's okay." She leant over and gently patted his thigh. "She's okay."

"What happened?" Craig asked.

"She was stabbed in the stomach and has a cut on her throat, but she's fine." Tracey watched as Craig's face turned ashen, as his hand instinctively moved to his own stab wound. "She's had surgery, and it went well. She's getting the best care."

He closed his eyes for a moment, breathing through his nose, to keep his anxiety down, remembering the moment he realised he'd been hurt. "Where is she?" he asked, finally opening his eyes.

"She's in a hospital in Missionly."

"Missionly!" Craig looked out towards the road and took a deep breath, filling his lungs, before exhaling slowly. "That's so far away!"

"Yes, it is." Tracey sighed deeply.

"How did she get there?" He asked, turning back to face her.

Tracey offered him a biscuit. "Eat. This is not a good story, I'm afraid." Craig frowned but took a biscuit, anyway.

"The guy who kidnapped Amber was her husband, and drove her back home, to their house in Barrister, just outside Missionly." She placed the plate back on the table, picked up a biscuit herself, and leaned back into the chair.

Craig choked on the half-eaten biscuit as he looked at her with wide eyes. Carefully, he sipped his drink, washing the biscuit down, before placing the glass onto the table and slowly looking up at Tracey. "She's married ..." he uttered. "So, he was right, when he called her, his wife." he added, nodding his head.

"Yes, from what Sheriff Hadlock told me, Amber, or Rachel, her actual name, ran away from her abusive husband and ended up here in Parker. From what he knows, they've been married for about ten years; they were high school sweethearts. Eventually Amber, oh sorry, Rachel, must have had enough of his abuse and escaped. She stole a car and drove through three states to get away. Her husband somehow found out where she was and, as you know, took her back."

She paused, looking at Craig with compassion, allowing him time to take it all in.

"She stole the car!" A small chuckle escaped him as he smiled. "I *was* dating a car thief!"

"Apparently," Tracey smiled too, seeing the humour in Craig's comment. "I guess she was desperate."

"And this guy ... her husband." Craig's face went serious again. "How *did* he find her?"

"I don't know the details or how he ended up here in Parker. Sheriff Hadlock didn't comment on that."

"And is he the one who stabbed her?" he asked, his hands trembling slightly.

"Yes. There was an ... altercation at their house when the police showed up, and Amber was stabbed by her husband."

"And what about him?" Craig's asked.

Tracey shook her head. "I don't know. The sheriff wouldn't tell me."

Craig nodded, "Okay, so what now? Am I able to see her?" he asked, sitting forward in the chair, the half-drunk glass of orange juice still resting on his knee.

"I don't see why not." Tracey said, finishing her juice. Craig smiled; his heart raced at the thought of seeing her again.

"Does she understand what's happened?" he asked. "This whole thing might be very scary and overwhelming for her."

"Oh, yeah." Tracey's eyes lit up, knowing there was a positive side to these unfortunate events. "Her memory returned. She remembered everything once she woke up in her house."

"Oh, wow. That would have been horrible." Craig sighed with relief, but his heart dropped with trepidation.

"I dare say, yes. I was thinking ..." she paused, looking at Craig with a hint of eagerness about her. "If you're interested, maybe the two of us should fly out to see her. I don't know what will happen next, but I'm sure she'd be happy to see us again. I know I will be happy to see her."

Craig's face lit up. "Yes. Yes, please. I think that's a great idea." His face slackened and his shoulders dropped at the suggestion.

Lifting the glass, and drinking the rest of the orange juice, all Craig could think of now, was how quickly could he get to her and tell her how much he loved her. How sorry he was he couldn't protect her, and how much he never wanted to let her go-ever again.

Chapter 63

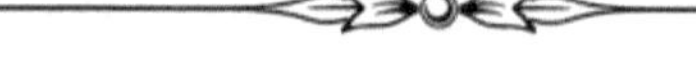

Tuesday, December 11ᵗʰ - 2:30pm

Opening my eyes and allowing them to focus, I glanced around the brightly lit hospital room, and my heart skipped a beat. Panic and confusion hit me in one second.

Where am I? Am I back in Parker?

Just as I was about to search for a remote, hoping Tracey would come to my aid, I heard a knock on the door. I glanced up to see two well-dressed gentlemen standing in the doorway.

"Good afternoon, Rachel. How are you feeling?" The taller of the two men spoke.

"Sore," I frowned a little, not recognising them.

"I can imagine. Do you remember who I am?" he asked as he walked into the room, pulled up a chair, and placed it next to my bed. I shook my head. "That's okay. A lot has happened in the past twenty-four hours," he said with a warm smile. "My name is Detective Martin Collins, and this gentleman behind me is Detective Tony Smitten." He indicated to the other officer standing behind him. "We are the two officers who entered your house yesterday afternoon." Detective Smitten gave me a small wave and nodded his head.

A flash of recognition of the chaos of yesterday morning suddenly played out in my head. "Oh, it's you two." I tried to sit up a little more in bed, but a jolt of pain rippled through my stomach.

"Stay there." Detective Martin moved forward and placed his hand on mine, calming me. "It's okay. We wanted to check in on you. See how things are and ... have a little chat if you are up to it."

"Thank you, thank you both for rescuing me!" Tears sprang forth and ran down my cheeks.

"It was our pleasure," Detective Tony said quietly.

"You've been a hard person to identify, Mrs Stowick," Detective Martin said, looking at me, his eyebrows raised.

"Oh, please don't call me that!" I shook my head again in disgust. "And what do you mean, I was hard to identify?"

"Oh, I'm sorry. Is Rachel, or Amber, okay?"

"Rachel is fine."

The detective sighed. "We work for the Bureau of Investigation. I work in the Missing Persons Unit, while Detective Smitten works in the Traffic Unit. A few months ago, we received your hospital picture from the Sheriff in Parker, and until just a few days ago, we had no idea who you were."

"Really? You've had my picture since then?" My eyes widened.

"Yes, but unfortunately, we didn't have much else to go on. Just that you had been in an accident in a stolen vehicle, in Parker, and you had amnesia." He looked at me with a soft kindness in his eyes. "So, if you can, we might need you to fill in a few blanks."

I looked at them and swallowed hard. "What do you need to know, Detective Martin?"

"Just call me Martin. For a start, do you have your memory back?" Martin asked, a small smile of hope on his lips.

I nodded. "Yes, I do."

"Excellent. Firstly, are you okay with us taking notes of this conversation?" Martin glanced over to Tony, who had a notepad out and was writing something down. I nodded in agreement. "Okay, well, I'll start with the basics. Can you please tell me what you were doing in Parker?"

I sighed nervously but knew it was time to tell my story. "I was running away."

Martin blinked and looked steadily at me. "Running away from what, exactly?"

"My abusive husband ..." I wiped away a tear that rolled down my cheek. I couldn't look either of the detectives in the eye, so I looked at my hands in my lap. "I couldn't take it anymore."

"That's okay. I understand." He paused. "And the car you were travelling in when you had the accident?"

"I stole it." In the corner of my eye, I saw Detective Tony write in his notebook. "And I *am* sorry for that. I just ... needed to get away." I paused and nervously glanced at Martin. "Are you going to arrest me?"

Martin smiled at me. "We can discuss the car situation later. Right now, we just want to get your statement." I smiled weakly at him. He smiled back and continued his questioning. "Were you heading to Parker specifically?"

"No. I was trying to get to Cape Gorge."

"That's a long way to travel!" Detective Tony commented.

"It was the furthest place I could think of, without leaving the continent," I admitted, and he gave an understanding nod.

Martin frowned. "What made you want to go there?"

"I didn't have any actual destination when I left. I just wanted to get away. I picked Cape Gorge after looking at a map I found in the car."

"Fair enough." Martin continued, bringing my focus back to him. "I would like to work out a time frame for the events. Can you tell me approximately when you left your husband?"

"At the beginning of September."

Martin nodded. "And after the accident, you stayed in Parker?"

"Yes."

"Did you know anyone in Parker?"

"No. No one."

"So, where did you stay and what did you do for those months you were gone?" Detective Tony asked with curiosity.

I leant back against the pillows and told the two detectives everything that happened to me, from the moment I woke up in the ICU to them breaking into my house. They both listened intently to my story, giving me plenty of time to explain everything. After I had finished talking, Detective Martin sighed deeply.

"Did you know your husband never put out a missing person report for you?"

I huffed through my nose; a small laugh escaped my throat. "Wow! Really?" I stared at the detective and shook my head softly with bewilderment.

"Is there a reason why he wouldn't have alerted the authorities?"

I shrugged. "His pride, no doubt! I knew he would search for me once I was gone. He has always threatened to find me if I left him, and he would never get the police involved. Gavin is a hands-on guy, would rather do things himself. I guess he stuck to his word. I never felt safe while I was running, always thought he would catch me, but I'm not sure why it took him so long to find me ..." I paused, then stared at Martin. "He truly is an arsehole!"

"Forgive me for prying, but you said you were running away from an abusive husband. I take it you didn't have a good marriage?" Detective Tony asked.

"No. Not at all." I looked at him. His eyes softened and a small smile of empathy tipped his mouth.

Detective Martin placed his hand back on mine. "Rachel, I don't want to put you in an uneasy situation, or make you feel uncomfortable, you are in a safe place now, but we need you to please tell us exactly what happened before you left, specifically the reasons you wanted to leave your husband."

"Before I tell you everything, can you at least tell me what happened to Gavin? The last thing I remember is watching him bleeding on the kitchen floor."

Martin glanced up at Tony, who looked at me. Neither of them said anything.

Chapter 64

Wednesday, December 12th

"Amber, Amber!"

Laying in the hospital bed, trying to sleep, I heard a voice I honestly never thought I would hear again. My eyes flew open, and I looked eagerly towards the door.

The door bursts open, and my eyes fell onto the most handsome face I had ever seen, and it was like I was seeing it again for the first time. Craig rushed up to the bed and grabbed my hand, and raising it to his lips, kissed it lovingly. As he looked at me, and I saw tears running down his cheeks.

"Craig!" I uttered as I lifted my hand and placed it tenderly against his cheek. He perched on the edge of the bed and leaned in to hug me, whispering my name, over and over. "You're alive!" I cried, gripping him harder, despite the pain in my stomach.

"I never thought I'd see you again," he said, releasing me a little so he could look at me.

"Neither did I. I thought you were dead." I glanced down at his waist.

"Na," He smiled. "Just a flesh wound." he laughed it off, but I saw a shadow of pain flash across his face.

"It was more than just that!" A female voiced stated behind Craig.

"Tracey?" I called out, excited to hear her voice.

"Of course, my dear, where else would I be?" She came around the other side of the bed and gave me a loving kiss on the forehead and took my hand in hers.

"You're here. You're both here." I started crying. Big fat tears rolled down my cheeks as I studied the faces of the two people, I had become so incredibly close to.

"I'm sorry, I'm so sorry for what happened to you," I said to Craig, again looking down at his waist, trying to envisage what his scar looked like.

"Don't think anything of it. I would do it all again, if it meant next time I could save you, instead of letting that man take you away." He leaned forward and kissed me tenderly on my cheek.

"That man," I said sadly, "That man is my husband and ..."

Tracey cut me off. "You do not need to explain anything, love. We know enough about him, and you don't need to talk about it right now. All we are concerned about is how you are feeling and when we can take you home."

"You know?" I felt ashamed. I'd never wanted anyone to know about the life I had led with Gavin, and I withdrew my hands, wanting suddenly to be alone.

"Hey, look at me Amber, or is it, Rachel?" Craig paused; a slight crease crossed his forehead, as though suddenly unsure what to call me.

"Does it matter?" I asked quietly, dropping my head.

"Yes. Yes, it matters. It matters to me," Craig said softly, as he gently lifted my face and peered into my eyes. "I fell in love with a girl named Amber, but I need to know if I still call her that, or if I call her Rachel, her real name." His blue eyes never left mine.

"You love me?" I stared back at him, shocked to hear him say those three words.

"With all my heart."

A new wave of emotions crashed over me, and I started crying again. "I love you, too," I blubbered between sobs.

He moved closer, took my face in his hands, and gently brought his lips to mine. I had forgotten how nice it was to have a man kiss me tenderly and softly. I melted into his lips and wrapped my arms around his shoulders.

"I think I'll head off and see the Doctor about when you'll be released," Tracey said discreetly, as she stepped away from the bed, allowing Craig and I some privacy.

Pulling away from Craig, I wiped the tears from my cheeks and grabbed a box of tissues. Craig used one to dry his own cheeks, smiling sheepishly at me.

"We are a pair, aren't we?" I giggled.

"I'd say a matching pair!" replied Craig. I looked at him with a puzzled expression on my face. "Some people get matching tattoos; we have matching stab wounds," he laughed.

I looked at him, my brows creasing with annoyance. "That's not funny Craig. You could have died," my voice suddenly firm.

"As could you. But we didn't. We're still here. And we're together again. Fate brought us together in Parker and now again here in Missionly, and I don't ever want anything like this to happen again."

He looked at me with those deep blue eyes. I studied his face—the shape of his nose, the lines of his jaw, and the way his hair perfectly framed his face. This man, who was so kind to me, who had treated me like I was worthy, this man I had fallen in love with. Yet, as I gazed at Craig, I realised I couldn't be with him the way I wanted to.

His forehead creased, and he tilted his head slightly. "What are you thinking about?"

"I can't be with you," I whispered.

"What do you mean?" He pulled back slightly, his frown deepening.

"I'm married."

"To a monster!" his voice deepened.

Tears welled again. "How much do you really know?" I asked, but honestly not wanting to know the answer.

"Enough to know I would *never* do those things to you. I know enough about him, to hate him and wish the bullet ended his life instead of just wounding him in the shoulder."

"Either way. I was a married woman when I met you. We had an affair. It doesn't make me look like a nice person."

"And you're a car thief," he said, his eyes wide in mirth, "but that doesn't matter to me. Neither of us knew and from what I've heard, it wasn't a good marriage. You had your reasons for leaving. Clearly, you wanted to break away from him and the abuse."

"I did, and well ... I did break away, for a few months, at least."

"And now you've broken away for good," he said, looking at me tenderly.

"I guess." I felt unsure about what the next steps of my life would look like. "I don't know what to do now?"

"Well, for a start, we'll wait for Tracey to get back and tell us what the doctors said when you can leave. Then we can take it from there.

"But where do I go?"

Craig gave a little shrug. "I'm not sure. Let's just take it one step at a time, okay?" He kissed my hand and smiled at me. I cherished these tender moments. After what I'd been through over the past ten years with Gavin and seeing another way to live with Craig—there was no comparison. Craig was everything Gavin was not.

Sitting in the room with Craig, I felt at peace again, grateful he had flown in just to see me. Cuddling on the bed, Craig looked at me, a cheeky grin on his face.

"I brought you a flower, but I wasn't allowed to take it out of the airport. Customs and all."

"Did you now?" I said, bemused by his actions.

"It was a daffodil." He looked at me, questioning with his eyes, if that was my favourite flower.

I laughed and shook my head. "Sorry, not right."

He frowned. "Do you ... remember what it is?" he asked hopefully.

"It's a frangipani." I said, smiling at how dedicated he was, still trying to make me happy.

"Finally!" He wrapped his arms around me, holding me tight. "Duley noted. I will have to plant a frangipani tree in the garden." I tried desperately not to laugh, the action painfully pulling at the muscles in my abdomen.

Within a few minutes, our peace was interrupted when Tracey returned, accompanied by the doctor.

"Good to see you, Rachel." he said politely as he came to the side of my bed. "I hear you might want to leave us already. Not happy with the accommodation?" he chuckled.

"The accommodation has been wonderful, thank you, but yes," I sighed. "It would be nice to go home ... or at least ... somewhere." I realised as I said it, the last place I wanted to go back to—was that house.

"Well, due to your injuries, I would like you to stay with us for one more night, just to monitor you and make sure your wounds are stable and infection free. The last thing we want is for you to leave too soon and accidentally rip the stitches open." He peered at me, making sure I understood.

"Fair enough," I replied, a little disappointed, as I wanted to stay with Craig.

"When you do leave, will you have anyone to look after you?"

"Yes, she has us," Tracey quickly pipped up.

"That's good. You need to make sure you don't do anything too strenuous. You'll need a lot of rest. It's going to take some time for your abdominal muscles to heal."

"How long?" I asked.

"At least six weeks. Maybe more. The more rest, the better. No heavy lifting. No over doing it. Nothing that will risk the muscles."

"Just like me. Maybe we should have bed rest and physiotherapy together," Craig said with a playful wink. I battered him slightly on the arm. The Doctor looked from Craig to me and back again, his brows furrowed. Craig lifted his shirt, wincing slightly at the movement, and showed the Doctor his stitches. "Her husband stabbed me when I tried to stop him from kidnapping her."

"I see," the doctor replied, his eyes wide. "The two of you have been through it! But he is right, though. You will need physiotherapy, and I'd like you to see a trauma councillor too, please."

"Don't worry, Doctor," Tracey said, looking at me. "I'm a nurse at Parker Hospital, and I've had the pleasure of looking after Amber, oh sorry, Rachel, before. I would be more than happy to look after her again, and she has a trauma councillor there too."

At her comment, my eyes welled, and I turned my head, embarrassed to be crying again. Tracey had been a pillar of strength for me for so long, and the thought she would so willingly take on the responsibility again made me cry with gratitude.

Chapter 65

"Amber! It's so good to see you again," Doctor Wilkins beamed as I walked through her door. "Or should I call you Rachel?"

"Amber, please. I'm getting it legally changed in a few months," I said with a grin.

"It's wonderful to have you back! I am so sorry for everything you've been through." She motioned for me to sit.

"Thank you. It's nice to be back in Parker."

"So, what can I do for you?" She sat down next to me.

"I wanted to thank you for everything you did to help me, but I also wanted to share with you what actually happened to me."

Doctor Wilkins lent forward, placing her hand gently on my knee. "You don't need to tell me anything you don't want to."

"It's okay. Really. I wanted you know the truth and let you know some interesting things."

"Okay." She rested her hands in her lap and watched me carefully.

"After I was kidnapped from the carnival, I was taken back to my home in Barrister. When I woke up in my old bed, my memory snapped back into place." I paused, looking at her, knowing this wasn't an easy story for me to tell. Even with Craig, I hadn't told the whole story, perhaps I never would, I didn't want him to look at me differently, but with Doctor Wilkins, knowing she was a councillor, and someone better equipped to understand what I had been through, I felt a bit more comfortable with her, so without any further hesitation, I opened my heart.

"I was married to a bad guy. Well, still married, but that will end soon. We met in high school and started dating just before we graduated. A few years later, we got married, much against my family's wishes. Although the relationship started off, like a picture-perfect romance, things began to change." I paused, readjusting my position in the chair.

"After about two years, the abuse started. It began slowly. Verbal abuse and gas-lighting me first. He started calling me fat, lazy, telling me I wasn't good enough at my job, criticising my looks, or what I wore. He would constantly nag me to clean the house better, cook better. Be a better wife in bed." I paused again, forcing myself to take a deep breath.

"The physical abuse came next. A few slaps or punches. He would push me over when he got angry over insignificant things he thought I did wrong. He apologised once, after the first time he hit me, but after that, he always blamed his behaviour on the stress at work, or the fact I hadn't done the *simple things* he asked." I shook my head, recalling some of the times he hurt me. "Alcohol didn't help the situations, either. That's usually when he would sexually abuse me. He would say he wouldn't do it again, but he always did."

"I understand how hard that must have been for you to go through this," she said patiently.

"It was. He isolated me from my family and my friends. I really didn't have anyone to go to for help. He would threaten me. Tell me he would hunt me down or kill me if I left him."

A few tears ran down my cheek. Tears of shame, of regret, of embarrassment. Doctor Wilkins handed me a box of tissues, her eyes gazing at me with understanding. "He threated to hurt my family and friends as well. So, I stayed loyal to him, no matter what he did to me." Saying these things, putting my life on the table, made me realise how lucky I was to be here.

"Did you ever report anything?" she asked.

"No." I dabbed the tears from the corners of my eyes with a tissue. "I didn't have the confidence to do that, and I was scared he'd act on the threats he made. I couldn't leave the house whenever I wanted. A few years into the marriage, he kept pushing for us to have kids. So, I quit my job to be a full-time housewife, hoping to have children. He also sold my car, so I had no way to escape."

"Do you have children?"

"No," I shook my head. "Well. Yes, sort of." She looked at me with curiosity, her eyes searching my face. "I've had three miscarriages."

"Oh, Amber. I'm so sorry to hear that." She leant forwards again, resting both hands on my arm. "Was he the cause of those miscarriages?"

"Yes. He knew about the first two of my pregnancy's, the third, he didn't know. He used to hit me in my back, or stomach and my chest. Places if I bruised, no one could see. After the first two miscarriages, he blamed me for losing the babies. He told me, if I were a better person, I could have carried them to full term."

Doctor Wilkins placed her hand over her mouth, her eyes wide with shock. I smiled weakly back at her.

"After I fell pregnant the third time, I kept it a secret. I hoped he wouldn't find out until I was well into my fourth month, that way, when I showed, he might stop the abuse. I hoped if he could see I was having his child, he'd change."

"Did he find out?"

"Yes. Called me a whore. Accused me of cheating on him. Not that I ever had a chance to even consider the possibility.

He shoved me into the corner of our square dining table. I lost the baby a few hours later."

"Oh, Amber. My heart breaks for you." She grabbed my hands, squeezing them tenderly. Tears fell down my cheeks in grief.

"If you don't mind me asking, how did you end up here in Parker?" she asked.

I smiled. "I knew after I lost the baby, I had to get out. That the next time, it would be me who died. So, I slowly began to hide money away, which wasn't easy. He controlled everything. Six months after the miscarriage, I left after he went to work. I hadn't planned to leave that day. I think I just woke up that morning and knew it was now or never. I took nothing with me other than the money and walked in the opposite direction from where he worked. I went down whatever side road, or back road I came across, anywhere I could stay out of sight." I paused again, letting the realisation of what I did finally sink in.

"I walked for a few hours. Far enough away from my house, where I hoped no one would recognise me. I found a motel where I stayed for a night. Locked myself up in the room and never left. I was so paranoid, he would turn up that I hardly slept, didn't eat anything. Every noise was frightening. I kept expecting him to barge through the door." I paused again as the remnants of that fear echoed through me.

"I left the motel early the next day. The sun wasn't up yet, but I knew my husband would be undeniably furious by then, and I had to keep moving. I think ... a new sense of urgency came over me. I was terrified, but I had no choice. I needed to keep moving. I walked for about another twenty minutes and caught the first bus I saw. Stayed on the bus until a few blocks passed. Got off. I had no idea where I was, so I walked down a few side roads until I saw an old car in the driveway of a small house. I'm not sure what came over me, to be honest. I've never stolen anything, but I couldn't keep walking—I needed to put more distance between me and Gavin."

Doctor Wilkins nodded, squeezing my hand.

"I went to the back of the house. Thankfully, found the kitchen door unlocked. I snuck in and saw a set of keys on the kitchen bench. I knew I wasn't doing the right thing, but I took them, plus an apple and banana that were sitting in a bowl on the table and left." I grimaced at my foolish behaviour.

"What did you do next?"

"I drove. Just drove. I had no idea where I was going, just that I had to get away. Once I hit the highway ... I headed in the opposite direction from home, only stopping for petrol and lunch. By late afternoon, I'd crossed the border into Chesterfield."

"Did you find somewhere to stay?"

"Not really. I went to a fast-food restaurant, bought some dinner, and drove around until I found a quiet park. Slept in the car. In the morning, I found a map book in the glove box. Decided right there, I wanted to go to Cape Gorge. I couldn't remember the last time I went to the beach, plus, it was really the furthest place I could go without physically leaving the continent. So, I drove through Chesterfield, into New Hampton."

"That's a long drive," Doctor Wilkins noted, looking at me with her eyebrows raised.

"I know. It was tiring. I slept in the car again that night, once more, only stopping for fuel and food. The adrenaline of leaving was pumping through me. The further I went, the braver I felt. Even though I was paranoid Gavin ... my husband, was following me, I felt a sense of freedom."

"So, you kept driving until you reached Camberton?"

"Yes."

"Did you make it to Cape Gorge?"

I smiled. "No. Fate brought me to Parker instead. A drunk driver ran a red light and slammed into me. It's weird now, all these months later, I can see the accident so clearly. I can remember the car heading straight for me. I know the accident happened extremely fast, and nothing I could have done differently, would have changed the outcome. It feels weird to know my brain shut everything out."

"The brain is a marvellous organ. It protects us when we least expect it."

"Yes, it is."

After a brief pause, Doctor Wilkins sighed and looked at me with a profoundly serious expression. "Can you tell me why you stayed with your husband for so many years? Other than the threats to you and your family?"

I swallowed hard. "Despite all the bad times—the verbal and sexual abuse, the beatings ... when he was good to me, he was wonderful. At times, he would spoil me—buy me flowers. Dance with me in the lounge room after dinner. The sex ..." I paused; a small laugh of bewilderment escaped me. "When we were both in the mood, the sex was great. I suppose I hoped he'd get better; go back to the Gavin I first fell in love with. The good moments seem to out-way the bad. Looking back now, I see so many times where things could have gone terribly wrong, where he could have hurt me much more than he did." I swallowed; grateful I had survived the abuse.

"Over the last few years, I began to see our relationship wasn't normal. It just took a long time for me to talk myself into doing something about it. Because the abuse started slowly, I never saw the ... what do you call them? ... red flags!" I looked at her with a quizzical gaze.

"Yes, that's right." She nodded in confirmation.

"I see them now, but at the time, I felt like I was drowning in my lack of self-worth. I didn't value myself anymore, and I guess he used that to his advantage."

"And now?"

I smiled so widely; Doctor Wilkins smiled too.

"Craig opened my eyes to a whole new world of love. Tracey and everyone at the Post Office, treated me in ways I was never privy to before. Not knowing my past for those few months allowed me to see there is a better life, and I *am* worth loving and deserve kindness and respect."

Doctor Wilkins nodded knowingly. I was finally healing. "And your husband? Where is he now?"

"In prison. Awaiting trial for assaulting and stabbing both myself and Craig, of kidnapping me, resisting arrest and all the other stuff that happened on the drive back home."

She frowned at me. "What happened on the drive home?"

"My husband tied me up and drugged me. Just enough to keep me docile and compliant. I was never really aware he was drugging me. He put sleeping tablets in the orange juice he gave me." I rolled my eyes at the thought of how cruel he was. "Each night when we stopped, he would rape me after feeding me dinner. We were always somewhere dark and alone, so no-one would be able to help me, and he kept me bound, so I couldn't run away."

"Oh Amber, I am so sorry." Her eyes searched mine in sympathy.

"He blamed me every time. Telling me I deserved it, for leaving him, for staying away for so long. It was my punishment for cheating on him with Craig."

Doctor Wilkins sighed; her head shook softly in disgust. "Is he being charged with domestic violence? For beating and raping you during your marriage?"

"Yes, and no. For now, the charges against him are only for what happened to me in the days after he abducted me. Prior incidences can't be used, as there is no evidence he physically or emotionally abused me. I never reported any of it. I was too scared. The miscarriages were recorded as of the result of natural causes, not the result of injuries."

"I can testify for you if that is an avenue you want to go down. I can explain how the brain blocked the trauma of what you endured at the hands of your husband. I can discuss this conversation with your permission, or if the police decided to raise a case against your husband, they may subpoena the conversations we have recorded."

"Thank you, Doctor Wilkins. That would be helpful."

"And your relationship with Craig?"

"He has been wonderful. He had been by my side the whole time. I am incredibly lucky to have him in my life." I could not hide the smile, knowing how happy he made me.

A genuine smile crossed her face. "I am truly thrilled to see you happy, Amber. You have been through so much."

"Thank you. There was something else I wanted to share with you. Do you remember all the times I told you heard a cat meow?"

"Yes?" She tilted her head and looked at me with new interest.

"I was in the kitchen the day after I got home, when I heard cat a meow, just like the ones I heard here in Parker. Well, when I looked out the kitchen window, there was a beautiful ginger cat outside. Mr Floofy, my neighbour's cat." I smiled, recalling the moment I saw him again. "He used to visit me every day, and he would always meow to let me know when he arrived."

"Well now, that's interesting. And the footsteps and breathing?" she asked.

"My husbands. We had wooden floors in the house. I could always hear him walking around, and as for the breathing. He slept behind me every night, always facing my back, so I always felt his breath on my neck."

"Maybe your brain hadn't quite forgotten everything."

"Maybe."

"So, what are your plans now?" Doctor Wilkins shifted positions in her chair.

"Well, I can't live in that house any longer. The Detective and sheriff have allowed me to live here in Parker, but I need to be available to fly back to Missionly for the court hearings."

"When will they be?"

"In a few months, I believe. Then hopefully if he is sentenced, I'll be free to live here permanently. Craig has asked me to move in with him."

"Well, as I stated earlier, if you need me to testify to anything in relations to what happened, I'll be more than welcome. I am incredibly happy to hear you have your memory back and your life is moving forward in a happier direction." She got up and moved over to me. I stood, and Doctor Wilkins hugged me tightly.

"Thank you so much for always being there to listen to me and for trying to help me remember my past."

"Think nothing of it. I am so sorry you had to go through a traumatic experience for your memory to return, but I'm glad you finally remember who you are."

I left Doctor Wilkins' office, feeling like a huge weight had lifted off my shoulders. Finally, I could appreciate what it felt like to be a free woman. Yes, I still had a long way to go in the healing process, but I felt lucky to have such wonderful people surrounding me and giving me all the support I'd need over the next few months and years.

Prologue

They say time flows faster the happier you are. I would agree, one hundred percent. At the beginning of February, I flew back to Missionly to attend the court case for my husband. The hearing spanned two days and took only four hours for the jury to decide his fate.

Gavin Stowick was charged with two counts of grievous bodily harm against Craig and me. One count of kidnapping, multiple counts of sexual offences and in the end, multiple counts of domestic violence. Doctor Wilkins, as promised, submitted written and recorded evidence of our sessions and testified regarding my retrograde amnesia.

My family and I were reunited at the hospital in Barrister after being kept from them for so long. Upon being discharged from hospital the day after Craig and Tracey arrived, I stayed with my parents for two weeks, while I recovered, eternally grateful to have them back in my life. Craig and Tracey stayed in a hotel, close to the house, with both visiting every day. Tracey, true to her word, cared for me, nursing my wounds.

It was also wonderful to see my family connect with Craig and accepted him into my family. To my surprise, my parents attended the trial and testified against Gavin. The information they provided to the court on how Gavin prevented us from having any contact assisted in my plea.

It was never easy to sit in the same room as the man I once thought I loved—a man who I had believed would love me for the rest of my life. There were many moments I couldn't look at him, especially when I had to take the stand. Tracey and Craig were my rocks during those times. Both attended the trial and smiled at me in support when they saw me struggle.

Gavin never denied any of the charges. He sat in the courtroom, stone faced and said nothing. Craig later told me he never once looked in my direction. He kept his head down the whole time, allowing his lawyer to speak on his behalf. For all the times he had something to say to me, it was weird to have him so quiet.

When the jury returned a guilty verdict, my head dropped, and my heart thumped so loudly, I thought the entire room heard it. Tears of relief that the ordeal had finally ended rolled down my cheeks as Craig's arms wrap around me from behind.

"It's all over," he whispered into my ear. "I love you so much." He kissed me gently on the cheek.

Gavin was sentenced to twenty years in prison. Five years for each of the stabbings, three years for the kidnapping, and seven years for the sexual, physical, and mental assault he inflicted on me over the course of our marriage. With his head hanging low, accepting his fate, Gavin was escorted from the courtroom. That was the last time I saw him.

Within the year, I'd signed my divorce papers, and I legally changed my name to Amber Cooper. I'd also sold my house in Missionly without having to split the money with Gavin. Although I didn't want to take it initially, Craig suggested I use it to set up a charity to help other women and men who are in Domestic Violent relationships and need somewhere safe to stay.

So, with help from Craig and Tracey, we purchased a large house in Parker, and it became a safe environment where people could get whatever assistance and advice they needed to escape from the horror of their abusive situations.

On the day we opened the doors, to my greatest surprise, one of my closest high school friends who had married a co-worker of Gavin's arrived. Seeing everything I had been through; and watching me find the strength I needed to survive; she finally found her own courage and left her abusive husband. Not only had I finally gotten one of my best friends back, but after all her issues were dealt with, and with her husband also imprisoned for sexual and physical abuse, she moved to Parker and worked alongside me in our rescue house.

A year later, on the eve of my twenty-sixth birthday, Craig took me to The Sapphire Bar, the restaurant he took me our first date. While eating dessert, he dropped to his knee and pulled out a little red box from his jacket pocket.

"Amber Cooper, I have never met anyone as strong as you. You have inspired me and so many people to find the strength they need to better their lives. I couldn't imagine my life without you. Will you please do me the honour of becoming my wife?"

"Yes, yes, yes!" I called out. The whole restaurant broke out in loud cheers and applause. With my face the colour of beetroot, Craig slipped a beautiful gold ring with a sapphire stone and two diamonds onto my finger.

Our wedding was a beautiful event, which we shared with our wonderful families and friends. We married in a small garden gazebo down at the lake, and held our reception at The Sapphire Bar, as the sun set over the town, the restaurant now holding two wonderful memories for us.

To my surprise, Craig booked us into a lovely little cottage down at Cape Gorge. I finally got there! We spent a week in the beautiful, warm, blue water, enjoying the beach, the shopping and nightlife, and all the attractions the small coastal town had to offer, including a bright orange and yellow cocktail I drank, as the sun set over the blue water.

As a post wedding gift, Craig and Tracey organised a special surprise for me when we got back to his, or should I say, our house. Sitting in the middle of the kitchen, in a small wicker basket, was a small, but very fluffy ginger kitten. I squealed so loud in delight when I saw him, I almost scared him away.

"Is he mine?" I asked tentatively, after picking him up.

"Absolutely. He's all yours," Craig laughed, watching me rub my nose into the little kitten's fur. "What are you going to call him?" he asked as he wrapped his arms around me and stared down into the face of the cat, I held so close to my chest.

"I think ... Phoenix."

"Phoenix?" he questioned.

"Yes. Everything in my life now feels like I've been given a second chance. It's like I'm rising from the ashes of my old life. I have you and Tracey and my family, and now this beautiful kitten. I don't think my life could be any better."

"Then Phoenix it is." He scratched the kitten behind its ears.

Yet, it did. Almost a year later, two weeks shy of our first wedding anniversary, I gave birth to a beautiful baby girl. We named her Hannah. I'd spent so many years believing I'd never be a mum. Craig was so loving and caring during the pregnancy, ensuring nothing would go wrong this time.

The joy she brought to our lives was immeasurable. Her laughter, her smiles, her tiny hands, and feet. We were both so in love with her. The look in Craig's eyes every time he picked her up made my heart swell, and I knew we were in the best place we could ever be. Tracey became an honourable godmother. There was no better way I could thank her for everything she'd done for me when I first arrived in Parker—and since.

A year and a half later, we welcomed another daughter, Jasmine, into our family. Two precious girls, to steal our hearts and fill our time. Our family was complete. Nothing would ever break us apart.

Two years later, Detective Martin Collins called to respectfully inform me, Gavin had been found dead in his cell, a few days earlier. Apparently stabbed to death by his inmate. I felt no pain, no sorrow, no pity for the man who had treated me so poorly during our time together. I didn't attend his funeral. As far as I was concerned, my time with him ended a long time ago.

Now, I dedicate my life to my family and friends who bring me more joy than I could have wished for, and to helping those who are going through the same terrible ordeals I did.

I am a victim of mental, physical, and sexual assault, who crawled out of the ashes and created a whole new life.

I am a survivor, who finally found a man who treats me as his equal.

I am a warrior who helps others like me to find their strength to live a better life.

I am worthy and loved by so many people. My heart is full every day.

I am free.

Acknowledgments.

When I first started writing this novel in 2010, I was young, eager, excited and determined to become a writer and took to it like water off a ducks back but over the last fifteen years, being a single mum to two kids, a move from one side of Australia to the other, buying my first house and working within the medical industry, my writing took a back seat many times but was never far from my mind. I admit I had many doubts it would ever make it to publication.

But here I am, publishing my debut novel.

My first thanks are for my sister Lana, for her support, constructive input, feedback and her enduring love. She was the first person to read this book many years ago and her encouragement along this long journey has been a rock for me. I hope you will be there for me as I write more novels.

To Liz Butcher, my editor. Thank you for taking on a new writer, for your patience, your advice (despite my stubbornness) and your wisdom. I have learnt a lot but still have a long way to go. I am forever grateful.

To Jason Smith and the team at Clark-Mackay, thank you for your patience, your time, for answering the many questions I kept throwing your way and for not giving up on me. You have helped me make a dream come true.

To my parents for your support when I finally shared with you that I was writing. Thank you for embracing my passion and taking an interest. Thank you to my friends and co-workers who I have told and who responded positively and supportively. It has been hard to share this adventure, as I never believed it would happen, and it took me a long time to admit ... I am a writer.

And finally, to my two wonderful children, Peta and Travis. For watching me sit in front of the computer for hours on end, fingers tapping away mercifully trying to get the story in my head out, you were both never far from my mind. Thank you, for your support and belief in me. I love you both from the bottom of my heart.

As a survivor of DA relationships, it took me a long time to see the abuse and to recognise the signs and red flags.

Abuse in relationships is not always given via a hand or fist but can be given verbally, mentally and emotionally. Being made to feel ignored, unworthy, unloved, pressured into situations you are not comfortable with, strung along, shamed, gas lit, humiliated or belittled by your partner, are all forms of violent and domestic abuse and are not tolerated.

If you are in a domestic abuse relationship, whether it is physical, verbal, emotional or mental, **you are not alone**. You can create a better life for yourself and those around you.

Please seek help. Please talk to your family, your doctor, a councillor or the police. Get your story out there. Raise your voice and put yourself first.

If you know of someone who is in a DA or DV relationship, please *talk to them, listen to them, believe them* and offer your assistance in whichever way you can. No one deserves to be treated less than they are worth.

Find your worth. Find your strength, Find your freedom.